BLACKWELL

THE ENCOUNTER BEGINS

THE FIRST OF
THE BOOKS OF KLYV

Michael E. Gunter

As much as I would like to believe otherwise, this is a work of fiction. While some of the locations exist in reality, the characters, circumstances, and dialogue are products of the author's imagination. Any resemblance to persons living or dead is entirely coincidental.

Blackwell
© 2011 by Michael E. Gunter LLC
Published in 2011 by Michael E. Gunter LLC

ISBN: 978-0-9837522-2-6

Contact the publisher at
Michael@GunterBooks.com

Cover Concept, design and art by Janine Krokus, JKrokus Illustrated Design. http://jkrokusillustrateddesign.com

Publishing Consulting, Book Design, Project Management and coaching provided by Alane Pearce Professional Writing Services, LLC, and Publishing Coach http:MyPublishingCoach.com or alane@ MyPublishingCoach.com

Inside front cover art by Carson Jones

ACKNOWLEDGMENTS

First thanks to my wife, Tammi, who has been listening to me go on and on and on about Aldi and Elsa-Eska since 2001. Thank you for believing and never letting me give up. I love you more than I could ever say in a hundred books, but I'll keep trying.

To my kids, thank you for the love and laughter and letting me feel cooler than I really am. Erik and Shea, you inspire me in countless ways.

Thanks also to those who read early drafts and offered so much encouragement. Sorry about all the typos and changes along the way.

To Marjorie Preston, my first 100% objective reader. Thank you for the months of correspondence and advice that enabled me to trim the excess and craft a better book. Goo-goo-g'joob.

To Alane and Brandon Pearce, my bridge between book and business. Thank you for your expert guidance and keen literary eyes. Without you, BLACKWELL would still be in my drawer.

To the café staff at my local Barnes & Noble, thank you for making all those Grande Decaf Extra Hot Mochas. And to Rick in the music department, thanks for providing an excellent musical ambiance.

To Jane Monheit, Jesse Cook, The High Kings, and the Trans-Siberian Orchestra, thank you for providing the best writing music in all the world. Music for every mood.

Dedicated to my son, Erik

PROLOGUE : ROSETTA

∴

"You're wasting your time, Carl. There's nobody out there."

Carl Drake heard those words so many times they no longer bothered him. He didn't even argue anymore. He'd just smile and nod and strike that person's name from the short list of people he cared to remember. But when *she* said them and then added the stinger, "But if there were, they wouldn't care about someone like you,"—those words were carved into his memory just like her name was permanently etched onto his short list. How could he forget her? How could he forget the last words she ever spoke to him? Even after a year, they still haunted him.

Carl sat motionless in his car, a dark green 1965 convertible Mustang he bought new from the dealer four years earlier. It still looked like it did the day it rolled off the assembly line. He liked it because it had the kind of style that made people look twice. In a car like that, a guy like Carl could feel normal, maybe even cool. And though there was no one out there in the lonely Nevada desert to notice him, he still felt good in it. With the top down, radio on, and the seat leaned back all the way, he watched the smoke from his cigarette drift straight up in the still night air. Above him, the moonless sky glittered with the billions and billions of stars that seemed close enough to touch.

The young man stared straight up into the cosmos and let his mind go as far and as fast as he could. Somewhere out there—beyond the tiny Sputnik, past the astronauts aboard Apollo 11, further out than anyone had ever peered through a telescope—there had to be someone; some kind of intelligent life. He knew it in his soul. And he wanted nothing more in life than to make contact, to see and hear them, to actually know them. He wondered if they were at all like him. Did they laugh and cry? Did they make love and war? Did they have hopes and dreams and fears? Did they wonder if they were all alone in the universe? Did any of their kind mock them for having such absurd thoughts? Carl imagined someone like himself on a distant planet like Earth. Maybe he or she or whatever else there could be was staring out into the same space, but from the other side. If only they could bridge the gap that separated their two worlds. Carl cursed the distance that rendered their meeting unlikely, if not impossible.

More than an hour had passed since Carl began his night vigil. The ground beside his car was littered with cigarette butts, and the RC Cola on the floor between his feet had long since become warm and flat. At some time in the evening (Carl was unaware when it happened), the radio faded out as the last bit of power drained from the car's battery.

It was fifteen miles to the nearest town. Even if he wanted to try to make it on foot, his legs could not have carried him that far. While the thought of being stranded alone in the desert should have given him cause for at least some concern, Carl Drake was content to stay and keep company with the stars. Automotive problems could wait until the last star surrendered its light to the new day. Besides, he knew he would not be spending this night in the desert alone.

Carl heard the rumble of the 1937 Indian motorcycle a few moments before he saw the light from its headlamp. He did not bother to watch the motorcycle approach since he knew who was on it. When the Indian finally came to a stop next to the Mustang, its rider switched off the engine, extended the kickstand and took off his helmet.

"Any problems?" Carl asked, still gazing up into the sky.

"Naw. The old man's on the verge of another breakthrough. He'll be locked away in his lab for days. As of this morning, I became just another echo from the Big Bang."

"Well, I'm glad to see you Frank. Did you get the key?"

"Yeah. Took it right off his key ring. He'll never miss it."

"You're sure we've got the place all to ourselves?"

"For days if we want it. Not much interest these days in listening to static. No one's scheduled to come out 'til next week."

"Guess it's meant to be then." Carl opened the door to his Mustang and swung his legs out. The metal braces on his legs rattled and clicked as he locked them into place. Without much effort, he heaved himself into a standing position. From the back seat he retrieved two crutches, the short kind with the wrist cuffs. It was a maneuver he had performed countless times. "So what's on tap for tonight?

Hendrix? Jefferson Airplane? Grand Funk?"

Frank unbuckled the leather pouch behind the seat of the Indian and pulled out a metal case about the size of a shoebox. "I don't think it really matters, Carl. Whatever you want is fine."

"Oh, but it does matter. You don't want them to think the earth is square, do you?"

Frank stared blankly at Carl. Then the light came on. "Oh, square Earth—good one." Frank snorted. "I doubt they'd judge us by our musical preference."

"You may be right. But they probably do have style. What if they like to, you know, get down?" Carl made an awkward attempt at a dance move. "I'd hate to think they passed on us for a better party."

"Carl, you have a bizarre view of the universe."

Beside them was a steel building about the size of a double car garage. Frank unlocked the door and felt along the wall for the light switch. Light spilled out of the door and cut sharply into the black desert. Carl took one last look at the stars and hobbled his way into the building. Frank followed and closed the door behind him, sealing every bit of light back into its container. On the door, in simple block letters, a sign read: **CETI BROADCAST STATION ELVIS**. Beyond the building, about fifty yards away, was an enormous radio telescope with its dish pointed straight up. From a distance, it looked like a big salad bowl balanced atop a thin pedestal.

Inside the building, Carl took his usual chair and laid his crutches on the floor beside him. "What's in the case?" He asked as he pulled a ten-inch reel of audiotape out of his leather satchel.

Frank was checking the printouts from the last several days. "Oh, something I've been working on." He shook his head as he leafed through the yards of paper, studying the rows of squiggly lines. "Hmm. Not much here."

"Patience, man. Patience." Carl attached the reel to a machine and fed the tape through the reader head and onto the empty retrieval reel. "What's in the case?"

"Uh-huh." Frank was lost in the squiggles. He had zeroed in on one particular section and was scribbling some notes onto the paper.

"Earth to Frank," Carl said a little louder.

"Oh, sorry. Did you say something?"

"The case. What's in it?"

"Oh, yeah, that." Frank placed the printout back in its tray and slid the case to the center of the table between them. "This is Rosetta."

"Rosetta," Carl repeated, flashing an impish grin. "Ah, your new girlfriend? Why don't you let her out so I can meet her?"

"Girlfriend? Cha!" Frank brushed his greasy hair back with one hand and pushed his thick plastic-framed glasses back into place with the other. "Like I would go out with a girl who could fit in a box that small."

Carl shrugged. "Yeah, you're right. Guys like us must have our standards. I'll just go and tell all those girls lined up outside that we only want the tall good-lookin' ones. Cha!"

Frank chose not to be drawn into another one of Carl's cynical rants. "Seriously, you've heard of the Rosetta Stone?"

Carl nodded. "Yes. The stone Napoleon's army found in Egypt."

"That's right," Frank said. "It had the same text written in three languages: Greek, Latin, and Egyptian hieroglyphs..."

"I knew that."

"... which provided the key for deciphering the previously undecipherable hieroglyphs."

Carl nodded. "I knew that, too."

"Well," Frank said as he patted the case, "this is sort of the same thing, only it's electronic. Here, let me show you." Frank found a piece of graph paper and placed it on the table. "Let's say you wanted to communicate human." He drew a stick figure on the paper. "Using a geometric grid, you can figure out the plot points of the picture and assign them numerical values like this." Frank scribbled out a series of numbers that represented the plot points for his stick figure. "If you transmit the plot points along with an audio recording of what the object is, whoever receives it can re-produce the object and hear an audible word designation."

"You're telling me you invented a machine that transmits a signal that draws a picture along with an audio track?"

"Yes," Frank said proudly. "That's right."

"I hate to break it to you, Frankie, but I think someone beat you to it. They call it television."

Frank shook his head. "Rosetta is nothing like TV. It doesn't even use a picture tube. The code for the picture is an audio signal as well."

Carl thought for a moment. "Okay. Aliens might not have a TV, but they probably have a radio. Come on, Frank. Don't you think if they're smart enough to travel through space, they'd be smart enough to have a TV on board their ship?"

Frank frowned. "I'm sure they're smart enough. But we can't assume compatibility between alien and human technology. They probably do have some form of video technology, but the likelihood of it being able to receive and translate one of our television signals is...well, it's hardly likely. Radio signals are much simpler."

"Hmm." Carl knew Frank had given this a lot of thought. He also knew that he was probably right. "So, you've created an electronic

Rosetta Stone?"

"Yes, that's why I call it Rosetta. You know, Carl, for a smart guy you can be kind of slow."

Carl shot him a sneer, but cut off the sarcastic comeback that Frank probably wouldn't have gotten anyway. "Tell me, Frank, what's the point?"

"The point is, we can broadcast your record collection for a thousand years, but it won't mean anything. If aliens are out there and they can detect our radio signals, they still wouldn't understand our music. I hate to sound like my old man, but to an alien race with no human point of reference, our music would just sound like noise. This isn't like Star Trek where all the aliens speak English. Rosetta uses what many scientists believe is the true universal language—mathematics. It's a key for them to begin the process of understanding us. Check out these symbols I've already programmed into the machine along with their verbal cues."

Frank drew the following symbols on the sheet of paper:

Carl studied the symbols and muttered to himself, "Okay. That's the sun and our solar system and there's Earth. What's this? Oh, I see—mountain, tree, water, human. And a peace sign?" He looked at Frank. "You seriously believe an alien who has never been to Earth is going to figure this out?"

Frank was disappointed at Carl's sudden lack of confidence. "It's a start. And I think it communicates a lot better than, *I can't get no satisfaction.*"

Carl smiled. "Okay, you've got a point. Let's just hope they've got plenty of graph paper."

"Very funny. You can play around if you want, but at least I'm trying to really do something here."

Carl stiffened. "Oh, so now I'm playing around? Look at me. Do I look like I'm playing around? Let's take stock. I'm a twenty-three year old cripple. Except for you, all my friends are either in Nam or Canada or getting stoned in a field of daisies somewhere. My parents think I'm a loser, and…" Carl stopped himself.

There was a long pause. "Look, Carl, maybe this wasn't such a good idea after all. You've been on edge since we got here. Let's just pack it up and try again some other time. Maybe tomorrow, huh?"

Carl leaned forward and pressed the palms of his hands against his temples. "No, tomorrow won't be any better." There was another long pause. "It's Amy. She's getting married."

"Oh, man, I'm sorry," Frank said. "When did you find out?"

"This morning. Her mom called."

"What'd she say?"

"I really don't feel like talking about it. Sorry I brought it up." Carl picked up the piece of paper and studied the symbols again. "I guess if they're smart enough to travel through space, they're smart enough to figure out these symbols. Tell me how this contraption works."

Frank spent the next thirty minutes explaining the Rosetta machine and patching it into Elvis's mainframe. After several minutes of Frank's fiddling with the dials and switches, Carl was getting restless. He had no understanding of computers and believed Frank purposefully engaged in excessive fiddling just to prove he could. When he couldn't take it any more, Carl got up and started hobbling around the station.

"Hey, Frank," Carl said, "what's a pulse burst transmitter?"

"A what?" Frank said from behind a large rack of electronic equipment.

"A pulse burst transmitter," Carl repeated. "It's printed on this crate. There's also some letters I can't read. I think it's Russian."

Frank climbed out from behind the rack and walked over to where Carl was standing. "Let me take a look at that." He examined the crate. "See if you can find a hammer or a pry bar."

"Now this is more like it," Carl said. He found a hammer in a drawer and brought it back to Frank.

"I know this. I read about it last year." Frank strained to get the pry bar into the crack between the crate and its lid. "But it was only a theory then."

"What theory?"

"There was this Russian scientist who claimed to have figured out how to transmit a signal at a super high speed over a tremendous distance. I can't remember the exact figures he used."

"Estimate."

"Think of it like this: If we ever put a man on Mars, it would make communication sound like a phone call across the street. But remember, it's just a theory."

"By the looks of it, that Russian guy went beyond theory. Let's take it out and fire it up."

"I doubt the thing even works."

"Why do you say that?"

"Look. It's never even been out of the box. I don't think anyone's ever even hooked it up."

Carl shook his head. "If they're never going to use it, what's the big deal? Besides, I thought CETI stood for Communication with Extraterrestrial Intelligence. You and I seem to be the only one's who actually send any messages out. If they're going to stop trying to communicate, they ought to change the name to LETI—Listening for Extraterrestrial Intelligence."

"LETI? That's kind of lame."

Carl thought for a moment. "How 'bout SETI? *Search* for Extraterrestrial Life. At least it still sounds the same."

"Why don't you mention that to my dad?"

"I think I will. Now let's test drive this pulse burst transmitter and see what she can do."

"I don't know. If my dad ever found out…"

"How could he find out? You're just an echo, remember?"

The image of his father on the verge of another breakthrough popped into Frank's mind. It was an image he knew well. In fact, Frank could not remember a time when his father was not working on the discovery of the century. "You're right. What's the worst that could happen?"

Thirty minutes later, Frank stood up and announced, "That's it. I think I got it." Frank had a concerned look on his face like he might have missed something important.

"Finally," said Carl. He had been reading one of the many technical manuals laying about. "How do you guys read this stuff? No wonder they put these places way out in the middle of nowhere. I want to slap somebody." He tossed the manual onto the table. "Let's fire it up."

"Not so fast," Frank replied. "According to these specs, this thing requires an awful lot of power. I had to hook directly into the main line coming into the building. I'm not sure what's going to happen.

We could blow something and lose power to the entire building."

"I guess we better make sure we get it right the first time then. You got your Rosetta thing ready?"

"Yes. We'll transmit the first sequence. If it works, we can send more later."

Carl held up a hand. "Wait a minute. Can this pulse thing transmit music?"

Frank thought about it. "Sure, but not an entire song. The pulse is too quick. You'd have to somehow compact the music down into a much smaller package. Maybe in the future we'll be able to do something like that. Hmm, compact music. That would be cool."

"It was just a thought. Go ahead and pulse the Rosetta signal. I'll stick to sending musical smoke signals." Carl gave Frank a nod and a thumbs-up.

Frank looked as if he were about to meet Miss America. He was perspiring, his eyes were wide open, and his hands were shaking. "Here goes something, I hope."

Carl stared hard at the Rosetta machine as if he expected it to do something. Every muscle in Frank's body tensed, and then he pushed the transmit button. There was a click followed by an amazing display of…nothing. Both men stood transfixed, their eyes locked onto the Rosetta machine. Still nothing.

"Try it again," Carl whispered.

Frank pushed the button a second time.

Another ten seconds elapsed.

Still nothing.

"A dud," Carl said. All the hopeful tension of the moment was let out like air from a balloon. "Oh, well, at least we still have lights."

"I don't understand. Maybe I didn't hook it up right." Frank began checking connections and reviewing the spec documents.

"Don't worry about it, Frank. We still have several hours. Let's just patch Rosetta into the system the old way. Besides, maybe the pulse machine never worked. That's probably why it was in the box. Good effort though."

"Yeah, you're probably right. I'll drop some hints to my dad. Maybe he knows something."

Sixty seconds earlier…

Outside Broadcast Station Elvis, the steel frame holding the radio telescope began to rattle and the dish atop started to vibrate. Three seconds later, the moonless black night became ablaze in a shower of sparks, and streams of blue electrical energy shot out in all directions. Bolts of electricity congregated on everything in the vicinity that was made of metal—the steel lightening rods atop the building, the Indian motorcycle, the Mustang, the metal "Keep Out" sign in front of the building. Fifty miles to the south, every light in Las Vegas blacked out.

Then, as quickly as it all began, the light show outside of Broadcast Station Elvis ended. Vegas flickered back to life and everything seemed to be as it had been before.

Four hours later...

The eastern sky was showing the first signs of morning as Frank and Carl emerged from the broadcast station.

"That was a bust," Frank said.

"It wasn't a complete loss," Carl replied. "You got me through my first night of knowing the only woman in the world for me is going to live happily ever after with another man. Besides, we can search the stars for intelligent life anytime."

Frank laughed. "I hope we find it soon 'cause there's not much of it down here. Hey, listen." Both men stopped. "Your car is running."

Carl looked at the Mustang. Sure enough, the car was idling like a new sewing machine.

Four years later and several light-years away...

A tone sounded in a darkened room, waking its occupant from a sound sleep. He spoke calmly in a language never before heard by human ears. Translation: "This is Ido."

From a speaker somewhere in the room, a female voice said in the same language, "Ka-Rel was correct." There was an edge of excitement in the voice.

PART I
INCIDENT AT BLACKWELL RANCH

CHAPTER 1:

WHAT ED TYLER FOUND

$\triangleq$

Rick Blackwell stepped out onto the back deck of his single-story house and walked to the railing at its furthest edge. He shivered as the cold air enveloped his body. The steam from his favorite coffee mug mingled with his breath to form a white cloud that rose up in sharp contrast against the clear blue sky. He relished this moment. Although it became his daily ritual, it never got old. It was his favorite part of the day.

The thirty-year-old transplant from the East Coast surveyed his massive back yard. Stretched out before him as far as he could see, the Wyoming desert was white from the light dusting of snow that fell the night before. Randomly scattered tufts of desert sage punctuated the landscape, providing definition to the brilliant swath of white. The only man-made object in sight was a split-rail fence about fifty yards out from the house. Fifty miles beyond, the Rocky Mountains rose up out of the desert like the back of a great serpent. Rick could think of nowhere else in all the world he would rather be.

Rick and his wife Jane moved to their Wyoming ranch in the summer of 1996. When they arrived, the locals politely told them that most city folks were lucky to last a year before the harsh weather and loneliness drove them back to wherever it was they came from. Like many things in life, they were told, the idea of wilderness adventures and a lifestyle of simplicity is appealing to those who have only glimpsed such things in books and movies. The reality, it turns out, is a shock to the system; and few stick with it long enough to experience the benefits that come only after the heart has been conditioned to receive them. To the surprise of all who knew them, Rick and Jane survived the first year, endured the second, and thrived with each year that followed. After five years, the Blackwells had paid their dues and earned the respect of their fellow pioneers. Now they seemed as much a part of the land as it was a part of them.

Gazing out at the Big Sky country, Rick felt small and obscure. The sheer bigness of it made him feel vulnerable, like at any moment the land might swallow him up. He liked the feeling. He said it gave him the perspective he had sorely lacked in the corporate world where he was revered as a modern day warrior of sorts—foolish things uttered by small men to make themselves feel bigger than they are. Here in the untamed, as he called it, he knew there were things much greater than himself. He did not know what they were, but he was certain they had to be out there somewhere.

As he pondered these greater things and how one might find them, he caught a movement out of the corner of his eye. He could tell immediately by the odd gait (something like a barefoot speed walker on hot asphalt) that it was Ed Tyler. The little bouncing form beside him was Bonko, a three-legged dog of unknown breeding.

Ed was all of five feet tall and maybe ninety pounds with full pockets. He wore blue denim overalls, a faded North Carolina Tar Heels sweatshirt, and a red hunter's cap like the one worn by Elmer Fudd. Chugging up the hill to the house, the breath-vapor rising from his mouth made him look like The Little Engine That Could. When he got within earshot, he started waving his arms and calling out, "Kevin! Kevin!"

Ed called everyone Kevin. Rick knew there must be a good story behind it, and maybe one day he would get around to asking, but for now he decided to let it remain one of life's great mysteries.

"Good morning, Ed. What brings you and Bonko out on such a cold morning?"

"Kevin! You gotta come quick. Quick! QUICK!" The little dog tried to bark, but he could only manage something that sounded like a sick walrus.

"How 'bout a cup of coffee first?" Rick asked. Ed never turned down coffee.

"Oh," Ed dug a finger deep into his ear and started to say something, but interrupted himself by shaking his head. "No, no, no time for that. Come on. Come On!"

The locals said Ed Tyler was the way he was from years of living alone, but no one could remember how or when the old guy came to live in the trailer that seemed to grow out of the earth in the southeast corner of the Blackwell Ranch. Rick inquired about him before he bought the place, but no matter who he talked to, he always got the same answer: "That's just old Ed Tyler. He's harmless. After awhile, you won't even know he's there." It was the same kind of logic he got from a realtor who sold him a house next to a freeway. After several attempts to get the story, Rick gave up asking and just accepted Ed as part of the deal—like everything else left on the property by the previous owner. Over the years, Rick got used to Ed and didn't mind so much when the old guy came around, which was only about once or twice a month.

By the look on Ed's face, Rick could tell something had rattled his cage. He set his mug on the deck rail and jogged down to meet him. "What is it?"

As Rick approached, the hair on Bonko's back raised up and the muscles in his muzzle began to twitch. He bared his teeth like a rabid badger, but made no sound.

"Come!" Ed snapped.

For an old guy, Ed was surprisingly quick. For a three-legged dog, Bonko was able to hold his own. Rick followed the pair across the driveway and out onto the snow-covered desert. They walked for several minutes. Ed was muttering to himself something indiscernible, and Bonko was making an unnatural grunting sound. Rick was beginning to feel the effects of the cold air in his lungs and he knew it must be even harder on his two companions.

When they finally reached the fence line, Ed grabbed Rick by the arm and began pulling him along with surprising force. After another quarter mile, Rick could see where Ed was leading him. A five-foot section of the fence was smashed to pieces. When they finally reached the breach, all three of them were breathing hard. Ed pointed to the break and Bonko commenced to sniffing.

Rick took a few steps closer and stopped. There, where the fence had once been, was a crater about five feet in diameter littered with splintered pieces of fence rail. In the center of the crater, half buried, was an object about the size and shape of a basketball. It was caked with dirt and it looked like it had been scorched. Rick knelt down to get a closer look.

"You think it's a meteor?" Rick asked.

"Ain't no meteor," Ed replied, kneeling down beside him.

"What else could it be?"

"Don't know, but I got an idea 'bout where it come from."

Rick looked around at the surrounding ground for tracks. There were none. Then he looked up. "I'd say it came from the sky. It must have fallen out of an airplane."

Ed looked up and scanned the blue sky. "Yup. That's where it come from alright. Commies maybe."

Bonko conjured up a menacing growl that was quickly interrupted by a coughing fit.

"Communists?" Rick said. "Ed, you do know the Cold War is over, don't you?"

Ed gave him the squint-eye. "Uh, huh. And I'm guessin' you believe America won it."

Rick knew better than to respond. He was not in the mood for another one of Ed Tyler's conspiracy theories.

Ed shook his head and muttered something under his breath about public education. "Then again," Ed said as he leaned in closer to the object. "Could be aliens."

Bonko let out a faint yelp and scampered off.

Rick watched the little creature go. For a three-legged dog, he was quite agile. Then he turned his attention back to Ed, who was standing and looking up into the sky.

"Just a matter of time now," Ed said in a spooky sort of way. "Just a matter of time." Then he looked down at the still kneeling Rick and said in his normal voice, "I'll take that coffee now."

Rick stood to his feet and brushed his hands on his pants. Turning around, he found Ed already on his way back to the house.

Rick didn't think much more about the broken fence or the strange object responsible for the damage. He would call Burt Cooper, a handyman who lived at the ranch during the summers and came in occasionally throughout the rest of the year as needed, to come out and fill in the crater and repair the fence. That section of the ranch was not in use, so there was no danger of any cattle getting out. Rick had a more pressing matter on his mind: The deadline for the final draft of his first book. He spent the rest of the day locked away in his study.

Later that evening, he told Jane about the fence and how Ed thought it was the work of either Communists or aliens. They had a good laugh about it and then spent the rest of the evening talking about a hundred other things, including the new addition to their family due in six months. Sleep came easily for both of them just as it always did in their home on the range. Maybe it was the clean air or maybe it was nothing more than the contentment that comes when everything seems to be as it should.

Sunday mornings were usually quiet at the Blackwell Ranch. Jane would soon be heading into town for church, leaving Rick at least four hours of solitude; more than enough time to put the finishing touches on his manuscript and email it back to his publisher before the Monday morning deadline. He might even have time to go back out to the site of his wrecked fence and take another look at the object at the bottom of the crater.

Rick was already in the kitchen when Jane appeared. Staring intently at the coffee maker with cup in hand, he looked like a sprinter in the blocks waiting for the bang of the starter's pistol. Jane crept up behind him and slipped her arms around his waist.

"Oh, hey!" Rick jumped and dropped his cup, sending it bouncing across the kitchen counter. He turned around in her arms to face her. "Jeez, Jane, you scared the Vitamin C right out of me."

"Maybe you should be drinking orange juice instead of that stuff." She nodded toward the coffee maker.

"That stuff is *Fred & Lulu's Roguish Mountain Blend.*"

"Oh, I see your Coffee of the Month delivery came."

"Yeah, it arrived yesterday. Want to try some?"

"Ugh, not on your life. If you want to kiss me, you better do it now before you pollute yourself."

Rick pretended to ponder his options. "Hmm."

Jane pulled his face close to hers and planted a long, passionate kiss full on his lips. She let the kiss linger until she was sure he had forgotten all about *Fred & Lulu's Roguish Mountain Blend.* Then, as cool as a cat, she pulled away from him, unhooked his arms from around her waist and announced, "Gotta go."

"You are too cruel."

"You could come with me, you know."

Rick turned his attention back to the coffee machine. It was burping out the last few drops. He said nothing.

"You'd like the new preacher," Jane said casually.

"Doubt it."

"He's different." Jane wanted to say more, but she was afraid it might cause him to start thinking about the disaster that happened the last time he went to church with her.

Rick wanted to fire back, but he didn't want to think about the disaster either. "I've got work to do."

"I see." Jane slipped her arms back around Rick's waist and rested her head on his shoulder. "Hey," she said after taking a moment to regroup, "they're going to love your book. I know I do." She could feel the tension melt as Rick faced her again.

"Thanks."

"How about one more for the road." She flashed him the sly, crooked grin that first caught his attention years ago in the cafeteria at the university.

"It is pretty cold outside," Rick noted.

"Let it snow, let it snow, let it snow!"

They kissed again. This time it was for real. Then Jane laid her head on Rick's chest and rested in his embrace. "Maybe I could skip today."

Rick wanted more than anything to spend the morning with her, but in spite of his own religious reservations, he knew church was important to her and she would regret not going. "You wouldn't be trying to tempt me now, would you? You know I have to finish those edits before tomorrow."

"I know," Jane said in a pouting voice.

"I tell you what," Rick said. "You go and I'll finish while you're gone. Then we can have the rest of the day together. I'll have a fire set when you get back. Maybe we can watch a movie or something."

"That sounds nice." She hugged him once more before putting on her heavy coat and gloves.

"Be careful. The bridges will be icy."

"I will." Jane lingered at the door. "I hope your editing goes well."

"Thanks. There's not much left."

"And don't drink too much of that Fred & Wilma stuff."

"You mean *Fred & Lulu's.*"

"Whatever."

It might have been the glow of anticipated motherhood or the crooked grin or the fact that he thought Jane was especially attractive in her winter parka, but Rick found it difficult to let her go. "Hey, you better get out of here before I talk you into staying."

"Okay, okay, I'm going." She stepped through the door and out into the cold. "Love you," she called over her shoulder.

"Love you, too." He watched her until her Jeep disappeared around the curve by the barn.

Rick took his time getting to work. He drank a cup of *Fred & Lulu's* while he thumbed through a hiking magazine. After refilling his cup again, he stepped out onto the back deck and let the cold morning air fill his lungs.

The sky was its usual deep blue. A thin white line was etching its way westward. It was too high for Rick to make out the airplane, but he imagined the passengers peering down at him through the tiny windows. He knew they could not see him, but he waved anyway. He followed the line until it reached far into the west, maybe as far as Nevada. Several unrelated thoughts passed through his mind before an involuntary shiver brought him back. Both he and his coffee were cold, so Rick returned to the warmth of his house and set himself to the task at hand.

When he finally settled down at his computer, he discovered there was far less work to do than he thought. In less than an hour, he was finished and ready to send his manuscript to his publisher. He started to click the send icon, but something didn't feel quite right. As he stared at the blinking cursor, he thought of the passengers on the jet. He thought about how maybe someday some of them might read his book never knowing that its author watched them fly by. He knew it was silly, but he often thought about the ironies of life and the many connections that existed unbeknownst to those connected.

He looked at the cursor again and tried to capture the feeling of the moment. With the click of a button, two years of work would be done. His book—his baby—would be in the care of his publisher, the printers, the distribution warehouses, and then bookstores around the country. He felt a wave of nausea come over him and he wondered if that was how parents feel the day they send their child to school. Finally, with all the courage and trepidation of a novice parent, he clicked his book into the hands of strangers.

Rick didn't know what to do now that the deed was done. Had this been the old days, the finished manuscript would have been delivered in person. There would have been smiles and handshakes and a verbal "Thank You" or "Good Job." Maybe there would have been a congratulatory toast or a celebration dinner. But in the modern world, no one had time for such extravagances. The only acknowledgment Rick received was a pre-programed, "Message Sent."

Left wanting by the cold efficiency of it all, he pushed back in his chair and stood to his feet. He decided to take a walk and let the frigid air revive him. At least that was supposed to be cold. As he stepped out onto his back deck, he thought of what Ed Tyler found.

CHAPTER 2:

GESUNDHEIT

↗

Rick was outside no longer than a few minutes when he noticed the contrail of another jet. This was not unusual, for the skies over Wyoming were often crisscrossed with jets destined for places like Seattle, Salt Lake City, Reno, Las Vegas, and San Francisco to the west and everywhere else to the east. These jets were always very high, and their contrails were arrow strait. What Rick saw was different. This jet was much lower, and its contrail was arcing in a great circle that suggested it was making an approach to land. But where? The airports in Riverton to the south and Casper to the east did not accommodate jets.

Rick continued to watch the mystery plane descend lower and lower, its contrail now spiralling around on itself. He suspected the plane must be in some sort of trouble. When it disappeared behind a hill, he braced himself for the sound of impact or maybe even an explosion. He waited a full minute, but there was no report. All was quiet, and the winds were beginning to erase the jet's imprint upon the sky.

Suspecting the worst, Rick raced back into the house, grabbed the keys to his pickup, and tore out of his parking spot beside the house. All he could think of was that the plane might have crashed and there might be injured people. Given the fact that there were probably only two people within a twenty mile radius, and the other one was Ed Tyler, it was likely Rick was the only witness to the crash and therefore the only one who could help. He pushed the old truck to its limits, dodging potholes, spraying gravel and dirt around curves, and startling the horses as he sped past the barn. When he got to the end of his mile-long driveway, he rumbled across the cattle grate and squealed out onto the paved main road. As he raced along the deserted highway, he kept his eyes trained on the location where he thought the plane went down. So far, there was no trace of smoke. He took that as a good sign.

Up ahead, the road curved sharply to the left around a large outcropping of rocks that resembled the profile of an old Indian. At any other time, he would have slowed down because it obstructed his view around the curve. He also liked to look upon the rock and pay his respect to the people who lived in this land long before the white man came. But this was not any other time, so he took the curve hard and fast—a little too hard and fast. In the shadow of the outcropping, he failed to notice a patch of ice that spread across the road. With no dry pavement to grab onto, the back wheels spun freely and the rear of the truck began to come around. Rick whipped the steering wheel hard to the right to compensate, but the ice rendered his efforts ineffective. When he came out of the shadow, his tires regained traction and grabbed at the dry road, propelling the truck straight for the embankment on the right. Rick instinctively turned the wheel back to the left, but the truck already slipped off the embankment and was threatening to roll over. He fought to regain control, but could not climb back onto the road. When it finally came to a stop, the truck was a good twenty feet off of the road and resting near a patch of sagebrush.

Rick let out the breath he had been holding since he hit the ice. He willed his hands to loosen their grip on the steering wheel.

"That was close," he said aloud. Then he noticed the engine was still running. He patted the dashboard. "Toyota."

Rick shifted the truck into first gear and eased out on the clutch. There was a horrible sound of metal on rock as the truck struggled to dislodge itself from the boulder it was straddling. After a few seconds, the truck rolled forward, free from all obstruction. Rick stopped the truck, opened the door, and leaned down to examine the underside of the truck. Everything appeared to be intact. He patted the dashboard again and cautiously made his way back toward the road.

Climbing the embankment was no small feat. His first attempt failed, as he did not get enough speed; the back wheels just dug into the dirt. For his second attempt, he got a running start and gunned it at the base of the incline. The little truck attacked the embankment like its monster truck cousins, sending a torrent of rocks and dirt thirty feet behind it. The engine whined, and for a moment Rick wasn't sure he was going to make it. Then, as if the truck had something to prove, it shot up and over the edge and back onto the flat road. Rick slammed on the brakes to keep the truck from shooting across the road and down into the ditch on the other side. When he finally came to a stop, all sense of triumph was displaced by what he saw not a hundred yards in front of him.

There, in the middle of the road, was the jet. It was sitting there as if on display. There was no sign of damage or anything else that would suggest an emergency landing. Rick eased the truck to within thirty feet of the plane and turned off the engine. The silence was the first thing he noticed. There was no sound whatsoever coming from the jet. Its engines had been shut down. Rick got out of his truck, but resisted the impulse to approach the aircraft. Something did not seem right, and since there was no immediate sign of damage, he assumed the jet's occupants were in no immediate danger.

Now that he was close enough to get a good look at the jet, he began to take note of its features. Rick inherited his father's enthusiasm for aircraft (they used to go to the annual air show when he was a kid) and he was familiar with most military and civilian aircraft designs. What he saw before him bore some similarity to a military jet, but it looked more like the experimental crafts he had seen in *Popular Science Magazine*. It had the basic shape of a fighter jet, but it was much larger. It could have easily accommodated a crew of ten. The fuselage looked like a squashed cylinder, narrow at the front and widening toward its rear. The wings were wedge-shaped, but they did not extend very far out from the body. In fact, they did not appear to be large enough to support a craft of its size. Rick guessed they might have been retracted, but he could not tell for sure. The tail section was most unusual. It was shaped like an inverted V, the point rising only a few feet above the back of the fuselage. The landing gear was also unconventional. Instead of wheels, it had skids that reminded Rick of snowshoes. He deduced that the plane must have the ability to take off and land vertically, like a Harrier Jet. The entire craft was flat black with no markings whatsoever, and its surface was seamless like it had been pressed out of a single piece of steel. There were no rivets or panels of any kind; there weren't even any windows. The craft looked more like an artist's conception of a futuristic spy plane than anything Rick had seen in reality.

Rick suspected he was looking at some kind of experimental craft, perhaps the world's largest drone. It probably had some kind of mechanical malfunction and had to make an emergency landing. This thought made Rick nervous. For if this were the case, the military probably did not want his civilian eyes checking out their secret weapon. Scenes from several movies flashed through his mind—black SUV's coming out of nowhere or maybe a black helicopter; men in dark suits with sunglasses and guns; no words, just strong hands and menacing faces. And then he would be gone, never to be seen or heard from again. He suddenly thought of Ed Tyler and wished he were there. He also thought about getting back into his truck and making a run for it, but then he remembered such desperate moves never worked in the movies. His Toyota was a good truck, but it would be no match for a military hit squad.

He could have stood there all day, terrifying himself with a hundred different scenarios, each one worse than the one before, but his thoughts were starting to sound a little too much like Ed Tyler's. He debated which was worse, to inadvertently stumble upon a secret military project or find himself in one of Ed Tyler's crazy conspiracy theories. He decided the secret military scenario would be the easiest to get out of. It wasn't like he was trespassing on a government installation. This was a public highway. Besides, what had he seen? Just an aircraft. Certainly, that was not enough to be deemed a threat to national security. If he wasn't supposed to see it, he would apologize and go home. On the other hand, if the crew (if there was a crew) were in any real distress, perhaps he could be of assistance. When he thought of it that way, his being there was actually his patriotic duty.

Rick was just starting to feel better about the whole thing when he heard a loud clank and a whirring sound from the craft. All of his imaginations ceased and his curiosity took over. He slowly approached the craft until he was about ten feet from the nose. From this vantage point he could see movement beneath the craft. A hatch opened and a ladder was being extended to the road.

Before Rick had time to decide whether to retreat or hold his ground, a black boot emerged from the hatch and stepped onto the top rung. Slowly, haltingly, another boot appeared and fumbled around until it found the next rung down. Rick was transfixed by the effort being exerted to descend the ladder. It was as if the person was exhausted or sick or perhaps drunk. When the figure reached the bottom rung, it hesitated as if unsure about taking the final step to the ground. Then, with all the care of a person walking out over a frozen pond, it placed one foot onto the road and then the other.

From where he stood, Rick judged there to be about six feet of clearance between the road and the bottom of the craft. He was surprised that the head of the figure was still concealed within the hatch. Rick guessed the person (most likely male) had to be nearly seven feet tall—much too tall for a fighter pilot.

The man, still holding firmly to the ladder, ducked down out of the hatch. He was wearing a helmet—flat black like the aircraft, but with a visor as reflective as a mirror. It was a good thing he was wearing a helmet because as soon as he had taken his first step, he raised up and smacked his head against the underside of the craft. The concussion must have jarred him because he immediately started to wobble. Rick thought the guy's knees were going to buckle, but he managed to steady himself with the ladder.

"You alright there, buddy?" Rick called out.

There was no reply. With head bent low, the man made his way out from beneath the craft and stood to his full height. Now Rick was sure he was at least seven feet tall.

"Hey," Rick said, waving nonchalantly in an attempt to hide the feeling of intimidation that was welling up inside.

Still, there was no reply. The mysterious figure just stood there looking at Rick. A moment later he raised his hand in imitation of Rick's wave.

Rick was about to say something else when he noticed another boot emerge from the hatch. A second figure began descending the ladder in the same slow, cautious fashion as the first. When he reached the bottom rung, his boot slipped off and he landed hard onto the asphalt with a bone-jarring jolt. The shock caused his knees to fold and he hit the road with a thud. There was an audible muffled grunt.

Rick cringed, as he knew the guy had to be in pain. He took a step toward the downed man, but stopped short as the man's partner had already returned to assist him. With some degree of effort, the two black clad figures climbed back out from beneath the craft and stood silently next to the wing. The second figure was just as tall as the first.

Rick tried a third time to communicate. "Is he okay?"

Again, there was no reply.

Rick's mind was working fast to make sense of what he was seeing – a futuristic aircraft in the desert, freakishly tall pilots wearing bulky black outfits that reminded Rick of the snowsuit he wore as a kid, and behavioral evidence that suggested there might be a party going on inside the plane. He was beginning to suspect this might be some sort of practical joke. But for whom? It wasn't like there was a crowd of people out there to entertain. If this was a Candid Camera gag, the set-up crew did a poor job choosing the location. A quick scan of the area revealed no hidden cameras, so he dismissed the idea. As curiosity trumped caution, he took a few steps directly toward the two men.

When he got to within five feet of them, caution kicked in again as he realized just how big they were. He stopped when he had to tilt his head back in order to look at their helmets. All he could see was a distorted reflection of himself in the reflective visors. He felt small and vulnerable. Then it occurred to him that there might be more of these giants inside the craft. If they meant to harm him, there would be absolutely nothing he could do to defend himself. Suddenly, one of Ed Tyler's wild stories popped into his mind, forcing him to take a step back.

"C-can I help you guys?" Rick asked, trying to sound confident.

He half-expected more of the same silent treatment, but this time there was a response. The man closest to Rick reached up and touched a button on the side of his helmet. With a click and a hiss, he began to lift the helmet from his head. Rick steeled himself for something, but he didn't know what. Most likely, it would be the brutish face of a soldier ready to read him the riot act. The reality was something altogether diffcrent.

Outside the protective environment of his helmet, thc man winced in the bright sunlight and lifted his hand to shield his eyes. Rick could see that the corners of the man's mouth were raised, not in a grimace, but a broad friendly smile. After a few seconds the man lowered his hand and looked at Rick through deep blue eyes that somehow seemed part of the smile. His expression was that of a child at Christmas—happy anticipation. But there was something else about the man that caused all of Rick's apprehension to melt away. He did not know how he knew it, but he was certain the man meant him no harm.

"Hello," Rick said. This time his confidence was genuine. He offered the stranger his hand.

The man looked down at Rick's hand, but did not take it. Still smiling, he closed his eyes, tilted his head back, and took a deep breath through his mouth. He held it in for a moment and then let it out. He took another deep breath, this time through his nose, and held it again. Suddenly, the smile faded and a look of concern came over him. He wrinkled his nose, took three rapid shallow breaths, and sneezed very loudly. His partner flinched and reached toward him as if to steady him. The sneeze was violent enough to dislodge a long mane of dark brown hair that had been gathered and tucked down the back of his suit. When the man straightened up, his eyes widened with surprise and his hair fell loosely down around his shoulders. He shook his head, wrinkled his nose again, and wiped the tears that were flowing freely down his cheeks. His partner placed a hand on his shoulder, but he waved him off. After a few exaggerated blinks of the eyes and another rubbing of the nose, the smile returned to his face.

"Gesundheit," Rick said.

"Gaw-zoon-tight," the man repeated slowly. He had an accent

that Rick did not recognize.

Rick was so fascinated by the man that he did not notice the third figure climbing out from beneath the craft or the fourth descending the ladder. When they joined the others, Rick noticed they were not quite as tall; maybe just a few inches taller than himself. And there was something else different about them, but it was impossible to tell since they were dressed in the same bulky outfits.

The man who had already removed his helmet turned to the others and said something that sounded like, "Three banjos." The others responded by tapping the sides of their helmets. There were more clicks and hisses as helmets were being removed.

Rick's jaw dropped as he discovered what it was about the last two figures. They were women, but not just women. In addition to their Amazonian height, they were drop-dead gorgeous.

Now Rick Blackwell was undeniably a one-woman man; hopelessly, helplessly, head-over-heals in love with his wife. He was not one to look at other women, but he could not keep himself from staring at them. A pang of guilt sparked in his mind, but it was quickly extinguished by something he would not begin to understand for quite some time. While he was certainly aware of their unusual physical beauty, his attraction to them was not quite like when he was a young single man looking for a good time. In fact, whatever it was that attracted him to the two women was equally strong in the two men. This thought was as disconcerting to him as was the guilt, but it too quickly faded and was replaced by a sense of genuine fondness.

After a fair amount of nose twitching and eye blinking, the four strangers fixed their gazes upon Rick. Their stares were so intense upon him that he had to look away. It wasn't a sense of threat or even intimidation that he felt, but more like a sense of vulnerability. While he did not believe in such things, he felt as if they were reading his thoughts. Rick unconsciously began to fidget with his keys, which drew the attention of all four strangers. The one Rick assumed to be the leader seemed to pick up on Rick's unease and took a step toward him with his hand outstretched.

"Gaw-zoon-tight," the tall man said.

The man's voice broke the tension, making Rick feel better. He looked up into the man's face to see the same friendly smile he saw before. Rick grasped the man's hand; it felt huge compared to his own. He tried to shake it, but the hand was immovable and it had no grip whatsoever. After a moment, Rick felt the grip tighten slightly and he knew the man could easily crush his hand if he wanted to.

"Gaw-zoon-tight," the man repeated, gesturing toward him with a nod.

"Se habla Espanol?" Rick replied. It was the only thing he could remember from his high school Spanish class. Relieved that the man did not respond with a barrage of Spanish he would not have understood, he played his only other non-English speaking card. "You speaka da English?"

The man chuckled and turned toward the others who were watching the exchange with great interest. He said something that elicited laughter from them and they formed a semi-circle around Rick. There were smiles all around and various forms of "Gesundheit" as each one took turns holding Rick's hand. Rick's only option, it seemed, was to laugh along with them and shake each hand; though he had no idea what was so funny.

CHAPTER 3:

FALLING OFF THE EDGE

Q

Russians. That was Rick's first guess, but now that he took a closer look at them he wasn't so sure. All of them had the same olive complexion and similar facial features—exotic, perhaps Mediterranean or maybe a mixture of Asian and something else. And they all had longish hair that, except for their leader's, remained neatly tucked down the backs of their flight-suits. The attribute he could not reconcile in his mind was their height. He had seen a documentary on the *Discovery Channel* about a condition called gigantism and he knew that those who suffered from it exhibited some distinct characteristics: Pronounced brow ridge, elongated jaw, and curvature of the legs and arms. These people had none of these traits. They were perfectly proportioned and good looking; and they appeared to be as fit as athletes. Rick imagined that in their own country they might be celebrities. Unable to think of any other ethnic group known for its unusual height or a country that possessed the ability to produce an aircraft so advanced, he settled on his first guess. They had to be Russians.

Somewhere in the back of his mind, he heard Ed Tyler's voice from the day before: *"Commies maybe."* For a brief instant there was a flicker of plausibility to the suggestion. But then he saw the two men grasping each other by the hand and saying, "Gaw-zoon-tight" over and over. *Commies,* he mused. *Communists wouldn't act like that.*

Then again, who would? The entire situation just did not fit into the context of Rick's world. Here was a futuristic airplane, piloted by a crew of freakishly tall, yet stunningly attractive people who were just a little too excited about landing out in the middle of nowhere.

They were like children, Rick thought, but not in the way adults find annoying or inappropriate. No, it was more like how children are naturally curious and unashamedly enthusiastic about everything. It was as if everything was new to them. Everything they saw, every rock and shrub, was like a rare treasure. One of them found a stick and happily showed it to the others. Another had gotten a handful of dirt and was letting it trickle though his fingers, watching with fascination the affect of the breeze as it blew it away. Interestingly, they did not seem to notice the majestic Rocky Mountains in the distance or the nearby entrance to a canyon. Every few moments, one of them would try to look up into the sky, but then they would squint and shield their eyes as if it were too bright to look at. A jet flew high overhead. It was too high for Rick to hear its engines, but all four of the strangers looked up at once and squinted in its general direction. Then they dismissed it, apparently unable to see it though its contrail shown silvery against the clear blue sky. Like children in a toy store, they rushed from one new discovery to the next as if there wasn't time enough to see them all. Still, they maintained a constant awareness of Rick. Every few seconds, one of them would smile at him and call out, "Gaw-zoon-tight!"

This continued for several minutes until one of them, the smiling leader, motioned for Rick to join him by the side of the road. Rick discovered that he used a stick to draw something in the dirt. The man knelt down and, after making sure Rick was watching, retraced it. Then, pointing to one particular design, he said in clear English, "Peace."

Rick blinked in astonishment. So the guy did know some English. But what surprised him more was the image the man was pointing to. It was a peace sign.

"Okay," Rick said. "Peace."

The man smiled at Rick and repeated, "Peace." Then he retraced another image, a wavy line. He pointed at it and said, "Riffer."

"Riffer?" Rick studied the image. "Oh, you mean river." He moved his hand in a wavy motion. "River."

The man studied Rick's hand. Mimicking the motion with his own hand, he said in a voice that sounded very much like Rick's voice, "River."

"Now we're getting somewhere," Rick said as an idea formed in his mind. He knelt down next to the man and used his finger to sketch out a fairly good representation of the aircraft. By now the others gathered around them and were watching with great interest. When he was finished, Rick pointed to the picture he had just drawn and then to the real aircraft. "Airplane," he said.

"Airplane," all four repeated in unison.

"That's right, airplane." He buzzed his lips and made a motion with his hand to illustrate an airplane landing.

The others imitated him, but the looks on their faces suggested they were not making the connection.

"Never mind," Rick said, "that was a prop plane, anyway."

"Never mind," said one of the women, "that was a prop plane, anyway." Her English was perfect without a hint of accent, and her voice inflection was a near perfect match of Rick's.

Rick spun around in surprise. The reply sounded so natural, yet it was obvious she had no comprehension of the meaning of her words.

Compared to "Gaw-zoon-tight" this was progress, but if all they did was mimic, there was not much hope for any real communication. Rick thought for a moment and then turned back to his makeshift sketch pad. He drew a large circle and outlined the shape of the continents in the western hemisphere. When he was finished, he waved his hand above North America and said, "America." Next, he tapped the region of the west and said, "Wyoming." Then, gesturing around at the surrounding dessert, he repeated, "Wyoming." Rick was hoping the man would understand his intention and follow suit by indicating where they came from. What he got was something Rick did not expect.

The man studied Rick's drawing for a moment and then smoothed out a spot beneath it. His excitement was evident as he drew a large circle with several small circles in a straight line to the right. He tapped the first small circle and flashed a wide grin at Rick. Glancing back at his drawing, he tapped the second circle and turned back to Rick, still smiling. Then, very deliberately, he tapped the third circle and said, "Earth." He tapped Rick's drawing and his voice intensified with excitement: "Earth." Finally, he waved his hand toward the surrounding landscape and nearly shouted, "Earth!"

It was a full minute before the implication of what Rick had just witnessed began to sink in. Even then it was too fantastic to believe. In fact, he refused to believe it. There had to be some other explanation—a joke, a mistake, a military experiment gone horribly wrong. Or maybe he was dreaming. Or—dread thoughts raced through his mind: *What if that close call in the truck wasn't just a close call, but a real accident? What if I hadn't been able to keep the truck from rolling over? What if I'm unconscious or wandering around in the desert delirious from a head injury? What if this is just a hallucination? What if…what if I'm dead?*

He closed his eyes tight and pressed his temples with the palms of his hands. Of all the possible scenarios, he was hoping it was just a dream. That had to be it. On the count of three he would open his eyes and find himself back in his bed.

One…two…three…wake up! Rick opened one eye and saw four giants smiling at him.

"Gaw-zoon-tight," the tall man said, his hand extended.

Rick's mind quickly checked off his list of possibilities. He had never dreamed about dreaming, so he could only assume he wasn't dreaming now. Death and hallucination would be impossible to test, so he quickly dismissed those two options. Nobody would go to such elaborate lengths to play a joke on one man out in the middle of nowhere. The behavior of the giants cast a considerable shadow of doubt on the theory that they were military, at least not any military he knew of. Not only that, they did not seem to be in any distress, so even if their landing in the desert was a mistake, it was not a serious one. That left only one possibility and his mind refused to form the mental words for it. It just was not possible.

From a dark corner of Rick's mind, a section reserved for those thoughts he kept under close wraps, came a voice. It was the raspy voice of Ed Tyler: *Then again, could be aliens.*

Try as he might to put the thought away, it refused to obey. Like a caged animal set free, the thought ran freely through his mind, becoming more bold with each echo of its unbelievable suggestion: *Then again, could be aliens.* If he had not known better, Rick would have thought Ed was standing right there with him. He could almost smell the old guy's pungent cologne.

"Okay, okay," Rick said as he regained his composure.

The leader of the giants was still smiling with his hand extended toward him.

Rick was halfway to belief, but there was still a chance everything could go back to the way it was. He had one more play.

"Wait right here." Rick ran the short distance back to his truck and rummaged through the debris behind the seat until he found a crumpled up atlas of the world. Thumbing through the dirty and bent pages as he walked back to the alie…tall people, he found the page depicting all the continents of the world. Handing it to the leader of the crew, he pointed to North America.

The smiling man looked at the map and proudly proclaimed, "Wyoming."

"Well, actually…okay, yes, Wyoming." Rick pointed again at the map, then to the surrounding area, and finally to himself. "This… all this is Wyoming. I…" He patted his chest again. "I am from Wyoming." Then, with a degree of apprehension, he put his hand close to the leader's chest as if intending to pat it.

The leader must have understood Rick's intention. Still smiling, he grabbed Rick's hand and pulled it to his own chest.

"Yes," Rick said, nodding. He placed his free hand on his own chest and said, "I am from Wyoming." Then patting the leader's chest, he said, "And you are from…" He gestured toward the atlas with a nod of his head. He slowly removed his hand from the leader and placed it on the atlas. Tapping his finger on Russia, he continued, "… Russia?" Rick's heart was pounding in anticipation. Common sense said anyone capable of piloting an aircraft of any kind had to have some geographic knowledge.

The leader did understand. He handed the atlas to Rick and led him back to the sketches in the dirt. Pointing to the third small circle and then to Rick, he said, "Earth." Then, after he pointed to himself and the others and their aircraft, he took the stick and began drawing a line in the dirt. The line extended far beyond the rest of the circles he had drawn.

Rick stared at the line in the dirt for a long time. He could hear Ed Tyler laughing in his head. Suddenly, he felt himself teetering on the edge of belief. As the edges of his field of vision began to blur, he heard another voice in his head—it was the voice of his college philosophy professor:

> *It's not always easy to believe. Sure, there are many things we accept without giving them much thought at all. When we were children we even believed fantastic things. But when it comes to something that carries with it extreme implications, belief can be a fight. This is especially true if the new belief requires us to accept something we've always rejected as false or rejecting something we've always accepted as true. We may encounter such life-changing moments only once or twice in a lifetime, but when we do, we find ourselves in the thick of a mental battle between two opposing forces. Part of us wants to reject the new idea in order to maintain the old system. We are wooed by the comfort, security, and familiarity of all that we have ever known. But another part of us wants to give in, to accept the new idea and all the changes that accompany it. Both parts know that a decision must be made, a threshold must be crossed, a new reality must be entered from which there is no return. This wrestling of the mind, and that is exactly what it is, can be exhausting. It can even manifest itself in physical ways.*

Everything in Rick's world began to tilt and swirl. The muscles in his legs began to relax. Although he could not at that moment reason through this mental struggle, he was all too aware of its weight upon him. He had heard the stories of those who claimed to have had just this sort of close encounter, but he never believed them. In fact, he questioned the very sanity of those who believed in such fantasy. After all, it was the stuff of science fiction. But now, with the evidence smiling at him, his fundamental view of the universe was being called into question.

After what seemed like a very long time, but in actuality was only a few seconds, Rick let go and tumbled over the edge. Mentally spent, his brain directed his last bit of energy to bodily preservation. Just before he fainted he managed to reach out toward the very thing he had not wanted to embrace. Then everything went black.

The smiling man caught Rick and gently lowered him to the ground. Then, placing his large hand upon Rick's head, he closed his eyes and spoke words in a language that had never been heard in Rick's world.

CHAPTER 4:

LIKE WAKING FROM A DREAM

⚔

AS Rick was in the process of regaining consciousness, the particulars of the moment came to him one at a time. The first thing he noticed was how good he felt, like the third morning of the best seven-day vacation ever. The second thing was the faintest recollection of the strangest dream he'd ever had. It was blurry and disjointed, but it had something to do with an airplane out in the desert and a freakishly tall guy with a goofy grin. *Must have been all that cheese I ate last night*, he thought. The third thing he noticed was the chill in the room. Shivering, he reached for the blanket, but came up empty-handed. *Jane must have left a window open again; and she's hogging the covers.* The fourth thing that occurred to him was the brightness. Even though he had not yet opened his eyes, he could tell the sun was shining directly in through the window.

"Jane, would you mind closing the curtains?" Rick squeezed his eyes shut tighter. Then the light dimmed as a shadow fell across his face. "Thanks, honey." He let his eyelids relax, but kept them closed.

"Thanks, honey," replied a soft and sultry voice.

The voice was so close that Rick could feel her breath upon his cheek. It was warm and pleasant. He could also feel her hair tickling his forehead. "Jane," he said playfully.

"Jane," replied the voice, imitating his exact inflection.

The fifth thing that occurred to Rick was that the voice did not belong to his wife. He snapped open his eyes and gasped. There, not six inches away from his own face, was a pair of the most mesmerizing eyes he had ever seen. Dark brown, almost black, with flecks of luminous gold, they looked as if they might have been digitally enhanced. And the face to which they belonged had an exotic look—olive complexion and striking features framed with a cascade of silky dark brown hair.

He tried to pull back, only to find the pavement beneath his head would not allow it. The woman slowly backed away, but she held her gaze firmly upon him as if she were looking at the answer to a long mystery. Although he was now aware that he was outside, that detail became irrelevant in comparison to the woman before him. She was stunningly beautiful, to say the least, but there was something else about her that made it impossible for him to avert his eyes. Had she been some random woman in a restaurant or on a bus, Rick would have immediately turned away, but something was overriding his sense of propriety. All he could do was stare.

After what seemed like a very long time, the woman stood up to her full height (about six inches taller than Rick) and held her hand out to him. Her grip was surprisingly strong, and Rick felt the bones in his hand shift as she lifted him to his feet. Standing before him, with the sun behind her creating a halo-like glow around her long dark mane, she looked like an Amazon Warrior Princess. Not that Rick had ever actually seen an Amazon Warrior Princess, but that's what he imagined one would look like.

It was at that moment that everything came rushing back to him—the beautiful woman in her bulky flight suit, the strange aircraft, and the others. Others? Where were the others? Rick took a step backward and bumped into the answer. The other three had been standing right behind him the whole time. The one with the goofy grin was smiling from ear to ear. "Gesundheit!" he said and his smile became even broader.

Rick thought he might pass out again, but he held it together. Shaking his head, he sidestepped away from them. This can't be real, he thought. But as he ran through his mental list, it was the only option that made sense. He started to laugh at the lunacy of it. How could aliens be the only thing that made any sense? "This is crazy!" he shouted. "How could…?"

"This is crazy!" echoed the grinning man.

"How could," said the other man.

Rick did a double-take at the alien parrots. Then he made his final argument as to why they simply could not be who he just admitted they were: "It's just not possible!" It was his last ditch effort to preserve the world view he had held his entire life, but he came up short. He had nothing else to say. There they were—beings that shouldn't be—undeniably there.

"It's just not possible!" the woman with the brown and gold eyes said in an exact imitation of Rick's voice inflection.

Okay, Rick thought to himself, I'm just going to have to say it. He walked up to the grinning man, looked him square in the face and said, "You, my friend, are a…" The word wouldn't come out.

"You, my friend, are a," the grinning man said. His grin was now a toothy smile.

Rick shook his head and held up his hand. Then, clearing his throat, he tried again, "You are a very, very tall…alien from another world." Rick said the last four words so fast that they all ran together. "There, I said it." He spun around and shouted out into the empty desert, "You're right, Ed Tyler! I admit it, you were right! Aliens are real and I've got four of them right here!" He started laughing because he couldn't think of anything else to do.

All four aliens tried to mimic this barrage of new vocabulary, but it came out as a cacophony of gibberish and forced laughter. The scene was so odd that all Rick could do was stare at them. Finally, he threw up his hands and shouted, "Now, what?"

The other female alien cocked her head, looked directly at Rick and said, "Aliens are real and I've got four of them right here."

It sounded so intentional and believable that Rick could only respond with, "I know!"

The odd exchange could have gone on all day, but the four visitors seemed to have gotten their fill of English for a while. With no further attempt to communicate, they turned and headed back to their ship, which was obviously not an airplane.

Thinking they might leave, Rick felt a tinge of disappointment. "Hey, where're you goin'?"

It's funny how quickly the human mind can assimilate new information. Just a few moments earlier, Rick was fighting hard not to believe what he was seeing. Now, he was fearful they might leave so soon. It would be just his luck to make the greatest discovery in history and not be able to prove it. He had no camera, and there was not another soul around for miles who could verify the encounter. Emboldened by his new belief, Rick caught up with them just as they reached the edge of the ship's wing.

The grinning man looked down at him and said, "Hey, where're you goin'?" Then he stooped low and made his way to the ladder.

"Oh, sorry, I was just…" Rick started to answer, but then realized the man was merely parroting the last thing he heard Rick say.

The grinning man climbed the ladder and disappeared through the hatch. The woman with the brown and gold eyes had also crawled beneath the ship and was waiting at the base of the ladder. The other two aliens stood next to Rick, conversing with one another in words Rick had never heard before. When they realized Rick was listening, they interrupted their conversation and smiled at him. The woman said something he thought was intended for him, but the way the man chuckled made him suspect it was actually about him. Rick blushed and turned his attention back to the ladder where a long metallic case was being lowered from the hatch.

The woman grasped the case, but struggled under its weight. Rick hurried to her side and helped her lower it to the ground. She smiled at him in a way that seemed to say thanks. Another case appeared through the hatch and would have crashed to the ground had Rick not grabbed it. He placed it on the ground next to its twin.

"Thanks, honey," a masculine voice said.

Rick looked up and saw the grinning man's head poking through the hatch. Then an arm appeared and made a gesture that Rick took as an invitation to approach. Not knowing whether his interpretation was correct, he glanced toward the woman. She was sitting on one of the cases; she looked tired and had not noticed her companion. He looked toward the other two and saw that something had caught their attention. They were kneeling beside the road, unaware of the activity beneath the ship. When he looked back at the hatch, the grinning man was still waving his arm at him. Rick shrugged and made his way up the ladder.

The interior of the ship was dark and it felt much smaller than it looked from the outside. Rick waited at the top of the ladder for his eyes to adjust before climbing the rest of the way in. Once inside, he scanned the compartment and was surprised at how un-alien it looked. There was a control console, seating for a crew of six, and a cargo area. The only un-earthly thing about it was what Rick guessed were decorations. The flat surfaces of the walls and ceiling were adorned with lighted symbols which cast the interior of the ship in a golden glow. The symbols reminded him of the hieroglyphs the ancient Egyptians used to decorate the insides of their temples and tombs. But unlike Egyptian hieroglyphs, these symbols had no correlation to anything in the natural world, at least not anything in Rick's natural world.

The grinning man was sitting in what appeared to be the pilot's seat. He was looking straight ahead at a blank screen and tapping on the armrest of this chair; a flurry of lights danced to the cadence of his drumming. When he saw Rick, he patted the seat next to him and said something in his own language.

Rick maneuvered his way into the seat. As soon as he sat down, the panel in front of him lit up with symbols and diagrams. Although none of it made sense to him, he thought it was beautiful. He turned toward the grinning man, and when he did, the display vanished.

When he faced forward again, the display reappeared. Rick slowly turned his head to the right. The main panel vanished again and a smaller panel to the right of the seat lit up. After a bit of testing, Rick discovered four panels of various sizes and shapes, each one becoming visible only when he looked directly at it. "Cool," Rick said as he turned his attention back to the main panel.

The grinning man, who's smile no longer seemed so goofy to Rick, reached forward and touched a symbol on the console. A three-dimensional, basketball-sized image of a planet appeared directly in front of Rick's eyes. Not recognizing the shapes of any of the land masses, he guessed it might be a depiction of some other planet; perhaps it was the grinning man's home world. But then something struck him as oddly familiar. He tilted his head first to the left and then to the right. Then it became clear—the unmistakable boot shape of Italy. From there, he could easily recognize the rest of Europe and Africa.

The image looked real. Every detail looked exactly as he had seen it a thousand times before in books and movies. The continents were clearly recognizable in contrast to the deep blue oceans. As the earth rotated downward, he saw an arc of clouds from a weather system moving toward the northeastern United States. Not only did it look real, it was accurate. Rick saw the same image on *The Weather Channel* earlier that morning.

The image began to increase in size, taking up more and more of his field of vision until Rick could no longer see the entire planet without turning his head. It seemed to be growing, or rather his perspective was changing as if he were being pulled into it. He looked up and saw the blackness of space eclipsed by the horizon of the earth. He looked down at his feet and saw beneath them the same effect. That's when it occurred to him exactly what he was seeing.

Rick subconsciously tightened his grip on the armrest of his chair as the image turned and flattened out before him. It was like being in a flight simulator, except there was no sound or vibration, and the landscape was as lifelike as if he were actually viewing it from an airplane. Although he could not pinpoint his location, he knew he was somewhere over North America (maybe Canada) and moving west at an incredible rate of speed. He was now low enough to pick out certain land features like mountains and forests, but he had to keep his eyes on the distant horizon because whenever he looked down, the blur of the earth beneath him made him woozy.

Suddenly, the landscape changed, and Rick gasped as he shot out over the Pacific Ocean. There, over the deep blue expanse, the speed was not so noticeable, but he kept his eyes fixed on the horizon which was starting to tilt. He gripped the armrest even tighter and held his breath as the horizon became nearly vertical. When it flattened out again, he exhaled in a whistle. There before his eyes was the most beautiful postcard-like image of San Francisco he had ever seen. He was much lower than he had expected, and his speed had decreased significantly. He saw boats in the bay and he could even make out cars moving on the Golden Gate Bridge. For a moment, Rick forgot that he was still on the ground in Wyoming. He wondered if the people on the bridge could see him.

Then without warning, San Francisco disappeared beneath him and the ship was back up to speed. Had he actually been moving, he would have surely been thrown back into his seat. But as it was, his body was not sensing the same information his eyes were relaying to his brain. The sensation was disorienting. He felt a wave of nausea build as he followed Interstate 80 eastward.

In what seemed like an impossibly short amount of time, he passed just to the north of Sacramento, crossed over the Sierra Nevada, and flew directly over Reno and out over the desert. Within seconds, he spotted what he believed to be Salt Lake City on his right. Continuing along Interstate 80, he was now flying low over the Rocky Mountains into Wyoming. Banking left, he flew north back over the desert. The city of Casper came into view. He recognized Casper Mountain where he and Jane once tried to ski. The image tilted to the left again, and he was flying due west.

Now he was close enough to the ground to see antelope grazing on shrubs along State Road 20 toward Riverton. The Rocky Mountains appeared again on the horizon, and he began to decelerate and descend in a slow counter-clockwise spiral. Finally, his forward movement ceased and he was hovering like a helicopter only a few hundred feet above the ground. He continued his descent until he touched down; then everything came to a stop. In front of him was an image of the road and a little round hill.

Rick felt as if he just watched a scene from a documentary about Planet Earth. The only thing missing was a stirring soundtrack. He was almost sorry it came to an end. As he stared at the scene in front of him, the documentary turned into an action flick as a white pickup came speeding around the hill and skidded off the road, disappearing over the embankment in a large cloud of dirt. A minute elapsed in real-time before the truck reappeared back onto the road, skidded to a stop, and then rolled to within thirty feet of him. Rick's mouth fell open as he watched himself get out of his truck.

As he watched himself walk slowly toward himself, a funny thought came to him: This was the most amazing thing that had ever happened to him (or anyone for that matter), yet all he could think of at the moment was that his wife was right—he really did walk like a cowboy. In the seat next to him, the grinning man was laughing. Did he think Rick walked like a cowboy, too?

"What's so funny?" Rick said defensively. He was getting used to the man and half expected him to answer. But all he heard the man say was something that sounded like, "Pass the can of peas." Then the alien got out of his seat, moved to the rear of the ship, and disappeared through the hatch.

Rick thought it strange that he was left unattended in their ship. It wasn't like he could steal it, but he was fairly certain he could break something. Looking at all the lighted symbols in front of him, he felt like a little kid again; and being left alone in the alien spaceship was like some kind of cosmic test to see if he could resist the temptation to touch something. Maybe he was over-thinking the situation, but he took it as a gesture of trust. For some reason, that was important to him. Rick took one last look around the ship and reluctantly made his way down the ladder.

Outside the spaceship, Rick found the four aliens huddled near the tip of the wing. They were engaged in deep conversation, so Rick kept his distance. Watching them, it dawned on him that he had progressed way past shock. In fact, the whole thing now seemed almost normal to him. Actually, normal might be a bit of a stretch, but his skepticism had completely disappeared and he no longer felt even the slightest hint of fear or apprehension. In fact, he was beginning to sense an affinity for them. Rick was not one to accept new ideas without long careful consideration, but these last thirty minutes opened the door to a universe of possibilities, and he had stepped fully across the threshold. It was like waking from a dream.

Although he could not hear or understand what the aliens were discussing, he could tell it was serious. They were huddled close and speaking with noticeable intensity. His earth-norms made him feel a little awkward for staring at them, but the aliens didn't seem to mind. Every few seconds one of them would glance toward him and smile. Perhaps privacy was not as important on their world.

Time didn't seem to matter much to them, either. They spoke for a very long time, and Rick was starting to get antsy. He wondered if on their world they might have a different perspective on time. Rick, however, was very much a product of Earth culture. Although he and Jane had moved to Wyoming in order to slow down, Rick's mind was still prone to efficiency. So he used this indeterminate pause to work out a few problems.

First, there was the matter of the ship. Rick was no rocket scientist, but he knew a ship that small was not built for deep space travel. The only solution he could think of was that it was a transport ship, which meant there had to be a much larger ship orbiting the earth. And if there was a larger ship, that meant there had to be a crew to maintain it. Granted, this assumption was based on the science of *Star Trek* and *Star Wars*, but it still seemed logical.

Second, there was the matter of their physiology. Except for their unusual height, these aliens were quite humanlike. Obviously, they were able to survive in earth's atmosphere, which meant their world must be a lot like Earth. But there had to be differences. A hundred questions flooded Rick's mind, but he knew he would never begin to answer any of them until they could learn to communicate…if they could learn to communicate. This was one aspect of alien encounter the science fiction movies had gotten wrong. Apparently, English was not a universal language after all.

Rick's train of thought was interrupted by what appeared to be the conclusion of the aliens' conversation. He would soon come to understand the meaning of their actions, but in the moment, all he could do was watch. The two men faced each other, as did the two women. Placing their hands on the sides of the each other's head, they drew each other toward themselves so that their foreheads touched. Then, the four of them spoke in unison something that sounded like a chant. After about a minute, they changed partners and repeated the whole routine. Rick expected a third round, but instead they approached him. As they drew close to Rick, he could see moisture in their eyes and that the grinning man's smile had faded. Rick sensed in his soul that something significant was happening between them. He felt like an intruder.

Rick wanted to disappear until the man who was not the grinning man stepped toward him. He gently placed his hands on both sides of Rick's head and leaned down until his forehead touched Rick's. Heat radiated from the point of contact throughout his entire body and he heard the man speak the same chant he heard earlier. Rick wanted more than anything to be able to understand what was being said. As the man stepped back, a smile appeared on his face. He bore a strong resemblance to the grinning man. Rick wondered if they might be brothers.

Rick felt his knees weaken when the other woman stepped toward him. She was every bit as beautiful as the woman with the brown and gold eyes, though her eyes were deep blue. She placed her hands on Rick's head and leaned toward him, touching her forehead to his. The warmth returned and Rick felt the sting of tears forming in his eyes. She spoke the chant softly, but now it sounded to him more like a song. His longing to understand it intensified. When she stepped back in line with the others, the expression on her face mirrored theirs. As Rick beheld them all, he saw such a strong resemblance that he wondered if they might all be siblings.

Rick readied himself for the grinning man or the woman with the brown and gold eyes, but they did not approach him. Instead, the other two ducked beneath the wing of the ship and made their way toward the ladder. The woman climbed up first and then the man. As the ladder was retracting, the head of the woman reappeared through the hatch. Her long hair reached nearly halfway to the ground. She smiled and called out something in her own language. Then she looked directly at Rick and called to him, "Gesundheit!"

Rick smiled and waved. "Gesundheit!"

Rick jumped as a large hand grasped him by the arm and pulled him backwards. The grinning man said something that sounded like, "Connie Chung" and led him to where the woman was already standing about twenty feet away from the ship.

There was a loud pop followed by a low whirring sound as the engines fired up. The ship lifted straight up off the ground and retracted its landing gear. When it was about a hundred feet above them, it turned toward the west and tilted in that direction. Rick, the grinning man, and the woman with the brown and gold eyes watched as the ship climbed another hundred feet. Then, in an impossible maneuver, it banked sharply to the right and took off like a shot toward the east. In a matter of seconds it was out of sight.

Sometime between the ship's departure and seeing the two remaining aliens walking directly toward his truck, it occurred to Rick that his encounter was not over. He didn't know for how long, but it was obvious these two intended to stay. And since Rick was the only human they knew, he guessed they intended to stay with him. At first, he was pleased, but before he reached his truck another thought brought panic. How was he going to explain them to Jane?

CHAPTER 5:

BACK AT THE RANCH

≈

Toyota did not design its 1982 line of pickups to accommodate three adults, much less one 6'3" human and two even taller aliens. But somehow, after the aliens conducted a thorough inspection of the vehicle, Rick was able to convince them to squeeze into the cab.

Although they were only a few miles from the ranch, it took nearly an hour to make the trip. Rick quickly learned that his new friends, in spite of the fact that they traveled across the universe in a supersonic spaceship, had a problem with ground speed. At 30 mph, the grinning man stopped grinning and the female just closed her eyes and held on. When Rick stopped the truck, they jumped out and backed away from it as if it were a wild and dangerous animal. At first, they refused to get back in, deciding instead they would rather walk while Rick drove beside them. But after about a hundred yards, they were both breathing hard and looking faint. After a bit of coaxing, Rick managed to get them back into the truck, though he had to keep the speed below 10 mph.

The other delay occurred when they came upon a bridge that crossed over a small stream. At the sight of water, the two aliens became very excited, so Rick had to let them out for a closer look. The stream was hardly a stream at all, but it may as well have been the Rio Grande. The aliens were like children on their first visit to the ocean. When the female put her hand in the water, she squealed and pulled it back, surprised by its frigid temperature. Then the male tried it and said something that sounded like, "Crabbit sun sun." After about ten minutes of patting, swishing, splashing, sniffing, and an attempt to taste (which Rick had to deter given the fact that they were down stream from a cattle ranch), they seemed satisfied and returned to the truck. By now, they were both shivering from the cold. The female huddled close to the male in a way that made Rick wondered if the two might actually be a couple.

When they finally pulled onto the road leading to the Blackwell Ranch, Rick kept a sharp eye out for Ed Tyler. He was relieved to find the ranch was as quiet and desolate as a ghost town. Glancing at his watch, he was also relieved that Jane would not be home for at least another hour, maybe two if she decided to stay in town for lunch with some of her church friends.

The main house was typical for central Wyoming—comfortable, but built more for function than for elegance. Though it was Spartan compared to the million dollar mansions in Jackson Hole, the aliens seemed to be as impressed as any human would be standing in front of Buckingham Palace. They took in every detail, pointing to and discussing the pitch of the roof, the fake shutters, the faded paint, the steps leading up to the front door. Even the scrawny leafless tree in the front yard warranted a close examination. Their curiosity was irrepressible. They literally ran from one new sight to another—and that was just the front yard.

Rounding the side of the house, the male caught sight of the barn. He called out something, and the female quickly joined him. Without hesitation, they made a beeline in the direction of the open barn door. Rick, who was sitting on the hood of his truck, jumped down and ran toward them.

"Stop!" he yelled. But it was too late. They were about ten feet away from the building when Jake, a large black stallion, stuck his head out of the half-door of his stall and snorted. The two aliens froze at the sight of the strange creature.

"Whew!" Rick said as he caught up to them. "You shouldn't get any closer to Jake. He's a feisty one."

Jake stared at them with his menacing black eye and shifted nervously in his stall. His ears were bent back and he snorted threateningly. Any normal person would have taken that as an invitation to give the great animal his space. But these were not normal people. The female cocked her head, her eyes wide with curiosity, and took a step closer.

"Um, miss, uh..." Rick wished he knew her name. When he reached out to stop her, the male stepped between them. Against his better judgment, Rick let her go.

The female approached the horse as if it were a lamb. She exhibited not a trace of fear or apprehension. Jake threatened with another boisterous "Neigh!" but it did not faze the alien in the least. Rick winced in anticipation of a terrible scene and started to call out again. But before he could get the words out, Jake put his head down; his ears turned forward and twitched almost playfully. The female placed her hand on the horse's head and murmured softly. She did not pat it like Rick expected, but touched it in the same way the other aliens had touched Rick's head before they departed in their ship. Rick had seen horse whisperers in action, but he had never seen anything like this. Jake, a horse deemed unmanageable, bowed at the female alien's touch. The once wild and dangerous beast was now as calm as a show horse.

"Well, I'll be," a gruff voice said from behind them.

Rick spun around to find Burt Cooper standing there in all of his cowboy glory. He could have been the inspiration for the Marlboro Man; Levi's tucked into leather cowboy boots, rawhide coat, and well-worn cowboy hat. He turned his head and spewed a brown stream of tobacco juice from his mouth.

"Ain't never seen ol' Jake cozy up to anyone like that before," he said, motioning toward the horse with a gloved hand.

"Hello, Coop," Rick said, his mind working fast. "What brings you out here?"

Burt Cooper (or Coop as he was known) was a friendly sort, although he tended to be a bit over-protective of the ranch and its occupants, mostly the four-legged kind. "Ed called. Said there was a fence that needed mending. Thought I'd better get on it before he has a hissy. He can be right ornery, that one."

"He can be right ornery, that one," the grinning man said as he approached Coop for a closer look.

Coop was also very protective of his personal space. He took a step back as the towering alien closed in on him.

Rick knew he had to act fast. "Uh, this is my, uh…my cousin." He put his arm around the grinning man's shoulder and gently pulled him back.

"He ain't from around here, is he?" Coop drawled, sizing him up.

"No," Rick chuckled. "He's from out-of-town. Actually, he's from out-of-the-country. They just flew in this morning."

"Uh-huh," Coop grunted. "I take it that pretty young lady over there's his wife." Coop nodded toward the female who was walking toward them. She was blinking and wiping her eyes with the back of her hand.

"Yes," Rick guessed. "Yes, she is."

There was a long pause. Then Coop said, "Well, ain't you goin' to introduce us?"

"Oh, I'm sorry," Rick said, his face turning red. "How rude of me. Burt Cooper, I'd like you to meet my cousin…" Rick's mind went blank as he tried to think of an appropriate name. Then he blurted out the first name that came to him. "Boris."

Coop offered his hand to the grinning man. "Glad to meet you, Boris. Where do you call home?"

The grinning man looked at Coop's hand and then at Coop.

Rick quickly stepped forward. "They're from Russia." Rick chuckled nervously. "They don't speak English."

"They don't speak English," Boris repeated.

Coop eyed the tall alien and then gave Rick the squint-eye.

Rick chuckled again. "But they're learning."

By now the female joined them. She took a great interest in Coop's hat. When she reached out to touch it, Coop took another step back. The female sneezed unapologetically and took another step toward Coop.

"And this," Rick said, putting his arm around her shoulder to dissuade her encroachment on Coop's space, "this is Natasha." Rick looked unusually short between the two aliens.

"Boris and Natasha, eh?" Coop said, rubbing his gloved hand across his unshaved chin. He looked as if he were on the verge of remembering something long forgotten, but whatever it was eluded him. His expression relaxed and he tipped his hat to the lady. "Welcome to America, ma'am." Then he addressed Rick, "You say they just flew in this morning? Huh. Didn't think Riverton had any flights before noon."

"Well, actually, they landed in Casper. We just got back."

Coop looked at Rick's Toyota and then up at Boris and Natasha. "That must have been some trip."

Rick seized upon the opportunity. "Yes it was. They've been traveling for days, and you know how it is, jetlag and all. I think I better get them settled in the house."

"Here, let me help you with their luggage." Coop started toward the truck.

"Luggage?" Rick said, "Um, it's lost. Yep, that's what they told us... in Casper, they told us that. You know how those airlines are. I just hope they find it. We'd love to stay and chat, but we better get going." Rick started moving Boris and Natasha toward the house. "See you later, Coop."

"See you later, Coop," Natasha said.

"Ma'am," Coop replied with a nod of his head and a tip of his hat. He watched them disappear into the house. On his way to the tool shed, Coop noticed the two large cases in the back of Rick's truck. He glanced back at the house and scratched his chin again. "Ruskies, eh," he said and then spit a stream of tobacco juice onto the white snow.

Inside the house, Boris and Natasha discovered the mother load of new sights and smells and things to touch. Though they were both showing signs of fatigue, they seemed to find new energy in the unexplored environment. Uninhibited by human etiquette, they proceeded to open every door and drawer, and handle every loose article as if they owned the place.

Rick attempted to steer them toward the couch in the living room because that's where he and Jane always entertained guests, but he would have had better success steering a bull through a room full of red capes. There was just no way to stem the tide of their curiosity. Realizing there was nothing he could do until they had completed their inspection, Rick went into the kitchen to put on a pot of coffee.

A few minutes later, Boris ducked through the doorway into the kitchen, leaving Natasha in the living room in front of a well-stocked book case. He scanned the kitchen as if he were looking for something in particular. The coffee maker made a gurgling sound. Boris zeroed in on it. Cocking his head like a puppy, he sniffed twice and approached the machine. He leaned in close and took a deep breath, held it in, and exhaled slowly.

"Coffee," Rick said.

"Coffee," Boris repeated. Then he reached for the pot.

Rick reacted like a startled parent. Grabbing the alien's hand just inches away from the hot glass, he yelled, "No! That's hot!" Rick's voice came out much louder than he intended, and Boris responded with an expression of confusion. A question flashed through Rick's mind: Which is worse, to yell at a seven foot tall alien or let him burn himself? He quickly let go of Boris's hand. "That's hot," he said more calmly.

Boris seemed to understand. He withdrew his hand and stood to his full height. "That's hot," he said and walked out of the kitchen.

Rick breathed a sigh of relief. *That was close*, he thought. *I'll have to be more care...*

Just then, loud music exploded from the living room. Rick sprinted from the kitchen expecting to find Boris and Natasha...well, he didn't really know what to expect. What he found were two aliens staring intently at a speaker on the top self of the book case. Rick rushed over to the stereo and switched it off. To his surprise, the aliens spun around and started speaking excitedly in their own language. Boris grabbed Rick by the arm and pulled him toward the speaker, while Natasha kept pointing and repeating something.

"What?" Rick said, "What is it?"

The aliens continued repeating the same words over and over.

"I'm sorry, I don't understand."

Natasha said something to Boris and he stopped, although there was an excitement about him as he kept looking from Rick to the speaker and back to Rick. Natasha moved closer to Rick and, like a teacher driving home an important lesson, repeated the mysterious phrase slowly.

"I'm sorry," Rick said, "I just can't..."

She placed her hand on his mouth. It was soft and warm. She repeated the phrase once more, slower still. This time part of it sounded vaguely familiar.

"Weega taco," Rick said, trying to repeat what he heard. "Weega taco. We-ga-ta-co. We got taco? Is that it? We got taco? Are you hungry?"

Natasha smiled and pointed to the speaker. Then they both continued repeating the entire phrase. It sounded like they were singing, "Oo-ee, oo-ee, oh, oh, weega taco."

Rick still didn't have a clue, but he did have an idea. He went to the stereo and turned it on. An old Rolling Stones song came blasting through the speakers. The aliens froze, as if hypnotized by the music. Then they started singing again.

"Okay," Rick said, and he joined in the song. "Weega taco! Weega taco!"

This went on for some time and the aliens seemed pleased at this breakthrough in communication. Rick smiled and nodded, though he still had no idea what it meant. After a few more rounds, Natasha pulled Boris over to the book shelf. The singing ended.

Natasha carefully pulled from the shelf an illustrated copy of Jack Finney's *Time and Again* and showed it to Boris. Gently, as if she were handling the original Guttenberg Bible, she opened the book. Boris felt the paper, sniffed it, and ran his finger over the print. Flipping through the pages, they came upon one with a picture. They examined it closely, flipping back and forth to its reverse as if expecting to find the reverse of the picture on the next page.

Rick watched with fascination. A fan of science fiction, he had seen hundreds of fictional aliens in movies, but none of them came close to the real thing. Movie aliens were savage conquerors or super-intelligent snobs or clumsy little creatures that behaved more like animals than intelligent beings. Boris and Natasha were none of these; they weren't even green. They were so human-like that he supposed a casual observer might not take notice of them at all, except for their unusual height and beauty. Yet the longer he was with them, the more aware he was becoming of something altogether non-human.

Rick was now convinced that Boris's perpetual smile was absolutely sincere. He also believed Natasha was completely unaware of how stunningly beautiful she was. Rick had known hundreds of smiling, beautiful people in his life, and he trusted only a few. In his experience, smiles covered ulterior motives and feminine beauty was a tool (and sometimes a weapon). He had been burned by both more times than he cared to admit, and as a result he constructed a protective wall of cynicism. How odd that these visitors from another world could so quickly penetrate his defenses.

"Say," Rick said when he caught himself staring, "I'll bet you guys are hungry. I don't know if we have any tacos, but I'll bet I can find something."

Boris looked up from the book and said to him, "Weega taco."

Rick started to reply as if the alien had spoken to him in English, but caught himself. "Yeah, well, there's that." He shook his head and went back into the kitchen.

As Rick searched the cupboards for something to serve his guests, he was hit by another wave of reality that made him chuckle. "This is crazy," he said aloud. "There are aliens in my living room, and I'm in here looking for snacks like it's the most natural thing in the world." He leaned on his elbows on the counter and messaged his temples. "I don't even know what aliens eat." When he looked up, he spotted a new box of 'Nilla Wafers. "I guess this'll have to do." He grabbed the box, three cups, and a carton of milk, and returned to the living room.

Boris and Natasha had replaced the Finney book and were now flipping through book after book looking for more pictures. When they saw Rick set the milk and cookies on the coffee table, they joined him. They sat next to each other on the couch while Rick pulled up a chair and sat opposite them across the table.

Natasha looked tired and her eyes were watery and red. Every few seconds, she sniffled and wrinkled her nose. Rick found it oddly attractive. He retrieved a box of tissues from under the table and set it in front of her. She did not appear to know what to do with it, so Rick demonstrated by plucking a tissue out of the box and wiping his own eyes and nose. She understood and pulled a tissue from the box. Although Boris had no need for one, he was intent on trying out this latest discovery. After much dabbing and rubbing and blowing of his nose, he smoothed out his used tissue and stuffed it back into the box.

Rick decided it was not worth the effort to demonstrate the proper disposal of used tissues, so he let it go. Instead, he reached into the box of 'Nilla Wafers and withdrew a cookie. "Cookie," he said, holding it up for them to see. Then he took a bite. "Mmm," he said, patting his stomach.

Boris picked up the box and looked inside. He sniffed at it and then retrieved a cookie of his own. Taking a small bite, his smile broadened as his taste buds relayed the new sensation to his brain.

"Cookie, mmm," he said and patted his own stomach. After popping the rest of the cookie into his mouth, he reached into the box for another one and handed it to Natasha. She took it and put the entire cookie into her mouth. "Cookie, mmm," she said, but she neglected the stomach patting part. Within minutes, the box was empty and Natasha seemed to perk up a bit.

Next, Rick poured three cups of milk and pushed two of them toward Boris and Natasha. They looked at the cups and then at Rick.

"Coffee?" Boris asked.

Alas, a statement that actually made sense. Rick smiled at the first real communication. "No, it's milk."

"No, it's milk," they echoed in unison.

Rick nodded. "Drink up," he said, taking a sip from his cup.

Boris and Natasha took their cups, drained them, and set them on the table.

Rick bit his lip to keep from laughing. His two alien visitors each had perfect milk moustaches, just like in the commercials. Not wanting to embarrass his guests, Rick plucked a tissue from the box and dabbed his upper lip. As expected, Boris and Natasha did the same.

Rick's amusement turned to concern when he realized he was wiping his mouth with the same tissue Boris used to blow his nose. Now Rick was not a germaphobe, but the thought of alien germs invading his body made him recall learning about how whole tribes of Native Americans had been obliterated by diseases introduced to them by the first European explorers. In the span of ten seconds, Rick's imagination played out the entire scenario: Fever and chills, a trip to his doctor, a frantic call to the Center for Disease Control, and then agents in hazmat suits taking him and Jane away in a special van never to be seen or heard from again.

Rick reigned in his imagination and forced the worst-case scenario thoughts out of his mind. Of course, playing host to visitors from another world had to come with certain risks—hundreds of reasons to get all worked up about. He couldn't let a little ET cold ruin the greatest discovery of all time. (Later that evening, Rick brushed his teeth twice, gargled with anti-bacterial mouthwash for twice the recommended time, and brushed his teeth again—just to be safe.)

Whatever energy-inducing affect the cookies might have had, the milk counter-acted it. Natasha yawned once and laid her head on Boris's shoulder. She was asleep within seconds, her breathing soft and steady.

Had the situation been reversed, and it was Rick and Jane visiting someone for the first time, Jane would have been mortified and Rick would have tried to keep her awake. For Boris, however, human embarrassment had no meaning. He simply responded in the way Rick only wished he could. He gently laid Natasha down on the couch so that her head rested on a pillow. Although she was too tall for the human-sized couch, he somehow managed to position her in a way that looked comfortable. Then he leaned over and touched his forehead to hers and tenderly ran his fingers through her long, silky hair.

Rick grabbed a throw blanket from the back of his chair and handed it to Boris. He understood the function of the blanket and draped it over Natasha. Now that she was all curled up on the couch, nestled beneath the blanket, no one could have guessed she was a six and a half foot tall alien. Rick was struck by how natural she looked lying there on his couch in his home. He was struck also by the thought that Boris and Natasha no longer seemed as strange to him. To be sure, they were visitors from another world, and he knew nothing about them, but he was beginning to sense affection for them.

With one last stroke of Natasha's hair, Boris left her to sleep and walked over to the window. Rick joined him and gazed out at the familiar sight of his backyard. It was a view he knew well; so well, in fact, that he could see it clearly with his eyes closed. It was a sacred place for him, as sacred as the church was to Jane. Though he tried to experience it that way with her, she didn't take it the same way. To Jane, it was just barren desert. So, every morning for the past several years, Rick experienced it alone. But now, in the silence of the moment, standing next to this stranger who had dropped into his life from who-knew-where, something was stirring within him. He looked up at Boris and noticed his smile had taken on a look of contentment. There was no way to know what he was thinking, but Rick sensed a connection forming. He liked the man and wanted to believe the man liked him. If only there was some way to bridge the language barrier, to communicate, to understand who they were and why they had come.

As Rick considered these things, he became aware of a thought. It was not like a thought that took on the shape of words, nor did it sound like his own voice. It was more like a wordless notion. He almost dismissed it, but the thought grew until he could not ignore it. Though he struggled to put it into the form of a sentence, the words refused to come. It felt like the idea entered his mind from an outside source that refused to let him take control of it. For the writer, this was frustrating, so Rick used a technique he discovered early in his writing career. He focused his gaze on a notch in the distant mountains and let his mind relax. At first, the thought faded as Rick let the contour of the mountains register in his mind. Then, like the first rays of dawn appearing in the eastern sky, the thought returned. This time it was so clear that it actually took form—though not in a sentence, but two distinct words repeating over and over.

Supposing he was actually hearing the words with his ears, Rick glanced up at Boris expecting to see his lips moving. The alien's eyes were closed and he was swaying slightly from side to side like he was watching a tennis match; and he was humming something that could have been a tune. Rick could still hear the words, though they were definitely not coming from Boris.

How is this possible? Rick heard himself think. *Mental telepathy? E.S.P.?* He had heard of these phenomena, but never put much stock in them. But after this morning, Rick had become much more open-minded. It made perfect sense that visitors from another world would possess mental abilities far beyond his own.

Concentrating further on the words, Rick decided that they were not being repeated after all. Rather, it was a single utterance that just hung in his mind. Had it been a single sound, it might have been like a singer holding out one long note. But it wasn't like that at all. It was definitely two words—four distinct syllables. It was impossible, but they hung so steadily in his mind that Rick was beginning to think they might have been there long before he noticed them, and may remain even after he put his mind upon something else.

As he marveled over this new experience, he felt a presence in the room. He turned around expecting to find Natasha had gotten up to join them, or that Jane had slipped in unannounced, but nothing had changed. Natasha slept soundly. Jane was not there. Then quite abruptly, the sound of the words ceased; though it left an echo in Rick's mind, kind of like how a bright light that is quickly extinguished leaves an imprint on the retina. Rick looked up at Boris who was now smiling down at him. Whatever had just happened, Rick had the feeling that even if Boris had not caused it, he was somehow aware of it.

Rick felt the need for some fresh air. When he opened the back door, a blast of cold air rushed into the house. Boris tilted his head back and breathed deeply. The cold air seemed to revive him, and he nearly ran out onto the deck and down the steps into Rick's massive back yard. Looking up into the sky, he raised his arms and laughed, "Tolis anuk! Tolis anuk!"

Rick could hardly believe his ears…or was it his mind? Even though he heard Boris speaking in his alien language, somehow he knew exactly what the man was saying. They were the same words that hung in his mind just a few moments earlier. Even stranger, he knew what they meant—*home*.

CHAPTER 6:

A FUNNY THING HAPPENED

WHILE YOU WERE AWAY

Å

Jane was not the jealous type, and Rick never gave her a reason to be. But when she walked into her living room and saw a strange beautiful woman sleeping on her couch, she became nauseated. Now it could have been any number of factors—the hormonal effects of pregnancy, the fact that she was starting to show and felt less attractive, the spiritual disconnect between Rick and herself—or it could have been a combination of all three. Whatever it was, Jane suddenly found herself getting angry. The bad part was she didn't know what she was most angry about. Was she angry at Rick for having another woman in the house while she was gone? Was she angry at this other woman? Or was she angry at herself for being angry?

She had no reason to not trust Rick, so surely there had to be an explanation. Maybe there was an accident or maybe the woman's car had broken down. Maybe Rick was working on the woman's car right now and she came inside because it was cold out and she just happened to fall asleep. That was a likely scenario except for the fact that Rick didn't know anything about cars and it wasn't that cold outside and the woman was so…so…well, who did she think she was invading her home?

Anger rose up inside her again and she no longer felt nauseated. She threw her Bible onto the coffee table hard, making a noise loud enough to wake Ed Tyler out of his medicated sleep. The woman didn't even flinch. Jane became all the more irritated that this woman was so comfortable in her house that she could sleep so soundly. Jane stomped through the room toward the back part of the house. As soon as she found him, Rick was going to get it.

As she passed by the window, she spotted Rick and a very tall man standing out by the split-rail fence. With her characteristically calm rationalism cowering in the corner of her mind, Jane jerked the door open and slammed it hard behind her. A tiny notion called out from that same corner suggesting that the tall man might be the strange woman's husband, but her anger drove it back. She stood on the edge of the deck and sweetly called out, "Rick dear, may I have a word with you?"

"Jane!" Rick called back.

"Now!" The sweetness had melted away.

There are times in a man's life when he knows it is best to keep his thoughts safely in check behind closed lips. This was one of those times. Rick gestured to Boris that he should remain at the fence while he went to talk to Jane. As he closed the distance between them, he noticed certain details about his lovely wife: Her arms were fixed in a pretzel shape across her chest, the muscle in her jaw was twitching, her eyes narrowed menacingly, and she looked much taller than her 5'4" frame. Gone was the "religious" peace and joy he had grown to resent, but now he wanted it back. When he got to within spitting distance of the deck, he stopped. "You're home."

"Surprised?" She said it with an icy tone that made it difficult to tell whether she meant it as a question or a statement.

"No," Rick replied, "I just didn't realize it was so late. Are you okay?"

She glared at him, trying to decide why he couldn't read her mind.

"Hey, um, a funny thing happened while you were away," Rick said, glancing back toward Boris.

Jane followed his gaze to the tall man. She could see the stranger's broad smile even at that distance and she could have sworn she had just heard him call out to her, "Gesundheit!" Something popped in her mind and rationalism crawled out from its hiding place. Her expression softened and her shoulders relaxed enough for her arms to fall to her sides. "Who is that man?"

Sensing it was safe to approach, Rick walked up the steps and onto the deck. "Honey," Rick said, taking her hands in his own, "this is going to sound a bit odd, so please just let me finish before you say anything."

Jane noticed something different about Rick. There was a gleam in his eyes she hadn't seen in years. "Okay."

"Maybe we better sit down." Rick took a seat on the bench and waited for Jane to join him.

"What is it, Rick?"

He thought for a moment and exhaled loudly. "This is really going to sound crazy, but you're just going to have to trust me."

"Okay, I trust you already. What's going on?"

"You see that man?" Rick nodded toward Boris who was now waving.

"Yes." Jane timidly waved back.

"And I guess you saw the woman inside."

"Yes, I saw her." Jane stopped waving and put her hands in her coat pockets.

"Well, they are…oh boy." Rick ran his fingers through his hair.

"Just say it!" There was a hint of anxiousness in Jane's voice.

"Okay, here goes." Rick looked down at his shoes and took a deep breath. "They're aliens." He chuckled as he heard the words come out of his mouth. He waited for a response, but there was none. Slowly, he turned his head and tried to get a glimpse of his wife out of the corner of his eye. "Did you hear what I said? They're aliens."

Jane's mouth fell open and she looked as if she had become paralyzed. It was not exactly the response Rick expected, but it was better than he had feared. At least she wasn't laughing at him.

"Jane? Did you hear me?"

"Uh-huh." Jane slowly rose to her feet. She looked back at the house and then out across the backyard.

"Aren't you going to say anything?" Rick asked.

"How did they get here?" Jane's voice was calm. She moved toward the steps and started down.

"They came in a ship. Hey, wait a minute." Rick joined her on the steps and put his hand on her shoulder. "Oh, I get it. You think I'm kidding, don't you?"

"No, I don't." There was something unnervingly calm about Jane's demeanor.

"Yes, you do. You're just playing along so it doesn't look like I got you."

"No, I'm not." She continued down the steps.

Rick watched her walk across the yard. "Jane, wait up." He jogged to catch up with her. "You mean you believe me?"

"Yes." Her pace quickened.

"You do? Why?" Rick had been rehearsing in his mind how he might convince her that he was not crazy or joking or lying. He was not prepared for this.

When they finally got to the split-rail fence, Jane stopped about ten feet from Boris and looked at him with childlike amazement.

Rick looked at his wife, then at Boris, then back at his wife. "You don't look all that surprised."

"Oh, I'm surprised," she assured him.

"No, I mean you don't seem…Jane, this isn't a joke."

"I know, Rick, I know."

"How do you know?"

Jane turned and looked directly into Rick's eyes. "Rick. I believe you. I just never thought I would actually meet one." With that, she turned back toward Boris and took the few steps that put her directly in front of him. She looked like a child standing in front of the tall alien who was nearly two feet taller than she.

"Wait a minute," Rick said. "Are you telling me you believe in aliens?"

"Yes," she said without turning to look at Rick.

"I mean before today, you believed in aliens?"

"Yes."

"How could I not know that?"

"You never asked."

"I never asked?" Rick laughed nervously and shrugged. "Why would I ever ask such a thing?" How could he not have known something this important about the woman who was carrying his child? "What else do I not know about you?"

"I don't think this is the time to get into that," she whispered back toward Rick. Then turning her attention back to Boris, she held out her hand. "Hello, I'm Jane."

"He doesn't speak English," Rick said, still musing over this revelation about his wife. Not the right time to get into that. She said that. "This isn't the right time to get into what?"

"Rick, this is incredible."

"Apparently, not all that incredible," he said under his breath. Then louder, "So, how long have you believed in aliens?"

"I've always believed. My dad and I used to talk about it when I was a kid. He said it was only a matter of time before they visited us."

"Well, yeah, I'm not a bit surprised that your dad would believe in aliens, but you?"

Jane shot him a look. "My dad was a brilliant man. Besides, it looks like you believe in them, too."

Rick started to say something smart, but didn't. She had a point.

Boris had been watching the exchange with great interest. Finally, he grasped Jane's hand and said, "Gesundheit."

"Gesundheit?" Jane asked. "Did he just say Gesundheit?"

"It's a long story," Rick said.

Jane stepped back and whispered to Rick, "Does he understand what we're saying?"

"No," Rick answered. There was a note of disappointment in his voice. "I've spent the entire morning with them. All they do is repeat what I say."

Jane frowned. "I guess it's not like in the movies."

"Not really."

"So, you haven't been able to communicate with them at all?"

"Well," Rick thought for a moment. "We drew some pictures in the dirt."

Jane nodded. It was a start.

"And they got pretty excited about the radio. We sort of sang along to an old Stones song." Jane wrinkled her nose—not a Stones fan. "And there was this thing. I can't really describe it, but I think Boris might have tried to use E.S.P. on me."

"Boris?"

"Oh yeah. We ran into Coop. I told him they were my cousins from out of the country. I introduced them as Boris and Natasha."

Jane started laughing. "Boris and Natasha? Like from *Rocky and Bullwinkle*?"

Boris started laughing, too. "Like from Rocky and Bullwinkle?"

Jane stopped laughing and stared in amazement.

"See what I mean?" Rick said. "They'll repeat anything you say."

"Hmm." Jane thought for a moment. "Let me try something." She took a step toward Boris and spoke slowly and deliberately. "I am Jane."

Boris smiled and said, "I am Jane."

Rick chuckled. "Not as easy as you thought, is it, smarty pants?"

Jane bit her lip and then tried again. She pointed to Rick and said, "Rick." Then she pointed to herself. "Jane." Finally, she pointed to Boris and waited.

Boris immediately imitated her. He pointed to Rick and Jane, saying their names correctly. When he pointed to himself he said, "Aldi."

"Aldi," Jane said, pointing to the man in front of her.

"Aldi," he repeated.

Jane shot Rick a sly grin. "His name is Aldi," she said triumphantly.

Rick frowned. Why hadn't he thought of that? "Maybe you can get Aldi to tell you where they came from and why they're here."

"I intend to," Jane said, "but first I'd like to meet our other guest."

Inside the house, Natasha was still sleeping soundly.

"Do you think we should wake her?" Jane asked.

"I don't know," Rick answered. "She was pretty tired and she hasn't been asleep that long. I'd hate to disturb her. Besides, you know how grumpy you get when I wake you."

"I do not get grumpy. It just takes me a little while to get my awake face on."

Rick rolled his eyes.

Aldi rolled his eyes.

"Rick," Jane whispered to him, "you're going teach him a bad habit."

"He's not a child, you know. He's just curious…about everything."

"What should we do?"

Aldi walked over to the couch and began stroking Natasha's hair. Then, looking back at Rick and Jane, he said, "Elsa-Eska."

"Elsa-Eska," Jane repeated. "That's her name. It's beautiful."

Aldi gently touched Elsa-Eska's shoulder, and she began to wake. He leaned down and spoke something into her ear. Elsa-Eska pushed herself up into a sitting position and brushed long strands of hair from her face. She blinked sleepily and gazed into Aldi's eyes, then she reached up and pulled his head toward hers until their foreheads touched.

"I think that's how they kiss," Rick whispered to Jane.

"Aw," Jane sighed, "how sweet."

Elsa-Eska turned toward them and flashed a smile of recognition at Rick. When she saw Jane, her face lit up with such warmth that Jane nearly blushed. Then she turned back toward Aldi and, looking deeply into his eyes, gently caressed his face. She pulled him close to her again and rubbed her cheek against his.

"That's new," Rick said.

"Not very shy, are they?" Jane assessed. She glanced at Rick and elbowed him in the ribs. "Don't stare."

Rick quickly turned away and scratched the back of his head, but Jane continued to watch.

A few seconds later, Aldi took Elsa-Eska by the hand and helped her get up from the couch. Jane's eyes widened and she gasped as Elsa-Eska stood to her full height. Meeting Aldi outside, Jane was not quite so overwhelmed by his height. But inside, seeing the woman's head come within a foot of the ceiling, the effect was much more dramatic.

"She's so tall," Jane said, not realizing she was voicing her thoughts.

"It's a bit of a shock at first," Rick said, "but I'm already getting used to it."

"Maybe we better all sit down," Jane said. She moved quickly around to the opposite side of the couch and took a seat in the reading chair next to the bookcase. She was experiencing one of those waves of reality that had buffeted Rick earlier.

"Are you okay?" Rick asked when he noticed the color had drained from Jane's face.

"I'm fine," she replied. "but I could use some water. Would you mind?"

"Not at all," Rick said. He disappeared into the kitchen.

Had Jane any idea of what was about to happen, she would not have sent Rick on an errand out of the room. He was just reaching for the cupboard when he heard Jane call to him. It wasn't actually a call of alarm, but it was close enough to make him forget all about the water. When Rick came back into the living room, he stopped in his tracks, not quite sure what to make of what he saw. Jane was leaning as far back in the chair as she could, and Elsa-Eska was kneeling in front of her with her hand on Jane's stomach.

"What happened?" Rick asked, holding back his amusement.

"I-I don't know," Jane said. "All of a sudden she got this strange look on her face and came over to me and…well, look."

Elsa-Eska said something and Aldi joined her on the floor in front of Jane.

"Rick," Jane said nervously as Aldi placed his hand on her stomach. "Do something."

Rick walked over to the examination and placed his hands on the shoulders of the two visitors. Aldi looked up at him and then at Jane. He seemed to understand and moved back to the couch. Elsa-Eska, however, did not appear to get the hint. With one hand still on Jane's stomach, she placed her other hand on Jane's head. With eyes closed, she rocked back and forth and began to hum. It was the same kind of humming Rick heard from Aldi earlier.

"It's okay," Rick whispered. "Try to relax. And listen."

Jane looked at Rick out of the corner of her eyes and then at the woman in front of her. A few seconds later, she felt the tension leave her body. She closed her eyes and concentrated on the humming that sounded like it might be a lullaby. A minute passed. Then two. Finally, Elsa-Eska took her hands off of Jane and moved back to the couch next to Aldi. She sat close to him, laying her head on his shoulder. When Jane opened her eyes, the color had returned to her face and she was completely relaxed.

"Did you hear something?" Rick asked eagerly.

"I-I can't explain it," Jane said. "It was like some kind of connection or something. Rick, I don't know how, but she knows I'm pregnant."

Rick chuckled. "I wouldn't have believed it yesterday, but today I'm not a bit surprised."

Jane reached for Rick's hand and looked up at him. "We're going to have a little girl."

Rick was not one to show emotion, but the words tapped a well within him he did not know existed. His throat tightened and he felt a slight tingling sensation in his right eye. On impulse, he brought his hand up and pressed his knuckle into the corner of his eye. Examining his hand, he was not at all surprised to find it moist.

CHAPTER 7:

THEY CAME, THEY SAW,

THEY STAYED FOR SUPPER

λ

After ten years of marriage, there were some questions Jane Blackwell no longer needed to ask her husband: Have you made coffee yet? Do you have an opinion on that? Would you like to try that in zero gravity? The answer was always, without exception, unequivocally "Yes."

There was one question, however, that had never come up before. Neither Jane nor Rick, nor anyone else for that matter, had ever asked this question, had ever been asked this question, and would not have known how to answer it if it had been asked. That question was this: "What do we do with them now?" Had anyone asked such a question of Rick Blackwell as recently as that morning, he would have laughed it off as absolutely absurd. But by the time evening rolled around, the question had been asked many times. What a difference a day makes.

Rick and Jane (human as they were) felt obligated to make sure their guests were properly entertained at every moment. They gave them a tour of the remainder of their home, offered them books and magazines, showed them countless photographs of holidays and vacations, and even let them play with their computer. The computer held their interest for about as long as the light switch. After several long and awkward moments of silence, Rick violated the most sacred Blackwell Rule of Guest Etiquette. He turned on the television.

All the while Rick and Jane were knocking themselves out trying to be the perfect hosts, Aldi and Elsa-Eska (non-human as they were) seemed completely oblivious to all the fuss that was being made on their behalf. They let their curiosity go unchecked, investigating areas of the Blackwell home that Rick and Jane would have preferred they didn't. They seemed to enjoy the magazines and pictures at first, but lost interest after a few minutes, wandering off just as Rick was about to show them photographs from their vacation in Nova Scotia. There were several moments when they dozed off, sometimes together, giving Rick and Jane pause to ask once again, "What do we do with them now?"

Ironically, what held their attention most was when Rick and Jane stopped scurrying around and just sat with them in the living room. They listened intently to every word either of them spoke and repeated them back as carefully as if they were practicing for a play. During the silent moments, the ones when they were not asleep, Aldi and Elsa-Eska seemed content to simply watch them. They spoke very little to each other, except for once when Rick swore they were using some sort of Vulcan mind-meld.

This gave Rick an idea, and for almost thirty minutes he got them to imitate lines from science fiction movies. Jane thought it juvenile, but Rick was impressed with Aldi's imitation of the Vulcan Live Long and Prosper hand signal. Jane did, however, smile when Elsa-Eska repeated, "Help me Obi-wan Kenobi. You're our only hope."

When they had exhausted all the best sci-fi lines, Jane decided it was time to start making supper. It was still early, but she needed something to do. Besides, when she learned that all Rick had served their guests was milk and cookies, she assumed they must be hungry. She excused herself and retreated into the kitchen.

Rick reached the limits of his hosting tolerance and was getting tired of all the mindless imitation. He reasoned that since they could not actually carry on a real conversation, it might be okay to turn up the volume on the television and catch the headlines from CNN. Flipping the channel, he was stunned by what he saw.

"Jane," Rick said, "come here, quick. Look at this."

"What is it?" Jane asked as she came back into the living room.

"Look. On the news. That's them!"

On the television, a fifteen-second segment of amateur video footage was repeating for the third time. The image was grainy and shaky, but Rick knew exactly what it was. A pretty reporter described the scene:

> Traffic came to a halt this morning on the Golden Gate Bridge as commuters got out of their cars to look at what many are calling a UFO. As seen in this dramatic amateur footage, an aircraft can be clearly seen hovering about fifty yards away from the bridge.

Eye witnesses say the craft appeared out of dense cloud cover, dropped down and hovered for about ten seconds before flying off toward the east. A spokesperson from the FAA said they are calling the incident an accidental fly-over by a non-registered aircraft. According to officials, the maneuver posed no immediate danger to the public, although it did violate federal air traffic regulations. A full investigation is underway. If you have any information leading to the identification of the person or persons involved in this incident, please contact your local authorities.

Jane and Rick looked at Aldi and Elsa-Eska. The two aliens had discovered a book of photographs taken by the Hubble Space Telescope and had ignored the news flash. Jane gave Rick a head-nod toward the kitchen and left the room. Rick waited a few moments to make sure Aldi and Elsa-Eska were adequately occupied and then made his exit.

"What's wrong?" Rick asked.

Jane had a concerned look on her face. "What are we going to do with them now?"

"Oh, I don't know. I guess we could show them the rest of the ranch. You should have seen how ol' Jake warmed up to Elsa-Eska. He was like a different horse."

"That's not what I mean. I'm talking about that news report. There's an investigation."

Rick considered this for a moment. "And your point is…?"

"Think about it, Rick. There are two aliens in our living room. Don't you think someone's going to notice? And if there's an investigation…well, somebody's looking for them."

"Jane," Rick said, trying to sound more confident than he felt, "first of all, we're in the middle of Wyoming. I doubt what happened in San Francisco will lead any investigation way out here. No one will ever know they're here."

"Coop knows," Jane offered.

"Okay, one person. But I hardly think he is cause for alarm. I already told him they were my cousins. He's probably forgotten all about them by now."

"What if somebody else sees them?"

"We'll just keep them out of sight."

"For how long?"

"What do you mean?"

"How long are they going to be here?"

Rick thought for a moment. "I don't know. They didn't say."

"I'm serious, Rick."

"So am I."

Jane opened the refrigerator and stared into it. "Their ship." She spun around to face Rick. "You said they came in a ship. The ship on the TV?"

"Yeah, so?"

"Well, where is it?"

"I don't know. It flew away."

"Flew away? Where? How?"

"I don't know. The others took off in it."

"Others? You mean, there are more of them?"

"Oh yeah, I forgot to tell you. I met four of them this morning. The other two took off and left Aldi and Elsa-Eska here."

Jane's eyes widened. "You might have told me that *earlier*." Jane crossed her arms and huffed. "Do you think they're coming back?"

"I don't know." Rick suddenly felt dumb for saying I don't know so much.

"That's my whole point, Rick. We don't know anything about them. We don't know where they came from, how they got here..."

"They came in a ship," Rick offered sheepishly. "I know that."

She ignored him. "We don't know why they're here or how long they plan on staying." She leaned on the counter and rested her head in her hands. "Rick, what if they stay for a long time? I mean, if you went to another world, wouldn't you want to stay for awhile? You know, check things out?"

"I suppose."

"How long do you think we can keep them here at the ranch? They're going to want to see more than this place. They're going to want to see more than just us."

Rick had not considered any of these possibilities. He had been so caught up in his own encounter with aliens that he had not thought about their encounter with humans.

Jane continued. "And what if the others come back? They got lucky the first time. Apparently no one but you saw their ship land. But next time, what if someone else sees it? I know this is nothing like in the movies, but if anyone else saw them, who knows what could happen? It could get ugly."

"I see what you mean," Rick said, nodding in agreement. "We've got to think this through and come up with a plan."

Rick stared at the ceiling while Jane closed her eyes and rested her head on the counter.

Finally, Rick broke the silence. "I got nothin'. What about you?"

Jane did not move, except for her hand that she held up. Rick took the hint and kept his mouth shut. After another minute, Jane stood up. There was a hint of optimism in her expression.

"Okay," she said, "help me think this through. Communication is our biggest obstacle. Let's focus on that. There must be a way for us to talk to them."

"Well, they are intelligent. That much is certain," Rick said. "I mean, you don't send morons into space...or do you?"

"Rick, this is not the time to make jokes."

"Okay, okay. I'm sorry. That was uncalled for. They're intelligent. That's a plus."

"And they're curious."

"You can say that again."

"Intelligence and curiosity are great allies in learning," Jane said, slipping into her teacher mode. "Most of my students are intelligent, but if they don't want to learn, there is nothing I can do to teach them."

Rick smiled. "That's it, you are a genius."

"What?"

"It's so obvious. You're an English teacher."

Jane smiled as the light of awareness came on. "And we have two willing students in our living room." Her smile faded as quickly as it had emerged.

"What's wrong?"

"Where would I start? It's not like we have a grammar or vocabulary to work with."

"No, but you understand language; and remember that old Indian man last year? He couldn't speak a word of English, but you taught him."

Jane nodded. "And he taught me." She ran her fingers through her hair. "Say, you mentioned something earlier about drawing pictures in the dirt."

"Oh yeah, I almost forgot. Aldi drew a fair representation of our solar system; he even knew which planet was Earth." Rick paused and thought hard, trying to remember the encounter. It seemed so long ago after all that had happened. "I think he even called it 'Earth' and...no, he couldn't have."

"What?" Jane prompted.

"You won't believe it."

"Rick, we have two aliens in our living room. I'm prepared to believe just about anything?"

"Okay. Aldi drew a peace sign in the dirt and actually said *Peace*."

Jane cocked her head.

"I'm serious," Rick declared.

"How could that be? Unless…unless we aren't their first human contact."

Rick looked disappointed. "I guess it's not out of the realm of possibility."

"If that's the case, they may know more than we think," Jane offered.

"Well, after you figure out how to communicate with them, we'll ask. But first, we have a more immediate need."

"What's that?"

"I'm getting hungry. And I'll bet our guests are, too."

"You're probably right. I guess we can figure this out later." Jane opened the refrigerator again. "What do you suppose they eat?"

"They sure liked those cookies."

Jane thought for a minute. "I was going to make chili tonight."

Rick grimaced.

"That might not be the best first Earth meal. We should probably start with something bland. Here." She handed Rick several apples. "Cut these up. Fruit is probably a safe bet. I'll slice up this bread, and we better drink water."

A few minutes later, Rick and Jane returned to the living room with plates of apple and bread slices, a pitcher of water, and four glasses. Aldi and Elsa-Eska perked up at the sight of food and joined them around the coffee table. After some sniffing and tasting, they made quick work of cleaning off both plates. When they finished, Aldi and Elsa-Eska initiated a round of forehead touching. Rick and Jane took it as a gesture of thanks.

With supper out of the way and evening falling upon them, Jane was eager to begin dismantling the language barrier. She found some paper and placed a few sheets on the coffee table in front of Aldi and Elsa-Eska. Next, she showed them a pencil and demonstrated its function. Apparently they understood the device and Jane's intention. Aldi held out his hand and nodded at the pencil. When Jane gave it to him, he began sketching out a series of symbols. When he was finished, he turned the paper around so Jane could see it.

"Hey, those are the same symbols he drew in the dirt," Rick said. "Those are the planets of the solar system. Now watch this." Rick pointed at the third planet from the sun.

Aldi tapped it with his pencil and said, "Earth."

"You didn't teach him that?" Jane asked.

Rick shook his head.

"What about the other symbols?" She placed her finger on the stick figure.

"Oo-mun," Elsa-Eska said.

Jane and Rick looked at each other. "Human," they said in unison.

Elsa-Eska corrected herself. "Human."

"How could she know that?" Jane asked. She pointed to the next symbol.

"Riffer," Aldi said. Then he looked at Rick and corrected himself. "River."

"Amazing," Jane said. She pointed to the next symbol.

"Tree," Aldi replied.

Jane moved on to the next one.

"Mountain," Elsa-Eska said. She reached for Jane's hand and moved it to the final symbol. "Peace."

Jane sat back. "Obviously, they got these from somewhere. But where? How?" Jane turned the paper back toward them.

Aldi looked at her and then at the paper. Understanding her intent, he sketched out another series of symbols and turned it back toward her. This time he did not wait for her to point to them. Instead, he pointed to them one at a time, naming each one in turn: "Heart…moon…star…clover."

Rick started to laugh. "Look, it's *Lucky Charms.*"

"That's weird," Jane said.

"That's weird," Elsa-Eska repeated and made the same face that Jane made.

Rick leaned back in his chair. "This might not be as hard as you thought. In fact, it looks like they've started without you."

Jane could hardly contain her excitement. "I think we're going to need some more paper. And Rick, would you please get me the picture dictionary and that photo journal?"

For the next several hours class was in-session. Jane systematically linked words with pictures in books and hand-sketched symbols while Aldi and Elsa-Eska watched, listened, and repeated each one of them. Next, she tried simple non-tangible ideas (tired, happy, sad), demonstrating them with actions and animated facial expressions. Their capacity for understanding was beyond anything Jane had ever encountered. Several times, they anticipated Jane's intent, demonstrating their comprehension before Jane could finish. While Jane drew energy from the exercise, Rick found it tedious and soon fell asleep. He missed the breakthrough that occurred at around two o'clock in the morning.

At three o'clock, Jane was trying to demonstrate the concept of time when Aldi interrupted her.

"Jane," Aldi said, "Elsa-Eska and Aldi sleep."

"Okay," Jane said, pleased at the progress, but disappointed that they could not continue. "It is getting late. We can continue in the morning."

"Yes, it is very late," Elsa-Eska said. "We will continue in the morning."

Jane smiled. It was obvious that she was not simply repeating what Jane had said.

"Thank you, Jane," she added, "for the teach to us."

"You are very welcome," Jane replied. "Come, I will show you where you can sleep." Jane led Aldi and Elsa-Eska to the guest room and showed them the features in the bathroom. "Well, goodnight then."

"Well, goodnight then," Aldi repeated. And then, "Night is good. Jane and Rick is good." Placing his hands on Jane's head, he leaned down and touched his forehead to hers. "Jane is good," he whispered. With that, he ducked into the guest room.

Next, it was Elsa-Eska's turn. "Aldi say the true. Jane and Rick are very good." She placed her hands on Jane's head and leaned toward her. As soon as their forehead's touched, Jane felt a warmth course through her body.

In her own bed, Jane could still feel the warm sensation as she drifted off to sleep.

CHAPTER 8:

GOOD AND BAD PEOPLE

Σ

Before moving to Wyoming, Rick Blackwell hated mornings. Each one was like the start of a race he had been running everyday for years. It began with the weather and traffic report that seemed to always be on when his clock radio woke him at 6:00 am. Like a starter pistol, it launched him out of bed and into the fray. It was a race against time to get out of the house and on the road before the traffic got too bad. Then it was a race against all the other commuters who were trying to beat the same bad traffic. Then at work it was a race against his fellow associates to impress the boss. And then it was a race against time again to make all his contacts and file all his reports before the end of the workday. Evenings were a welcome respite, but they were tainted with the knowledge that in just a few hours the race would start all over again.

All that changed when Rick and Jane relocated to the Blackwell Ranch. Now, instead of hitting the ground running, Rick eased into the day. In the beginning of this new way of living, he thought about all those poor rats still running the race while he sipped his coffee and watched the desert wake to the gentle rays of the rising sun. But now he hardly thought of them at all. Each day put him further away from the race that seemed like another life.

The house was dark and silent when Rick slipped out of bed, careful to not disturb Jane. On Mondays, her first class wasn't until after lunch, so she usually slept in a little later. He pulled on a pair of sweat pants and a t-shirt and tiptoed out of the room, closing the door behind him. His first stop was always the kitchen where he conducted the first order of the day. The routine was so well rehearsed he could have performed it in his sleep —insert filter, measure out four scoops, fill water to the eighth line, and push the button. Five and a half minutes later, more than enough time to take care of the second order of business, the morning fuel would be ready.

With his favorite coffee mug in hand, Rick moved stealthily through the house to his favorite morning spot, a high-backed chair positioned in front of the large picture window that looked out upon his massive backyard. He tiptoed quickly across the cold hardwood floor, more in an effort to minimize the foot-to-floor ratio than to mask any noise his bare feet might have made as they slapped the hard surface. When he got to the thick rug in front of his chair, he let his feet sink into its warmth. He was just about to sit down when a voice from somewhere in the darkened room broke the silence.

"Morning good, Rick."

"Who's there?" Rick said with a start. He squinted into the direction of the voice, but could just barely make out a very tall silhouette. "Oh, Aldi, I didn't expect to…hey, wait a minute. You spoke. I mean you spoke my language. Wow, that was fast."

"Jane give teach. Aldi learn." The alien stepped into the pale moonlight that filtered in through the window. "Aldi speak human words."

"Wow, that's great," Rick said. "Whoa, Aldi, where are your clothes?"

The naked alien looked down at himself and then at Rick. "Clothes?"

"Um, covering." Rick tugged at his own t-shirt.

"Clothes good?" Aldi asked.

"Yes." Rick tried to avert his eyes to the window, but he could not help noticing Aldi's reflection in the glass. "Yes, clothes are very good."

Aldi pondered what seemed to be new information. "Clothes good inside house?"

"Yes, clothes are good all the time."

"All the time, clothes are good?"

"Yes." It was like talking to a giant child. "Here." Rick grabbed a throw blanket from the back of the couch. "Wrap this around yourself. You must be freezing."

"Freezing?" Aldi asked, taking the blanket.

"Cold." Rick simulated a shiver and rubbed his hands on his own arms. "Aren't you cold?"

"Ah," Aldi nodded his head like he had seen Rick and Jane do several times the day before. "No."

Rick didn't know which Aldi meant. Apparently there were still more language lessons needed. "Would you like to sit down?" Rick offered his favorite chair. Aldi wrapped the blanket around his chest and sat in the chair; fortunately, the blanket was extra-large enough to cover the essentials. Rick pulled another chair from the dining table and sat next to Aldi. Since he had slept through most of the language lesson, he wondered how much Jane had been able to teach them.

They sat in silence for a long time. Rick found it difficult to enjoy the moment. He felt like Aldi expected him to say something, but with every minute that passed, the silence grew until it became a nagging sound-void daring him to challenge it. He became so distracted by it that he could not think of a single thing to say. *And you call yourself a writer?* The void taunted him. Aldi, on the other hand, did not seem to mind the silence. He gazed out the window at the desert that was beginning to reflect the first rays of dawn. Then he closed his eyes and gently rocked back and forth, humming. Remembering yesterday's supposed E.S.P. encounter, Rick concentrated on whatever Aldi might be trying to communicate. But try as he might, all he could hear in his mind was the blaring silence.

"Good," Aldi said after several minutes. "Good night. Good morning. Good clothes."

Rick nodded, not knowing what to say. "Good is…good."

"Rick are good man," Aldi said, still looking out the window.

"Uh, thanks," Rick said. "Aldi is a good man, too."

"Rick is a good man," Aldi practiced. He turned his attention to Rick. "Earth is man, man, man, man?"

Rick pondered the question. "Are you asking if there are other men on Earth?"

"Other men?"

Rick pointed to himself. "Man." Then he pointed to Aldi. "Man." Then he waved both hands toward the scene outside the window. "Man, man, man—other men."

Aldi thought for a moment. "Yes, other men. On Earth other men is a good man?"

The question took Rick by surprise as another wave of awareness washed over him. He was only beginning to consider the extent of Aldi's alien-ness, and the reality of it frightened him. Who was he to represent humanity to this visitor from another world? What if he said or did something wrong? What if he told him too much or not enough? He felt completely inadequate to bear such an enormous responsibility.

Rick weighed the question: "On the earth, are other men good?"

Aldi waited patiently.

"Good…and bad," Rick finally said.

"And bad?" Aldi asked. "What are…is and bad?"

"Bad means not good."

Aldi looked back out the window for another long moment of silence. He seemed to be processing this information. Then he spoke again. "Rick Aldi happy."

"Sorry, I don't understand."

"Sorry? What is *sorry*?"

Rick gained a new appreciation for his wife. In spite of his own eagerness to communicate and Aldi's amazing capacity to learn, the language barrier was still daunting. There was so much meaning in a single word, how could he even begin to explain it with words that possessed even more meaning themselves?

Rick forced his mind to slow down. "Well, sorry means you are sad about something. Do you understand sad?" He simulated an expression of sadness.

"Sad," Aldi said, mimicking the expression. He seemed to understand. Then, waving his hand as if to erase the idea, he tried again. "Aldi sad no. Happy…" He looked out the window again as he processed all the words and grammar he had learned just a few hours earlier. Then turning back to Rick, he said more confidently, "Aldi happy Rick see Aldi." He placed his big hand on Rick's arm. "Other men on Earth is good and bad. Aldi happy good Rick see Aldi."

"Oh, I get it," Rick said as the light of understanding came on. "You (he pointed to Aldi) are happy that I (he pointed to himself) found you yesterday. Yes, I am happy, too. If…" Rick shuttered at the thought. Had Ed Tyler found them, Aldi and Elsa-Eska would be in jail right now; or worse, on a plane heading to some lab at an undisclosed location. Rick forced himself to smile. "I am very happy I found you."

A few more minutes passed, but this time the silence seemed less threatening.

"Coffee that's hot," Aldi said, nodding toward Rick's cup.

"Would you like a cup?" Rick asked. "Wait here, I'll be right back."

Less than a minute later, Rick returned with another cup and handed it to Aldi.

"Like this." Rick showed Aldi how to grasp the cup by the handle. He wondered if he might be acting too much like a parent, but he had no idea what Earth things might prove dangerous. Having been the recipient of spilled hot coffee in the past, he decided to err on the side of caution.

Aldi took the cup like Rick showed him and brought it up to his lips.

"Careful now, it's hot," Rick warned.

"Yes." Aldi nodded. "Coffee that's hot."

"Here, do it like this." Rick blew into his own cup.

Aldi imitated him.

"Now take a small sip." Rick brought the cup to his lips and took the smallest sip possible.

Aldi watched closely, and then took a sip. He made a face and stuck out his tongue.

"What are you guys doing?" a voice said from behind them.

"Jane," Rick said, turning toward her. "I thought you were still asleep."

"I don't think I slept a wink. Not after last night. Good morning, Aldi."

"Good morning, Jane," Aldi replied.

"Is that coffee?" Jane asked, peeking into Rick's cup.

"Yeah, I thought he might like some."

"I hope it's not that roguish stuff you had yesterday."

"*Fred & Lulu's Roguish Mountain Blend*. Why?"

"Rick, you have to work up to that. Here, Aldi, let me get you something better." Reaching for his cup, her eyes widened when she noticed he was wearing nothing but a blanket. "Rick, would you like to help me?"

Aldi started to get up.

"That's okay, Aldi," Rick said. "You stay here. I'll only be a minute."

Aldi looked confused. "Jane say Rick and you like to help. Rick say you stay here. Aldi like to help me and stay here?"

Rick cocked his head as if it would help him understand what the alien had just said. "Uh, let me get back to you on that."

In the kitchen, Jane poured the remainder of *Fred & Lulu's Roguish Mountain Blend* into the sink.

"Hey, what are you doing?" Rick protested. "That's not cheap, you know."

She grabbed a can of *Don Francisco's Butterscotch Toffee* and started a fresh pot. "Why isn't he wearing any clothes?"

"I don't know." Rick watched the last bit of *Fred & Lulu's* swirl down the drain. "That was a fresh pot."

"Rick. He's naked."

"Yeah, I know. Be glad I came out here before you."

"You mean…"

Rick shook his head. "Not even the blanket."

A curious look came over her.

"Jane," Rick said, as if she had just done something completely out of character. His back was to the door so he could not see what Jane saw.

"Oh my," she said.

"What?" Before Rick could turn around, Jane had him in a vice-grip hug that prevented him from turning his head. "What are you doing?"

In the doorway, Elsa-Eska was standing in the same state in which Rick had found Aldi.

"Elsa-Eska," Jane said, trying to sound natural. "Good morning." Then, in a move that only a woman in just such a situation could make, she slipped out of Rick's arms and positioned herself in front of Elsa-Eska before Rick could turn around.

"Jane and Rick," Elsa-Eska said.

Rick's reflexive curiosity turned his head in the direction of Elsa-Eska's voice. Realizing the situation, his reflexive self-preservation forced him to spin back around and concentrate hard on the coffee maker. "Good morning, Elsa-...." he mumbled, his voice trailing off.

"Good morning, Jane. Good morning, Rick." Elsa-Eska smiled at them as casually as if they were all fully clothed old friends meeting at a coffee shop. She took a deep breath, exhaled slowly, and disappeared into the dining room.

"Stay here and tend to the coffee," Jane ordered on her way out of the kitchen.

Rick did as he was told.

When Jane turned the corner into the dining room, she stopped. Aldi stood to greet Elsa-Eska, and in the process had left the blanket in the chair. Their foreheads were touching and Aldi was speaking to her in their own language. When they noticed Jane, they turned toward her. Jane's face immediately turned red and she became very interested in the chandelier that hung over the table.

"Jane," Elsa-Eska said, "Aldi say..." She paused as if searching for the right words. "Inside clothes are good?" She stepped toward Jane and touched her shirt. "Clothes good inside?"

"Yes," Jane said eagerly. "Yes, we wear clothes inside."

"Aldi and Elsa-Eska wear clothes inside. Yes?"

"That would be...yes, that would be good."

Elsa-Eska reached back and found Aldi's hand. They made no attempt to cover themselves as they walked past her toward the guest room. Passing the kitchen, Aldi called to Rick, "Inside clothes."

Rick emerged from the kitchen with a tray of coffee cups just in time to see Aldi and Elsa-Eska turn the corner into the guest room. "Now that's something you don't see everyday." He placed the tray on the table and picked up his cup.

Jane stood next to him, looking out the window. "How long do you think they'll stay?"

"I hope they stay at least 'till tomorrow morning." He took a quick sip to hide his grin.

Jane shot him a look. "I better get up with you."

A few minutes later, Aldi and Elsa-Eska returned wearing their flight suits. They did not seem to be the least bit embarrassed. Jane, on the other hand, was still red-faced, and Rick couldn't keep from chuckling to himself over his wife's embarrassment.

"So, who wants coffee?" Rick asked.

Aldi made a face and nodded his head, but Elsa-Eska indicated an interest.

"This is better, Aldi," Jane assured him. "I put a little creamer in it."

"A little creamer," Aldi repeated, receiving the cup. This time, when he took a sip, his eyes widened. "A little creamer is good. You like a little creamer." He quickly took another drink.

Rick leaned close to Jane and whispered, "We're having trouble with the pronouns."

Elsa-Eska sampled her cup, but was not nearly as enthusiastic about it. After a few more sips, she set her cup on the table and did not touch it again.

In spite of the incredible progress Aldi and Elsa-Eska had made with their first language lesson the night before, conversation was still slow and tedious. Aldi, whom Rick and Jane were discovering was the more talkative of the two, was eager to move beyond the casual talk and get on to the more pressing matters that were on the minds of them all. His limited vocabulary, however, prevented him from articulating his thoughts and his frustration was beginning to show. Elsa-Eska, on the other hand, seemed content to listen and observe, speaking very little at first. She hardly took her eyes off Jane and Rick. Even when Aldi spoke, she kept her attention trained on them in order to catch even the subtlest nuances as they responded to him. By the end of the second round of coffee, it occurred to Jane that Elsa-Eska was systematically processing every bit of new information. This prompted Jane to pick up the pace and expand her vocabulary usage. Elsa-Eska seemed up for the challenge, and after just thirty minutes, her speech had improved noticeably.

"Elsa-Eska," Jane said, "would you like to help me prepare breakfast for us all?"

Aldi started to get up, but then sat back down when he realized Jane had not addressed him.

"What is breakfast?" she asked.

"Food of the morning," Jane replied.

"Yes. I would like to help you prepare breakfast for..." She hesitated, looked around the table, and then continued. "...for you and Rick and Aldi and me."

Aldi, who was listening very carefully, smiled and shook his head.

"Thank you, Elsa-Eska." Jane winked at Rick; he was clearly impressed.

After the two women disappeared into the kitchen, the two men looked at each other. Aldi's grin grew into a wide smile.

"What?" Rick said.

"I like a little creamer." He handed his empty cup to Rick. "You..." He made a pouring motion with his other hand. "Please."

Breakfast consisted of cereal, toast, and sliced oranges. After sampling each, Aldi piled his plate with orange slices and asked for more. Elsa-Eska tried a little of each, but hardly ate much at all.

"Jane and Rick," Elsa-Eska said, "Aldi say some humans are good, some humans are bad. Where are the bad humans?"

"Every place has both good and bad people," Jane replied.

"Do you..." Aldi started to say, but had to finish in his own language.

Elsa-Eska translated. "Do you have a picture of Earth?"

"A map," Rick said. "Sure, I'll get one." He got up from the table and pulled an atlas from the book shelf. Opening it to a two-page image of the earth, he placed it in the center of the table.

Aldi and Elsa-Eska studied it, turning it first one way and then another. After about a minute, Aldi pointed to North America and looked at Rick and Jane.

"That's North America," Jane said. "And we are right here." She moved Aldi's finger to the Pacific northwest. "Wyoming. All this area is called North America and this place here," she placed her finger next to his, "is called Wyoming. Do you understand? You, Aldi and Elsa-Eska, are in Wyoming."

Elsa-Eska asked, "Wyoming humans are good?"

Rick and Jane glanced at each other and shrugged simultaneously. "Yeah, sure," Rick said.

"Mostly good," Jane corrected.

Aldi pointed to another location on the map.

"Australia," Rick said.

"Australia humans good?" Aldi asked.

"We've never been there," Jane said, "but I suppose people there are probably like people here. Mostly good."

Elsa-Eska and Aldi studied the map again. Elsa-Eska pointed to another location.

"Ah, Ireland," Rick said. "It's beautiful there."

"You see Ireland?" Elsa-Eska asked.

"Just pictures," replied Rick. "We'd love to go there some day."

"Ireland people are good?" she asked.

"I guess so. Why are you so interested in these places? Will you be going there after you leave here?" There was a hint of disappointment in Rick's voice.

The question was left unanswered, as Elsa-Eska had moved on to another location. She pointed to the center of the map and looked up at Rick and Jane.

Rick and Jane bent down to see where she was pointing. "That's Iraq," Rick said.

"Iraq," Aldi repeated. "Iraq humans are good?"

"Hmm," Rick began. "That one is a little hard to explain. The people who live in Iraq are probably like people anywhere. But their..."

Jane touched Rick on the arm. "Rick's right. The people of Iraq are just like people in Wyoming and Australia and Ireland. Most of them are good people, but there are also some bad people."

Elsa-Eska said something to Aldi in their language. Both of them had a look of concern and confusion. "Good and bad humans in the same place?" Elsa-Eska asked.

"Yes," Jane replied. "There are good and bad people all over the earth. Why are you so interested in these places?"

Elsa-Eska looked at the map again and said, "Our people are in these places."

"Rick," Aldi said, looking into his eyes as if he could see into his soul. "You know in these places. Humans in these places happy to see...our people?"

Rick tried to avoid Aldi's penetrating stare, but he found it impossible to turn away. He tried to think of a way to answer him without really answering him, but again something was compelling him to just tell the truth.

"I'm sorry, Aldi. I just don't know."

Aldi reached for Rick's arm and gave it a squeeze. "Sorry is sad."

Rick knew there was no way on Earth he could explain the complexities of human civilization to Aldi and Elsa-Eska. Besides, Aldi and Elsa-Eska had not been on the earth that long. How much could they understand? Rick also did not know how the people in Ireland, Australia, or Iraq would react to meeting their people. He was truly sorry.

CHAPTER 9:

EVERYBODY'S CURIOUS

➤

If there is one constant in the universe, it's this: Intelligent beings, be they human or otherwise, are curious. And when intelligent beings from opposite ends of the galaxy encounter one another, things get interesting.

In the minds of the four intelligent beings who were gathered at the Blackwell Ranch, countless questions were begging to be asked. The challenge, however, was the language chasm between them. True, a bridge was being built upon Jane's experience as a teacher and the inestimable learning capacity of Elsa-Eska and Aldi, but they had not quite spanned the gap. Communication was still quite elementary. But if the morning's conversation was any measure of progress, answers were close at hand. Jane said the best thing they could do was simply keep talking. With every exchange, Aldi and Elsa-Eska expanded their vocabulary and refined their understanding of the English language. Rick was getting tired of sitting in the house, and since they could talk just as easily outside, he suggested they might all benefit from some fresh air. Jane reluctantly had to decline because she had to get ready for her class.

The air was cold and dry and there was a steady breeze coming in from the west. Protected by their flight suits, Aldi and Elsa-Eska seemed to tolerate the cold, but something outside was having an adverse effect upon them. After walking only fifty yards from the house, they were both breathing heavily and Elsa-Eska was beginning to look pale.

"Rick," Aldi said between breaths, "Wyoming is hard to walk."

"And breath," Elsa-Eska added.

"Let's stop and rest for a minute," Rick said.

Aldi looked back at the house and then around at the wide-open dessert. "Wyoming is big."

"Doesn't your world have big spaces?" Rick asked.

"Yes," Elsa-Eska said, but she did not elaborate. She sneezed and wiped at her eyes with the back of her hand.

"Look!" Aldi pointed toward the horizon.

Rick followed his gaze. "Those are called mountains."

"Ah, mountain." Aldi smiled as he made the connection between the symbol he knew and the real thing.

Rick made the connection, too. "Say, Aldi, those pictures you drew, where did you see them?"

Aldi said something to Elsa-Eska. She answered for him. "Our ship…" She thought for a moment. "Like the TV. We found…I do not know the word."

"A signal maybe," Rick offered. "Your ship must have sensors that picked up some kind of radio or television signal from Earth. At least that's how they did it on the Enterprise."

"Enterprise?" Aldi looked intrigued. "What is the Enterprise?"

"It's from an old television show I used to watch when I was a kid."

"Earth has ship?"

"Well, not really. I mean, yes, we have spaceships, but we never got very far. We went to the moon a few times, but that was it."

"What is the moon?"

Rick looked up, but saw nothing but an empty sky. "The moon is a…" He could not think of what the moon actually was. "Well, it's kind of like a small planet that orbits, moves around, the earth." He tried to simulate the movement with his hands. "You can see it at night."

"We see the moon," Elsa-Eska said. "We see no humans there."

"Oh, you saw it? What, on your way here?" A thought suddenly struck him. "Wait a minute, were you actually on the moon? I mean, did you land your ship on it and walk around on it." The idea that they might have visited other worlds had not occurred to Rick until that moment.

"Yes," Elsa-Eska said. "Good to walk. No good to breath. Have you walk on the moon, Rick?" She said it as matter-of-factly as if she were talking about walking to the barn.

"No," Rick chuckled. "Only a few humans have ever been there. We call them astronauts."

"We not see astronauts," Aldi said.

"They aren't there anymore. They just went to look around and then came back. That was a long time ago." Rick did not know how much of what he was saying was being understood. By the look on

Aldi's face, Rick guessed he either did not understand much or he was disappointed that humans had not ventured any further than their own moon. "I guess going to the moon doesn't seem like much to you, but it was big news here for awhile."

"The astronauts came back to Earth?" Aldi asked.

"Yes. Now they just go up, fly around the earth for a few days, and come back down." Hearing himself describe the extent of human space travel, Rick realized how unimpressive it really was. "How far have you travelled? How long did it take you to get here from your world?"

Apparently, the concepts of time and distance were beyond the range of their English lesson. They did not understand the questions.

Suddenly, a strange sound could be heard in the distance.

"What is?" Aldi asked, pointing to a small white object hobbling toward them.

"Oh, no. That's Bonko."

"Bonko?" Aldi and Elsa-Eska repeated in unison.

Rick scanned the area. He did not see Ed Tyler, but he knew the old man could not be too far away. Bonko seldom wandered very far from him.

"We better get back in the house." There was urgency in Rick's voice.

The walk back to the house was more difficult than the walk out. Rick was moving faster in an effort to avoid an encounter with Ed Tyler. By the time they got back to the house, Elsa-Eska's breathing became raspy. She was limping, and Aldi had to help her climb the steps up to the back deck.

"Is she okay?" asked Rick.

Aldi replied in his own language.

"Get her to the couch. I'll get some water." He took one last look across the desert and closed the door behind them.

Jane heard them come in and met Rick in the hall. "What's wrong?"

"I don't know. It's Elsa-Eska. She's having trouble breathing. I'm getting her some water."

When Jane entered the living room, she found Elsa-Eska lying on the couch. Her eyes were closed and her breathing was labored. "Aldi, has this happened before?"

Aldi looked confused.

"Her breathing," Jane said, mimicking Elsa-Eska's panting, "Does she breath like this at other times?"

"No."

Rick arrived with the water. Jane dipped the corner of the blanket in the water and gently wiped Elsa-Eska's face. "She feels warm to me, but I don't know if that's normal." Jane put her hand on Aldi's forehead for comparison. "I think she might have a fever. Aldi, help me get her to the bed. We need to get her out of her flight suit."

Aldi lifted Elsa-Eska into his arms and followed Jane to the guest room.

"I'll just wait here," Rick said. There was a knock at the door. "And answer the door."

Before Rick got to the door, the knocking turned into pounding.

"I'm coming." Rick looked through the peephole, but he could not see anyone. "Oh, great," he muttered under his breath and opened the door. "Hello, Ed." Then looking down, "Hello, Bonko."

Ed tried to push his way into the house, but Rick had already put his hand on the door jam, blocking his way. Ed craned his neck, trying to look inside. Bonko did the same.

"Need something, Ed?"

"Where they at?"

"Where who at…where are who?"

"I wanna see 'um."

"See who?"

The little man stood up as tall as he could and stuck out his chest. "Kevin told me you got some visitors yesterday. Said they was from Russia. That right?"

Rick tried to make sense of what Ed was saying. So much had happened since yesterday, he had all but forgotten his conversation with Burt Cooper. Did he really tell him they were from Russia? That's the trouble with lies— they're hard to remember. He took a chance. "Yes, Ed, that's right."

"You sure 'bout that?"

"Yes, I'm sure."

"Well, I wanna see 'um."

"Well, Ed, you can't. They're asleep. And you shouldn't be so demanding."

Ed sucked his teeth. "I'll see 'um sooner or later. And when I do, I'll know."

"You'll know what?"

"I'll know I'm right, that's what I'll know." Ed glared at Rick, his right eye twitching.

Rick sighed. "I know I shouldn't ask this, but what are you talking about?"

"You're hidin' somethin.'"

"Goodbye, Ed." Rick started to close the door, but the little man stuck his foot inside the door just in time to keep it from closing.

Bonko let out his version of a bark.

Ed glared at Rick. "You told Kevin that you went to Casper yesterday. That ain't true. I seen ya. Lit on out in your little *Ty-ota* truck like a spooked deer. Kevin told me you come back in about an hour or so. Weren't no time to git all the way to Casper and back."

Rick opened the door. "And that proves...?"

"It proves you're hidin' somethin'. And I know what it is. It's what I told you day before yesterday. That thing that crashed the fence, it belongs to them, don't it? They come to git it and God knows what else. Well, they ain't gittin' me, that's for sure."

Rick processed what Ed was saying and found something that made sense. The object that destroyed the fence was the same flat black color as the spacecraft. Maybe Ed was right about that.

"I'd be careful if I was you," Ed continued.

"And why is that?"

"Association, Kevin. Guilt by association. You take two Commies into your house, that's as bad as you bein' one yourself." Bonko emitted a low growl at the mention of the word commies.

"Commies?"

Bonko growled louder.

"That's right, Commies!"

Bonko tried to bark, but it sounded as if he were drowning. The little dog shook his head and tried again, but it still sounded like he was trying to cough something up.

"Ed, they are not Communists. But what if they were? The Cold War is over."

Ed let out a low grunt and shook his head. "Well, just so you know, we're gonna be watchin'. And just so you know, we know people in the United States government."

"I thought you didn't trust the government." Rick rarely went down this road with Ed, but there were times when he could not resist pointing out the inconsistencies in the old man's reasoning.

"I ain't talking about that bunch of yahoo's they got out there in Washington, DC. I'm talking about the real United States government."

Rick knew where this was going and he did not have the time or desire to go there. "Okay, Ed. Thanks for letting me know." With that, he closed the door, but he could still hear Ed's rambling and Bonko's strange unearthly bark. "At least he thinks they're Communists."

"Who was it?" Jane asked. She had just come back into the living room.

"Oh, just Ed and Bonko."

"What did they want?"

"Nothing. How is Elsa-Eska?"

Jane sighed. "I don't know. I'm worried about her. She's breathing easier, but she's so weak. She fell asleep as soon as we got her to the bed."

Rick frowned. "Yeah, she looked tired yesterday, too. Maybe she's got a cold. Aliens probably get colds, too. Maybe it's not so bad."

"Aldi is clueless about it," Jane said.

"What do you mean?"

"It's weird. It's like he's never seen her this way before, but he's more confused than worried."

Rick thought for a moment. "Maybe they don't catch colds. Maybe it's something here."

"Aldi seems to be okay."

"I don't know, he got pretty winded just walking across the yard. But you're right; Elsa-Eska seems to be having a harder time of it. Maybe she's allergic to something. She was sneezing quite a bit yesterday and her eyes were watering."

"Hmm, I didn't notice."

"It was before you got home." Then a thought came to him. "It was when she was outside. I'll bet there's something outside that she's allergic to. Come to think of it, Aldi sneezed when he took off his helmet. In fact, they all did. Maybe Elsa-Eska just has a lower tolerance for, I don't know, dust or something else in the air. But she does seem to do better indoors."

Jane looked at her watch. "I wish I didn't have to go, but we're starting a new unit today. I'll try to get someone to take my other two classes and come home early. Just keep them inside while I'm gone and we'll talk more when I get back. I'm sorry, but I have to go." She put on her coat and hat and grabbed her car keys from the hook by the door. "Rick," she said, turning back toward him. "This really is amazing, isn't it? I can hardly believe they are here…in our house."

"I know what you mean."

"Do you think there's a reason?"

Rick shrugged. "I don't know."

"I get the feeling…" She paused.

"What?"

"It's probably nothing."

"Go on. What were you going to say?"

"It's weird," she began, paused again, and then continued. "It's just that when I am around them, I get this strange feeling like, I don't know, like it was supposed to be us. I know that sounds crazy, but I just feel like there's some purpose to all this—like maybe we are supposed to do something for them." She looked at Rick, expecting him to roll his eyes like he did whenever she started talking like that.

"That same thought has crossed my mind, too," Rick said.

Jane smiled at him. His words meant more to her than he knew. "Thank you. I wish I could stay, but I gotta go." Jane opened the door. "Rick, why is Ed Tyler staring at the house?"

Rick looked out the window and saw Ed standing by the fence. His arms were crossed and his eyes were locked onto the front door. Bonko was turning round and round on his three legs, trying to nip at something on his backside.

Rick shook his head and sighed. "He thinks we're harboring communists."

"Communists? Is he *crazy*?"

Rick looked at her.

"Never mind. You don't think he'll do anything…" She started to say crazy. "Do you?"

"Naw, I doubt it. Ed gets riled up easily, but he's harmless. We'll just keep Aldi and Elsa-Eska out of sight for awhile, and he'll forget all about them. I wouldn't worry about it."

"Okay, if you say so." Jane gave him a hug and closed the door behind her.

Rick watched her get into her Jeep Grand Cherokee and back out of the driveway. He saw Ed wave to her as she passed him. Yeah, he's harmless. When Rick turned around, he was startled to see Aldi standing behind him. "Aldi, I didn't hear you. How is Elsa-Eska?"

"She sleep. Jane is not here?"

"No, she had to go to class. She is a teacher."

"Teacher," Aldi repeated.

"Yes, she teaches English at the college in town."

Aldi's eyes widened. "Others like us?"

"Oh, no," Rick said when he realized what Aldi must have thought. "She teaches humans."

Aldi looked confused. "Why humans need learn human words?"

"That's a good question," Rick admitted. "There is more to English than words. That probably doesn't make much sense to you, does it?"

"Aldi learn more than words."

Rick could not tell whether it was a question or statement. "I guess you could say we are all learning more than words."

Aldi walked to the couch and sat down. "Teach me about Enterprise."

CHAPTER 10:

STAR TREK

++

When Jane returned home nearly four hours later, she found Rick, Aldi, and Elsa-Eska on the couch watching television. The air was heavy with the aroma of popcorn and there were empty glasses on the table, the bottoms of which bore the residue of Coca-Cola and melted ice.

"I'm home!" Jane announced when it was obvious no one heard her enter.

"Hey, welcome home," Rick called over his shoulder.

Aldi and Elsa-Eska turned as well. "Hey, welcome home," they said in unison.

"What is that, *Star Trek*?"

"Yeah," Rick said. "We should have thought of this earlier. You won't believe how much they're learning."

"From *Star Trek*?"

"You said the best thing for us to do was talk. I was running out of things to say. Aldi asked me about the Enterprise, so I figured it would be easier to show him than try to explain it myself."

"But *Star Trek*?"

"It *is* logical," Aldi said, and his right eyebrow raised slightly.

Jane bit her lip to keep from laughing. "Okay, well, I can go along with that. But if we are going to use television as a learning tool, we might want to be a little more selective with the programming." She hung her coat on the hook and pulled a chair next to the couch to join them. "Popcorn and Coke?"

"Yeah, they love it."

"Yeah, we love it," Aldi agreed.

"Bu po-corn icks oo y eeth." Elsa-Eska was working hard at removing a kernel from a back tooth.

Jane put her hand in front of her mouth to hide her amusement. "How are you feeling?"

Elsa-Eska removed her finger from her mouth. "Vital signs are normal, Captain."

"I see." She leaned close to Rick and whispered, "Let's not make a habit of this."

"I think they really like it," Rick said.

"I can see that, but..." she looked to see if Aldi or Elsa-Eska were listening, "...do they understand this isn't real?"

"I explained that to them," Rick said.

"Oh, I'm sure that took care of any misunderstanding," she said sarcastically.

"I think it did."

"Aldi, Elsa-Eska," Jane said, pointing to the television. "Do you understand what this is?"

Aldi answered without hesitation. "A five year mission to seek out new life and new civilizations."

"Uh, huh," Jane smirked. "Do you think it is real? You understand real?"

"Yes, real means the true." Aldi thought for a moment. "Enterprise is not the true."

"See, I told you," Rick said, feeling justified.

"Okay," Jane admitted.

A full minute passed. Then Aldi said, "Mission to seek out new life and new civilizations is the true."

"Huh?" Rick dared not look at Jane, for he could feel her stare burrowing into the back of his head.

"Aldi said the mission to seek out new life and new civilizations is the true," Elsa-Eska said. "That is mission of Aldi and Elsa-Eska."

Jane and Rick stared at her. It made sense, but hearing her say it brought another huge wave of reality over both of them.

Elsa-Eska continued. "These things on the TV we did not see. The galaxy does not have so many life...so *much* life."

"Well, how about that?" Rick said, his sense of justification returning. "Now we're getting somewhere."

"We come to seek new life. We come to seek you. Rick and Jane, you are mission. You are mission of Ka-Rel."

"Ka-Rel?" Jane asked.

"Ka-Rel is...I do not know the human word." Elsa-Eska paused. Then she placed her hand on Jane's stomach. "You have child. To this child, Rick is..."

"Father. Rick is her father."

Elsa-Eska nodded. "Ka-Rel is father father to Aldi."

"Aldi's grandfather," Rick offered.

"Ka-Rel is father to mission to seek life."

"Where is Ka-Rel now?" Jane asked, feeling herself being drawn into this new information.

"Ka-Rel is on Klyv," Aldi said.

"Klyv? Is that where you are from?" Jane asked.

Aldi did not respond.

"Is Klyv the name of your world?" Jane restated.

"Klyv is the world of Ka-Rel," Aldi replied.

"What about you?" Rick asked. "Isn't that your world, too?"

Aldi said something to Elsa-Eska in their own language. She interpreted. "Yes, Klyv is the world of our people. Aldi and I not see Klyv. We are of mission."

"Do you mean you were born on the way to Earth?" Rick asked. "You were born onboard your ship?"

"Yes, the ship is home world of us," Elsa-Eska replied. "Our home world."

"Wait a minute," Rick said, holding up his hands. "That little ship I saw yesterday."

Aldi started to laugh. "No, Rick, that is shuttle craft. Enterprise orbits the planet."

"Oh," Rick and Jane said in unison.

Then Jane asked, "Your parents, I mean your father and mother, are they up there right now?" She pointed up.

"Yes," Elsa-Eska said. "They are on the Enterprise."

"Okay, the Enterprise," Jane said, giving Rick a look. "The shuttle craft brought you here and then what? They just left you?"

"Yes. Imtulon and Tyba are in Australia."

As Rick and Jane processed all this new information, the picture was starting to become much clearer. "When are they coming back?" Rick asked.

Elsa-Eska responded, "They will come back when child…I do not know the words…when child is as we, not small." She held her hands together and then moved them apart.

"What does our child have to do with this?" Rick asked.

Elsa-Eska smiled at him. "Not the child in Jane. Child of Aldi and Elsa-Eska."

Jane's jaw dropped. "Oh! You're going to have a baby, too! That's wonderful!"

"Your baby?!" Rick exclaimed. "You're going to have a baby here? How? When? Oh, boy." Rick got up and went to the window as more waves washed over his head.

Elsa-Eska looked to Jane. "Is Rick sad?"

"No, I'm not sad," Rick said, sitting back down on the couch. "It's just a lot to take in, that's all."

Jane's initial joy gave way to concern. "When will your baby come?"

Elsa-Eska and Aldi spoke to each other in Klyvian for a full minute. Finally, Elsa-Eska turned to Jane. "The time will be soon."

Jane sat back in her chair and rested her chin on her hand. Rick sensed her mood change as if someone had thrown a switch. Aldi and Elsa-Eska, however, seemed not to have noticed. When an explosion on the television caught their attention, Jane mouthed something to Rick, but he failed to pick up on it. Finally, Jane stood up and moved next to Rick. "Would you two excuse us for a minute?" She quickly slipped out of the room.

"What is it?" Rick said once they were in the kitchen.

"It looks like we are starting to get some answers."

"Yeah, I know. Isn't it great?"

"We need to talk about one of those answers right now. Rick, I think they intend to stay. I don't know how long it takes for a…a Klyvian baby to become an adult, but I think we can assume it will take longer than a few days. And it sounds to me like they intend to stay here with us."

Rick pondered this. "I see what you mean."

"Can we…I mean, is it even possible to keep three aliens in our house for what will probably be years? We have no idea what that will mean. We hardly know them. And what about our own child? Do we want to raise our daughter in the company of…"

Rick put his finger up to Jane's lips. "Shh. They might hear you." He peeked into the living room to find Aldi and Elsa-Eska sitting on the edge of the couch engrossed in a conversation between Spock and Dr. McCoy.

Turning back to Jane, he said, "Jane, this is the most amazing thing that has happened, maybe to anyone. We have people from another world right here in our living room. Call it chance or fate or whatever, but we have been chosen to be a part of something really big. You're right, we don't know much about them or what it will mean to have them here, but think about it. We've always said we wanted to one day use the ranch to help people in need. Well, Aldi and Elsa-Eska are certainly in need. Maybe they are the reason we bought this place. Maybe all of this is because of them."

Jane never heard her husband talk like this before. She didn't know whether to hug him or cry.

Rick continued. "Jane, I know there are a lot of details that will need to be worked out, but we can do this. Why not?" Rick's expression lightened further as he got an idea. "We could build a house for them. Honey, think of it; we've got more than enough room and I've got more than enough time. We could build a house and they could raise their child right here with us. The ranch is perfect. What do you say?"

"I don't know, Rick. I just…" A thousand thoughts were rushing at her at once. Then one began to push all the others aside. She remembered the connection she felt with Elsa-Eska when she placed her hand on her stomach. "It is pretty amazing. And maybe…" She hesitated, not knowing how Rick would react to a thought she had been having all day.

"Maybe what?"

"Maybe we have been chosen to help them."

"Yeah, that's what I said."

"Maybe God has chosen us." Jane braced herself for a sarcastic response.

"Maybe." Rick shrugged. "Who knows?"

That was the confirmation she needed. She hugged him tight. "Okay, let's do it."

In the living room, the crew of the Enterprise had just boldly gone where no man had gone before.

When Aldi saw Rick and Jane come back from the kitchen, he motioned them to sit down. "We have question."

"What is it?" Rick asked.

"What is *alien*?"

The question caught Rick by surprise. "Well, an alien is someone who is different."

"Different," Aldi said. "McCoy say Spock is alien."

"Yes, he's a Vulcan."

Aldi looked confused.

"He's from the planet Vulcan," Rick explained.

"McCoy is human?" Aldi asked.

"That's right. He's from Earth."

"McCoy is different to Spock."

"Yes."

"McCoy is alien."

"Well, no." As soon as he said it, Rick understood what Aldi was getting at and he wished he could retract his last two words.

Aldi pondered this and then said, "All not human people are alien?"

Although there was not the slightest hint of accusation from Aldi, his question hit a nerve. Rick felt like he represented the entire human race in an inter-galactic trial. The charge: Human Arrogance.

Elsa-Eska was listening intently to the exchange. She brought it home. "Rick and Jane, are Aldi and Elsa-Eska aliens to you?"

Yesterday, Rick would have had to say they were. In fact, he had referred to them as aliens several times. But now, the word didn't seem to fit. Aldi and Elsa-Eska may not have been human, but Rick felt more of a connection with them than with most of the humans he knew.

Jane sensed Rick's dilemma and came to his rescue. "Actually, we are all aliens."

Rick looked as confused as Aldi and Elsa-Eska.

Jane was thinking about a sermon she had heard. Pastor Howerton said Christians were aliens in this world waiting to go home. She remembered thinking it was odd that he would use that word in church, and then when he read it from the Bible, it sounded even more strange. She intended to mention it to Rick, but the occasion never seemed right. Now she wondered if this was the time. Fast-forwarding the conversation in her mind, she heard herself trying to explain God to Aldi and Elsa-Eska. She imagined Rick rolling his eyes. Perhaps this was not the right time. She changed directions. "An alien is someone from another place. Sometimes it means another planet, but it also means another country or even another part of the same country."

"That's right," Rick said, remembering a news story he had seen recently. "We have a real problem with illegal aliens coming into America from Mexico."

"What is illegal?" Aldi asked.

Jane scratched her head. These Klyvians didn't miss anything. "Do you have laws where you are from; rules that tell you what you can and cannot do?"

"Yes," Elsa-Eska replied, "you speak of the true."

"If you broke the law…"

Elsa-Eska put her hand on Jane's arm, stopping her. "I do not understand. What is broke the law?"

Jane thought for a moment. She grabbed the bowl of popcorn and slid it in front of Elsa-Eska. "Okay, I make the law. I say, 'Do not eat the popcorn.'"

Aldi frowned. "I like the popcorn."

"All the better," Jane said. "You like the popcorn, but I say you cannot eat it. That is the law."

Aldi and Elsa-Eska nodded their understanding.

Jane continued. "If you eat the popcorn, then you have broken the law. That is illegal."

Aldi and Elsa-Eska continued nodding. Then Elsa-Eska asked, "Aliens are illegal in Wyoming?"

"Well, if you come into America without asking, yes." Rick knew there was more to legal immigration than simply asking permission, but he was trying to keep things simple.

"We did not ask to come to Wyoming or America," Elsa-Eska said. "Are we illegal?"

Jane sighed and looked to Rick for help.

Rick responded, "Our law is only for aliens who come from other countries on Earth."

There was silence for several moments as they all considered the uniqueness of the situation.

Finally, Aldi spoke, "Are others like us on Earth?"

"You mean people not from Earth?" Rick asked.

"Yes, like us."

"Some people believe Earth has been visited many times."

"Is the true?" Elsa-Eska asked.

"A lot of people want to believe it," Rick said, "but no one has ever been able to prove it."

"Now it is the true…the truth," Aldi said. "You can prove it. You will tell other humans of us?"

Rick shook his head. "No, we can't tell anyone."

"Why?" Elsa-Eska asked.

Rick hesitated, unsure of how to respond. "Sometimes people are afraid of what they do not understand."

"You understand," Elsa-Eska said. "Other humans will understand."

Rick smiled at her simple logic. Until yesterday he was the last person in the world he would have thought would ever believe in alie…in visitors from another world. He also knew humans, and had a pretty good idea of what some of them would do if they discovered the identities of Aldi and Elsa-Eska.

"Some people will understand," he conceded, "but others will not. You will have to trust us. For now, we cannot tell anyone. Do you understand?"

Elsa-Eska said something to Aldi and a concerned look came over both of them. Then she said in English, "Yes, we understand. Rick and Jane will help us know when tell other humans."

Jane switched the television off and sat on the coffee table facing Aldi and Elsa-Eska. "That's right. Rick and I want to help you understand much about our world. And to do that, we think it would be best if you stayed here with us."

"Yes, we stay here with you," Elsa-Eska said.

Jane smiled and touched her arm. "We, Rick and I, want you to live with us. Do you understand? We are asking you to live here with us for as long as you like—for as long as you are on Earth."

"Yes," Aldi nodded. "We understand. We live here. You teach us about Earth." Aldi paused and then added, "Aldi and Elsa-Eska teach you about Klyv ways."

"Yes," Rick said enthusiastically. "We would like that very much."

It was unclear whether Aldi and Elsa-Eska understood all that the invitation to stay at the Blackwell Ranch would mean. It was doubtful that Rick and Jane had any clearer understanding either. But in the moment, it seemed like the right thing to do.

Rick reached for some popcorn and whispered to Jane, "Why do I get the feeling they are one step ahead of us?" Then leaning back he said, "Well, I guess that's it then."

Aldi eyed Rick with a new sense of seriousness. "I think we cannot tell anyone of Rick."

"What do you mean?" Rick asked around a mouthful of popcorn.

"You break popcorn law." Aldi tried to suppress his grin, but it was too much a part of his natural expression. "Rick is illegal alien." He started to laugh.

Hmm, Jane mused to herself as she watched the two men laughing together. This ought to be very interesting. In the five years they lived in Wyoming, Rick put forth no effort to make any real friends. How interesting, she thought, that he would find one now in a man who was not even human.

"Aldi," Rick said after the laughter died down, "we should get your suitcases."

"What is *suitcases*?" Aldi asked.

"Your boxes. They're still in the back of my truck. We better bring them inside. Come on." Rick got up, and Aldi followed him out of the house.

After Rick and Aldi had gone, Elsa-Eska leaned toward Jane and placed her hands on Jane's head. She drew her close until their foreheads touched and whispered something in her own language. Then she said in English, "Thank you, Jane."

Jane sensed there was more to it than a simple expression of gratitude. She hoped that in time she would be able to understand it.

CHAPTER 11:

A KLYVIAN SORT OF WAY

☉

"You know," Rick said as he opened the tailgate of his truck, "you guys sure travel light."

"I do not understand," Aldi said.

"Jane and I pack twice this much just for a weekend getaway."

Aldi grabbed the first case and pulled it to the edge of the truck bed. He tried to lift it, but lost his grip. The case slammed back down into the truck with a loud bang.

"Here, let me help," Rick offered. "It must be heavier than it looks."

As the two men picked up the case, Aldi stumbled and almost fell.

"Hey, are you okay?" Rick asked.

"I'm givin' her all she's got, Captain." Aldi's voice had a hint of a Scottish accent to it.

Rick chuckled. "Jane was right. We need to go easy on the *Star Trek*."

They took the case into the house and returned for the second one. Sliding it onto the tailgate, Rick got into position for the lift. "Ready?"

Aldi held up a hand. "No." He tapped the corner of the case, and the top slid open with a hiss that sounded like the case was pressurized.

Rick was tempted to take a peek inside, but he didn't want to be nosey. He looked away until his curiosity got the best of him. *What would one take to a new planet?* he wondered. Aldi made no attempt to block Rick's view, so he looked.

The first case must have had all their clothing and accessories because the contents of this case looked nothing like what he and Jane would have packed. There was something flat and shiny, a clear-topped compartment with several neatly packed cylinders, and a smaller case with beautiful symbols etched into its top. Rick had no idea what he was looking at, but he thought it looked more like equipment than personal affects.

Aldi opened the clear-topped case and withdrew one of the cylinders. He opened it at one end and tapped some of its contents into his hand. Rick thought the substance looked like dried pine needles. Aldi took a pinch of the stuff and put it into his mouth, then he held his hand out to Rick.

"Chippick," Aldi said. "Not good like popcorn, but good." He gestured for Rick to take a pinch.

Rick sampled the chippick and discovered that it tasted exactly like it looked. He was not at all into the all-natural lifestyle, but he knew enough to suspect that chippick would be a hot item at any health food store.

"Mmm," he said, trying to not make a face. "You're right." *Right about it not being as good as popcorn, that is.* "Thanks. You should let Jane try some."

Aldi replaced the cylinder in its case and took out something that looked like a rigid magazine. It beeped on as soon as he touched it. "Tricorder," he said with a sly grin. "Follow." He held the device out in front of him and started walking.

"Where're we going?" Rick asked. "Whoa!" He had taken only a few steps when a rush of energy kicked in like a jolt of electricity. "Wow!" He felt better than he had in years, like he could run a marathon or climb a mountain. He put his hand on his chest and felt his heart beating strong and steady, but not fast at all. "Was that the…oh, man!" he said again as a second rush hit him.

"Chippick," Aldi said and kept walking.

"That stuff is amazing. I hope you brought a lot of it."

They walked for about a hundred yards. Aldi kept a close eye on the tricorder, and Rick kept commenting about how good he felt. It was apparent that Aldi was feeling better, too. He walked quickly, his breathing slow and steady. When they came to the split-rail fence, they followed it for a little over a quarter mile. Finally, Aldi came to a stop at a section of fence that looked newer than the rest.

"Coop must have already fixed the fence," Rick said. Then it hit him. "Oh, the fence."

Aldi was already on his hands and knees, waving the tricorder over the ground like it was a metal detector.

"That thing from the…" Rick said excitedly. "That ball thing, that was you!" He examined the area. "Coop must have filled in the hole." He got down on his hands and knees next to Aldi and felt around for soft dirt.

Aldi set the tricorder on the ground. It was emitting a steady tone. "This must be the spot," Rick said.

The ground was hard-packed and difficult to dig in, but Rick's energy-surge enabled him to make quick work of it. After just ten minutes of digging with his pocketknife, Rick dug a hole the size of a large washtub. He was beginning to wonder whether he was digging in the right place when he heard a metallic chink as his blade struck something hard. A few minutes later, he had uncovered enough of the sphere to get a hand underneath it. He tugged, but in spite of feeling like he could lift a small car, he couldn't budge it.

"It's stuck," Rick said, sitting back on his heels. "I can't get a good grip on it."

Aldi tapped Rick on the shoulder. "It must be heavier than it looks." He held the tricorder over the sphere and wiggled it from side to side. The object began to twitch in response. When he raised the tricorder to about waist level, the sphere freed itself from its earthen tomb. Aldi took a few steps backward and the sphere followed him, levitating at the same height as the tricorder.

"Now that's cool," Rick said. He waved his hand underneath the sphere like a magician performing the floating lady routine.

Aldi handed the tricorder to Rick and approached the sphere. He did something, Rick could not see what, and the top of the sphere slid open at its equator to reveal a smooth black surface. Aldi waved his hand over it and a three-dimensional shape appeared, rotating slowly. After one complete rotation, the image morphed into the figure of a woman. She was just over a foot tall, but Rick could see that she was stunningly beautiful; even more so than Princess Leia. She wore a sheer robe with an intricately embroidered design. Her long dark hair fell loosely down her back and in front of her shoulders; it seemed to almost float as if she were under water. Aldi spoke to her in his own language and she responded in kind, though her voice was difficult to hear for all the static.

Rick held the tricorder steadily and listened with amazement. He had heard Aldi and Elsa-Eska speak to each other, but it was always in short phrases and hushed voices. This was the first time he heard the Klyvian language spoken with a duration that allowed him to really listen to it. There were sounds and tones that seemed almost familiar to Rick, but it was unlike any language he had ever heard. It flowed smoothly and had a musical quality to it, almost like a song. It had an ancient feel to it, though it did not seem at all primitive. Although he had no idea what they were saying, he was mesmerized by it. He could have listened to them talk for hours. The Klyvian language was truly beautiful. Rick imagined it would be simply enchanting coming from Elsa-Eska.

After several minutes, Aldi finished his conversation with the holographic woman. He closed the sphere and took the tricorder from Rick. "Come," he said, turning toward the direction of the house.

Rick was confused that they did not take the sphere with them, but Aldi seemed intent on leaving it. They walked for almost a minute when something sped over their heads so close that Rick could feel the vacuum of its wake above him. He looked up and caught just enough of it to make out the shape of a black sphere ascending rapidly. Within seconds it was gone. He glanced up at Aldi and saw his characteristic grin.

"Warp speed," Aldi said, "back to Enterprise."

About twenty yards away, a small hump in the desert began to move. The figure of a man sat up and pushed aside the dirt-colored tarp that concealed him. He was in full desert camouflage, like the kind used during Desert Storm. His face was covered and his eyes were hidden behind dark tinted goggles. Standing to his feet, the man watched his targets until they disappeared from his sight. Turning, he headed off in the opposite direction, binoculars dangling from his neck. A little white dog hobbled next to him.

By the time Rick and Aldi returned to the house, the sun dipped low in the western sky and the temperature dropped into the twenties. Rick was glad to return to the warmth of the house and he knew Aldi must have felt the same. The living room was dark and quiet, but the delicate sounds of distant conversation and the filtered glow of lamplight spilled out from the guest room into the hallway. Rick balanced his end of the second case on his knee while he switched on a lamp.

"We may as well take it on back to your room," he said, regaining his grip.

"Rick," Aldi said as he sniffed the air. "What is in the air?"

Rick breathed deeply. "I don't smell anything."

Aldi sniffed again. "Yes. In the air is like food. I am hungry."

"I'm getting hungry, too. Let's see what Jane's got planned for supper."

In the guest room, Rick and Aldi found Jane and Elsa-Eska sitting cross-legged on the bed. The two women were deep in conversation, like best friends reunited after a long time apart.

"We thought we heard you guys come in," Jane said. "What took you so long?"

"Oh, nothing," Rick said. "Aldi just had to, uh, send a probe back to the mother ship." The expression on Rick's face said, *I can't believe I just said that.*

Jane nodded and returned a look that said, *I can't believe that doesn't surprise me.* "We're glad you guys are back. I just put a couple pizzas in the oven, not two minutes ago."

Rick glanced at Aldi who had not stopped sniffing the air since they had come in. "Just two minutes, eh?"

"Yes, why?" Jane asked.

"Oh, no reason. We were just getting kind of hungry, that's all. Say, where do you want this?"

"The other one's by the closet," Jane said. "Thanks for bringing it in. Elsa-Eska wants to change into something more comfortable."

Change into what? Rick thought. He had not seen any clothing in the case; maybe it was in the smaller case with the etching.

"Yes, thank you," Elsa-Eska said. "This clothes is...uncomfortable." She looked at Jane to make sure she said it correctly. Then, before Rick had a chance to react, she began to undo her flight suit.

Rick nearly dropped his end of the case as he and Aldi set it next to the other one. "Okay then. I'll just go out and, uh, make sure we've got enough...yeah." He was out the door before anyone but Jane saw his face begin to flush.

Aldi had already loosened his own flight suit when Jane excused herself. When she joined Rick in the kitchen, it only took one look from him to cause her to break out in a giggle. "I guess modesty is not a Klyvian characteristic."

"I think it's kind of refreshing," Rick said, trying to keep a straight face.

"Oh, you do?"

"Sure. I always felt like I missed out on the whole '60s thing. It's nice to know that some civilizations are still comfortable in their... skin."

"Why, Mr. Blackwell, I do believe you are blushing." Jane laid her southern accent on thick. "Perhaps it is getting a tad bit warm in here." She picked up an oven mitt and fanned herself.

"You know, Mrs. Blackwell," Rick said, putting on his own southern accent that sounded like a poor impersonation of Rhett Butler, "your Southern Belle ways become you. It may not be such a bad thing if you gave into them more often."

If there was one thing that could snap Jane out of her southern-ness, it was Rick trying to slip into his. Even though they were both born and raised in South Carolina, Rick never acquired the accent. And when he tried to put one on, it sounded like *Gone With The Wind* meets *Forrest Gump.*

"Back in the vault for another year," Jane said, her accent completely neutralized.

And not a moment too soon. Rick had nothing against the South. In fact, he held a great affection for that region of the country that had been his home for most of his life; and was still home to all of his family and many of his friends. But if the truth be known, he always felt like an immigrant there. The South never really fit him like it did the rest of his family. And Jane, though she too came from a rich southern heritage, never felt like she belonged there either. This mutual sense of being out-of-place was the spark in the conversation that initiated the date that led to the discovery of the many things upon which Rick and Jane built their relationship. It was that same sense, coupled with Jane's free-spirited love for adventure, which made it possible for them both to break with generations of tradition and move to the Great Northwest Territory.

"She really is quite lovely, isn't she?" Jane mused aloud.

"I beg your pardon?" Rick said. He knew what she meant, but he wanted to buy some time while he measured his response.

"Elsa-Eska—she's beautiful."

"I can see how some people might think that," Rick said cautiously.

"Oh, come on. I know you think she's pretty. Admit it. I won't be mad."

Rick tried hard to read his wife's mind. Honesty had been a hallmark of their relationship from the beginning. And while he believed she could handle it, he still felt awkward admitting that he found another woman to be attractive. He knew she wouldn't be mad if she said she wouldn't, but that did not mean his admission wouldn't sting. He had to use extreme caution. "Okay," he said. "She is quite hot."

Jane's playful smile diminished by a degree.

Then he added, "In a *Klyvian* sort of way."

The way he said it and the glint in his eye did the trick. "That's one of the many things I love about you," she said, wrapping her arms around his waist. "You know how to wiggle your way out of every tough spot I put you in. Keeps me on my toes."

Emboldened by his cleverness, Rick played the next card. "Okay, Miss Tip-toes, let's hear your honest appraisal of Aldi."

Jane didn't flinch or hesitate. "Oh, there's no question about it. Aldi is one good-looking man. Klyvian, human, either way."

Rick expected as much. Women can get away with much more than men.

Jane knew she had him, so she went a little further. "He's so tall and fit. That hair just invites you to run your fingers through it; and those eyes are so piercing, like they can see right down into your soul; and that smile is just so cute; and then there's the mystery..."

"Okay, okay," Rick said. "I get the point."

"Yes indeed," Jane said dreamily. "He is one good looking man."

Rick started to pull away. It was the moment Jane was waiting for. She tightened her embrace and looked into his eyes. "But he's not my man." She ran her hand up his back and buried her fingers in his hair. Then pulling his face close to hers, she kissed him gently, but with passion.

When they opened their eyes, they found they had an audience. Aldi and Elsa-Eska were standing in the doorway watching them.

"Oh, excuse us," Jane said. She stepped away from Rick and checked the timer on the stove. "We were just, um."

The two Klyvians ducked into the kitchen. They were wearing robes made of the most delicate material Jane had ever seen. They were the color of sunset, with intricately embroidered patterns that seemed to move within the material as they moved. As they came further into the kitchen, their robes shimmered and trailed behind them, giving them the appearance of gliding across the floor.

Except for the brief glimpse that morning, it was the first time Rick and Jane saw them out of their flight suits. The sheer material confirmed what they had imagined about them. Aldi was powerful, his muscles toned; yet there was a gentleness about him that kept his masculinity far from macho. Elsa-Eska was also very fit, but in a way that fully complimented her femininity. Together, they had the appearance of royalty. Had this been their first sight of them, Rick and Jane might have been tempted to bow before them. The thought passed through Rick's mind that on Klyv they might even be considered a king and queen.

"Please, Jane," Elsa-Eska said. "What was that with your mouth?"

Jane blushed. "It's called a kiss."

Elsa-Eska nodded. "Again. Kiss again." She nodded toward Rick.

"Okay." Jane and Rick kissed once more, though this time it lacked the passion. Of course, that could have had something to do with the fact that Elsa-Eska and Aldi were examining them like a science experiment.

When Jane stepped back, Elsa-Eska moved close to Rick and embraced him just like Jane had. Jane thought she was going to kiss him right there, and Rick got a panicky look on his face. Then she let him go and returned to Aldi. She wrapped her arms around him and planted a good one full on his mouth. She then turned to Jane. "Like that?"

Jane nodded. "Yup, that's pretty much it."

"Fascinating," Elsa-Eska said in a tone that sounded exactly like Spock.

Just then the buzzer on the stove timer sounded.

"Oh, good," Rick said. "The pizzas are ready."

"And just in time, too." replied Jane.

Rick and Jane welcomed the interruption and busied themselves with pans, plates, and glasses. On the way to the dining room, Aldi commented on how much he liked the kiss. That was the last word on the matter, but Rick suspected there would be a more thorough investigation later. He looked at Jane and thought that he would like to conduct further research himself.

After supper, Rick volunteered to clean up while Jane and Elsa-Eska and Aldi continued their language lessons. The lesson did not last nearly as long as the night before. Elsa-Eska looked tired, and by nine o 'clock Aldi was looking like he had enough for the evening. After about twenty minutes of casual conversation, which demonstrated the remarkable progress they were making, and a round of "goodnight" forehead touching, Aldi and Elsa-Eska retired to their room.

"What a day, huh?" Jane said as she dropped into her chair.

"You can say that again," Rick replied. He sat down on the couch and stretched his legs out onto the coffee table.

"I really thought Elsa-Eska was going to plant one on you."

"I know. That would have been awful," Rick said in mock disdain.

Jane picked up the nearest object and fired it at him. The television remote hit him square in the chest. "Rick, I need you to be serious for a minute."

"Okay. What's up?"

"I've been thinking. If this arrangement is going to work, we're going to have to really help them understand how things are here. I mean, they have no concept of what is, you know, appropriate. Not that they are ill behaved, but can you imagine how people will react to them? What if Elsa-Eska hugs a stranger?"

Rick let the scenario play out in his mind. "You're right. I guess we can't keep them out of sight forever. Eventually, they're going to have to mingle. After all, that's why they're here."

"I agree. And I think we should start tomorrow."

"Tomorrow?" Rick exclaimed. "It's too soon."

"Yesterday, I would have thought the same thing," Jane replied. "But after today, I really think they've learned enough English to pull it off. If we explain to them how to blend in and we stay close to them, I think it will be okay."

"Blend in? Do you really think people are not going to notice two seven foot tall super-models?"

"I'm sure people will take notice of them. But a month or a year won't change that."

"I don't know."

"Think about it, Rick. I bet they're ready to see more of Earth than this house, and more humans than us. After all, that's why they're here."

"Yeah, I just said that, didn't I?" Rick noticed a look on Jane's face that he had seen a million times before. "Let me guess, you've already got a plan?"

"As a matter of fact, I do."

"Okay. This is not a concession, but let's hear it."

Jane moved over to the couch and curled up next to Rick. It was a devious tactic that usually yielded good results.

"Don't think I don't know what you're doing," Rick said. "But I must warn you, this one might require some extra persuasion."

Jane smiled and started to lightly scratch the back of his neck. "Well, it's pretty obvious our two new housemates need a few things—clothes for starters."

"True."

"I think we should take them shopping."

Rick waited for more, but none came. "That's it? That's your big plan?"

Jane nodded. "It makes perfect sense. We go into town, pick up a few things, and come home. That way we keep interaction at a minimum, and if anything happens, we just leave. See? Simple and easy."

"What if we run into someone we know?"

"If we go to Casper, we minimize that possibility."

"Casper? That's over a hundred miles away. They had a hard enough time on the ride here, and that was only a couple miles. Speed kind of freaks them out."

"Okay, how about Lander. It's not as far. We can explain to them how safe driving is. They'll get used to it."

"What about your classes tomorrow?"

"I've got it covered. I told Dr. Bennett that I had a family emergency and that I would be out the rest of the week. That's why they have substitutes."

Rick thought for a moment. "Well, other than the fact that none of us knows what to expect, it looks like you've got it all figured out."

"And I even talked it over with Elsa-Eska. She thinks it's a great idea. They're ready."

"So basically this was already determined and you're just letting me in on the plan."

"That's another thing I love about you—your ability to see through all the reasoning and get right to my point."

"I see. You've got me all figured out, don't you?"

"I've devoted my life to it."

"Well then," Rick said, changing positions so that they were now face to face. "Now that the decision has been made, how about that extra persuasion?"

"Whatever you say, dear. Whatever you say."

CHAPTER 12:

JOHNNY TWO FEATHERS

It didn't take nearly as much convincing as Rick expected to get Aldi and Elsa-Eska back into a vehicle. Of course, Jane's Jeep Grand Cherokee was much more appealing; it had more leg room than Rick's old Toyota pickup. So after just a little investigation of the vehicle, all four were comfortably seated and on their way. Jane and Elsa-Eska quickly immersed themselves in conversation in the back seat, and Aldi distracted himself with every control on the dashboard in the front. By the time he was satisfied with the contents of the glove compartment, they were cruising down the highway at sixty miles per hour.

"We move fast," Aldi said, his eyes struggling to focus on the posts of the split-rail fence along the side of the road.

"See, it's not so bad," Rick reassured him.

"I can see the fence here." Aldi pointed out the windshield. "I cannot see the fence here." He pointed out the side window. "And the mountains move with us." Aldi pointed to the mountain range in the distance.

"That's called perspective. Those mountains aren't really moving, but because they are so far away, they only look like they are travelling with us."

"Fascinating," Aldi said, sounding just like Spock. "The sky is close to the ground."

"Those are clouds."

"Clouds," Aldi repeated. He leaned forward and peered out the windshield. "The clouds are come down."

Rick noticed a few flakes of falling snow when they pulled onto the main road, but now it was starting to snow more steadily. "That's called snow."

"Snow. Where is snow…from?

"When it's cold like this, the water in the clouds freezes and comes down as snow. If it was warm outside, it would be rain."

Aldi nodded, but it was unclear whether he understood exactly what Rick was saying. And so it was for the next forty miles. Aldi inquired about antelope, rock formations, desert brush, why the road curved as it did, and why the sky was grey since it was blue the day before. They met only two other vehicles between the Blackwell Ranch and the outskirts of Riverton. After the shock of what Aldi perceived as a near miss, he and Elsa-Eska both got very excited about seeing other humans. They asked Rick and Jane who they were, where they were going, and would they see them again on their way back home.

When they arrived in Lander, Aldi and Elsa-Eska were like children in a museum. As soon as they asked about one sight, another would grab their attention. Rick and Jane attempted to provide answers, but they simply could not keep up with the barrage. After a few minutes, everyone realized the futility of it. An excited silence fell upon them as they tried to take it all in. Rick and Jane enjoyed this fresh enthusiasm over things they had long taken for granted.

Rick found a parking spot at the corner of Arizona & Winslow and stopped the Jeep. Before they got out, Jane felt compelled to explain the plan one more time: "There's our store, and the guys will be in that one over there." She pointed to the shops lining the street. "We will go in, pick out some clothes, and meet back here. It will be easy." She said this mostly for Rick's benefit.

Before she could say anything else Aldi was already out on the sidewalk and heading straight for the first person he saw.

"Rick!" Jane said, pointing to the encounter that was about to occur.

Rick jumped out of the Jeep and nearly got taken out by a Ford flatbed truck. The girl driving it did not slow down or even look at him as she sped by. She just laid on the horn and offered an unfriendly gesture.

The sound of the horn caught Aldi's attention, slowing him down just in time for Rick to intercept him before he could get to the old woman who had just realized she was about be accosted. Paralyzed by the sight of the grinning giant coming toward her, the woman was unable to do anything but stare wide-eyed and open-mouthed. Rick caught Aldi by the arm and pulled him back around in the opposite direction. He apologized to the stunned woman and escorted Aldi safely back toward the Jeep.

"I'm really sorry, Aldi," Rick said. "I didn't mean to grab you, but you can't just go up to people like that. You are, well, you're kind of intimidating."

"Intimidating?"

"It's just that you are so tall, and that woman..." They looked back to where the old woman had been standing. She managed to duck into an antique shop and was now looking out at them through the storefront window. "Never mind."

When they got back to the Jeep, Jane and Elsa-Eska were standing on the sidewalk. Jane turned away when Rick gave her an I told you so look.

"Come on, Elsa-Eska. This way." The two women headed for *Tillie's Boutique.*

"Are you angry?" Aldi asked.

"No," Rick replied, summoning a smile. "I'm just a little cautious, that's all."

Although Aldi did not understand the word cautious, he did not ask Rick to explain. He could sense what Rick was feeling.

"I guess we better get on with it," Rick said, pointing to a store with a sign that read *Lander Outfitter*. Rick was not much of a shopper. He didn't even like to go with Jane. He didn't expect shopping with a seven foot tall Klyvian would be any better.

Inside the boutique, two other customers and the young woman behind the counter were trying hard to gawk inconspicuously. Jane noticed the frequent looks that were being cast their way. Every time she checked them, the customers would look away, and the cashier would hide behind her computer screen. Elsa-Eska was oblivious to the exchanges. She was overwhelmed by the amount and variety of clothing on the racks and shelves.

After the obligatory one-minute-browsing-allotment had expired, the cashier came out from behind the counter. "Good morning ladies," she said warmly. "Welcome to Tillie's. Are you looking for something in particular?" Sizing up Elsa-Eska in her bulky black flight suit, her smile took on an air of snobbery.

Jane read the cashier like a neon sign, but she reigned in the sarcastic comment that was threatening to launch. "We'd like to look at some outfits for my cousin. A few casual outfits and maybe a couple dresses."

The cashier saw dollar signs and became their best friend. "I think I can help you with that. My name's Connie."

"My name is Elsa-Eska. You are pretty."

"Oh, thank you," Connie blushed. "Elsa-Eska is it? What an unusual name."

"My cousin just moved here from Russia," Jane offered.

Elsa-Eska gave Jane a curious look, but did not correct her. "Russia? How interesting." Connie was good. Her manufactured interest was well rehearsed and flawlessly executed. "Welcome to Wyoming. Now let's see what we can find for you."

Inside the *Lander Outfitter*, Aldi and Rick were attracting a different kind of attention. The other male customers hardly noticed them at all, but the two young women behind the counter checked them out as soon as they walked through the doors. One of the cashiers whispered something to the other, and then jogged out from behind the counter, leaving her partner cross-armed and pouting.

"Good morning," she said cheerfully. "What can I help you guys with today?"

Rick stepped forward. "That's alright, we're just looking for some jeans and a couple shirts for my cousin."

The woman looked up at Aldi. "Mmm, you're nice and tall," she said with just the right mixture of courtesy and playfulness. She glanced at his left hand and raised an eyebrow. "My name's Kari."

"My name is Aldi." He smiled at the young woman and sniffed the air. He leaned close to her and sniffed again. "I like the air from you."

Kari didn't miss a beat. "And I like the air from you, too." She flashed a sly grin that said, *yes, I am interested.*

Rick cleared his throat. "He's not from around here."

"Oh," Kari said. "Where are you from?"

Aldi started to answer, but Rick cut him off. "He's from Russia."

"Wow, I've never met anybody from there. Welcome to America, Aldi from Russia." She stuck out her hand.

Aldi looked down at it. Remembering the earth custom, he shook it.

"How long will you be in town?"

Aldi looked to Rick for help.

"Actually, he just got here," Rick explained. "He's not sure how long he'll be staying."

"Maybe if you see something you like, you'll stay awhile." She smiled at him coyly and flipped her long blonde hair. "Now let's see if I can help you find something you like."

Rick rolled his eyes and fell in behind Kari as she led them to the big and tall section of the store.

Thirty minutes later, Rick and Aldi returned to the Jeep with two large bags and a phone number scribbled on the sales receipt. Had

Rick been with any of his college buddies, they would have had a good laugh over Kari's flagrant flirtatiousness. But Aldi seemed not to have noticed it at all, so Rick decided to let it go.

"I guess the girls are still shopping," Rick said as he put the bags into the Jeep. "Would you like to go find them or wait out here?"

Aldi did not answer. He was too distracted by a man and woman who were walking toward him on the sidewalk. Aldi beamed and looked as if he wanted to shake their hands. When they got to within arms reach, they both looked down and quickened their pace.

"I am Aldi," he said. "From Russia." The couple hurried by without returning the greeting. "Hey, Aldi," Rick said. "Let's go find the girls."

On their way to Tillie's, which was only a couple stores down, they passed by an elderly Native American man in dirty blue jeans and a worn flannel shirt with no coat sitting on a bench on the sidewalk. Rick entered the store and let the door close behind him. He would have noticed that Aldi had not followed him in had it not been for the vision in front of him.

Elsa-Eska was standing just inside the store. She was wearing a white western-style blouse and a pair of blue jeans tucked into brown moccasin boots. The outfit was simple, but she looked great in it. When she saw Rick, she flashed him a smile that made his jaw drop.

"What do you think?" Jane said coming up behind him, her arms loaded with purchases. "This is so much fun. She looks great in everything. Do you like the boots? That was my idea. They didn't have any pants long enough for her, if you can imagine that. Pretty clever, don't you think? We got three really cute outfits for everyday and a couple dresses for going out and a few other things. I might have gone over just a little, but I didn't think you'd mind, considering. So, how'd you and Aldi do? Where *is* Aldi?"

Rick looked behind him and then out the glass door. Aldi was nowhere in sight. "Oh, great!" Rick said and he ran out of the store.

Outside, he found Aldi sitting on the bench with the old Indian. As he approached them, he heard the old man say something about his brother. Then he noticed the old man was wearing the new coat and gloves he had just bought for Aldi.

"Ah, Rick," Aldi said. "He is Johnny Two Feathers."

The old Indian bowed his head and stuck out his hand. Rick looked at the brand new leather glove and shook it. "Nice to meet you, Mr. Two Feathers." Rick was cordial, but not enough to conceal his annoyance.

"I am glad to meet you," the old Indian said. He stood to his feet. Although he was barely five feet tall, he looked Rick right in the eye. His braided hair was gray and his face was weathered like he had been around for many, many moons; but his pale blue eyes were clear and youthful. "Aldi says you are generous and honorable. He is fortunate to know such a man."

"Aldi is a good man, as well," Rick replied, keeping his guard up.

"He has a good spirit—wise like the elders and pure like a child. You will learn much from him, and he from you."

Rick wondered what Aldi told the man about himself. "Well, we need to get going. Stay warm."

"I will now." Johnny Two Feathers grinned a toothless grin and held up his newly gloved hands. Then turning to Aldi, he did something Rick did not expect. Johnny Two Feathers hugged him. Then Aldi leaned forward until their foreheads touched, and the old man whispered something Rick could not hear. Aldi whispered something back and then stood up to his full height.

Jane and Elsa-Eska came out of the boutique in time to watch Johnny Two Feathers shuffle down the sidewalk and around the corner.

"What was that about?" asked Jane.

"Beats me, but it looks like I'm going to have to buy Aldi another coat." Rick looked at his watch. "Hey, it's getting close to lunch time. Is anybody hungry?"

Everyone was feeling the cold. Aldi was shivering and Elsa-Eska was studying her breath as it drifted up in a cloud. It was agreed that they were all ready for a warm restaurant and some hot food.

After they loaded themselves into the Jeep, Rick asked Aldi, "What was all that about with Johnny Two Feathers? Why did you give him your new coat and gloves?"

Aldi gave Rick a quizzical look. "He was cold."

"That was very nice, but I bought those things for you. They were yours."

"I am not cold," Aldi said. "The Jeep is warm inside. The house is warm inside. I do not need now."

Rick found it hard to be frustrated with Aldi, but the coat and gloves were not cheap; and he had already reminded Aldi once that he shouldn't try to talk to everyone he met. "You didn't tell him about yourself, did you?"

"I say to Johnny Two Feathers I am Aldi and I live with Rick."

"I see. If you don't mind me asking, what did he say to you before he left?"

"Johnny Two Feathers say to me I must trust Rick. I say to Johnny Two Feathers that is what Rick say to me."

"Oh." That pretty much ended the discussion of Johnny Two Feathers, though Rick could not stop thinking of those pale blue eyes.

CHAPTER 13:

THE NEW NORMAL

<<

"Look," Jane said, pointing to an empty parking place in front of *The Gannet Grill.* "There's a spot there."

The Gannett Grill was one of Rick's and Jane's favorite restaurants. It had great food and a cozy rustic atmosphere. The only problem was that it was also a favorite restaurant of everyone else who lived in Lander, and one of the first suggestions offered to hungry tourists.

They were lucky to get a parking spot so close to the front door, especially since the wind had picked up and the temperature felt like it dropped another ten degrees. When they stepped out of the Jeep, they were buffeted by a blast of cold air. Elsa-Eska gasped in surprise and grabbed Aldi's arm. Even the short walk from the Jeep to the restaurant seemed to take its toll. By the time they got indoors, Elsa-Eska was coughing and gasping for air. Even Aldi seemed to be struggling to catch his breath.

"Are you two okay?" Jane asked. She took Elsa-Eska by the arm and helped her to the nearest chair. Aldi sat down next to her and let her lean against him.

After a few moments, Elsa-Eska brushed her snow-flecked hair out of her face and wiped the tears from her eyes. "I will be good," she said, sighing heavily.

"Maybe we should just go home," Rick offered.

"No, stay please." Elsa-Eska's breathing had eased some and her tears stopped flowing. "We are here now. I will be good."

Just then the hostess appeared and greeted them. "Good afternoon. Welcome to The Gannett Grill." When Aldi and Elsa-Eska stood up, the hostess did a double-take. "Where are you folks from?" she asked, trying to maintain her professional demeanor.

"Just north of Riverton," Jane replied. "We came in to do some shopping."

"You picked a great day for it. Looks like it's getting pretty nasty out there," the hostess said. "The weatherman said a cold front will be moving in this afternoon."

"I think it's already here," Rick observed.

"Well, it's always warm in here," the hostess said with a smile. She led them into the dining room, past several tables of gawking patrons, to a table next to a large window. "Is this okay?"

"Yes. Fine. Thank you," Rick said.

"Jamie will be with you in a few minutes to take your orders. Enjoy your lunch." With that, she was gone.

Once they were seated, Rick and Jane immediately started looking at their menus. Aldi and Elsa-Eska looked at theirs, but put them down after only a few seconds.

Jane noticed. "Oh, I'm sorry. Here let me tell you what they have." She explained to them about appetizers, soups and salads, main courses, and desserts. Then she read aloud some of the menu items she thought they might like, trying to explain such ideas as fried, baked, and grilled. When she described to them what a hamburger was, a strange look came over the two Klyvians.

"Jane," Elsa-Eska said. "Do you mean the cow like we saw in the field?"

"Yes. Ranchers raise them for food."

"You *eat* the cow? That is life." There was a look of confusion in her eyes. Aldi did not say anything, but he wore the same expression.

Jane gasped and looked at Rick.

"Yes," Rick said. "Humans eat animals. We call it meat."

"We cannot," said Aldi. "It is, what do you say? To eat the life is illegal."

The mood at the table became noticeably tense.

"I am so sorry," Jane said. "We had no idea."

Rick started to say something about the sausage pizza they ate the night before, but the sudden sharp pain in his shin stopped him before he could utter a word.

Jane tried to smooth the awkward situation. "Aldi. Elsa-Eska. I can't lie to you. Most humans do eat meat, although some do not. We don't have to. In fact, if it offends you, we won't eat it either. Isn't that right, Rick?"

"We won't? I mean, yes, of course we won't."

Jane continued. "Is that okay? Are you okay with us?"

Elsa-Eska put her hand on Jane's arm. "We know the human ways are different from our ways. We do not...I do not know the word." She thought for a moment. "You do not stop your ways for us. But we cannot eat the life. Aldi says the true. It is the law. Is there food that is not life?"

"Oh, yes," Jane said. "There are lots of vegetarian dishes. Here, let's take a look at the menu." Jane scanned the menu for any kind of vegetarian meal. Then she remembered they were in Wyoming. "There's salad," she said. "And they might have vegetable soup."

Rick sighed at the thought of all the meals he might never get to eat again.

A young woman introduced herself as Jamie and asked if they were ready to order. Aldi looked like he wanted to shake the woman's hand, but he restrained himself. He looked at Rick like a child looking at his father to make sure he saw the good deed. Rick suppressed a chuckle and placed their order.

It didn't take long for the soup and salad to arrive at their table. Although it had a good flavor, it still felt like an appetizer to Rick. Aldi and Elsa-Eska seemed to enjoy it, which was all Jane cared about. She kept asking them if it was okay and was it enough?

All the while they were eating, they watched the weather outside the window worsen. The snow was falling heavily, and the gusting winds were creating near blizzard-like conditions. Rick suggested they start heading back to the ranch before the roads got too bad, but Jane wanted to make one more stop for some personal items. Rick reiterated his concern, and Jane agreed that they would wait until they got to Riverton (about half the distance to the ranch). If the roads were not too bad, they would stop at the Wal-Mart there.

Aldi and Elsa-Eska did not understand Rick's concern or Jane's insistence that they see this Wal-Mart, whatever that was. They were content to just sit in the warm restaurant and watch the snow come down. Elsa-Eska discovered that she could make designs in the fog that was forming on the window next to her. She drew a woman's face that looked remarkably like Jane. When she was finished, she touched her drawing finger to Aldi's face. He chuckled and placed his entire hand on the glass. Then, reaching across the table, he put his cold, wet hand on Jane's cheek.

Jane recoiled from the shock of it. "Aldi, that's cold."

"Yes, that's cold," he repeated. "And wet." He wiped his hand on his new shirt.

The childishness was starting to get on Rick's nerves. When Jane tried to give him a sampling of the cold and wet, he brushed her hand away and gave her an irritated look. Finally, he had enough.

"I hate to break up this little experiment, but we really need to get on the road." Rick snatched the check and credit card from the edge of the table and headed to the cash register.

Inside the Jeep, and back out on the road, Rick's mood had not improved. He could not find the ice scraper, so he used a cassette tape case to clean the ice and snow from the windshield. He had forgotten his gloves, so now his hands were red and prickly. During the snow removal, he stepped into a slush-filled pothole, soaking his left foot. His jeans were also cold and wet from the blowing snow. And to make matters worse, in his rush to get on the road, he opted not to use the restroom. He was now wishing he hadn't drunk that third glass of water. He was thoroughly uncomfortable and facing a drive that may take longer than his bladder could endure. If he could make it the twenty miles to Riverton, he would have to stop.

Jane, now riding in the front passenger seat, picked up on the signs of Rick's tension—his set jaw, hands at ten and two on the steering wheel, the slight forward lean to his body as he focused all of his attention on the road that was quickly disappearing beneath the wind-whipped snow. After several minutes of silence, she looked over her shoulder. Elsa-Eska had lain down in the back seat with her head in Aldi's lap. Aldi was staring out the window and gently caressing her hair and face. Jane reached over and began to massage Rick's neck. His muscles were tight, but she could feel his shoulders relax just a little.

"I'm sorry," she said after another minute of silence. "I was hoping this would be a fun trip for all of us."

"That's okay," Rick said. "It's not your fault."

"What's the matter? I sense something's bothering you."

Rick glanced in his rearview mirror and noticed Aldi's eyes were closed. "I don't know," he said in a hushed tone. "I guess I'm just a little overwhelmed by everything that's happened the last couple days. Before they came, everything was, well, normal. We were happy, my writing was finally coming together, we had our baby to look forward to."

"We still have all those things," Jane said.

"I know, but now everything is different. Don't get me wrong, I think they're great and I like having them with us, but..." He sighed. "It's just so huge. I keep getting hit with these waves of reality. You know, I haven't thought about my writing once since they arrived. And I hate to admit it, but I haven't even thought much about our baby. All I can think about is them and this mission of theirs, whatever that is. I just hope we haven't jumped the gun."

Jane thought about their conversation the day before. It was Rick who had been so optimistic about inviting Aldi and Elsa-Eska to stay with them, and she was the hesitant one. Now it seemed they traded places. She decided not to bring that up.

Jane shifted in her seat so that she was looking directly at Rick. "It's going to be okay. Yes, it will take some adjustments for all of us, but I really think that in time we'll find our rhythm. I will teach, you will write, Aldi and Elsa-Eska will...well, I'm not sure what they will do, but they'll find their place here. And yes, things will be different from the way they were, but it will be good. Rick, I know you've felt the same things I've felt. Elsa-Eska and I have really bonded. I like her so much and I believe she likes me, too. And Aldi is great. You guys look like brothers together. You know, I'm even starting to not think so much of them being alie...I mean Klyvian."

"Really?"

"Yeah, I know that sounds weird, but when we are together I see them as people just like us."

"Just like us?"

"Well, maybe not exactly like us." She paused. "Okay, so they're not much like us at all, but you know what? I don't care. So what if they aren't human? Does it really matter? I feel closer to them than any human I've ever known – present company excluded, of course. I'm glad they're here with us and I hope they stay for...for good. I'm also glad that our daughter is going to grow up with them." Expressing these thoughts strengthened Jane's resolve in the matter.

Hearing Jane express her thoughts brought Rick back to his own resolve that he felt so strongly the day before. "You're right, as usual. They really are great to be with. I understand how you feel. I feel it, too. But it's hard to explain. It's kind of like love, but a different kind of love, if there is such a thing."

"I think I know what you mean." Jane let a full minute of silence pass. Then, "Can I tell you something?"

"Sure."

Jane looked back to make sure Aldi and Elsa-Eska were asleep. She thought they were, but she leaned closer to Rick anyway and spoke in a quiet voice. "I was a little jealous when I first saw Elsa-Eska."

Rick gave her a questioning look.

"I thought maybe you would..." Jane blushed, "I thought maybe you would be attracted to her."

Rick found the conversation getting a bit uncomfortable, but he felt a need to go there. "Can I tell you something?"

"Of course."

"And you won't be mad...or hurt?"

"I won't be mad. What is it?"

Rick took a deep breath. "I was, um, I was attracted to her at first." Jane bit her lip and nodded.

"When they first arrived and she took off her helmet, I thought I was looking at an angel. I just didn't expect to see anyone that beautiful, you know, in that circumstance. But then when she touched me, when they all touched me, you know that forehead thing, I felt something come over me. It was the strangest thing. Somehow I knew I just couldn't think of her in that way. I mean, not that I was unable to, but more like I was not allowed to. I know that sounds weird. Elsa-Eska is beautiful, I can't deny that, but she's not you." Rick thought for a moment. "I know it sounds sentimental, but being around them makes me want to be a better person. And that better person really wants to love you more. Does that make any sense at all?"

Jane rubbed her eye and scratched the end of her nose. "Yes it does." She leaned over and kissed him on the cheek. "Thanks for being honest with me. I love you so much."

They rode in silence for the next several minutes, letting the moment sink in.

"Jane," Rick said. "How old do you think they are?"

"I don't know. About our age, I guess. Maybe a little older, or younger. I can't tell. Why?"

"That Indian back in Lander…"

"Johnny Two Feathers?"

"Yeah, Johnny Two Feathers. He said Aldi has a good spirit, wise like the elders and pure like a child. It just made me wonder how old they are. For all we know they could be a lot older or younger than they look. Klyvian time is probably not anything like Earth time. And since they've spent their entire lives on a ship speeding through space, could they even measure time? They may not even know how old they are themselves. And if they did, would it mean anything to us? How would you calculate an equivalence that we could even begin to understand?"

"You have the strangest thoughts," Jane mused.

"I think maybe strange might be the new normal, don't you?"

"What do you mean?"

"Well, given our situation, strange might not be so strange after all. I've been thinking about a few other things. For example, you know how they are always so tired?"

"Yes."

"Gravity."

"Gravity?"

"Sure. There's no gravity in space. I'm guessing they must have some kind of artificial gravity onboard their ship. It could be that their gravity is less than ours. Maybe a lot less. That would certainly explain why they get tired so easily."

"I suppose."

"It might even explain their height."

"What do you mean?"

"Think about it. If you were born and grew up in a gravity that is, let's say half of what we have here on Earth, that would have to affect the way your bones grow and fit together. You know, Aldi and Elsa-Eska may actually be a lot taller than the average Klyvian. I wonder what long term exposure to the earth's gravity will do to them. Will they get shorter? Or could it cause some health problems?"

Jane pondered what Rick was saying. Normally, such ideas would have sounded to her like pointless speculation, but given their new circumstances, they seemed much more relevant.

Rick continued. "Think about all the dust and pollen and germs on the earth—all that stuff is alien to them. Its no wonder Elsa-Eska gets those episodes. Aldi must have a greater tolerance for some reason. And then there's food."

"I know. Let's never say anything about that pizza we ate last night."

Rick nodded. "We need to be careful. Something that is perfectly fine for us could be poison to them. And what about viruses and bacteria? What if they get hurt and need to go to a hospital?"

"Okay, enough already. You're going to make us paranoid. We're just going to have to be careful and take things as they come. It's not so different from having a baby."

"How so?"

"Our daughter will be exposed to all those same things for the first time, too," Jane explained.

"Yes, but she's suppose to live on this planet."

Jane thought for a moment. "Maybe Aldi and Elsa-Eska are, too."

"What do you mean?"

"Oh, nothing."

"Oh, no you don't. I told you my strange thoughts. Now you tell me yours."

"Okay. Remember yesterday when we were talking about how maybe this isn't a coincidence? That maybe we were meant to help them?"

"Yes."

"Well, if this is supposed to be, if God brought them here, then it makes sense to me that they should be able to adapt and survive here. Don't you think?"

Rick pondered this side of it. "Yeah, what about God?"

"What about, 'what about God'?"

"You bring up an interesting point," Rick said. "I would be interested to know where Aldi and Elsa-Eska stand on the whole God issue. What god or gods do they believe in? Do they even have a concept of God?"

Jane had already asked herself the same questions, but she was afraid to bring them up. Religious differences caused enough problems between humans. The thought of what they could mean to people from different worlds was almost too much to consider.

"I'll tell you one thing," Rick continued. "If they do have a god, I'd be a lot more open to exploring what they believe than listening to another sermon from the last preacher I heard."

"I told you that was a guest speaker. He doesn't even live here."

"Yeah, well, he was invited to speak at that church you go to."

Rick had a point. Her church had invited the man to preach, and as much as she did not want to admit it, she knew many in her church absolutely loved what he had to say. Jane sat back in her seat and propped her feet up on the dash. "I think we'll learn as much from Aldi and Elsa-Eska as they will learn from us."

"Hey, that's what Johnny Two Feathers said."

"He did?"

"Yeah, he said the same thing. Weird, eh? Hey look, we're coming into Riverton. And not a moment to soon. My bladder's about to bust."

Rick pulled the Jeep into the parking lot of the Wal-Mart and found a parking space. When he switched off the engine, Aldi woke up.

"We are home?" Aldi asked.

"No, not yet," Rick replied. "I have to stop for a restroom break. Does anybody else need to go in?"

Aldi looked through the window at the Wal-Mart. "I will go."

"Let's all go in," Jane said. "Aldi, would you wake Elsa-Eska?"

Inside the Wal-Mart, Rick made a dash for the restroom. Aldi and Elsa-Eska stared in wonder at the abundance of merchandise.

"So much," Elsa-Eska said.

"Are there so much people on the earth for so much?" Aldi asked.

Jane looked around at Riverton's small Wal-Mart. It was tiny compared to stores in larger cities. She wondered what Aldi and Elsa-Eska would think if they ever saw a Super Wal-Mart or a mall.

"There are more people here than you know," she said.

CHAPTER 14:

IF SPOCK ONLY KNEW

⊙

The rest of the drive home was uneventful. The snow tapered off, leaving the road dry and clear. Rick was in a much better mood after his pit stop. When they finally turned off the main highway onto the dirt road leading to the ranch, everyone was relieved to be back home.

It took several trips, but they managed to get all the bags into the guest room. As Jane began to help Elsa-Eska unpack the new clothes and personal items, she made a surprising discovery. It started when Aldi disappeared for a few minutes and then reappeared without his shirt and pants (Jane later found the missing items laid neatly on her bed). Then Elsa-Eska asked if they would be returning all the stuff to Lander the next day. After some discussion, Jane realized that neither Aldi nor Elsa-Eska understood that it all now belonged to them.

The evening's language lesson was spent discussing the concepts of ownership and possession. The humans were surprised to learn that such ideas had no equivalence in Klyvian culture. The Klyvians were equally surprised to learn that these concepts formed the basis for much of human society. At first, Aldi and Elsa-Eska were unwilling to accept the items. But after Rick explained that it was a contribution to their mission and necessary for further human interaction, they accepted them with great appreciation. This was expressed with much forehead touching, and Aldi even kissed Rick on the cheek. By nine o'clock, Aldi and Elsa-Eska were both looking tired. They thanked Rick and Jane again with another round of forehead touches and turned in for the night.

It was still early for humans, so Rick and Jane raided the kitchen on their way to the couch for an evening of mindless television watching. After a few minutes of channel surfing, Rick landed on the *Discovery Channel*. Of the more than two hundred channels to choose from, none prompted Jane to find a magazine more than the *Discovery Channel*.

"Two," Rick said to the television.

The voice of Leonard Nimoy had just posed the question: "Out of the billions of planets, how many may be home to intelligent life?"

Jane looked up to see what Rick was watching. "Seems kind of pointless now, doesn't it?"

The voice of Spock continued with another puzzler: "How deep into the vastness of space will we have to look for evidence that we are not alone in the universe?"

"Look in the guest room, Mr. Spock," Rick taunted.

"And what will that evidence be? A signal from a distant planet? A message from the stars? SETI, the Search for Extraterrestrial Intelligence, has been searching for just such a signal for over forty years. With their enormous radio telescopes pointed toward the heavens, they constantly listen for a signature within the static of outer space. Skeptics scoff at what many consider a futile and wasteful effort, but long-time proponents of SETI argue that The Big One, as they call it, could be found at any moment. Dr. Carl Drake has a word for those who doubt."

The image changed from a computer animation of a swirling galaxy to a man in his 60's with thick dark-framed glasses. He was sitting in front of a bank of electronic equipment. "Wouldn't it be a shame if we stopped listening just before the call comes in?" the man posited.

The voice of Spock continued: "And so he and others like him continue their vigil in hopes that one day their waiting and watching (or listening, as the case may be) will pay off."

Rick punched a button on the remote, and the television blinked off. "I used to laugh at guys like that," he said, pointing to the blank television screen with the remote. "Now it doesn't seem fair that a skeptic like me should be living with what that guy's been looking for his entire life. The universe is weird like that I guess."

"Or maybe the universe is smart like that," Jane suggested.

"What do you mean?"

"What if Aldi and Elsa-Eska landed in that guy's back yard?"

Rick pondered the possibilities. "I don't know."

"He'd be famous, that's what."

"Yeah, and he'd get the last laugh," Rick mused. "He would be vindicated."

"And the world would own Aldi and Elsa-Eska."

Rick shuddered at the thought, and a new weight of responsibility fell upon him.

The Blackwells went to bed with the sober thought of Carl Drake and others like him investing their lives into the search for what? An impersonal signal or some scientific proof of life from another world? Rick remembered hearing about a meteor that had been discovered somewhere. The scientific community was beside itself with excitement because some expert, probably one of Carl Drake's buddies, determined the chunk of rock was from Mars. He said it contained something that looked like it might have once been a Martian microorganism. Rick had wondered then how so many supposedly well-educated people could make such a huge leap, for one thing, and then get so gaga over it as if it settled the question once and for all. What would they do with two live, intelligent, smiling, beautiful, forehead-touching Klyvians? The thought only reinforced Rick's non-scientific gut instinct to protect Aldi and Elsa-Eska from public scrutiny. He fell asleep pondering the many things that would have to be done to ensure that his new friends had a chance for a peaceful life in their new home on Earth.

PART II
A MUSICAL INTERLUDE

CHAPTER 15:

TIME AND TIMES

The days of summer are long in Wyoming. It's nature's consolation for short changing the north during the winter months. The people who live in these regions are used to these conditions and they order their lives accordingly. Winter time is for indoor activities, but summer is outdoor time. Once the days get longer, and the weather gets warmer, folks begin their list of outdoor projects that must be completed (if they are to be completed) before the snow returns.

At the Blackwell Ranch, these outdoor projects usually consisted of a small garden, minor repairs and routine maintenances, and maybe a fresh coat of paint on one of the barns or the main house. These inconsequential projects took place in and amongst the comings and goings of town folks who boarded their horses at the ranch, the wilderness tours that laid over for a night or two, and the occasional drifter passing through to anywhere or nowhere. The atmosphere at the Blackwell Ranch was intentionally slower than the frenetic pace of the city Rick and Jane left five years earlier.

This summer, however, an unexpected project had been placed at the top of the list and it *had* to be completed before winter. A guest house was being built next to the main residence. The contractor Rick hired worked fast and honored Rick's unusual request to stop all work by four o'clock each afternoon. By 4:30, as the dust from the last carpenter's truck settled, Aldi was onsite exploring what the carpenters had done that day. His inspection was not the least bit critical, as some new homeowners are prone to look for the slightest indication of a cut corner or shoddy workmanship. Aldi's inspection was born purely of curiosity. He had never seen anything like it in his life. He stood looking up at the newly installed roof trusses when Rick joined him.

"It's coming right along," Rick said. "Won't be long before you and Elsa-Eska will have your very own home."

"It is so very big," Aldi observed. "All of this is for us?" Actually, it was not all that large. Only about half the size of the main house, it consisted of two bedrooms, one bathroom, a very small kitchen, and living area. The two unique features of the building were the extra-high ceilings and eight-foot tall doorways.

"When your baby comes, you'll be glad for the extra space," Rick offered.

"Klyvian babies are very small. Are human babies so big?"

Rick noticed the glint in Aldi's eyes and his irrepressible smile. "That's a good one," Rick said. "Come on, let's go sit on the deck."

The back deck of the main residence had taken on a special meaning for the two men. It had always been Rick's favorite spot since he and Jane moved to the ranch. He loved the view of his massive "backyard" and began each day by watching the desert wake up to the first rays of dawn. When Aldi and Elsa-Eska arrived, Aldi seemed to sense Rick's affinity for the spot, and although he was never actually invited, he joined Rick there each morning. Surprising to Rick, who was usually protective of his personal time, sharing this time with Aldi was the most natural thing in the world. Now, after three months, Rick looked forward to this time with Aldi as much as he looked forward to the sunrise.

Aldi followed Rick to the deck where each man settled into his usual deck chair. Neither of them spoke for several minutes, allowing the desert to reset itself after the cacophony of hammers and saws from the day's work.

Finally, Rick spoke. "You have something on your mind."

Aldi pointed skyward to a tiny sliver of silver radiance.

"That's the moon," Rick said. "You can see that?"

Aldi nodded.

"That's great!" Rick was truly impressed. "Two months ago you could barely see the moon when it was full. Your eyes must be getting used to this atmosphere."

"The Enterprise is there," Aldi said.

Rick squinted up toward the moon expecting to see a high altitude jet or a bird. Then he remembered. "Oh, yeah, your ship. You can see your ship from here?" Rick got excited at the prospect of seeing a genuine UFO—although technically it would not have qualified as an Unidentified Flying Object because had he been able to see it, he would have known exactly what it was.

Aldi explained, "The distance from the earth to its only natural satellite is approximately 240,000 miles. Although it's diameter is one fourth that of the earth, it appears to be about the size of a thumbnail at arm's length. The Enterprise is miniscule by comparison and therefore is not visible from the surface of Earth."

Rick smiled and shook his head. "I see you've been watching the *Discovery Channel* again."

"Yes," Aldi replied. "Did you know an earthbound observer would require the use of a telescope to see an object of that size from this distance?"

"I have a telescope. I'll go get it." Rick started to get up.

"You still cannot see it," Aldi said. "The Enterprise is on the other side of the moon."

"Oh." Rick slumped back into his chair. "How do you know this?"

"I spoke to my father."

"You did? When?"

"I have seen the moon four times since we spoke."

"And you're just now getting around to telling me?"

Aldi smiled at Rick. "I think you are happy as we are to talk with our people."

"Sure I am," Rick said enthusiastically. "After all, you haven't communicated with them since that flying sphere thing. I was beginning to think they might have…how are they? What have they been doing all this time?"

"*Time,*" Aldi mused. "Humans think much of time."

"It's been three months," Rick noted.

"Three months has no meaning to us," Aldi said. "We are here. They are there. Knowing is enough for us. To hear their voice is happy for us, too."

Any other time, Rick would have gladly delved deep into the difference between the human and Klyvian perspectives on time, but he was more interested in what news had come from the Enterprise. "What did they say?"

"We spoke of many things," Aldi explained. "Mostly the mission. Imtulon and Tyba have found good people in Australia."

"Are they the ones I met when you arrived?"

"Yes."

"Australia is a long way from here. Too bad. It would be great if they were close enough to visit from time to time."

Aldi's confusion over Rick's comment was genuine. "We cannot all be in this place. Tyba and Imtulon must be in Australia. It is the mission."

"Right, the mission. It was just a thought. Go on."

"Kai-Tai and Mallia are in Ireland. They have found good people. Ido say there are many who welcome them. They called it a *parish.*"

"I've heard that term before," Rick said. "I think it means a small town. That's great news." Rick tried to hide his concern over the fact that so many humans had become aware of the Klyvians' presence. "What about the team in Iraq?"

Aldi's expression became grave. "Yes, Iraq is the place. Ido has not heard from Jalamin and Arkel."

Rick suspected his fears might have been confirmed, but he did not want to worry Aldi. "I'm sure they're fine. Maybe their communications are down."

Aldi nodded. "Maybe. Maybe they will hear next time."

"Next time?"

"When the moon is dark again, that is the next time we will speak. Ido say there are many signals from Earth and many objects orbit. He has moved the Enterprise to the other side of the moon. When the moon is dark, he will move the Enterprise from behind the moon. That is when we will speak."

"That's pretty clever," Rick mused. "Using the moon as a shield and a signal."

"Ido say he remembers the moons of Klyv. Our people use them to speak of time and times when there is need."

"Humans used to do the same thing. Now we use calendars."

"There will be seven more times and then the Enterprise will go."

"Go?" Rick asked. "Go where?"

"The mission," Aldi said. "We have found life here on Earth. Maybe there is life on another planet. The Enterprise must seek out new life and new civilizations."

Rick smiled at Aldi's reference to *Star Trek*. Then another more sobering thought occurred to him. "Will you go then?" He felt a pang of disappointment.

"Do you not remember? Our child will be born here and grow up here. Then we will go."

"Oh, that's right. How long do you think it will be before the Enterprise returns for you?"

Aldi thought for a moment. "Time. Time is difficult for us to say. When our child is as we are, then it is time. The moon will become light and dark very many times."

Rick did some quick mental calculations. "Okay, let me see if I've got this straight. You said there will be seven more moon times and then the Enterprise will leave."

Aldi nodded.

"That's about seven months. It's the end of June now." Rick counted seven months on his fingers. "January. They will leave in January. Then you will be stranded here until they return whenever your child becomes an adult. That's…that's a long time."

Aldi eyed Rick for almost a minute. "Is it too long for us to stay here with you?"

"Oh, no," Rick replied quickly. "That's not it at all. I'm just thinking about you and your people. My family is just on the other side of the country, and I sometimes feel like they are on another world; I miss them so much. But you and Elsa-Eska, your family really will be on another world, sort of. I imagine you will miss them very much."

"Yes, we miss them, but it is the mission. It is our way." Aldi placed his hand on Rick's shoulder. "Now we have family that is not far away."

Rick wanted to say something, but the words eluded him. He just sat there and stared up at the tiny silver sliver that marked the location of Aldi's biological family. After several minutes, he finally worked up the courage to say what had been weighing heavy upon his mind. "Aldi, I want to talk to you about something."

Aldi turned to face him.

"You and Elsa-Eska have been here for three months now. I think it's working out pretty well. Jane and I love having you here."

"Elsa-Eska and I love having you here, too," Aldi replied.

"That's great. I'm very happy to hear that." Rick moved to the edge of his chair. "But there's something that's kind of been bothering me."

Aldi moved to the edge of his chair and locked eyes with Rick. "What is in your mind?"

"This is difficult to explain, but here goes. You and I have become very good friends. In fact, I feel closer to you than I do my own brother."

Aldi's wide smile grew wider. "Yes, we are as brothers."

"That's just it. You say we are like brothers, but I hardly know anything about you. I feel like I'm always telling you things about me and my world, but you haven't told me much about you and your world. I'd love to know more about Klyv. Is it at all like Earth? And your people, I want to learn your history, your culture, your customs. I want to understand you."

Aldi nodded. "I also want to know those things."

Rick remembered that Aldi and Elsa-Eska had been born onboard their ship and had never actually seen their home world with their own eyes. "Haven't your parents told you about your world?"

"We know of Klyv from what they say to us, but it is not as they know it."

"Can you tell us what you *do* know?" Rick asked.

Aldi thought for a moment. "There are still many words in your language I do not know."

"But you have learned so much," Rick encouraged.

"Yes, we have learned much of your language, but there are things of Klyv I do not know how to say."

Rick nodded.

Aldi sensed Rick's disappointment. "Elsa-Eska knows many more Earth words." It was true. Although Aldi could understand a tremendous amount of the English language, speaking it was another matter. He could parrot long, intricate excerpts of what he heard, but he still found it difficult to articulate his own thoughts. Elsa-Eska, however, seemed to have a knack for language and could speak English almost as fluently as if she had lived in America her entire life. She was even able to imitate various accents she heard on television or from Rick and Jane as they were prone to put them on from time to time.

"Do you think she feels up to giving us a lesson in Klyvian history?"

Aldi nodded. "Yes. She feels better today. She had good sleep last night."

"I'm glad to hear it." Rick looked at his watch. "Hey, the girls should be home soon."

Aldi cocked his head and looked off in the distance. "They come now."

Rick looked in the direction of the highway. The mile long dirt road that separated it from the ranch house was deserted, and Rick could detect no sound whatsoever. Then he saw it, a tiny cloud of dust showed just above the rise in the land between the house and the highway.

CHAPTER 16:

SONG OF MY PEOPLE

✝

Rick and Jane sat anxiously on the couch waiting for Aldi and Elsa-Eska to emerge from their room. It had been nearly half an hour, and Rick was getting more fidgety by the minute.

"I wonder what's taking so long?" he asked.

Jane sighed. "I'd think you would have learned by now that they don't get in a hurry for anything. Be patient."

"I only asked her if she would tell us a little about Klyv," Rick said. "It's not like I asked her to perform or anything. It's not that big a deal."

"Apparently it is to them," Jane snapped. "Didn't you see how Elsa-Eska's eyes lit up when you asked?"

"Yeah, but..."

"Yeah, but nothing. Obviously, this is important to them. The least you can do is show some respect."

"Respect? I asked because I'm interested in the people I care about. I asked *because* I respect them."

Jane crossed her arms, resting them on her growing belly. "Just try to keep your jokes to a minimum."

"What's that supposed to mean?"

Jane rolled her eyes.

"What?" Rick inquired.

Jane was about to answer his question with a response that would have certainly started a discussion neither of them wanted when Elsa-Eska and Aldi appeared from the hallway. They were wearing their Klyvian robes and Aldi was carrying a small box.

Though Rick and Jane had seen them in their robes before, they could not keep from staring. Their robes were light and shimmering and they billowed as they moved across the room. Through the translucent material, Jane could see the effects of Aldi's involvement in the work around the ranch. Rick decided to not rehire the usual crew of cowboys to work the ranch during the summer, so all the work fell to him, Aldi and Coop. Aldi's muscles were becoming bigger and more defined. She also noticed that Elsa-Eska's stomach was just starting to reveal that she also was with child. Rick noticed her as well and was surprised again by the effect she had upon him. Stunning as she was, and revealing as their robes were, Rick beheld her with the deepest respect. She was, after all, the wife of his closest friend. If Aldi was becoming his brother, then Elsa-Eska was his sister.

Aldi placed the box he was carrying upon the coffee table. He waited for Elsa-Eska to sit down in the easy chair and then pulled Rick's early morning chair from its spot in front of the window and placed it next to her. Gently, he lifted the ornately decorated lid from the box and placed it on the table next to it. Then, with the greatest of care, he lifted from the box something that looked like a scroll made of the same material as their robes. He laid it on the table and unrolled it. It seemed to glow as if illuminated by a light beneath or within it. Jane and Rick leaned forward to get a closer look. The scroll was small, only a few inches wide and about ten inches long. It was covered with delicate script that shimmered like rays from a late afternoon sun upon a mountain lake.

Elsa-Eska smiled warmly at Rick and Jane and reached for Rick's hand. Her touch was soft and warm, and Rick felt a sensation travel up his arm and settle into his chest. Aldi took Jane's hand in his left and Elsa-Eska's hand in his right. Jane got the idea and reached for Rick's hand. He hesitated long enough for Jane to notice, but then took her hand.

After about a minute of silence, Elsa-Eska took a deep breath and exhaled slowly. Then she began to speak in her native tongue. Her voice was soft and low and had a musical quality to it, almost as if she were singing. Although Rick and Jane could not understand her words, they sensed they were important, perhaps even sacred. What they heard with their ears was actually brief, no more than thirty seconds, but they were left with the impression that what Elsa-Eska had said was an excerpt from something much longer.

When she finished, Elsa-Eska allowed another moment of silence in which the sound of her voice seemed to linger. "This is the Song of my people," she finally said in English. "It began with Kalan and Dorran in the time when there was no before time. It will continue until the time when there is no after time. The Song tells of our world, our people, our mission. It is how we know and remember."

"It's beautiful," Jane heard herself say. "What does it mean?"

"It is difficult to say in human words. I will try." Elsa-Eska thought for a moment as she translated in her mind.

According to the desire of our father, we have come out of our place. According to the desire of our father, we are. Always becoming until become and then return to the place of our beginning. From all our knowing, we search the great space that is only blackness. In silence we hear the voice from a far place. It says, 'We are your searching.' According to the desire of our father, we are and do. The star pictures change, but our hearts do not change.

She paused and then added, "It is very difficult to say in human words. When I learn more, I will try again."

"I think I got it," Jane said. "It's your mission, right?"

"Yes, they are the words of my father," Aldi explained.

"When humans write songs, they write them in sections called *verses*," Jane offered. "Your father wrote this verse?"

Aldi and Elsa-Eska nodded their understanding.

"You said it will continue," Jane noted. "How is that?"

"The Song is the story of our people," Elsa-Eska explained. "Every Klyvian adds to it. We learn the verses of our fathers and mothers. Aldi and I will add verses and teach them all to our children. They will add verses and teach them to their children."

"That's amazing," Jane said. "It's like a musical genealogy. How much of the Song do you know? I mean, how far back can you sing?"

"To the time of Kalan and Dorran."

"You mean you can recite the entire Song all the way back to the beginning?"

"Yes, Jane, to the time of Kalan and Dorran in the time when there was no before time."

"Do you know *every* verse of every Klyvian since then?"

"This is all very interesting," Rick interrupted, "but can you just tell us about your world and your people?"

Jane glared at him and muttered something under her breath.

Elsa-Eska did not seem to notice Jane's irritation. "What would you like to know?"

"For starters, what can you tell us about your planet?"

Jane crossed her arms with a huff and leaned back on the couch.

"Klyv is the fourth of ten in its planetary system. It has two moons and the memory of a third. The rotation to revolution ratio is two hundred twenty-seven to one. Klyv has an atmosphere comparable to Earth, and many of the basic elements are the same. Klyv is a water planet with three lands and the memory of a fourth." Elsa-Eska sounded like she was reading from an encyclopedia.

"I see," Rick said. "That's very interesting. But can you tell us what it's like on the planet? What does it look like?"

"I am sorry, Rick, this is what I know. The Enterprise has images of Klyv, but we have none here."

"I see."

Elsa-Eska sensed Rick's disappointment. "My mother once told me of the place where she and my father lived before the mission. It was close to the ocean. She said she liked to listen to the sound of the water at night. And the stars—at night, my mother and father would look up at the stars and talk about the mission. That is how they found sleep at night. She said it was very beautiful."

"They slept outside?" Rick asked. "Every night?"

"Yes, it is the way of our people. But we, Aldi and I, have never slept outside. We have never been outside until we are here. That is interesting, I think." It was as if the thought had not occurred to her until that moment. "The planet Klyv is as strange to us as it is to you. Yes, that is interesting."

"Hmm, I never thought of it that way, but I guess you're right." Rick mused over the idea that Aldi and Elsa-Eska had more experience with Earth than with their own home world.

"Are there no houses on Klyv?" Jane asked. Curiosity had trumped her irritation with Rick and pulled her back into the conversation.

"Not like this." Elsa-Eska gestured around the room. "There is no need."

"What about shelter from the cold or heat or storms?" Rick asked.

"Our parents never spoke of such things. I do not believe there are storms or cold where they lived."

"Sounds like paradise," Jane noted.

"What about the people?" Rick asked. "Can you tell us about Klyvian civilization?"

Elsa-Eska closed her eyes. Aldi whispered something in his own language and closed his eyes as well. Jane shook her head at Rick who shrugged and mouthed the words, "What did I do?" He was about to apologize for whatever he had done when Elsa-Eska and Aldi opened their eyes.

Aldi nodded and Elsa-Eska spoke. "Our people remember these things in the Song. We do not speak of them in common words."

"That's okay," Jane said. "If you can't tell us, we understand."

"It is not that we can't tell you," Elsa-Eska assured her, "or that we do not want to tell you. But the Song has meanings that I cannot explain in human words."

"Really, that's quite alright," Rick added for Jane's benefit. "If you'd rather not."

"We, Aldi and I, want to tell you what we can. We want you to know us and understand our ways."

"Thank you," Jane said. "That means a lot to us."

Elsa-Eska nodded slightly and then began: "In the time of Kalan and Dorran, Klyv was one people. We lived on the large land called Klyv. So the land and the people were both called Klyv. It was this way for many generations. Then the Hori came. But Klyv was strong and the Hori disappeared. Many times passed, and a new generation was born. When the Hori returned, they came in secret and turned many of the young ones from the ways of Klyv. This was the Time of Trouble. The Hori became very bold and caused the young ones to rise up against their fathers and mothers. In the rebellion, many were killed and many were put into something like what you call prisons. A small number escaped from Klyv and crossed the waters to Muur. Muur is a smaller land. What was once one people became two—the true Klyv live on Muur and the Raphim remain on Klyv. Do you understand these words?"

Rick and Jane nodded in unison.

"Then do you understand why this is a great sadness for us?" Elsa-Eska asked.

"Humans have seen many rebellions and wars," Rick said. "It is sad, yes, but sometimes you just have to learn how to accept the way things are."

"We do not see it that way." There was an edge to Elsa-Eska's voice that caught Rick by surprise. "The Raphim have turned, but they are still Klyv. The Hori have done this to our people. We cannot accept it as the way things are." The gold flecks in her eyes burned bright with intensity.

Rick started to say something, but Jane cut him off. "Elsa-Eska, please. Rick didn't mean anything. We…we don't understand. We want to, but we don't. Please accept our apologies."

Aldi took Elsa-Eska by the hand and spoke to her in their own language. Then he spoke in English. "Rick, I have seen what you speak of on the TV. I know of your many wars. Humans war with humans, and it is, as you say, accepted by many of your people. With Klyv, it is different. The Hori are…I do not know the word."

"Very bad," Elsa-Eska said, her words barely above a whisper. "The Hori are very, very bad."

"Who are these Hori?" Jane asked. "Where did they come from?"

"They are not of Klyv," Aldi replied.

"Did they come from one of the smaller islands?" Rick asked.

Aldi shook his head. "They come from another place."

"You mean from another planet?"

Aldi did not answer. An awkward stillness fell upon them—awkward, that is, for Rick and Jane. Although Elsa-Eska's eyes had stopped glowing, she had not taken them off of Rick. Her stare made him very uncomfortable. He felt as if she were evaluating him, judging him. He tried to turn his attention toward Aldi, who was his usual calm self, but he could not escape Elsa-Eska's penetrating gaze. Jane just looked down at the floor.

After several minutes of agonizing silence, Elsa-Eska spoke. "Rick, please try to understand." Her voice was once again gentle, and her countenance had softened, yet it retained an urgency. "There is much more of the Song that we must tell you, but it is not the right time. For now, you must understand that all things are connected; what I have told you today, what I will tell you soon, it is all part of the mission."

Rick nodded.

Elsa-Eska continued. "You and Jane are now part of the mission. Please understand how important this is to us. Please."

Rick suddenly felt a weight, not falling, but being placed upon him. "I'm sorry about…"

Elsa-Eska placed her hand on his. "There is no need to be sorry. We are from different worlds. It will take time for us to understand each other. But the time will come soon."

"May I ask you a few questions?" Rick asked as his confidence returned.

"Of course. I will try to tell you anything you want to know."

"You said there was a memory of a third moon and a fourth island. What does that mean?"

"In the time of Kalan and Dorran, there were three moons and four lands. Just before the Hori came the first time, one of the moons broke apart. We believe it was hit by what you call a meteor. The hit took most of the moon out into space, but pieces of it remained in orbit. In the Time of Trouble, when the Hori returned, one of the lands disappeared into the ocean. All that is left is a memory."

"All things are connected," Rick said.

"Already you see," Elsa-Eska replied. "The Hori bring trouble and leave only memories. Bad memories."

As a product of humanity's Scientific Age of Explanation, Rick's first thought was that these occurrences on Klyv were purely coincidental. There had to be a rational explanation that had nothing to do with these Hori, whoever they were. Then again, Rick's own rationalism had taken a hit, leaving him much more open to unconventional thinking than he had been just three months earlier. He decided to keep his human logic to himself on this one and take a different track. "And you believe these things have something to do with your mission?"

"It is the true," Aldi replied.

Elsa-Eska simply nodded.

Jane had been making her own assessment of what she had just heard. There was one question she wanted to ask, but felt it was not yet time. She too took a different approach. "Elsa-Eska, can you tell us about the mission? How did it begin?"

Jane could tell by their expressions that Aldi and Elsa-Eska preferred talk of the mission more than Klyvian history. Aldi's eyes lit up and he leaned forward in his chair. Elsa-Eska's mood seemed to brighten as well.

"You have heard us speak of Ka-Rel?" Elsa-Eska asked.

"Aldi's grandfather?" Rick guessed.

"Yes. Ka-Rel is of the first generation born on Muur. His father was of those who escaped from Klyv in the Time of Trouble. It is the way of Klyv to give the younger ones the work of exploring. All people of Klyv are curious, so the young ones are happy to take this work."

"Klyvians are curious?" Rick teased. "I would have never guessed."

Jane shot him a look.

Aldi took the question as an honest inquiry. "Yes, we are."

Elsa-Eska continued. "Can you understand this is a great honor?"

"Sure," Rick agreed.

"Muur was an unknown land. There was much to explore. Our people were happy there, and they were safe."

"Couldn't the Hori or the Raphim follow them to the island?" Jane asked.

"No. The Hori fear water. They gave the fear to the Raphim. They will not cross the ocean."

"That's good," Jane acknowledged.

"Yes," Elsa-Eska agreed. "It is the way that is provided for the true Klyv."

Provided? Jane thought. *Provided by whom?*

Elsa-Eska looked at Jane as if she could read her thoughts, but continued her account. "Ka-Rel and his generation explored Muur until they had learned all. Then…" She leaned forward and began to speak as if revealing the secret to a great mystery. "…one day, Ka-Rel went up to the high place to look into the night sky. There he saw a star that was not there before. It seemed to him as if the star was moving toward him, or he was moving toward it, he did not know. The star came closer and closer until Ka-Rel could see its planets. He heard something that sounded like many voices. Then the voices became as one voice. They said to Ka-Rel, 'We are your searching.'"

"Hey, that's part of the Song," Rick blurted out.

"Yes, it is," Elsa-Eska replied, and her eyes flashed for a moment. "The words stayed with Ka-Rel. Every night when the sky became dark and the stars returned, he could hear them."

Rick and Jane were on the edge of the couch. They looked from Elsa-Eska to Aldi and back to Elsa-Eska, waiting for the rest of the story. "Then what?" Rick asked.

"Then we are here," Aldi answered.

"Just like that?" Rick asked. "Ka-Rel heard the voices, and your people launched a ship to go find them?"

"Yes," Aldi said. "It is the mission."

What Rick wanted to say was: *You're kidding, right? You don't just launch a space program because somebody hears voices. Ol' Grandpa Ka-Rel must have found some kind of Klyvian weed on that high place.* But Elsa-Eska's gaze bore into him like an x-ray into his mind. What he actually said was: "Wow! That's really interesting." For a writer it was less than stellar, but it was the best he could come up with on the spur of the moment.

"Interesting?" Jane countered. "That's fantastic! It's like Noah and the Ark."

Every eye turned toward Jane. Rick was trying to communicate *don't go there* with a slight shake of his head. Elsa-Eska and Aldi were waiting to hear more.

"Noah?" Aldi asked.

"What is ark?" Elsa-Eska asked.

Jane glanced at Rick. He was rubbing the bridge of his nose between his thumb and forefinger. "Well, Noah was a man who lived a long, long time ago, and he built this big boat called an ark. Then he put his family and some animals on it and…"

Rick blew out the breath he was holding and muttered to himself, "*Oh boy.*"

"…and they were saved from a flood that covered the earth."

Aldi and Elsa-Eska listened intently. Rick wanted to crawl under the couch.

Jane almost stopped there, but something inside caused her to go a little further. "You see, Noah knew the flood was coming because God told him."

"God?" Aldi and Elsa-Eska said in unison.

Jane tried to ignore Rick who was now sitting back with his arms crossed. "Noah heard the voice of God," she said meekly.

"The voice of God," Aldi repeated. "Who is God?"

Jane shrugged. "We believe God is the Creator of, well, everything."

Aldi and Elsa-Eska looked at each other and then back at Jane. Elsa-Eska bowed her head reverently and said, "You speak of the One who was before Kalan and Dorran, the One who was in the time before there was time."

"Yes," Jane said, "I guess so."

Rick moaned.

"We know the One who created all," Elsa-Eska said.

"What do you call Him?" Jane asked, her excitement growing. "What is His name?"

Elsa-Eska pondered the question. "The One who was before there was time does not have a name."

"We call Him God," Jane said.

Why have you not spoken of this before?" Aldi asked.

"I, uh," Jane stuttered.

"Why haven't you?" Rick asked. There was a hint of a challenge in his voice.

"We didn't know if you knew of the One who was before there was time," Elsa-Eska said, her excitement matching that of Jane.

"Well, we didn't know if you knew of the One who…was… before…of God, either," Rick replied. The challenge in Rick's voice had morphed into justification.

"We know the Before One!" Aldi exclaimed. There was laughter in his voice.

"So do we," Rick said. As soon as he said it, it occurred to him that it was the first time he had ever expressed any kind of belief in a deity.

Jane's jaw dropped, and a lump began to form in her throat.

Aldi and Elsa-Eska spoke rapidly to each other in Klyvian.

Rick was trying to figure out what had just happened. Did he really believe or was it just something he said to put himself on equal ground with Aldi and Elsa-Eska? And what was that ground? The Before One, God —were they even talking about the same thing? A sharp pain began to grow behind his right eye.

Jane was wrestling with the same questions, but instead of a headache, she felt a little nauseous. There was, however, a sense of relief. Now that the cat was out of the bag, she could explore the matter further with Elsa-Eska and Aldi. Judging from the scowl on Rick's face, she decided to rescue him from further inquiry by steering the conversation back to the mission. "Elsa-Eska," she said, "how long did it take to launch your mission?"

"I do not understand your question," she replied.

"Our space program is forty years old," Jane explained. "And we haven't gotten very far at all compared to you. I doubt we'll get past the next planet in my lifetime. I was just wondering about Ka-Rel. A lot had to happen between his hearing the voice and you being here. Did he ever get to see your ship?"

"The Enterprise was made by Ka-Rel," Aldi said.

"He must have been an engineer," Jane suggested.

"I don't know the word *engineer*," Elsa-Eska said. "Ka-Rel and the others received the idea for Enterprise from the Before One. The Before One told them how to build it."

Just like Noah, Jane thought. "It's too bad Ka-Rel couldn't be here to see that his mission has succeeded. It's kind of sad that he doesn't know you made it."

"Do not be sad for Ka-Rel," Elsa-Eska said. "The mission of Ka-Rel is the mission of Klyv. Ka-Rel gave the mission to his children. Ido and Naya gave the mission to their children. Aldi and I will give the mission to our children. Do you understand?"

"I think so."

Elsa-Eska reached across the table and took Jane and Rick each by the hand. "Rick and Jane, this is very important. Ka-Rel gave the mission to all of us. Now Ka-Rel gives the mission to you. Rick and Jane, if you are our brother and sister, you are Klyv as we are Klyv. Do you understand?"

The implication of her words, strengthened by the sense of her touch, weighed heavily upon Rick and Jane.

Aldi reached across the table and joined his hands with theirs. "The Song," he said. "The Song of our people is now the Song of you."

Elsa-Eska smiled and spoke softly, but with a conviction that moved even the entrenched skepticism of Rick Blackwell to the periphery. "You will learn the Song and you will teach the Song to your children. From now until the time when there is no after time, the Song of our people is the Song of your people."

"How are we supposed to do that?" Rick asked.

Aldi let go of Elsa-Eska's hand and gently moved the shimmering cloth across the table. "This is the Song. It will help you learn."

Rick and Jane looked down at the piece of cloth. The delicate script looked ancient, but not at all primitive.

"But we can't read this," Rick protested.

"We will teach you," Elsa-Eska said. "Just as you are teaching us the ways of your people, we will teach you the ways of Klyv."

The only language Rick had ever studied was Spanish during his junior and senior years of high school. He didn't learn it then and he surely didn't know it now. The notion of learning a language from an entirely different world seemed incomprehensible—even laughable, which is what Rick was doing. Elsa-Eska's eyes flared briefly and then returned to normal, but it was enough to catch Rick's attention. He stopped laughing.

"You do not believe you can do this," Elsa-Eska observed. "You do not know that you have already begun."

"Kel siblema-a fi."

Rick turned toward Jane. "What did you just say?"

"Kel siblema-a fi," she replied, astonished by the words that had just come from her own lips. "I don't know how I know it, but I just said, 'Yes, I will learn.'"

Elsa-Eska and Aldi nodded and said in unison, "Kelim lema-a. We will teach."

Apparently, language classes were back in session.

CHAPTER 17:

A DAY TO CELEBRATE

≃◁

The next week, the Blackwell Ranch was quiet and still—more so than usual. The construction crew was off for the Fourth of July holiday, Coop had gone to visit a relative, and Ed Tyler had not been seen in nearly a month. Rick stepped out onto his back deck, expecting to find Aldi waiting for him. For the first time in three months, he was not there.

Things had changed since "the conversation" a week ago. Even though Elsa-Eska assured him she was not upset with him, Rick felt like he had somehow offended her. They hardly spoke since that evening. Jane and Elsa-Eska, however, seemed to have discovered a new level of closeness. They spent nearly every waking moment together. For Jane's sake, Rick was happy, but he sensed something had come between Elsa-Eska and him. Aldi was his usual happy and carefree self, but even he seemed different somehow. The day after "the conversation" Aldi asked him about God, but Rick avoided the subject. After a couple of unanswered questions, Aldi didn't bring it up again.

Rick gazed out at his massive backyard, trying to recapture a sense of the normal he had once associated with the desert. Over the last week, different aspects of the Klyvian Song invaded his mind, refusing to leave. This morning he had been awakened by thoughts of the Hori. Whoever they were, he was glad they were held within the confines of a planet in some other solar system. Earth had enough trouble of its own. As he scanned the early morning landscape, he spotted a little silhouette of a man off in the distance. He watched the figure kneel down and pick up something from the ground. At that distance he could not identify the object, but he could see the figure was holding it in both hands. Curious, Rick went back into the house to retrieve his binoculars. He smiled when he saw that it was just Aldi examining a stick. Rick was just about to lower the binoculars when he noticed the stick bend in the middle. Now it looked more like a piece of rope or cable. Then one end of it raised up by itself and bent back away from Aldi's head.

Rick tossed the binoculars aside and broke into a full sprint across the backyard. When he got to within ten yards of Aldi, he stopped. "Aldi," he called out, panting from the exertion so early in the morning. "Don't move."

"Good morning, Rick," Aldi said happily.

Rick took a few cautious steps closer and froze in his tracks. His fears were confirmed. The rattlesnake in Aldi's hands was a big one. Its head was still bent back like it was ready to strike, but its tail twitched lazily back and forth like the tail of a contented cat. The clicking sound it made struck Rick as odd.

"Listen, Aldi, I want you to do exactly as I say. Very slowly, you need to put that down on the ground."

"Okay, Rick." Aldi's voice was that of a child—joyfully naïve. He lowered the snake to the ground and let it go. The snake slithered itself into a coil and began to shake its tail more vigorously.

"Oh boy," Rick said to himself. Then to Aldi, "Good. Now don't move a muscle." Rick searched the area for a stick or rock or anything he could use to kill the snake.

"What is it?" asked Aldi.

"That's a rattlesnake. They're very dangerous. Just hold still." Rick scanned the area again, but found nothing suitable for the execution.

"It is okay, Rick." Aldi started to kneel.

"Aldi, don't…" Rick braced himself for the strike that was sure to come. But instead of striking, the snake put its head down as Aldi stroked it with his finger. The rattling returned to the lazy click, click, click. Then, like an affectionate house cat, the snake rubbed against Aldi's leg as it slithered off into the desert.

Rick breathed a sigh of relief. "That was close. Aldi, you can't just go around picking up snakes like that. It could have bitten you."

Aldi nodded. "Why?"

"Why?" Rick shook his head and threw his hands up. "Because that's what snakes do. They bite. And they're poisonous."

"What is poisonous?"

"It means you could get very sick or even die."

"Oh." Aldi pondered the new information. "Then it is good you are here to tell me these things. Thank you, Rick."

"No problem. Let's go back inside."

When they got back to the house, Jane was in the kitchen. "Where have you guys been?" she asked.

"Just out for an early morning walk," Rick said. Jane was deathly afraid of snakes, and he saw no benefit in worrying her.

"Rick saved me from a rattlesnake," Aldi said.

Jane's eyes widened. "A rattlesnake! What happened?! Aldi, are you okay?"

"It was nothing," Rick fibbed.

"Do you know snakes are poisonous?" Aldi asked.

"Uh-huh," Jane nodded.

"Really, it was no big deal." Rick gave her a reassuring hug. "Say, you're up early." Then he noticed a large glass of milk and an opened box of doughnuts on the counter. "Oh, I see."

"What?" Jane asked innocently, in spite of the incriminating powder sugar on her lips.

"Oh, nothing. Come on, Aldi, let's go into the living room." Rick kissed Jane on the forehead. "Love you, honey."

An hour and a pot of coffee later, Rick and Aldi were deep in conversation about the significance of the Fourth of July. Rick was surprised to find that Aldi already had a basic understanding of the discovery and settlement of North America and he was familiar with the events leading up to the Revolutionary War. Rick was about to describe the war itself when Jane and Elsa-Eska joined them. Elsa-Eska sat on Aldi's lap and laid her head on his shoulder. He breathed in her scent and rubbed his cheek against her hair. Rick's history lesson would have to wait until later.

"Would you guys like some breakfast?" Jane asked. "I'm starving."

"Sure, I'll give you a hand." Rick started to get up.

Jane sat down on the couch beside him and pulled him back down. "But first, I thought we could tell Aldi and Elsa-Eska about our surprise."

"Or we could do that," said Rick.

"Today is a very special day," Jane began.

"Independence," Aldi announced with great enthusiasm. "On this date in 1776, our forefathers formally severed ties with England by signing the Declaration of Independence. Considered by the crown to be an act of sedition, we now see it as a bold act of defiance against the tyrannical oppression of England."

"Wow, Aldi, that's very good. I'm impressed."

Rick leaned close to Jane and whispered, "He's been watching a lot of the *History Channel* lately."

"I see," Jane said. "Also on this date in 1991, Rick and I were married. Today is our anniversary."

"Married?" Elsa-Eska asked.

"It's when Rick and I became husband and wife. You know, together, like you and Aldi."

Elsa-Eska nodded, but her expression suggested she did not fully understand.

Jane continued. "Today is a day for celebration—America's Independence…" She winked at Aldi who smiled in return. "…and our marriage. Not exactly the same thing, but that's okay. Anyway, Rick and I want you to celebrate with us. We would like to take you to Casper for a nice dinner and then watch the fireworks afterward."

"What is fireworks?" asked Aldi.

"Fireworks are…" Rick started to explain. "On second thought, I think it would be better if you saw them for yourself. I think you'll find them very interesting."

"We will go to Casper for dinner and watch the fireworks," Aldi said.

"The restaurant is very nice," Jane added. "I'll need to go into town before we go. Elsa-Eska, if you're feeling up to it, I'd like you to come with me. I have something in mind for tonight."

"I would like that," replied Elsa-Eska.

"What is in your mind, Jane?" Aldi asked.

"You'll see." Jane said teasingly. "Another surprise. You'll love it. Now who wants breakfast? I'm starved!"

CHAPTER 18:

SOME ENCHANTED EVENING

Rick and Aldi paced around the living room like grooms before a wedding. How she did it, Rick had no idea, but Jane had managed to find a very stylish sport coat and shirt that fit Aldi like it had been tailored especially for him. He had to admit Aldi looked cool, like a musician. He tried not to think about how much it must have cost.

Jane came out of the bedroom first. Like a runway model, she swept into the living room, spinning around so Rick and Aldi could admire her new outfit. She was radiant—a combination of her true natural beauty and the glow of expectant motherhood. Rick gazed upon her with a renewed affection. He knew this evening meant a lot to her and he was happy to make it all she hoped it would be.

"Jane, you take my breath away." Rick took her hand and delicately kissed it.

Aldi watched the exchange with a keen interest. When Jane held her hand out to him, he looked to Rick for guidance.

"Go ahead," Rick urged.

"Jane, you take my breath away." He kissed her hand just like Rick had.

"Why, thank you Aldi. You look very handsome yourself." She slid gracefully next to Rick and slipped her arm through his. She looked him up and down and flashed him her trademark crooked grin. "And you, my dear, look delicious."

Rick stood up a little taller and gave her arm a squeeze. After ten years of marriage, he was still under her enchantment. Vast was her arsenal, and she always chose just the right look or word or combination to dazzle him. Had Aldi not been there, he might have planted one on her—good and long. He settled for a kiss on her temple, which enabled him to whisper discreetly into her ear, "If we were alone…"

"We will be," she whispered back.

When Elsa-Eska entered the room, time paused. The dress Jane had selected for her was an elegant black evening gown with a plunging back and a slit up one side. Her hair was styled in gentle waves, spilling gracefully down her back like a dark chocolate waterfall. The only make-up she wore was a hint of eye shadow and liner that accentuated her natural exotic look. To be sure, she was a creature of quintessential beauty, though she seemed completely unaware of herself. She entered the living room confidently, yet unassumingly, smiling sweetly like a child.

When Aldi saw her, his face lit up just like it always did. "Elsa-Eska," he said, "you take my breath away." Then he took her hand and kissed it. "This is the human way," he explained.

Elsa-Eska nodded and proceeded to extend the custom. She kissed Jane's hand first and then Rick's. Had it been anyone else, it would have looked goofy, but Elsa-Eska made it look sweet. Jane curtsied in appreciation. Rick felt his heart skip and he really did find it difficult to catch his breath.

"You look lovely," said Jane.

"You look lovely," Rick echoed automatically.

"This is so much fun," Jane said. "Shall we go?"

Driving eastward on Highway 20, with the sun behind them, the sky ahead was a deep purple. It was a clear night and the stars were just beginning to show. The mood in the Jeep Grand Cherokee was light and the conversation was casual. For Rick, it was a welcome change. The tension that had come between Jane and him seemed to have dissipated; it even seemed as if Elsa-Eska were warming to him again. It felt like the beginning of a truly magical evening.

When they arrived at the restaurant in Casper, after a two-hour drive across the barren desert, everyone was hungry. Rick did the honors of ordering for everyone—vegetarian, of course—to which the waiter gave him a curious look. Aldi had gotten much better about not trying to talk to every human he met, but when he noticed the couple at the next table staring, he took it as an invitation to engage them.

"Hello," he said and offered his hand. "I am Aldi. We came to Casper for dinner and the fireworks."

The couple suddenly became interested in their menus, although the man kept sneaking looks at Elsa-Eska.

"What do you think?" Jane asked. "Isn't this place great?"

Aldi and Elsa-Eska took in the details. The motif of the restaurant was that of a medieval castle. The room they were in (one of several) was large with a high vaulted ceiling; dark wooden rafters forming an intricate pattern overhead. The walls were of white plaster; random sections of red and brown bricks showed through. An enormous tapestry covered the large wall at the back of the room; on it the scene was that of a lush countryside with knights on horses and damsels in waiting. The room was dimly lit by open-flamed wall sconces and pewter pot candles at each table. The carpet was a rich burgundy color, though it looked nearly black in the dim light. Patrons sat in high-backed chairs around square tables set with pewter mugs and heavy flatware. From hidden speakers, baroque music set a jaunty mood.

"Rick and I came here last year for our anniversary and fell in love with the place," Jane said. She went on to explain how it was modeled after a real English inn and pub called *Klinkerdaggers*. Aldi and Elsa-Eska had no frame of reference, so they were not quite as impressed as Jane and Rick were on their first visit.

"Rick and Jane," said Elsa-Eska after Jane had finished her discourse. "Tell us about your married."

"Our *married*? Oh, you mean our *marriage*. Rick and I were married on this date back in 1991."

"Was that a long time?"

"Ten years."

"How many years do you have in your life?"

"Well, I'm thirty-one years old, and Rick is thirty-six."

Elsa-Eska had no sense of Earth time, but her understanding of mathematics enabled her to figure what percentage of their lives Rick and Jane had been married. Finally, she said, "That is not a long time."

"I don't know," Jane replied. "Sometimes it seems like it."

"Thanks a lot," Rick shot back teasingly. "I love you, too."

Jane blushed. "That's not what I meant. It's just that a lot of marriages don't last this long." Jane put her hand on Rick's. "Actually, it doesn't seem long at all. How long have you and Aldi been married?"

Rick leaned forward with interest. He had been curious about Klyvian time since they first arrived.

Elsa-Eska thought for a long time before answering. "For us, time is not the same. We do not say, 'We have been married for ten years.' We say, 'Aldi and I became as one in the time of the lighted ones.'"

"What are the lighted ones?" asked Jane.

"On our journey here, we saw lights. From a distance, they looked like moving stars. When they got close, we saw they were like us, but they had their own light."

"What were they?"

"We do not know," she replied as if ignorance were perfectly acceptable.

"That's amazing!"

"There are many things in space that are, as you say, *amazing*. The lighted ones come and go, but they do not stay long. Aldi and I became as one in the time when we first saw them."

"I see," Jane nodded.

"So, I guess you two met onboard the Enterprise," Rick said.

Aldi started to snicker.

"What's so funny?" asked Jane.

Aldi tried to sound serious, but his voice was tinted with laughter. "No, it was the Fish Under the Sea dance."

"I don't get it," Jane said, her eyebrows nit with confusion.

"It's humor," Rick explained. "Aldi is trying to understand human humor."

Aldi let out a loud guffaw. "Human humor. That sounds very much the same. That's funny. *Humans* have good *humor*."

Jane and Elsa-Eska had not been part of Rick Blackwell's School of Humor. "Aldi," Jane said, sounding very much like a mom. "Not all human humor is funny or appropriate." Then, directing her attention back to Elsa-Eska, "Seriously, how did you two get together?"

"Get together?" Elsa-Eska asked. "We are always together."

"No, I mean when did you fall in love?"

"*Fall in love*? I do not understand *fall in love*."

Jane's determination would not allow her to let this question go unanswered. She posed it another way. "When did you know that you loved Aldi?"

Elsa-Eska nodded her understanding. "I understand now. I love Aldi the first time I saw him."

"Aw, how sweet. Love at first sight."

Rick held up a hand. "Weren't all the children on the Enterprise born about the same time?"

"Close together," Elsa-Eska replied. "Four children were born in the first time. And then four more children were born the second time. Yes, all are close."

"But you were all together as very young children, right?"

"Yes. We are together always."

"Just one big happy family," Rick quipped.

"We are a family," Elsa-Eska agreed, "and we are happy. There is much love with us."

Jane got Rick's point and kicked him under the table. When he looked at her, she mouthed, "Show off."

Rick decided to make his point a little sharper. "I'll bet that made dating kind of awkward."

"I do not understand dating," Elsa-Eska said.

"Never mind him," Jane said. "What I want to know is how you and Aldi knew you were to be together as a couple like you are now—a husband and wife?"

Elsa-Eska finally understood what Jane was getting at. "It was told to us."

"An arranged marriage?" Jane thought she understood. "People used to do that here a long time ago. Did your parents set it up? Did they tell you?"

"No, not that way." Elsa-Eska thought for a moment. "I do not know the human word. We call it *Ka-noa.*"

"Ka-noa," Jane and Rick repeated in unison.

"Yes, Ka-noa is the deep part." Elsa-Eska placed her hand over her heart. "It sees what eyes do not yet see. It hears what ears do not yet hear. It knows what minds do not yet know. In the time for us to become as one, Ka-noa of Aldi and Ka-noa of Elsa-Eska became as one. That is how we know. Ka-noa told us."

"Wow," Rick said.

"That's beautiful," Jane said. "I'll bet your wedding was amazing."

"Wedding?" Elsa-Eska asked.

"A wedding," Jane explained, "is a time when your family and friends get together to watch and listen to you promise your love to each other. It's when people recognize that you are married—that you are as one."

"We do not have a wedding," she explained. "When it is time for us to be as one, we are as one."

"No weddings?" Jane was disappointed, but she tried to hide it.

"It's kind of like a sixth sense," Rick offered. "Like a feeling that you can't really put into words?"

"It is more than a feeling," Elsa-Eska explained. "We can say what Ka-noa tells us. We hear it as clearly as we hear you."

"That sounds like E.S.P." Rick said, determined to get to the bottom of it. "Some people claim they can hear the thoughts of other people. Is that Ka-noa?" Rick secretly tested his theory by concentrating hard on a thick, juicy steak.

"No, we cannot hear your thoughts here." Elsa-Eska reached across the table and touched Rick on the forehead. "Ka-noa is the deep part here." She placed her hand on his chest.

Rick felt a tingling sensation where she touched him, and all the sounds around him faded as if someone had turned the volume down. A wave of an emotion he could not quite identity washed over him. It felt something like when his mom hugged him as a child, but he did not feel like a child. The sensation carried a deep level of intimacy unlike anything he had ever known, not even with Jane. Then the emotion turned into a clear impression, though not articulated in words. Somehow, he knew beyond any doubt that Elsa-Eska loved him. He looked into her dark brown eyes and saw the flecks of gold sparkle and swirl. Then he looked at Aldi, who was simply smiling at him. He felt the same impression of love emanating from him as well. Suddenly, in a moment of clarity, Rick thought he understood how Aldi and Elsa-Eska knew they were meant for each other.

Jane, who had been watching the exchange, felt something, too. But her experience was different. She somehow understood that this moment was meant for Rick. Still, she did not feel slighted in the least.

When the waiter arrived with their meal, Rick felt himself being pulled above the sensation. As the sound of music and conversation returned to his senses, he was fascinated by the fact that the impression did not cease, but simply moved to the background in order to allow him to become fully cognizant of the waiter and everything else in the restaurant. The meal was excellent and the conversation light. Yet Rick and Jane remained keenly aware of something otherworldly flowing continually beneath the surface of everything around them.

Aldi took his last bite and leaned back in his chair. "That was very good food."

"Yes, very good," Elsa-Eska agreed. "Thank you for this. You are very kind to share your marriage celebration with us."

"It's our pleasure," Jane said.

"We're glad you're having a good time," added Rick, "but our evening has just begun."

"Fireworks?" Aldi asked, sounding like an excited child.

"Not yet," Rick said. "There's something we'd like to do first."

"What is it?" asked Elsa-Eska.

"You'll see." Rick stood up and took Jane by the hand. "Come on. It's in the basement."

Aldi and Elsa-Eska followed Rick and Jane through the crowded restaurant to a descending staircase. When they reached the lower level, they found themselves in another very large room crowded with people. The music was noticeably louder, modern, and up-beat.

"What is this?" Aldi asked.

"It's called dancing," Rick said. He had to speak loudly to be heard over the music.

Aldi and Elsa-Eska stared wide-eyed at the people dancing in a pulsating glow that alternated from blue to green to red to yellow. A band was playing on the far end of the basement.

"Follow me," Rick said. He led them through the crowd to a tall table next to the wall. They climbed up onto tall stools and took in the scene.

Jane leaned over and spoke into Elsa-Eska's ear. "Would you like to try it?"

Elsa-Eska looked unsure of what Jane was asking.

"It's fun," Jane said. "Come on, we'll all go together."

Jane hopped down from the stool and started to move to the music. She grabbed Elsa-Eska and Rick by the hands, pulling them out onto the dance floor. Aldi followed, bobbing his head up and down to the music. The crowd parted as those nearest to Aldi and Elsa-Eska gawked at them like they were celebrities. When Rick and Jane began dancing, Aldi and Elsa-Eska studied their moves. Then, timidly at first, Aldi started to imitate Rick. Elsa-Eska watched Aldi for a moment and slowly began to sway to the music. Jane smiled and nodded encouragingly. Before long, the two Klyvians were blending in (sort of), and the dancers around them turned their attention back to their own partners.

By the second song, Aldi had gotten the hang of it. Unfortunately, he did not yet understand that dancing is a sport for couples. He drifted into the pair next to him and formed a trio. At first the couple tried to ignore him, but then they succumbed to Aldi's infectious grin and unusual moves. The woman sized up Aldi and winked at him. The man, apparently secure in their relationship, shrugged and kept on dancing. As often happens on crowded dance floors, Aldi and his new friends disappeared into the crowd. Two minutes later, he returned with two young women who looked as if they had just landed the catch of the day. Rick did a double-take and Jane gasped, but they kept dancing. When Elsa-Eska saw them, she smiled cordially and joined them. The two friendly girls froze on the spot. Clearly intimidated by Elsa-Eska, and cooled by Aldi's vibe, the girls frowned dejectedly and receded back into the mass of humanity from whence they had come.

When the song ended, Elsa-Eska said she was tired and needed to rest, but Aldi looked like he had caught his second wind. Rick accompanied Elsa-Eska back to the table, leaving Jane and Aldi out on the floor. A few more fast songs later, Aldi had found his groove, re-attracting the attention of the dancers around him. Jane, no stranger to the dance, kicked it into high gear, and the two of them put on quite a show. When the song ended, the crowd around them actually applauded.

The next song was a ballad. Jane turned to go back to the table, but Aldi stopped her and said he wanted to dance some more.

"This kind of dancing is different," Jane explained.

Aldi looked at the other dancers who had settled into nice slow rotations around them. "I believe I can do this."

"Okay." She held her left hand up for Aldi to take and reached her right hand up onto his shoulder.

After studying the couple next to them, Aldi placed his left hand on Jane's waist. Then, awkwardly at first, they began to sway with the music. Jane tried to look up into Aldi's eyes, but he was too tall. Not wanting to stare into his chest, she laid her head against it. When they finally found their rhythm, Jane found dancing with Aldi to be the most natural thing in the world.

From the table, Elsa-Eska noticed the change in the music and the slower pace on the floor. She scanned the crowd until she found Aldi and Jane. "I want to try that," she said, pointing to their spouses. She headed out onto the floor without waiting for a response. Rick followed her like a new puppy.

When they got to an open spot on the floor, Rick noticed the guys around them stealing glances at Elsa-Eska, careful to not allow their dates to notice. For an instant, he was conflicted. Part of him enjoyed being the envy of so many guys, but another part of him surged with protective defensiveness. He wanted to shield her from their ogling. Elsa-Eska, however, didn't seem to notice. Looking at how the other women were dancing, she moved close to Rick and let him take her in his arms. Holding her like that, Rick quickly forgot about the other dancers.

"I like this dancing," said Elsa-Eska.

"It's nice, isn't it?"

"Rick?"

"Yes."

"I think you are getting taller."

"What do you mean?"

"Our eyes are the same now."

She was right. Before, Rick had to look up at her when they stood in close proximity, but now they were exactly the same height.

"I haven't gotten taller. I think you've gotten shorter. Must be the effects of Earth's gravity."

Elsa-Eska started to chuckle.

"What's so funny?"

"Not funny," she replied. "Interesting. The Before One is making me fit better into this world."

Rick felt a smile form on his lips. That Elsa-Eska would be so quick to attribute a scientific effect to the Before One seemed to him quaint. Typically, he would have rolled his eyes and come up with a sarcastic comeback. But sarcasm didn't seem as clever anymore. All he could do was smile and say, "That *is* interesting." Besides, she was right about one thing; this beautiful woman he was holding in his arms certainly did fit better into his world, literally.

Elsa-Eska glanced at the couple next to them and noticed how close they were dancing. Rick felt her snuggle in closer to him and lay her head on his shoulder. Her hair was warm and soft against his cheek, and it smelled like exotic spices. It was intoxicating. For the next five minutes, nothing else mattered.

When the song ended, a good number of the dancers walked off the dance floor. Elsa-Eska took a step back, but held on to Rick's hand.

"I want to dance like this again," she said.

Rick felt a tingle on the back of his neck like he did with his first high school crush. "I do, too."

"Let's find Jane and Aldi."

Those were not exactly the words he had expected to hear, but they brought him back to the present. "Oh, right. I was thinking the same thing."

It wasn't hard to spot Aldi above the crowd, and the four were reunited just as the next song began. It was another slow dance. Elsa-Eska slipped gracefully into Aldi's arms and they began to dance like they had been doing it for years. Rick watched them for a moment, realizing how deeply they loved each other.

"Well?" Jane asked, taking his hand. "You up for another spin?"

"Yeah, sure." He took her in his arms and held her close. He breathed in her scent, trying to force himself to think only of her. But when he closed his eyes, all he could see was Elsa-Eska. He felt guilty and had to open his eyes to disrupt the image in his mind. When he did, he saw Aldi and Elsa-Eska dancing not three feet away from them. Their foreheads were touching and they were talking to one another. When Aldi caught sight of him, he flashed that big goofy grin of his and reached over to squeeze Rick's arm. Then he turned his full attention back to Elsa-Eska. That's all it took to chase away the last lingering remnant of desire. "Jane," he spoke into her ear. "I think we better go after this dance. The fireworks will be starting soon."

The fireworks were to be launched from the top of Casper Mountain out over the blackened desert. Given the topography of the area, there was not a bad place to watch them. A large crowd had gathered at the fairgrounds where food and novelties were being sold by local vendors, and patriotic songs were being played over loud speakers. Wanting to avoid the crowds, especially the long line of post-show traffic, Rick decided they would watch from a vacant lot on the outskirts of town and listen to the synchronized music selections on the Jeep's radio. The view from there was excellent, and not many watchers were present – mostly couples who were so caught up in each other, they paid no attention to the Jeep Grand Cherokee as it pulled into the lot.

"What is going to happen?" Elsa-Eska asked, getting out of the Jeep.

"Just wait and see," Jane replied. "It will happen over there." She pointed in the direction of Casper Mountain.

A group of teenagers about twenty yards away were partying and laughing. Aldi spotted them and asked Jane if they should go over to introduce themselves and see what was so humorous. She told him they were just having a good time and probably wanted to be left alone. That seemed to satisfy him.

After a few minutes, Aldi noticed Jane and Elsa-Eska were huddled together, shivering from the cool night air. He found a blanket in the back of the Jeep and draped it around their shoulders.

"Thank you, Aldi," Jane said.

"Aldi, kree fana," Elsa-Eska said.

"Aldi, kree fana," Jane echoed.

Elsa-Eska nodded.

Aldi bowed and said, "Kel tani fanim."

Rick suddenly felt like an outsider. "If it gets too cold, we can watch from the Jeep," he offered.

"Thanks, but I think we'll be fine." Jane reached over and gave his hand a squeeze. "Kree fana."

"You're welcome." Rick took a sulky step away from the trio.

Without warning, three streaks of light shot up from the top of Casper Mountain and arced out over the desert. Aldi was the first to notice and pointed them out to the others. They disappeared for a few seconds and then erupted into three enormous explosions of red, white, and blue. Aldi and Elsa-Eska both jumped and said something in their Klyvian language. The show had begun.

Veterans of numerous Fourth of July celebrations, Rick and Jane found more pleasure in watching Aldi and Elsa-Eska watching the display than in the display itself. Every few seconds they would glance over to see their reactions; the two Klyvians stood with their heads tilted up, eyes transfixed on the sky overhead, faces locked in wide-eyed, open-mouthed expressions of pure joy and wonder. They did not move during the entire twenty-three minutes of programmed pyrotechnics. During the finale, the excitement became too much and they both started laughing. When the show was finished and the last sparks trailed off, Aldi and Elsa-Eska continued to stare into the sky at the huge cloud of smoke drifting slowly eastward.

"That's it," said Rick. "What'd you think?"

"We have never seen anything like it," Elsa-Eska replied.

"Fascinating," Aldi said, sounding very much like Spock.

After standing outside in the chilly night air for over thirty minutes, no one had to ask if they were ready to get back in the Jeep. The four climbed in, and Rick cranked up the heater. Elsa-Eska and Jane continued to huddle beneath the blanket in the back seat, while Aldi joined Rick in the front. Cruising westbound again on Highway 20, the only sound in the Jeep came from the radio, which had returned to its regular programming of classic rock.

After a few minutes, Elsa-Eska spoke. "Thank you for a very nice evening. Everything was much fun."

"We're so glad you enjoyed it," said Jane.

"Yeah, it was fun," Rick chimed in.

Aldi, who had been staring out the window into the darkness, turned to Rick. "Please tell me about fireworks."

As Rick tried to explain the science behind pyrotechnics, Jane and Elsa-Eska fell promptly asleep. When he finished what he thought was a fair explanation, Aldi nodded though it wasn't clear how much of it he understood.

"I hope to see them again," he said.

"I'm sure you will."

CHAPTER 19:

TOLIS ANUK

Z

Somewhere on Highway 20, the headlights of Jane's Jeep cut through the night. Rick set the cruise control on sixty and leaned his head back against the headrest. He kept the volume on the radio low and faded to the front speakers. The DJ spoke in a cool, laid-back voice as one song bled into the next: "You're listening to the Voice of a Generation, baby—echoes from the Decade of Revolution."

Aldi transferred his gaze from outside to the light on the radio. "I like this human music."

"I do, too," Rick said, happy for the conversation. "Klyvians have music, don't they?"

"Yes."

"What's it like?"

"It is the Song of our People."

"Is that it? Just the one Song?"

"I don't know," Aldi replied. That there could be more than one song had never occurred to him. "Maybe there is another, but we have only heard the one."

"Wow." Rick could not imagine going through life with only one song. His CD collection had become massive over the years, and he still felt the need to buy new music from time to time. "Now that you're a resident of this planet, you may as well start learning about our music." Rick pointed to the radio. "The Doors." Then he sang along with the chorus: "Come on baby light my fire."

Aldi noticed Rick drumming on the steering wheel. He began tapping his right hand on the door beside him. "Come on baby light my fire," he repeated, but he was out of time with the music. When the chorus came around again, Aldi bobbed his head to the beat. He tried again. This time he got the timing right, but his pitch was off.

Aldi chuckled out loud. "I like this door." He tapped the door again.

Rick suppressed his amusement. "Not the door to the Jeep. The name of the band is *The Doors.*"

"What is the band?"

For the next fifteen minutes, Rick introduced Aldi to rock-n-roll. With each song that came on the radio, Rick explained to him about the musicians, the instruments they were playing, and the subjects of the songs. Aldi was particularly interested in what the songs were about. When the opening riff to the next song began, before Rick could name it, Aldi began singing, "Oo-ee, Oo-ee, oh, oh, wega taco. Yeah, yeah, yeah, yeah."

Rick shot Aldi a look of surprise. Then the singer began: "Louie, Louie, oh baby, we gotta go. Yeah, yeah, yeah, yeah."

"How do you know that?" Rick asked.

"I have heard this."

"Where?"

"On the Enterprise. It came with the pictures and words of Earth. It is how we found you."

Rick thought for a moment and then started to laugh. "*Louie, Louie* was part of the signal you detected coming from Earth? Oh, man, that's classic."

Aldi nodded enthusiastically.

Through his laughter, Rick said, "That figures. Out of all the electronic garbage we've been sending out into space for the last fifty years, you found us with *Louie, Louie.* That's great."

"Rick," Aldi said, "I have heard this my whole life. Please tell me, what does it mean?"

Rick stopped laughing. "Gee, I've never really thought about it. Louie is the name of a guy, but I have no idea what the song is about."

Aldi seemed disappointed that Rick could not explain the meaning of the most important recording of all time—the song that brought two worlds together and answered one of the most puzzling mysteries of the modern age. When The Kingsmen recorded *Louie, Louie* in 1964, rumors about the song's meaning prompted an FBI investigation. Now, after thirty-seven years, if this piece of the song's history were to become known, the FBI would have to re-open its investigation and the song would undoubtedly shoot straight to the top of the charts. Nothing sells like a good conspiracy theory. As the song played on, Rick tapped the steering wheel to its beat and Aldi listened to it for the first time in its entirety and free from the static that accompanied it on its long journey through space.

They drove on through the night, the Jeep a tiny oasis of warmth and life in the emptiness of the cold, dark, lifeless desert.

"Rick," Aldi said after the musical portion of the broadcast paused for a newsbreak at the bottom of the hour. "This is like space."

"Excuse me?"

"This." Aldi nodded toward the blackness outside. "On the Enterprise, it is always like this. Outside is dark. No house, no tree, no mountain, no Jeep, no book, no snow, no blue sky, no people. Just dark. No life."

Rick nodded courteously. He had always considered space travel to be the ultimate adventure. This was a different side of it from someone who had actually been there.

Aldi continued. "When I was on the Enterprise, I did not like to look out. Outside is dark and cold. Inside is light and warm and life. Inside is…" He looked at Jane and Elsa-Eska still asleep in the back seat and then at Rick. "Inside is…"

Rick heard what Aldi had said and he may even have responded, but in his mind, it seemed that he was caught up in a strange dream. He had not fallen asleep, however, as he was still very much aware of the road ahead of him. But in another part of his mind, he was somewhere else.

In this daydream, if that's what it was, he was in a room with four television sets, each one replaying an event from the day. On the first set, he saw Aldi holding a rattlesnake. It was so real, he could sense the emotions of the moment—first curiosity when he thought it was a stick, then raw fear upon realizing it was a snake, and then relief as the snake slithered harmlessly away. He moved to the second set and saw Elsa-Eska reaching toward him from across the dinner table. Somehow he knew she had just explained Ka-noa and now he could feel the tingling sensation as she touched his chest. The emotion of this scene was almost beyond words —joy, contentment, and the purest form of love he had ever known. He wanted to stay, but he felt himself being pulled to the third television. There he saw himself slow dancing with Elsa-Eska and he felt the rush of desire followed by the sting of guilt. Part of him wanted to remain, but a sensation of nausea forced him to move on. At the fourth and final set, he saw the fireworks. The emotion that came with this scene was a combination of boyhood wonder and the joy of sharing it for the first time with Aldi and Elsa-Eska. Then the televisions began to move, forming a semi-circle in front of him. As the scenes played over and over, Rick felt the emotions of each scene converging upon him, first in turn and then all at once. The emotional overload was becoming more than he could stand. He felt that he must run away or pass out, but he could not move his legs. Then, from somewhere a long way off, a voice cut through the clatter. "Tolis anuk." It was Aldi's voice as he heard it that first day on the back deck of his house. The word hung in his mind and drew closer. Then the voice morphed from that of Aldi to his own. Without realizing it, he himself was repeating the Klyvian words, "Tolis anuk."

"You are learning," said Aldi.

"What?" Rick snapped out of the daydream.

"Tolis anuk," Aldi replied. "I was thinking inside here with you and Jane is home, and you said, 'Tolis anuk.' Tolis anuk is home."

"You were thinking it?" Rick could still sense the end of the daydream.

"Yes," Aldi chuckled.

"But I could hear you."

"That is Ka-noa."

"I thought you said Ka-noa was not mind reading."

"It is not. I hold tolis anuk in here." Aldi pointed to his heart. "I was thinking it, too, but you did not hear my thoughts. You heard the deep part."

It was true. Aldi was still thinking in his own Klyvian language. What Rick had become aware of was Aldi's deep affection for tolis anuk as he was trying to translate it into English. The awareness (or daydream, as Rick thought of it) was a surge from Aldi's Ka-noa. The entire experience had happened in a fraction of a second, but even now, a remnant of it still lingered.

"That is so strange," Rick said. "It was like we were connected." He tried to process what had just happened. If the experience really was a connection, and Aldi could sense Rick's deep part, then maybe he sensed the emotions of Rick's vision. If that were the case, then Aldi must also have sensed Rick's attraction to Elsa-Eska. The thought was alarming. "Aldi, I don't know what to say."

"You do not need to say anything," Aldi said.

"Then you must know what I was feeling."

"Yes. Ka-noa speaks your feeling."

Rick glanced over at Aldi to get a read on him. He was looking back at him with his characteristic grin. What did it mean? Was he okay with Rick's feelings for Elsa-Eska? Or was he just toying with him? Rick swallowed and looked straight ahead. "So, uh, you're okay with that?"

"Yes," Aldi replied with enthusiasm. "You are feeling what I feel."

"I am? *You are?*" Rick didn't know whether to be relieved or horrified. "You mean you feel this way about Jane?"

"Yes," Aldi nodded. "And you. And Elsa-Eska has the same feeling for you."

"She does?" Rick rubbed his eyes and shook his head. For a brief instant, he felt a flash of schoolboy excitement. But it was over-ruled by the mature knowledge of Elsa-Eska's devotion to Aldi. *Then again, maybe Klyvians were not monogamous. What if the four of them...* "Wait a minute." Rick tried desperately to reign in his runaway train of thoughts. "What are we saying here? Tell me exactly what it is you feel."

"Tolis anuk," Aldi said. "Home. You and Jane are home with us. Together, we are all home. That is what you feel, too, yes?"

The train jumped the track and came to a screeching halt. Of course, that's what Aldi was talking about. Rick nodded and said, "Yeah, that's what I was thinking, too." Then, just to make sure, "Aldi, I know we're talking about home, but what exactly do the words *tolis* and *anuk* mean?"

Aldi thought for a moment. "Anuk has different meanings. Sometimes it is a place like here or there. Sometimes it is a time like now or when we first came here. There are other meanings, but I do not know how to say them in English."

"Spatial and temporal," Rick said nodding. "That's interesting."

Aldi continued. "Tolis is peace. There is no trouble or fear in tolis."

"Refuge," Rick said. "So tolis anuk literally means refuge place."

Aldi nodded.

"Aldi, that first day when you arrived and we were standing on the back deck, I sensed tolis anuk from you, but I understood it as home. Was that your Ka-noa saying you had found a place of refuge—a safe place to live?"

"Yes."

"But that didn't mean Wyoming or even Earth, did it? When you think of home, or tolis anuk, you think of Jane and me? We are a place of refuge for you and Elsa-Eska?"

"Yes. And we are the same for you. Together, Jane, Elsa-Eska, Rick, and Aldi, all are tolis anuk."

They drove the rest of the way home in silence. Aldi went back to his staring out the window. Rick pondered the implications of tolis anuk. It came naturally for Aldi and Elsa-Eska, and Jane seemed well suited to it. But what about himself? The concept was attractive for what it offered to him. But could he offer as much to the others? Tolis anuk would make no room for the selfish.

CHAPTER 20:

WHAT ED TYLER KNEW

It was very late by the time they got back to the ranch. Aldi and Elsa-Eska expressed their appreciation again for the enjoyable evening and went straight to bed. Jane turned in as well, but Rick lingered in the living room for a while. He was still keyed up from the road and needed to clear his head. After a few minutes of mindless channel surfing, he switched off the television and stepped out onto the back deck. The cool night air helped a little and he soon found himself looking up at the full moon.

"So, that's where you hang," Rick said out loud to the people onboard the Enterprise. "Glad you could stop by and visit our little planet." He picked a splinter off the deck rail and flicked it into the darkness. He looked up at the moon again. "In case you're listening somehow, there's something I'd like to say. Just between me and you, this is some kind of mission you've got goin'. I mean, all of you up there and your kids down here, all because Grandpa Ka-Rel had a dream. Well, I don't get it. You come all this way; you're probably not going to make it back home, and for what? Curiosity? Well, here we are! What do you think? I hope you're not disappointed!" Rick shook his head and picked at another splinter. "Man, I sure would be. All this way for what? A jerk like me? And what's worse, you dragged your kids into it. You didn't even give them a choice. Just a lot of talk about *The Mission of Ka-Rel*. Talk about an offer they couldn't refuse."

Just then, the splinter sank deep into his finger. He cringed in pain and stuck his finger into his mouth. "Now look what you made me do." Nibbling on his finger in a vain attempt to extract the splinter, he turned to go back inside. Before entering the house, he looked back up at the moon. "By the way, your kids are doing just fine...in case you're wondering. You should be proud of them." He was about to go inside when he sensed a presence behind him. "Hello, Ed. What are you doing out so late?"

Ed Tyler shuffled up to the deck and stopped at the first step. Bonko stopped at his feet and laid down. "We seen you folks come in awful late. Everything okay?"

"Yes. We just got back from Casper. Today's our anniversary. We went out for a celebratory dinner."

"You and them tall people?"

"That's right, Ed. We took my cousins with us."

Ed gave Rick a squint-eye. "How dumb do you think we is?"

"What are you talking about?"

"They ain't no kin to you. And they ain't no Russians neither. Good thing, 'cause if they was Commies, well…they ain't, so that's why we're here."

Rick didn't know what to say, so he didn't say anything.

Ed continued. "I done told you that day at the busted fence they could only be two things. If they ain't Commies, they gotta be aliens. And you, Mr. Smarty-in-the-pants, spent the last three months sneakin' around like you was gittin' away with something. Ya shoulda just told us from the git-go. Made us go to a whole lot of trouble figurin' it out ourselves."

Rick looked up into the night sky stalling for time. He realized there was no way to redirect Ed Tyler's thinking, so he decided to take him on directly. "I should have just told you, eh? I'm sure you would have been fine with that. If you remember, Ed, you threatened to call the *real* government, whatever that is. I didn't trust you."

"Kevin, Kevin, Kevin," Ed said, shaking his head. "I'da called the real government if they was Commies. Aliens is a whole 'nother matter. I had to make sure…" Ed stopped when he heard Bonko making a strange noise. The little dog was convulsing like he was choking on something. Ed knelt down and performed the Heimlich maneuver (apparently it is possible) and Bonko coughed up a large chunk of beef jerky.

Rick grimaced at the sight and waited for Ed to finish. When it appeared Ed had lost his train of thought, Rick asked, "Make sure of what?"

"Huh?"

"Had to make sure of what, Ed?"

There was another long pause as Ed re-boarded his train of thought. "Oh yeah, I had to make sure what kind they was."

"What do you mean, what kind?"

Ed snorted deeply and swallowed. "Well, there's good ones and…"

He looked at Bonko who was sniffing the beef jerky he had just dislodged from his throat. Then he climbed the steps and whispered, "...the other kind. Them aliens you got livin' in yer house—they's the good ones. We don't mind the good ones."

"So what? You've encountered a...um...a bad alien?"

"Shhh." Ed put his grimy finger on Rick's lips, then he pulled him close so he could whisper directly into his ear. "We don't speak of the other kind around Bonko. That's how he lost his leg."

Fortunately, the little dog was too busy with his second attempt at the beef jerky to hear what the humans were discussing.

"I see," Rick whispered.

"Okay then," Ed said. "Hey, you want to come over to the trailer for a midnight snack? I got Vy-anna sausages and pickled eggs."

Bonko's left ear perked up and he let out a happy yip.

"Yes, Bonko, you can have the extra sausage jelly."

Rick shuttered like he had just swallowed a raw oyster. Although he was starting to become intrigued by Ed's apparent knowledge of aliens, there was still a lot about the old guy and his dog that he just did not want to know. "No, I'm still full from supper. But thanks anyway."

"You sure? I got Frescas."

"Thanks Ed, but I think I'll pass."

"Them sausages are mighty good," Ed said temptingly. "Come all the way from Vy-anna, Australia."

"As good as that sounds, it's too late for me. I'm just going to go on in and go to bed."

Without another word, Ed turned and walked back down the steps. Rick watched as the strange little man shuffled off into the night, the little dog hobbling beside him. Then he heard Ed say, "You know what that means, Bonk? That's right, we each get our own can. I can taste those little yummies now. Mm-mm." As Rick turned to go inside, he could have sworn he heard within Bonko's grunting something that sounded exactly like, "Mm-mm."

Rick chuckled to himself. "Those two just keep getting weirder."

PART III

NATURAL BORN CITIZEN

All persons born or naturalized in the United States, and subject to the jurisdiction thereof, are citizens of the United States and of the State wherein they reside. No State shall make or enforce any law which shall abridge the privileges or immunities of citizens of the United States; nor shall any State deprive any person of life, liberty, or property, without due process of law; nor deny to any person within its jurisdiction the equal protection of the laws.

Section 1 of the 14th Amendment to the
Constitution of the United States of America
Ratified July 9, 1868

CHAPTER 21:

COMMUNIQUÉ

↘

The farthest human-to-human connection ever established was made in the late 1960s and early 1970s between controllers at NASA and astronauts on the moon. Those were the heady years of the Space Race when mankind was busy taking giant leaps and planting flags in order to expand the human domain. With the return of Apollo 17 in 1972, the last manned mission to the moon, those communications ceased, and the moon was reclaimed by silence. The sound of voice, it seemed, was a momentary blip in the moon's long quiet history. In early 2001, voices returned to the vicinity of the moon. But unlike those historic communications of nearly three decades earlier, these voices were not human.

On August 17, 2001, a mere sliver of the moon was visible from the surface of the earth. While most of the world's inhabitants went about their business without giving the waning moon even the slightest notice, a few new arrivals paid close attention. In the desert outback of Australia, on a green hillside in Ireland, and on the high desert plains of Wyoming, eager eyes kept careful track of the moon's phases.

The skies over the Blackwell Ranch were clear on Saturday, August 18. The temperature that day had reached a scorching 93 degrees. Fortunately, construction on the new house next to the main residence had been completed the week before. Its brand new air conditioning unit was keeping the interior of the home a comfortable 80 degrees—a bit warm for the human residents of the Blackwell Ranch, but ideal for the Klyvians whose new home it was.

It was late afternoon when the new doorbell rang. Elsa-Eska slipped on her Klyvian robe and answered the door. "Jane, Rick, please come in." She took a step back, pulling the edges of her robe together in the front. It was a courtesy she extended to her human visitors. When she and Aldi were home alone, they preferred to go without clothing. Such was the Klyvian way, and given Elsa-Eska's condition, it was more comfortable to forgo the restrictive human custom of covering up. But for the sake of her visitors, she had embraced her newly learned adage: *When in Rome.* Her very limited knowledge of Rome did not explain why Rome should set the standard for behavior in Wyoming, but thanks to Jane's explanation, she understood the meaning behind the saying.

When Jane came to visit alone, and their husbands were out on one of their frequent adventures, she thought of Elsa-Eska's home as a Klyvian domain; thus, she joined her in the Klyvian way. She too was in the final weeks of her pregnancy, which made 80 degrees unbearable with clothing on. She felt awkward at first, but in the company of Elsa-Eska, her Klyvian sister, it soon seemed as natural as wearing a bikini at the beach. When she told Rick about it, he simply shrugged and commented, *When in Klyv.* But he asked her to promise she and Elsa-Eska would not, *go all Klyvian* unless he and Aldi would be gone for awhile.

"How are you feeling today?" Jane asked.

"Very well. I believe I have gotten used to Earth's climate. I feel the best I have since we arrived. How are you?"

"I'm fine, but I've had about enough of this heat." Jane wiped a trickle of sweat from her brow.

"Yes, it *is* warm outside. Let's sit."

The small living room was sparsely furnished with a drab old couch the color and texture of oatmeal and a couple of mismatched chairs Rick found stored in the barn. Jane was embarrassed by it, but it met the immediate need until they could buy better furnishings later. Aldi and Elsa-Eska, however, thought the furniture was beautiful. They could hardly believe such human finery was all for them. Jane sat in a dark green swivel chair while Rick sat next to Elsa-Eska on the oatmeal couch.

"Where's Aldi?" Rick asked.

"He's in the bedroom getting ready to call the Enterprise."

"Oh, I didn't realize it was that time. Do you think he'd mind if I joined him?"

"Not at all," Elsa-Eska replied. "But first I want you to feel something." Before Rick could react, she grabbed his hand and placed it on her stomach.

Rick's face flushed. He looked at Jane only to find her enjoying his embarrassment. But then he felt a strong but gentle movement as a tiny hand or foot pressed against his hand. "Whoa! I can feel her."

Elsa-Eska beamed with delight. "I have told her all about you. She is eager to meet you."

Rick wondered if she meant it literally or sentimentally. "Yeah, well, I'm looking forward to meeting her, too."

"Do you know how much longer until your baby will be born?" Jane asked.

"Not long."

"Have you settled on a name yet?" Rick asked.

"We cannot know her name until we see her with our eyes. Then we will know."

"Hey, what a great idea." Rick looked directly at Jane. "Honey, we should try that." He turned his attention back to Elsa-Eska. "You should see the list we've got. There must be twenty names on it."

"Why so many?" Elsa-Eska inquired.

"We can't decide," Jane answered. "Rick likes the name Kathryn Mary, but I think that sounds too old fashioned. I've been stuck with *Plain Jane* my whole life, so I'd like to name our daughter something unique—something interesting."

"There are a lot of interesting Jane's," Rick noted. "Jane Mansfield, *Jane* by Jefferson Starship, Tarzan's Jane. And then there's my personal favorite, Jane Monheit. She's amaz..."

Jane Blackwell gave him a sideways look and cleared her throat.

"What I mean is, she's a mayyy-be second favorite."

"Did you say Aldi was in the bedroom?" Jane asked Elsa-Eska. "Maybe Rick should go see what he's doing?"

Rick got up from the couch just as Aldi entered the living room carrying a device that looked like a thin book.

"Rick, you are here. Hello, Jane. I am going outside to contact the Enterprise. Do you want to come with me?"

"Yes, please."

"I want to try a place past the fence. There is interference close to the house."

Before leaving, Aldi leaned over to kiss Elsa-Eska. She reached both hands around his neck and kissed him passionately on the lips for several seconds. Rick noticed the *aw-how-sweet* expression on Jane's face. Getting the hint, he followed Aldi's lead which elicited a surprisingly warm response from Jane.

As the two men walked out of the house, Aldi commented, "I like the kissing you showed us. We do that a lot."

Alone now, Jane loosened the top button of her blouse and wiped her brow with the back of her hand.

"You look uncomfortable," Elsa-Eska said.

"I'm just so hot. And carrying around all this extra weight sure doesn't help much. I just don't have any energy."

"I'll adjust the air conditioner." Elsa-Eska started to get up from the couch.

"Oh, no. That's okay," Jane objected. "Keep it where you like it." She wiped her face again on the sleeve of her blouse.

"I know it is warm to you, but the cold air gives me a headache. I'll be right back." Elsa-Eska stood up the rest of the way and exited the living room. When she returned, she had a glass of water in hand and Aldi's Klyvian robe draped over her arm. "Here, put this on."

When Jane took the robe, she noticed a small metallic vial in Elsa-Eska's hand. She quickly slipped out of her clothes and put on the Klyvian robe. It hung loosely on her, so light that it hardly felt like she had anything on at all. "Ah, that's better. Thank you." She rubbed her cheek against the material. Aldi's scent was noticeable and pleasant.

"Take some of this." Elsa-Eska poured some of the contents of the vial into Jane's open palm and handed her the glass of water.

Jane knew what the stuff was and took it without hesitation. "Wow!" she said as a jolt of energy surged through her body. "That chippick is good stuff. Thank you, I feel better already."

Elsa-Eska returned to the couch. She looked at Jane for a long moment and then said, "You have the look of new life about you."

Jane blushed.

"Your baby is strong and healthy. She will come soon."

"I'm still a few weeks away from my due date, but I'm ready to get this over with."

"Why are humans always in a hurry?"

Jane had been with Elsa-Eska enough to know that the comment was not meant as a criticism, but rather an honest enquiry. "I don't know. I guess we just get impatient sometimes. Also, I'm kind of nervous about the delivery."

"Why?"

"There's the pain for one thing. Then the recovery, and getting back into shape. And, well, sometimes things go wrong. I'm just a little scared about the whole thing."

Elsa-Eska considered this new information. "I do not know what it will be like. I was very young when my sister was born, and my mother never spoke to us about it. I guess I always thought I would know when it was time. I am very happy to share this with you. We will help each other." She reached over to give Jane's hand a squeeze.

"Yeah, we'll help each—whoa, whoa, wait a minute. Oh, Elsa-Eska, I can't believe we haven't thought about this yet."

"What?"

"You don't have a doctor."

"I am not sick."

"Not that kind of doctor. When a woman has a baby, she goes to the hospital. A special kind of doctor delivers the baby and takes care of the mother and child."

"I have Aldi. I will have our baby here. And you will be with me, too."

Jane started to object, but stopped herself. "I tell you what, come with me to my next appointment and meet my doctor. She's very nice. I just want you to talk to her."

"I don't need a doctor." Elsa-Eska shook her head. "Aldi is here. You are here. Rick is here."

"Believe me, Rick won't be any help. And I'm afraid Aldi and I won't be much help either. Please come with me and just talk to her. You don't have to decide anything now. Just come."

"No," Elsa-Eska replied firmly. "Aldi will help me here."

"Alright," Jane conceded. "I can respect your wishes." Then she thought to herself, *There's still time. I can talk her into it.*

Out beyond the fence in Rick's massive back yard, the two men stood looking up into the sky. Aldi was pointing to a spot where he said the moon was. Unable to see it, all Rick could do was believe him.

Aldi held the device he was carrying in one hand and tapped its surface with the other. Several symbols lit up. As his hand moved slowly across the symbols, the sound of static changed pitch until a voice could be heard from a speaker somewhere on the device. Rick leaned in close to listen and was surprised to hear English. He soon discovered it was the voice of a pilot requesting an approach to land somewhere. Aldi continued to move his fingers over the symbols, dialing in a variety of signals; an announcer calling plays at a baseball game, numerous cell phone conversations, a traditional native American chant, and some kind of transmission in a language Rick believed to be Arabic.

Aldi glanced over at Rick. "Hailing all frequencies, Captain." He grinned and looked back down at the device.

Finally, after another minute, Aldi drew back his hand. As he did, a six-inch three-dimensional holographic image of a woman materialized above the shiny black surface of the device. She wore a translucent robe and spoke in a language Rick recognized as Klyvian. Aldi spoke to the woman for several seconds before another voice could be heard. The woman stepped aside, disappearing into thin air, as the image of a man materialized in her place. He looked enough like Aldi to be his older brother. Aldi and the image spoke for several minutes. Rick could not understand anything that was being said, but he could tell there was a bond between the two men. There were several exchanges and then a bout of laughter. Rick could only guess it was Klyvian humor. He would have given anything to be able to understand what they were saying.

Several hundred miles away, in a tax-funded government installation that did not officially exist, two casually dressed young men sat before an array of computers and sophisticated listening equipment. Surrounding them on all sides of the room were racks of video monitors, reception boosters, signal enhancers and modulators, and digital archiving vaults. During the Cold War, uniformed men fluent in the Russian language occupied these same seats, listening to and translating captured radio transmissions from the Soviet Union. But now, in a world dominated by just one world superpower, things had changed. The Russians had fallen several notches down the list of enemies of the United States. The men who now occupied this command barely remembered the Cold War. They were young, talented, and considerably less conventional than their predecessors from the previous generation. Their technical skills were such that their superiors turned a blind eye to their disregard for military dress and protocol. These were agents of the new order. Their tools of the trade were Geosynchronous satellites, strategically placed long-range microphones, and the ability to hack into any wireless transmitting device anywhere in the world.

One of the young men was leaning back in his chair with his feet propped up on the console in front of him. He was flipping through the latest issue of *Sports Illustrated* and keeping a watchful eye on a live feed from a satellite positioned 35,790 kilometers over a terrorist training camp in Afghanistan. His partner was leaning forward, headphones on, eyes closed, and one hand making subtle adjustments to a dial on a signal enhancer.

"Hey, Dave," the man said, "your mystery signal is back."

Dave sat bolt upright, dropping the magazine on the floor. "Are you sure?"

"It's the same signature. Take a listen." Dave's partner, whose name was Jim, handed him the headset.

Dave slipped it on and closed his eyes to concentrate. The sides of his mouth turned up in a triumphant grin. "It sure is. Can you tell where it's coming from?"

Jim made several clicks on his mouse and watched a series of pages flash on his computer monitor until a map of the world appeared. He clicked on the region of North America, enlarging the continent until it filled the screen. "Definitely North America. Pacific Northwest. Could be Idaho, Wyoming, or Montana."

"What about the other end of the connection?"

Jim typed a command on his keyboard, then rolled his chair over to a rack of computers and monitors where he made some more adjustments. Rolling back to his station, he said, "That's odd. There is no other end, at least not one I can find."

"Dude, we're sitting in the most sophisticated spy thingy in the world. You're telling me you can't find out who this guy's talking to? Can you at least clean up the signal so we can listen in?"

Jim grabbed another headset and plugged it into the system. Reaching up, he tapped a button on another computer, linking it to his own. The monitor showed a graphic depiction of the signal. Jim shook his head. "This thing is compressed way beyond anything I've ever seen. Whatever it is, it's massive. It's like nothing I've ever encountered. In fact, I'm surprised we're getting this much of it."

Dave stared at the graphic, then back at the monitor showing North America. "Can you at least tell what direction he's transmitting?"

After several more operations, Jim leaned back in his chair. "Up."

"Up?"

"Well, it's just a guess, but it appears the signal is being transmitted straight up in a tight configuration. Our satellite must be in just the right position to snag part of it."

Dave scratched his head. "When did we get it last?"

"I don't know – three, four weeks ago."

"And the time before that?"

"Same. Why?"

"Pull the log. I need to know the exact dates."

While Jim pulled up the report file on his computer, Dave scanned the Internet.

"Got it," Jim said. "First contact was June 20. Second contact was July 18."

"And this is August 18," Dave added, looking intently at his computer screen. "No way."

"What is it?"

Dave turned toward his partner. "According to this website, on those dates the moon was in conjunction with the sun."

Jim raised his hands. "What does that mean?"

"I have no idea. But it means something. Do you know if we have any radio telescopes aimed at the moon?"

As Rick watched the exchange between Aldi and the Enterprise, he noticed a change in the tone of the conversation. Tiny Aldi's face became somber, and big Aldi's expression became etched with concern. He did not speak for a long time. Even when it seemed the holographic image had finished talking, Aldi just stared at it. A few moments later, the image resumed speaking for awhile longer. Finally, Aldi spoke for a long time, the image gave a short reply, and Aldi tapped a symbol that turned the device off. Tiny Aldi blinked out of existence.

"What just happened?" Dave asked.

Jim checked his equipment. The graphic depicting the signal was flat. "That's it. The signal's gone."

Dave reached down to retrieve his magazine from the floor and put his feet back up on the panel. "Log it, and set up a reminder on September…" He glanced back at his computer monitor. "September 16. That's the next new moon. I'll bet you a hundred bucks it'll be back then."

Jim glanced sideways at his partner. "You're on."

Aldi looked out across the desert at the late afternoon sun. He didn't say anything for a long time. Rick sensed he needed to remain silent. When Aldi turned toward him, there were tears trickling down his cheeks. He took a deep shuddering breath and let it out slowly. "Jalamin and Arkel are gone."

"What do you mean, *gone*?"

Aldi set the communication device on the ground and reached for Rick. Rick felt the weight of Aldi's pain as his Klyvian brother broke down. He held him for a long time until the silent sobs subsided. When Aldi stepped back, Rick knelt down and picked up the communication device.

"When we last spoke," Aldi said, his voice still shaking, "my father told me he was going to send Imtulon and Tyba to Iraq to search for them. They found the probe that Arkel was supposed to send back to the Enterprise. It was still buried in the ground. They could not find the shuttlecraft, but they did find a man who lived in the desert. They could not understand his words, but the man seemed to recognize the clothes of Imtulon and Tyba. He took them to a place and showed them where he had buried Jalamin and Arkel in the ground. They were there." Aldi buried his face in his hands and then looked up into the darkening sky. He closed his eyes and began to hum. Then his humming turned into a chant and then a song, The Song. He sang the Klyvian words that Rick could only assume were about his fallen friends. When he was finished, he turned to Rick, but said nothing.

"I'm so sorry," Rick said. "Is there anything we can do?"

Aldi shook his head. Then turning toward his home, he said, "Jalamin is Elsa-Eska's sister."

CHAPTER 22:

THE REMEMBERING

Elsa-Eska took the news about her sister better than Rick expected. When Aldi told her, she simply closed her eyes and bowed her head. She remained that way for several agonizing minutes. Jane's reaction was somewhat more expressive. Her initial impulse was to rush over to comfort Elsa-Eska, but she stopped mid-room and changed course to sit with Aldi. Tears flowed freely from them both as Jane held his hand and prayed.

Rick didn't know what to do, so he just stood watching and waiting. Though not one to show emotion, he felt his throat tighten and his eyes begin to itch. He was moved by the emotions of his grieving friends. He wanted to join Jane and Aldi, to pray with them, but a voice inside countered the desire with an accusation of hypocrisy. The truth, he knew, was that any attempt to pray would be a gesture of shared grief rather than the belief that God actually cared or could do anything. While the sharing of grief would have been reason enough to join them, the act of praying would have been just that— an act. Rick was all too aware of his own faults, but hypocrisy (the one he despised most in others) was not one of them. At least he didn't think it was. So, he continued his own frustrating vigil, sharing their pain from a distance, but unable to do anything to ease it.

Without looking up, Elsa-Eska raised her hand in Rick's direction. At first, he thought it was a gesture of prayer to the Before One, but then she motioned for him to join her. Tentatively, Rick made his way to the couch where she sat, her eyes still closed and head still bowed. When he got within reach, she took his hand and pulled him to the couch next to her. For the next several minutes, Rick just sat with her, holding her hand, not doing or saying or thinking anything. But at least that was something.

Several minutes passed before Rick became aware of a change in Jane's praying. She was no longer praying in English, but murmuring quietly in unison with Aldi. Rick tilted his head to listen more intently. He discovered they were actually singing. Looking back at Elsa-Eska, he saw that her lips were moving, and then he could hear that she too was singing in concert with Jane and Aldi. Rick readied himself for the ability to join them, but he felt nothing. There was no spark, no warm sensation, no clarity of thought, no sudden awareness that he too possessed the ability to sing the Klyvian Song. He was just an observer. While Rick thought of himself as immune to hypocrisy, he had to admit to a ready dose of self-pity. He felt slighted, like he was being left out of something truly fascinating.

How long all this went on, Rick could not tell. The internal confab of so many conflicting emotions caused him to lose track of the time; he had been staring vacantly at a spot on the floor that curiously resembled an old man with an enormous nose. Shame finally took the center stage and pricked his conscience with the realization that he was no longer sharing the pain of his friends, but had been taken for a mental ride by his own self-interest. Shaking his head to clear the internal room, his thoughts returned to Elsa-Eska. The curious face on the floor morphed back into the natural pattern in the grain of the hardwood. When he looked up at Elsa-Eska, he was startled to find she was watching him; luminous golden flecks swirled in the soft brown of her irises. It was not the same flash he had seen when she was agitated at him a couple months earlier, but a warm glow that suggested compassion. It was then that he felt a quiet echo of what he had felt at the anniversary dinner when she reached across the table to touch his heart.

"Thank you for being here with me." She let go of his hand and folded her hands in her lap.

As if on cue, Jane and Aldi stopped singing and turned their attention toward Rick and Elsa-Eska. Jane moved from the arm of Aldi's chair to the vacant green swivel chair next to Elsa-Eska's side of the couch. She reached for her hand. "I am so sorry. Would you and Aldi like to be alone for awhile? Rick and I can come back later."

Elsa-Eska took Jane's hand. "Klyvians draw strength from family. Please stay."

Jane nodded and sat back in her chair. "Is there anything we can do for you?"

Elsa-Eska did not hear the question. Something seemed to come over her. Her face hardened and the gold flecks in her eyes flashed brilliantly. Then as quickly as it came, whatever it was faded. Her face relaxed and her eyes returned to their normal soft brown. She smiled at Jane, but her smile was tainted with pain.

"Elsa-Eska?" Aldi said. "What did you see?"

Rick and Jane glanced at each other questioningly.

Elsa-Eska took a deep breath and exhaled slowly. "The day we arrived here, I had a dream. In my dream, we had just landed, but the desert looked different. Instead of Rick, there were many people. And instead of your truck, there were two large machines that made a loud noise. I did not know what they were. All the people looked the same, except for one man who stood apart from the others. He raised his hand like this..." Elsa-Eska raised her hand above her head, palm open and fingers tight together, "...and when he brought it down there were many loud noises. That's when I woke up."

Jane and Rick were on the edges of their seats, their eyes riveted on Elsa-Eska.

She continued. "I didn't understand the things I saw because we did not yet know your world. But now I know. The dream was not of our landing. It was of Jalamin and Arkel. The machines were helicopters, and the men had guns. That was the noise I heard— the guns. Jalamin and Arkel were..." She stopped as a wave of pain washed over her. Tears welled up in her eyes, and her bottom lip began to quiver. "Jalamin and Arkel were killed by those men. They had no idea they were in danger. Those men killed them." She fell into Rick's arms and wept without restraint.

Jane covered her mouth with her hand as tears dripped down her cheeks.

When Elsa-Eska collected herself, she sat back upright. She rubbed her eyes with her fingers and then her nose on the back of her hand. "I have suspected for awhile that my sister and Arkel were gone. But now I know how. This loss, it is the first of the mission, but not the first of our people. I have told you of the time of trouble, how many of our people were killed in the rebellion. The pain I have felt for my people is the same pain I now feel for my sister and her husband." She took another deep breath and sighed heavily. "But this pain is close."

"Oh, Elsa-Eska," Jane said, wanting to comfort her, but not knowing what to say.

Aldi spoke. "In the time of trouble, after the rebellion, our people were in great pain from our losses. My father told me that when they arrived in Muur, they gathered to remember those who were not with them. When the sun disappeared, they spoke of them through the night. They did not eat or sleep. When the sun returned, they sang the Song together. That is when the Before One visited them and spoke of their lost ones in another place. This night we will remember Jalamin and Arkel."

"Yes," Elsa-Eska said, "tonight we will remember. Jane and Rick, will you remember with us?"

"We would be honored," Jane replied.

Rick nodded in agreement.

Aldi got up from his chair and moved to Elsa-Eska's side, placing his hand on her back. "You can join us outside just before the sun disappears."

Rick and Jane got the hint at the same time.

As Jane stood up, she realized she was still wearing Aldi's robe. "Oh, I uh…" She quickly drew the ends of the robe around the front of her.

Noticing Jane's embarrassment, Rick interjected, "We'll be there, brother." Hiding his amusement over Jane's predicament, he put his arm around his red-faced wife and ushered her out the front door.

An hour later, Rick and Jane stepped out onto the back deck of their home. Jane was wearing a pair of Rick's sweatpants and an oversized jersey. The sun was barely kissing the tops of the mountain to the west. The temperature had already dropped ten degrees.

"You think one box will be enough?" Jane asked, holding up a new box of tissue.

"Beats me. I've never been to a Klyvian remembering. You can always use your sleeves."

"Poor Elsa-Eska. I can only imagine what she must be going through. This could be a very long night."

Rick pointed toward the sun. "We better get going. Don't want to be late."

They stepped off the deck onto the desert clay and walked hand-in-hand the distance between the two homes. Rounding the corner of the new construction, they found Aldi and Elsa-Eska standing regally, silhouetted in front of the golden sunset. A strong breeze raced across the desert, whipping Elsa-Eska's long mane to one side and billowing her robe out away from her body. Aldi stood strong and noble. He was shirtless; his long hair danced over the defined muscles in his back and broad shoulders. No movie director could have created a more mesmerizing effect. Rick and Jane stopped in their tracks, captivated by the sight of the two Klyvians standing on the plain of this alien world. In that moment, they seemed less human; not in a physical sense, but in a different way. Maybe it just seemed that way to Rick and Jane because they knew the truth and had been exposed to their Klyvian essence. Maybe it was the fact that humans had been the perpetrators of a senseless and evil act against two innocent Klyvians. Whatever it was, it caused Rick and Jane to hesitate.

Although they were still far enough away that Aldi could not have heard them, he must have sensed their approach. Turning, he extended his hand toward them, his characteristic smile clearly visible and inviting. The Blackwells approached reverently, aware of the sacredness of the observance to which they had been invited. Though no words were spoken, it was obvious Aldi and Elsa-Eska were pleased to see them. After a round of forehead touches, the four of them watched in silence as the sun dipped out of sight behind the mountain.

"My sister never got to see a sunset." Elsa-Eska's words were soft, but carried a strength that Jane had not expected. "She would have thought it beautiful."

It suddenly occurred to Rick that Aldi and Elsa-Eska had never experienced a sunset either until five months ago. So much of what he had taken for granted his entire life was still new to them.

Elsa-Eska continued. "Jalamin and Arkel never got to see many things that we have. They never got to meet a human."

Her words, though not intended to be, were cutting to Rick. The grim reality was that his kind had killed two of their kind. Rick had always argued that morality was a purely human invention. As such, the rules that governed human society must be fluid, adaptable to the ever-changing landscape of human culture. He even considered the extinction of the Neanderthals at the hands of the intellectually superior modern humans as simply the next necessary step in man's evolutionary journey. But the murder of two Klyvians at the hands of humans cast a shadow in the shape of a huge question mark over his worldview. That single heinous act forced him to consider the existence of a universal morality. And the disturbing truth of the matter was that if such a morality did exist, then it was his own species that violated it. Rick Blackwell, human that he was, emotionally overcompensated the idea to the point that he himself felt some responsibility for the deaths of the two Klyvians.

Whether Elsa-Eska sensed Rick's thoughts or not, the words she spoke next seemed to be aimed directly at him. She caught his eye and said, "They never got to know the kindness and goodness of humans as we have."

Her words were like balm to his soul—at least for the moment.

No one spoke again for a long while. As the sun dipped further beneath the horizon, the western sky turned from a bright orange to a pale blue and then to a deep purple as blackness edged its way across the sky. Stars blinked into appearance above the night watchers like a billion silent sentinels keeping watch over them; the absence of moonlight allowing them to shine with spectacular brilliance. Rick could not remember a more vivid Milky Way. It seemed almost alive.

It was Aldi who finally broke the silence. "From here it looks like the stars are close together. It looks like it would be easy to travel from one to the next. Did I ever tell you that I have seen only one other star close like your sun? I was very young, but I remember it. Arkel and I made a game of how long we could look at it. When we found your sun, we played the game again. For a long time, we could look as much as we wanted. As we got closer, Arkel measured our progress by how soon he had to look away. Our parents told us that on Klyv the warmth from their sun was warm on their faces. Arkel was very excited to know that feeling from your sun."

And so it went for more than an hour. Elsa-Eska and Aldi took turns remembering Jalamin and Arkel with stories of their life together. Listening to them, Rick and Jane got to know the two fallen Klyvians, and in turn, learned much more about Aldi and Elsa-Eska. They learned that Klyvians are playful by nature. Rick was especially intrigued to learn that they would often disengage the artificial gravity generators onboard the Enterprise and play floating games throughout the ship. It was Jalamin who discovered how two of them could focus their Ka-noa in such a way so as to create a kind of magnetic field that would enable them to actually maneuver in zero gravity.

The stories also revealed much about life onboard the Enterprise. There were many responsibilities ranging from routine tasks (cleaning, growing food, and ship maintenance) to scientific experiments and operations directly related to the mission. One of the most critical was the constant monitoring of the ship's sensors that searched for signs of intelligent life. There was also the ongoing education of the second generation by the elders. Lessons consisted of the history and ways of Klyv as well as the many aspects of the mission. All of this set the backdrop for countless stories about Jalamin and Arkel.

Through the telling of these stories, Arkel emerged as a man of endless curiosity. Rick could hardly imagine anyone more curious than Aldi, but apparently Arkel was. It was he who suggested to Aldi that they systematically disassemble and reassemble the ship's many computer systems. The elders, under their supervision, encouraged this *hands-on educational exploration*. But it wasn't long before their technical knowledge surpassed that of their teachers, and the duo became the ship's primary systems technicians. Routine system checks and the occasional minor glitch did little to quench their thirst for greater challenges, so the two began to experiment with certain *creative modifications*. It was their tweaking of the ship's sensors that enabled them to detect what Aldi called *small empty spaceships*. Rick guessed he was referring to NASA's deep space probes, but for all he knew, they could have originated from another planet. When asked how he knew they were empty, Aldi explained how they had once caught one and opened it up. Finding nothing of interest, they put it back together and let it go.

Arkel was also an artist. According to Aldi, the drawings of Arkel could have rivaled those of the Renaissance masters. But more than these impressive accomplishments, it was evident that Arkel was head-over-heals in love with Jalamin. Elsa-Eska smiled as she spoke of the many ways Arkel expressed his love for her younger sister. She was often the subject of his drawings, which showed up on the walls throughout the ship. This was not only acceptable, but encouraged by the rest of the crew who had their own Arkelian portraits scattered throughout the ship. The idea struck Rick as vaguely reminiscent of early man's cave drawings.

As for Jalamin, Jane and Rick concluded that she was a carbon copy of her older sister. Though Elsa-Eska did not put it that way, many of the things she described about her sister were the very things Rick and Jane had observed about Elsa-Eska. Her gentle, unassuming spirit concealed an intellect that may have exceeded that of the rest of her generation. When Aldi mentioned how much Jalamin resembled Elsa-Eska in appearance, Rick and Jane were surprised to learn that the sisters' eyes were something of an anomaly. Only one other Klyvian aboard the ship had eyes accented by luminous, swirling flecks—their mother.

Jalamin was one of the few Klyvians who found interest in the lifeless void of outer space. She would spend extended periods staring into the blackness, observing minute alterations in the star field as their tiny oasis of life groped its way through the enormity of space. As much as the mysteries that awaited discovery, Jalamin was fascinated by the sheer bigness of the universe. She never got over the fact that her entire life had been spent travelling in one direction at close to the speed of light, yet all that could be seen was still out there further than she could reach.

Though somewhat quieter than the others, she was by no means a loner. She often said, "Beauty is greatest when shared with another." More times than not, the *another* was Arkel. Though he did not share her enthusiasm for what he referred to as the *big empty* (his interests were much more local), he would join her at one of the ship's view ports and discuss the mysteries of the universe, their life together, the world of their people, the mission, and what awaited them when they arrived in the new world.

When the remembering had encountered a lull, Elsa-Eska said she was cold and wanted to go inside. The foursome made their way into the new home where they took their usual places in the living room; Aldi and Elsa-Eska on the couch, and Rick and Jane in the two mismatched chairs. Candles illuminated the room. A silver cylinder and a pitcher of water were placed on the coffee table. Once settled, The Remembering resumed.

For the next several hours, the humans listened with rapt attention as story upon story portrayed life onboard the Klyvian vessel. To be sure, some aspects of spaceship life were unique to the Klyvian explorers, yet Rick and Jane felt they were still gaining a better understanding of Klyvians as a people.

One recurring theme that especially impressed Jane and bewildered Rick was *family*. Rick could hardly imagine a more dreadful fate than having to spend more than the occasional holiday with his crazy extended family, and Jane never had much of an extended family with which to spend holidays. For them, any idea of family beyond their own was either tainted by bad jokes and clichés or haunted by an aching void. But for the eight Klyvians who set out on the mission of Ka-Rel and the eight children who were born into that mission, family was not just a good thing—it was the best thing. Family is an accurate word because, as it was now apparent, everyone onboard the Enterprise was related in some way. Out of the eight people who comprised the first generation, two were sons of Ka-Rel and the rest were cousins. When the mission called for children to be born, great care was taken to ensure that each couple produced two, and only two, children. When Elsa-Eska described this, she did not go into detail about how this was achieved or how it worked out to be an equal number of boys and girls. She simply explained it as necessary to the mission and attributed its success to the Before One.

Hours passed and the candles began to drown themselves in their own wax. Unbeknownst to anyone in the house, the eastern sky was beginning to show the first indications of the new day. Jane was beginning to sense a haze around the periphery of her vision and the edges of her mind. She yawned and stretched her neck to one side. Elsa-Eska's voice was hoarse from having talked so much. She poured herself a glass of water, drew her legs up onto the couch, and found a comfortable place in the crook of Aldi's arm. The break in the conversation also brought a wave of sleepiness over Rick, and he began to wonder if The Remembering was drawing to a close. Catching himself staring vacantly into the flame of a nearby candle, he shook his head, rubbed his face, and cracked his knuckles. He tried unsuccessfully to focus his blurred vision onto the face of his wristwatch. Aldi alone seemed to be unaffected by the lateness of the hour.

Elsa-Eska took a much-needed sip of water and set her glass on the table. "We were mistaken," she said, but didn't finish whatever it was she was thinking.

"Mistaken?" Jane asked. "About what?"

Elsa-Eska had a far away look like she was reliving a significant moment from the past. Then, as if allowing the others to enter into her thoughts, she began almost mid-thought. "When the radio transmissions started coming more regularly, we knew we were getting close. After so long— longer than my life—our mission became more than a hope. It was upon us. We studied the transmissions carefully, trying to make sense of the words, hoping to learn something of this new world and the people. When we discovered that there were many languages in the transmissions, we thought they might be coming from more than one world, maybe many." Elsa-Eska chuckled at her own naïveté. "I believed I would spend the rest of my life visiting many worlds, meeting people from so many worlds. Ka-Rel believed in many life-worlds, too. He once said that Klyv might have been pushed away from the rest of the life-worlds by the Hori."

Rick and Jane glanced at each other at the oddness of the idea. How could someone with the ability to build and fly an interstellar spacecraft not understand the concept of inhabitable zones around stars? Did they not realize that even if it were possible to push a planet to another part of the galaxy, it would mean the extinction of every living thing on that planet?

"Jalamin had a different idea. She believed the many languages came from one world with many different people. We did not agree because on Klyv there is only one language. We thought other planets would be the same. When we got closer to Earth, we realized Jalamin was right." She interrupted her story to ask, "Why does Earth have so many different languages?"

Rick started to offer an explanation that had to do with thousands of years of migration and isolation, but Jane interrupted him. She was too tired to go into the whole story, so she abbreviated. "There was a time when all humans spoke the same language, but God changed it and scattered the people all over the world." Surprising to Rick, Elsa-Eska and Aldi accepted this as a reasonable explanation.

Elsa-Eska continued. "Because Jalamin was right, we all agreed that she should help plan our landings. The first plan was to send all eight children to one place on the planet where there were many people and then explore the rest of the planet from there."

"Why send the children?" Rick asked. "Didn't the elders want to see it with their own eyes."

"You have forgotten," said Aldi. "It is the way of Klyv to give the younger ones the duty of exploring."

"That's right," Rick replied. "You did say that. So what happened to the first plan?"

"Jalamin said because this world had so many different people, it would be better to land in more than one place. Her idea was four places—two of us at each place." A grave look came over her. "Jalamin chose the landing places and where each of us would go. Jalamin and Arkel were very excited to go to the large land."

A hush fell upon the house as the four contemplated the consequence of Jalamin's plan. In effect, she had saved the others while dooming herself.

Aldi was the first to notice a brightening in the sky outside. Without speaking a word, he got up from the couch and helped Elsa-Eska to her feet. Rick and Jane joined them as they stepped out onto a smaller version of the Blackwells' deck. The crisp morning breeze was exhilarating after so many hours in the heavy indoor air. The foursome faced eastward and watched the sun rise from the distant horizon. It was a familiar sight for Rick, but Jane could not remember the last time she had watched a sunrise. In that moment she understood why her husband had become such an early riser.

Without comment or instruction, Elsa-Eska began to sing the Song, her voice as clear as the morning sky. Aldi joined her a moment later and the two of them sang the portion of the Song Rick guessed was about Jalamin and Arkel. He waited for Jane to join them, but she didn't. She just stood there, reverently listening. The Song continued for at least ten minutes—sometimes Elsa-Eska would drop out and let Aldi sing by himself and then they would switch. After awhile, the words they sang together started to sound familiar, as if this were the chorus and the solo parts were verses. At least, that's the way it sounded to Rick.

When it seemed as if another chorus was about to begin, they stopped abruptly and tilted their heads as if listening. At first Rick and Jane could hear nothing. Then very faintly, a voice could be heard far off in the distance. It was a male voice and it sounded like it was getting closer. Straining his eyes in the direction of the voice, Rick could barely make out a figure. It took several moments for his brain to interpret what his eyes were seeing. Something about it looked familiar. Then it came to him—it was dancing like he had seen the native Americans do in their Sundance festivals. Jane saw it, too, but didn't say anything. All four watched and listened to the figure's lone performance. Then, instead of coming closer, the figure reversed course and danced its way up and over a rise in the land. The singing faded to silence with the figure's disappearance.

It was Aldi who broke the silence. "Arkel and Jalamin are gone from this place. Now they are in another place."

"Was that…" Rick started to ask, but couldn't get the words out.

"The Before One?" Elsa-Eska finished for him. "No. But that one speaks the words of the Before One. He has told us that Arkel and my sister are well."

With that, The Remembering was concluded.

As Rick lay in his own bed, an image of the dancing figure flitted through his mind. Though he was too far away to make a positive identification, Rick had the distinct impression that he had seen the man before. Just before he drifted off to sleep, a name materialized in his mind. The man was Johnny Two Feathers.

CHAPTER 23:

JACQUES FABER

$$\hbar$$

Johnny Two Feathers danced wildly in the open desert to the sound of unseen drums. Spinning with arms outstretched, leaning deeply to the left and then to the right, he resembled a bird wrestling with the wind—or better, playing in it. His long hair whipped freely with every movement, and his feet kicked up little puffs of dust like smoke signals. He seemed to move in slow motion. The golden glow of the rising sun cast the whole scene in a sepia hue.

Rick watched the man from his familiar perch on his back deck. His bare feet and hands felt the drums resonating through the wood planks and rail. The beat was steady like a heartbeat, neither speeding up nor slowing down; relentless like an eternal heartbeat. It seemed to Rick as if it had always been there, but he was just now becoming aware of it. Johnny appeared not to notice his audience. He danced uninhibited in the freedom of his ancestors who roamed this land long before the first white men set eye or foot upon it. All the elements of nature converged in this place—earth, sky, wind, rain – each playing its part as it had since time immemorial. It seemed to Rick, as he watched Johnny dance without reservation, that the man was somehow playing his part in concert with the elements.

Soon two figures appeared from the new construction next door. Then another came from behind Rick and descended the steps from the deck down onto the desert clay. Aldi, Elsa-Eska, and Jane joined Johnny, mimicking his every movement as if they had rehearsed it. The drums pounded on, getting louder. The four dancers whirled and stomped and wove themselves in intricate patterns. Rick could not help but get caught up in the scene. He bobbed his head to the beat and swayed his body in an attempt to mirror their movements. He felt his own heartbeat sync to the rhythm and he felt an urge to leap from the deck and join in the dance.

He tried, but failed. Though he wanted to, he simply could not move his feet or let go of the deck rail. Looking down at his hands, he found that they had been grafted somehow into the wood railing. He looked at his feet and discovered that they too had sunk deep into the wood planks. To his horror, the wood grain began to creep up his arms and legs. Panic enveloped him. He tried to call out for help, but found he had no voice. And then a dread silence settled upon him like a thick cloud, quashing the sound of the drums. He had become mute and deaf—as mute and deaf as a tree. And the dancers danced on, seemingly unaware of Rick's dilemma.

Suddenly, a short burst of a shrill noise cut through the deafening cloud. Rick looked around for its source, but could see nothing. It sounded again. There was something vaguely familiar about it, but he could not quite place it. After three more bursts, Rick felt something jab into his side.

"Rick." Jane's voice was close to his ear. "Could you get that? It's probably for you."

Rick's eyes snapped open. Jane was laying next to him, her face tensing as the telephone rang again. On the seventh ring, the answering machine clicked on, and Rick heard his own voice telling somebody that he was unavailable. Relief came over him as he realized he had been dreaming and he was still safe in his own bed. When the pre-recorded greeting ended with the anticipated Beep, Rick waited to hear whom he was ignoring.

A male voice with a hint of a French accent came through the speaker. "Rick. I got your book yesterday and I am *loving* it. Call me when you…"

Rick snatched the receiver. "Jacques. I'm here." Rick looked as his hand. Flexing his fingers, he was relieved to see flesh rather than wood. "Say, can I call you back? I need to get to another phone. Great, give me just a minute." Rick replaced the receiver and rubbed the sleep from his eyes. Glancing over at Jane, he heard her soft purring and knew she was asleep. Quietly, so as not to disturb her, he slipped out of bed and pulled on the sweat pants that lay crumpled on the floor.

On his way into the living room, Rick grabbed the cordless phone from the wall in the kitchen and punched in a number from memory. He sat down in his morning chair, stared outside at the empty desert, and waited.

Jacques Faber picked up on the second ring. "Inky Blackwell— teller of tales, weaver of words. It appears congratulations are in order."

"Thanks, Jacques. How is my old roommate?"

"All is well here in the civilized world. How are things in...what did you used to call it? *The untamed*?"

"Fine, fine. Man, it's good to hear your voice. It's been way too long. So you got my book?"

"Yes, but I had to get it like the rest of the rabble. I can only assume my complimentary autographed copy got lost in the mail."

"Oo, sorry about that." Rick silently scolded himself for his absent-mindedness. "I should have sent you one."

"Don't worry about it. I'll let you make it up to me soon. How about dinner?"

"Dinner? When?"

"I've got business in Denver next month. I thought we could meet. Diane is coming. She'd love to see Jane. Think of it, the four of us together again."

"Gosh, I'd love to, but I may not be able to get away. Our baby is due in a few weeks."

"Wow, that's great news. First a book, then a baby—you're having quite a year. Anything else I should know about?"

Rick chuckled to himself as he thought of the last five months with Aldi and Elsa-Eska. "I hardly know where to begin," he said. "Things here are...different, very different. But enough about me. What about you? Are you still working for Cyber-Dyn?"

Jacques laughed at the inside joke. "I hadn't thought about that in years. Actually, I started my own company last year. It's called Saber Technologies. We're still pretty small, but we've got a few promising irons in the fire. That's why I'm coming to Denver."

"Tell me about it."

"I'm afraid it's rather dull. I know a guy who knows a guy who's in research and development for the Department of Defense. This guy, who works for the DOD, told this other guy that the government is not opposed to entertaining certain arrangements with interested parties for mutually beneficial exchanges."

"Huh? You just lost me."

"Oh, I'm sorry. I just spoke with the DOD guy before I called you. Apparently, at this early stage, vagueness is a necessary part of the game. They don't want to say or commit to anything until they're convinced you've got something they want. All I know is the DOD is working on some top secret surveillance system, which is nothing new or surprising, and they want an information delivery system with securities that can stay several steps ahead of the competition... which is also nothing new or surprising."

"Where does Denver come in?"

"Oh, right, Denver. A few months ago, I got a call from this guy who's been working on a new Internet application he claims is impervious to hackers. I didn't believe it at first. I mean, everything's got a weakness, right? But the guy kept calling, and last month he sent us a sample. I've had my team trying to get into it for weeks. We can't touch it. So, long story short, I'm flying out to meet him. If we can work out a deal, we might just have something that will move my talks with the DOD to the next level."

"That's complex."

"Naw, pretty dull, actually. And who knows? It may not even pan out. But that's business. You chase down ten to get one, right?"

"You just reminded me why I left all that behind. But I hope it works out for you."

"I do, too. Technology is a tough business, and the competition is brutal. You come up with something new, and by the next week three companies have taken your idea and made it better. It never ends and there's never any time to rest."

"Why do you do it?"

"Guttenberg, Edison, Ford, Gates," Jacques said without hesitation. "These guys took the technology of their day and pushed it to the next level. In effect, they advanced civilization and changed the world. Think about it, Rick, we do the things we do because of them. The routines of our lives consist of their innovations. Your book was made possible in part by each of those men. One day, people will do things that we cannot yet imagine. They will do them because of the technologies we will give them."

"Why do I get the feeling you've given that speech before?"

Jacques laughed. "I say something like it everyday—to my partner, our research teams, our developers, customers, investors, people I may meet only once. I say it because I believe it. You know, Rick, each generation shapes the next. We are who we are because of those who came before us. And those who come after us will be who they are because of us. For both good and bad, that's the way it works."

"That's an interesting way to look at it."

"Only because it's true. Sadly, most people never realize that they are part of the chain. So they never figure out how they fit in to it all. I know my part, so that's what I do. It's not any different from what you do."

"How's that?"

"Take your book, for instance. Why did you write it?"

"Lots of reasons. It's something I've always wanted to do. I enjoy it. I think I have something to say."

"And there it is. You have something to say. And not just because you like to say it; you have something to say because people need to hear it."

"But my book is a novel. Its just fiction."

Jacques laughed again. "Oh, Inky, how quickly you forget. You were the one who convinced me to expand my reading. 'Fiction is the vehicle of truth,' you said. Don't you remember how I used to read only business books, ugh, and all those boring technical manuals? I always thought fiction was a waste of time until you convinced me otherwise."

Rick chuckled. "Yeah, I remember."

"That's your part. And because you were so good at it...no, because you believed it, I recognized the better way. Now I've got a novel going all the time. You know, a lot of the stuff I read in science fiction has given me inspiration for what I hope to do for real. I'll never be able to write a novel, but I do enjoy them now. Which, by the way, is why I called you. I got your book yesterday, and it kept me up half the night. I only put it down because Diane kept after me to come to bed. It's great, it really is."

"Thank you, Jacques. I appreciate that. And thanks for reminding me why I started writing. I do love it, but more than that I believe in it. I guess I kind of lost sight of that with all that's been happening here lately. The whole publication process was a lot more involved than I thought it would be. Writing the book was the easy part. And then there's all the preparation for the baby. The first part of that process was the easy part, too."

Jacques laughed. "I can imagine."

"And then there's Aldi and Elsa..." Rick stopped mid-sentence.

Jacques waited for Rick to finish. Then after a moment of silence, he asked, "Who's Aldi and Elsa?"

"Just a couple we took in a few months ago."

Jacques picked up on the change in Rick's tone. "You okay, Rick?"

"Yeah, sure. It's nothing."

"It doesn't sound like nothing. You know, when you live with someone as long as we did, you learn to read them. I know it's been years, but I know you, Rick. There's something you're not telling me."

"It's complicated."

"Are you in some kind of trouble?"

"No, it's not that at all. It's just...well, I can't even...I really can't talk about it over the phone."

"Oh, well that sure puts my mind at ease." When Rick did not reply, he continued. "Rick, you know I'd do anything for you. If you need anything or if you need me to come out there, I can be there tomorrow."

"No, no, that's not necessary. Really, Jacques, it's…I shouldn't have said anything."

"For a writer you're not at all convincing, but I get the hint. Obviously, you've got a good reason for being…whatever. But please know I'm here for you. I mean, I can be *there* for you. You know that, right?"

"Yes, I know. And I appreciate it. I do. I tell you what…" There was another long pause.

"What?"

"You gotta trust me when I say I'm not in trouble. It's just that I can't…I mean, I would rather not explain this over the phone. Let me check on a few things, and if there is any way I can meet you in Denver, I might be able to explain it all then. When will you be there?"

"The dates aren't confirmed yet, but I'm thinking middle of the month. If it would help, I can nudge them one way or the other."

"I wish I could say. There's just no way of knowing when the baby will come. Jane's due date is September 14th. Her mom is planning on flying out on the 11th."

Jacques thought for a moment. "How about this? Forget about trying to get to Denver. I'd never hear the end of it if you missed your baby's birth because you were hanging out with me. I'll set my meeting for the 10th and then Diane and I will catch a flight up to you on the 11th. We haven't had a vacation in so long, this will work. Don't worry about putting us up. What's the nearest town?"

"Riverton."

"Okay, we'll get a flight into Riverton and book a room there. That way we can see you, Diane will be very excited to see Jane, and if our timing is good, we'll get to help you welcome your new baby. And then, if you want to talk to me about this Aldi and Elsa, well, we'll cross that bridge then."

A hundred different thoughts were bombarding Rick. If there was one person in the world he would trust with the truth about Aldi and Elsa-Eska, it was Jacques Faber. They met in college and became instant friends. Over the years, that friendship deepened to the point that they stood with each other as best men in each of their weddings. But it had been five years since they had seen each other. During that time, there were several phone calls, but with each passing year, they became fewer. It had been a year since they last spoke. Still, Jacques was a man Rick could trust. "That sounds good," Rick said. "Let me talk to Jane about it and I'll call you back in a few days to confirm."

"If it will help, I could have Diane call her."

"Jane would like that. But let me talk to her first and get back with you."

"Alright then," Jacques said. "I'll wait for your call. In the mean time, I'll go ahead and set my meeting time and check on flights from Denver to Riverton."

"Sounds good. It's great talking to you. And thanks...thanks for, well, everything. You're a great friend."

"The feeling's mutual. I'll finish reading your book before you call, but I'll look forward to giving you my review of it in person."

"I'll look forward to hearing it."

"Goodbye, Rick. Give my love to Jane."

"You do the same for me with Diane. Goodbye, Jacques."

Rick pressed the off button on the phone and stared out the window at his massive backyard. Two thoughts danced in his head, seemingly unconnected. The first was the fact that Jacques Faber was now in business for himself. Success was not a question in Rick's mind as he had never known Jacques Faber to not succeed at anything he put his mind to. The intriguing part was the nature of his business—cutting-edge technology. The second thought was that he had all but committed to telling Jacques about Aldi and Elsa-Eska. Up until now, he had not considered revealing their secret to another human being. But up until now, he had not considered Jacques Faber. Jacques was just the kind of guy who one, would not think he was crazy or trying to pull a fast one; and two, would not freak out and do something foolish, like tell someone else about it. Jacques was open-minded and he could be trusted. With some persuasion, he could be brought into the circle. It was a prospect that had some merit now that Rick thought about it.

Unconsciously, he chewed on the cordless telephone's little nub of an antenna, letting the two thoughts mingle in his mind: Jacques Faber / Aldi and Elsa-Eska...Saber Technologies / Klyvian technology...Jacques scouting out new talent / a way for Aldi and Elsa-Eska to participate in the human experience and generate an income. As the two thoughts finally melded into one, it was like someone had flipped a switch in Rick's brain: *Saber Technology: Better Living through Alien Technology.* It probably wouldn't work as a slogan for the company, but as a business strategy, why not? It's not like anyone could say, "Been there, done that, didn't work."

Rick glanced at the clock on the wall. It was almost nine o'clock in the morning. Yawning, he remembered that he had slept only two of the last twenty-four hours. He would have to wait a while before sharing his genius idea with Jane. And then he would have to figure out how to explain it all to Aldi and Elsa-Eska in a way they would understand. Yawning again, he doubted he would have any trouble getting back to sleep in spite of his excitement. Getting up from his chair, he noticed Aldi standing out in the backyard looking at something in the distance. *"Good grief,"* Rick said to himself. *"Doesn't that guy ever sleep?"*

Rick squinted in the direction of Aldi's gaze to see what had grabbed all of his attention. He gasped, rubbed his eyes, and looked harder. It was too far away to make out the details, but it looked disturbingly similar to his dream of the dancing Johnny Two Feathers—arms outstretched, spinning, swooping up and down like a bird caught in a strong wind. He snatched the binoculars off the window ledge and trained them upon his subject. Bringing the image into focus, Rick chuckled in relief. It wasn't Johnny, or even a person. It was a large bird, an eagle maybe, toying with something on the ground. Rick watched as the bird landed and then propelled itself backwards and up into the air with a flap of its mighty wings. Then it would turn and attack from another angle. Finally, the bird went in for the kill, landing with authority and delivering the fatal jab of its dagger-like beak. Then, in an amazing demonstration of power and grace, the bird lifted off the ground and flew away, a dead rattlesnake dangling from its talons.

Rick looked back at Aldi to see how the Klyvian would react to such a graphic display of wildlife carnage. He seemed unfazed. Still, there would be questions if Aldi knew Rick was awake and had witnessed it. Rick ducked out of sight just as Aldi turned toward the window where he stood. He was just too tired to explain the cycle of nature's food chain.

When Rick climbed back into bed, Jane rolled over and snuggled up against him. It was Sunday morning, but Jane had no intention of going to church. In fact, she hadn't been to church in months. It wasn't that she was having doubts about God, but the traditional church view of God did not account for the existence of people from other worlds. She felt she needed to figure out where Aldi and Elsa-Eska fit into her belief system before she went any further with her church. Rick believed he was getting the old Jane back.

CHAPTER 24:

PERSPECTIVE

ʃ\

Time is constant, but perception varies from person to person.

For Jane, time was slow—agonizingly slow—like the coming of Christmas for a child. The novelty of pregnancy had been worn thin by physical fatigue and discomfort as well as the emotional strain of it all. Rick's perception of time dwelt on the other end of the spectrum. The days were speeding by as his plan to introduce Aldi and Elsa-Eska to Jacques Faber continued to develop. For Elsa-Eska and Aldi, time held little meaning. In the half-year they had been on Earth (a measure that was completely irrelevant to them), they had demonstrated a decidedly slower pace of life than Jane and Rick—an ironic twist, since it was for that very reason that Rick and Jane left the city in the first place.

As a happy result, Aldi and Elsa-Eska were good for Rick and Jane. Elsa-Eska's easy demeanor had a calming influence upon Jane, making the unbearable final days of pregnancy bearable. And Aldi's optimism encouraged Rick whenever his Great Idea was assaulted by thoughts of self-doubt, the frequency of which seemed to increase as the moment of truth approached.

All in all, these were contented days. Jane and Elsa-Eska were inseparable, as were Rick and Aldi. Their routines were settled: Rick and Aldi would meet on Rick's back porch at sunrise each day and by mid-morning they would join the girls for a light breakfast. Then it was roaming the ranch for the guys, baby planning for the girls, a light supper together at sundown followed by an evening of conversation and reading. For Rick and Jane, life had returned to a semblance of normalcy—if living with people from another world can ever be considered normal.

Although these days were fairly uneventful, the conversations that took place at the Blackwell Ranch would have been earth-shaking had they been made public. With their increasing command of the English language, Aldi and Elsa-Eska offered more insight into their lives, the mission, the other teams and Klyv. Every conversation carried with it the fascinating satisfaction of fitting more and more pieces of a huge jigsaw puzzle into place. For Aldi and Elsa-Eska, the new normalcy was anything but normal. Earth and its inhabitants were still something of a novelty. Everything was research and exploration. As curiosity was part of their nature, satisfying that curiosity was part of their existence. As the sun set on the second Monday of September, all seemed right with the world—at least the little corner of the world that was the Blackwell Ranch.

"Jane," Elsa-Eska said from the dining table where several books and magazines were spread out before her. Ever since she had acquired the ability to read English, downtime at the ranch was an invitation to delve into the human documents. "What year were you born?"

"1970," Jane replied, looking up from the parenting book she was reading. She was sitting across the table from her.

"And Rick?"

Jane looked toward the couch were Rick and Aldi sat glued to the television. Normally, the television remained off whenever the four of them were together. It was an arrangement proposed by Jane for the benefit of Aldi and Elsa-Eska, and reluctantly agreed to by Rick. But this was the first Monday Night Football game of the season, the perfect opportunity for Rick to test his new secret weapon. Earlier that day, he mentioned to Aldi that humans enjoyed a game called football. When Aldi inquired about it, Rick told him that it would be much better to show him than explain it, and there just so happened to be a game on the television that night. The plan worked flawlessly. When Aldi told Jane he wanted to understand football, she could not resist his innocent inquisitiveness. And so…

> With one second remaining in the first half, Denver was up 14-7, but New York had regained possession of the ball on Denver's forty-five yard line. The Giants had one more play to close the gap before halftime. Rookie Owen Pochman lined up for a 63 yard field goal attempt—a long shot, but what else could they do? The ball was snapped…the defense rushed the line… the kick was executed…Giants fans held their collective breath as they watched the ball sail end-over-end toward the goal post…Owens pumped his clenched

fists in an effort to will the ball through the uprights…
Rick edged forward on the couch…Aldi watched Rick
with curiosity…the goal referees readied themselves to
make the call…and the ball—wide to the right, no goal!

"Ha!" Rick exclaimed and clapped his hands together. "That's the
half!"

"Rick," Jane said. "Elsa-Eska asked you a question."

"Huh? Oh, I'm sorry. What is it?" He hit the mute button on the
remote.

Elsa-Eska repeated her question, "What year were you born?"

"1965. Why?"

Elsa-Eska considered the collage of images from the books and
magazines on the table. "Do you know people who lived in…" She
flipped back to a page she had marked. "…1941 to 1945?"

"Sure. Why? What are you looking at?"

Referring to the cover of the book, she replied, "*The Century* Peter
Jennings and Todd Brewster. And these magazines: *The Twentieth
Century in Pictures, The Century in Review 1900 to 2000, The New
Millennium.* This year 2001 looks different from 1965, and very
different from 1941."

"Well, yeah," Rick said, getting up from the couch and moving over
to the table. Aldi followed him. "The world has changed a lot over
the years; actually, people have changed. Let's see what you've got
there."

When he got to the table, he found *The Century* opened up to a
two-page spread—a grainy black and white photograph of four
women and a young girl standing amidst bodies strewn over the
ground; Nazi soldiers stood in the background. The caption read
Global Nightmare 1941-1945. Elsa-Eska flipped through a few pages
of pictures: Soldiers moving through a bombed-out city; a young
Russian girl crying over the body of her dead mother; American
soldiers—on one page gathered for calisthenics in preparation for
combat, on the next page surrendered in a progression through the
ranks of their Japanese captors.

"What is all this?" Elsa-Eska asked. The look on her face was a
mixture of confusion and pain.

"That was World War Two," Rick replied, taking a seat at the table.

Aldi leaned over the table to examine the pictures, and then he
looked at Rick. "Was all of the world at war?"

"No, not really, but it must have seemed like it for a lot of people.
Mostly it was Germany, Japan, and Italy against Russia, the United

States, and Great Britain. Most of the fighting took place in Europe and the South Pacific Islands."

Maps were of great interest to Aldi and Elsa-Eska. They had studied the giant world map on the wall of Rick's office and asked if they could have one in their new home. They nodded as Rick named each country, plotting the locations on the maps they held in their minds.

"Did you say World War *Two*?" Aldi asked.

"Yes, World War One happened about twenty-five years earlier."

"Was there World War Three?"

"No," Rick replied. "At least not yet."

Aldi nodded.

"I knew there were wars in your world," Elsa-Eska said, "but I did not know they were this big." She flipped through several more pages depicting the war in graphic detail. "Or so frightening...so cruel. I have never seen such things."

Rick flashed on a memory of a previous discussion when Elsa-Eska found his ready acceptance of war so abhorrent. He decided to take a different track this time. "War is humanity at its worst." As disturbing as the photographs were, he was thankful they were few in number and not as horrific as others he had seen. Supposing another era might paint a more favorable picture of humanity, he asked, "What did you find out about 1965?"

Elsa-Eska turned to a section she had marked. It's title read: *Into the Streets 1961-1969*. The images were much less graphic, mostly gatherings of people—a protest of the Vietnam War; a reception for President Kennedy; a rally for Martin Luther King, Jr.; mourners lining the railroad track that would carry the funeral train of Robert Kennedy. Two pages were of particular interest to Elsa-Eska. "Tell me about these," she said, flipping back and forth between them.

Rick looked closely at the first photograph. It was a close-up of a crowd; their faces were solemn. A young woman was holding a sign that read: NO WAR OVER CUBA. "Well, these people are demonstrating against a war we almost got into with Russia."

Elsa-Eska turned to the other page, another close-up of a crowd. They were all young women, many of them open-mouthed as if screaming. Two of them sported buttons that read, I LOVE GEORGE.

Rick knew what it was, but he read the caption to get the details. "February 7, 1964. That's a year before I was born. These people were waiting at the airport to see the Beatles when they came to America."

"Beatles?" Elsa-Eska's expression was one of shock. "They must have been very big."

Rick tried to suppress his amusement. "The Beatles was the name of a rock band. They were men, not bugs." Rick turned the page and found what he hoped was there, a picture of the Fab Four. "There." He pointed to it. "The Beatles."

Elsa-Eska leaned in to examine the picture. "Oh," she said, relieved, but not nearly as impressed as the screaming fans in the photograph. She leaned back in her chair and retraced the path back to her original line of thinking. "I know there is more in this world than what we know here. Wyoming is big, but it is also small. These books and magazines show a much, much bigger world with many, many more people than we expected."

"That's right," Jane said. "There's a lot that Rick and I haven't seen either. We should plan a trip somewhere so you could at least see more of America."

"Yes," Elsa-Eska nodded, "we would like to see more of your world. But that is not what I mean. This…" She waved her hands over the books and magazines on the table. "The things in these pictures—we cannot travel to see World War Two or the almost war with Russia or the Beatles when they came to America. That's what I mean when I say 2001 looks different from 1965 and very different from 1941."

"Oh, I get it," Rick said. "You're talking about history. And you're right, those times were very different from today."

"Time," Elsa-Eska said. "Yes, *that* is a difference between humans and Klyvians. Look at this." She flipped through a magazine entitled *The Twentieth Century in Pictures*. "See, this says *The Roaring Twenties*. Look at how this woman is dressed. Now look at this." She flipped to the back of the magazine to a picture of Britney Spears. "See how this woman is dressed? It is so different. And this…" She found a picture of two children sitting on the floor in a living room that looked like the set of *Leave it to Beaver*. "This is 1952." She returned to the back of the magazine to a picture of a plush apartment with stylish furnishings and a large screen television. "See how different this is? Everything is different—the cars, the clothes, even the people." She thumbed through the magazine, pausing at various photographs so Rick and Jane could see them: A stern looking man and woman standing in front of a horse drawn wagon (1901); a sophisticated couple dressed for an evening at the theatre (1920); a handsome couple in military dress uniforms (1942); a traditional family (1959); hippies (1969); dancers at a disco (1975); punk rockers (1985); and finally, a tanned, athletic couple in tennis outfits (1999). "Humans change with time."

"In some ways, yes," Jane said. "Fashion, culture, technology. I guess we have changed a lot over the last hundred years."

"What about on Klyv?" Rick asked. "Wouldn't you find these same kinds of changes on your world?"

"Not like on Earth," Elsa-Eska said.

"There have been some changes on Klyv," Aldi noted. "The Time of Trouble made our people into two. The Hori brought strange ways to the Raphim, but the true Klyv live as they have always lived since the before time."

"But your life is different," Jane offered.

"Yes," Elsa-Eska agreed. "The mission has given us a very different life, but we are still the true Klyv. We still follow the ways of Klyv."

"I don't understand," Rick said. "You say the true Klyv live as they have always lived, yet they were able to launch a spacecraft to another world. Weren't your people changed by the technology they developed for the mission?"

"Changed?" Aldi asked, tilting his head questioningly.

"Yes, didn't the new technology change the way your people lived?"

Aldi shook his head. "No, the technology is for the mission only."

"Hmm," Rick said. "On Earth we use a lot of the technology that was developed for our space program. It makes our lives easier, better. I just thought that your people would use what they developed to make their lives better."

The assumption seemed odd to Aldi. "Better than what?"

"Well, it sounds like your people still live a primitive lifestyle."

"*Primitive*? I do not understand."

Elsa-Eska spoke up. "For humans, primitive is the old way like in this picture." She turned to the front of one of the magazine to a picture of a farmer plowing his fields with an ox. "Technology has taken them from this kind of life to this." She turned to the back of the magazine to a photograph of business people in suits sitting around a large oval table engaging in a teleconference. "Are you saying this way is better?"

"It's progress," Rick replied. "Sure, I'd say it's better than slaving out in the fields all day."

"You have told us of your life before you came to Wyoming. Was it like this?" Elsa-Eska tapped the magazine.

"Yes. Actually, it was a lot like that."

"Why did you leave it?" Aldi asked.

Jane saw where this was going and bit her tongue to keep from smiling.

Rick caught a glimpse of her and knew exactly what she was thinking. "It's complicated."

"Would these people think of your life here in Wyoming as primitive?" Elsa-Eska asked, her finger still pointing to the picture of the modern office.

Rick remembered the comment Jacques had made about his

untamed life in Wyoming. "Yes, I suppose they would."

"Is life in Wyoming easier than life in the city?" Elsa-Eska pressed.

"No, not really."

"But you are here. Is it better?"

Jane chuckled under her breath. Aldi looked at her, supposing there was a piece of human humor he wasn't getting. Elsa-Eska simply waited for the answer to her question.

Rick shook his head and threw up his hands. "Okay, you got me. I guess it's a matter of perspective. For *us,* life here in Wyoming is better. But we still use technology, and our lives are better because of it."

"How?" The question was not a challenge, but one of pure curiosity.

"Well, communication is one way. Television enables us to know what's going on in the world. The computer helps me do research for my writing. I can talk to friends on the telephone. Technology helps us stay connected."

"That is good in this world," Elsa-Eska agreed. "And technology is necessary for the mission. But on Klyv, it is not this way. Muur is a small place. Our people all live together. They have no need for these things. They are happy. Easier...better. As you say, it is a matter of perspective."

CHAPTER 25:

THE TIME OF TROUBLE

◁:

Rick was impressed by her reasoning, and he felt no need to press the issue. But her last statement conjured up another question. "How many live on Muur?" For some reason he had assumed there was a great number of Klyvians, but now he suspected their numbers might be fewer than he thought.

Elsa-Eska thought for a moment. "I don't know the exact number, but I think there were about a hundred when the mission was launched. There must be more by now."

"Only a hundred. What about the Raphim? How many are they?" Rick expected an equally small number; maybe a few more.

"More, but I do not know their numbers," Elsa-Eska replied.

"Many, many more," Aldi said. "My father told me of the before time, before the Time of Trouble. He said there were more than could be counted. He said there were sina sina living in all the land."

"Thousands," Elsa-Eska interpreted. "Many thousands."

"How many thousands?" Rick queried.

Elsa-Eska shook her head. "We do not know exactly. Maybe hundreds of thousands.

Aldi continued. "But many died in the rebellion. The ones who became the Raphim—my father believes there might be thirty or forty sina…thousand left."

Rick's face fell as he calculated the tremendous loss of life in the time of trouble. He had thought of the rebellion on Klyv as a minor uprising, but now he understood it to be of a much larger scale, perhaps even close to that of World War II.

"And only a hundred true Klyv are left," Jane added softly.

"The Hori invasion must have been huge," Rick speculated.

"Invasion?" Elsa-Eska asked. "What is *invasion*?"

Rick flipped through one of the magazines until he found a photograph of the Allied Forces storming the beaches of Normandy. "That's an invasion. It's when one large group of soldiers moves into the land of their enemy."

Elsa-Eska and Aldi studied the photograph of D-Day for several moments. "No," Elsa-Eska said, shaking her head. "The Hori did not come like that. They were not that many."

"And not with fighting," Aldi added. "The Hori came as friends the first time. They showed our people many different ways: How to make the ground give more food, how to build great houses that reached into the sky, how to put the strength of a hundred into the arms of one. Our people liked these ways and they began to make a difference between the old ways and new ways. Then the Hori spoke of a strange thing. They said they had come from another place where there were others who were like our people and also different. When our people heard this, they knew the Hori did not speak good words. Even to the far edges of the land, the Song tells that all the people of Klyv came from Kalan and Dorran. Kalan and Dorran are the mother and father of Klyv. There are no others, only Klyv. The Hori tried to use many convincing words, but they had lost the ears of our people. When they could not speak anymore, the Hori disappeared."

Rick glanced at Jane and noticed her slight smile and raised eyebrows. It was an expression he recognized as her *see-I-told-you-so* look and it almost always touched a nerve. Had it not been for the fact that this new information sounded so much like a point of contention between Rick's scientific worldview and Jane's Christian worldview, he might have kept his thoughts reigned in. *The look* only made it easier for him to speak his mind.

"If I may," Rick said, holding up a finger. "We have a similar story. Some believe all humans are descended from just one man and woman. Their names were Adam and Eve. Some believe they were humanity's father and mother. Others believe Adam and Eve are just a reference to the appearance of the first modern humans in the long progression of human evolution. Adam and Eve were merely a new stage in humanity rather than two actual humans."

Jane looked at Elsa-Eska and Aldi to see their reaction, but there was none. Their expressions were that of a person looking at something for which there was no frame of reference.

"I'm just sayin," Rick continued, a little less confident, "maybe there *were* others on Klyv and your people just didn't know about them. You did say there were other islands that had not been explored. Maybe Kalan and Dorran weren't really..." Rick hesitated when he saw their bewilderment deepen. "...What I mean is, maybe there were others before Kalan and Dorran. Or maybe..." It was clear they were not following this line of reasoning. Rick felt like a man who had leapt before he looked only to discover he landed on cracked ice. There was no way to retract his words, so he pushed through with a suggestion that even he himself found unconvincing. "I don't know, maybe Kalan and Dorran were pioneers or just leaders of one group of Klyvians. I know the Hori weren't from Klyv, but maybe there were others somewhere else."

Elsa-Eska replied, "We do not know about your Adam and Eve, but we do know Kalan and Dorran. It is as Aldi has said. The Song tells us that Kalan and Dorran are the mother and father of all Klyv. There are no others."

"But couldn't the Song have been changed over time?" Once again, *the look* from Jane caused Rick to speak the thoughts that were racing through his cynical mind.

This time Aldi answered. "My father learned the Song from Ka-Rel. Ka-Rel learned the Song from his father, Aldakai. Aldakai learned it from Kalan herself. The Song has not changed in just three learnings."

"Is Kalan still alive?" Jane asked, intrigued by the possibility.

Elsa-Eska looked down at the table as Aldi explained. "No. Kalan and Dorran were killed in the rebellion along with all of the elders. Aldakai, I believe you would say he is my great-grandfather, is now the oldest of our people. Before the Time of Trouble, all of our people learned the Song from Kalan and Dorran. Now it is passed from parent to child." There was a long pause while Rick and Jane digested these new insights. "Do you want to hear more?"

"Yes, please, if you don't mind."

"The Hori disappeared for a long time. The elders did not speak of what they believed was a small thing, so the young ones did not know of them. When the Hori returned, they were only two in number and they appeared only to the young ones. In time, the Hori convinced the young ones of the others who would soon come to destroy Klyv. The Hori made lies about the elders and convinced the young ones that only they could save their people. The young ones believed the Hori and brought a great many of their generation to believe. Then the Hori put pictures into their minds and made them believe lies about the elders. They said the young ones must destroy the lies put into the minds of the elders by the others. That is how the rebellion began. The Hori watched as the young ones destroyed nearly all of our people. The fighting was not like your wars because the elders would not fight against their own children. In a very short time it was over. All but about a hundred true Klyv were left to escape to Muur. Then the Hori came in large numbers and turned our brothers and sisters into the Raphim." Aldi took a deep breath and let it out slowly. "Now we know—the others were the Hori."

Rick noticed that the gold flecks in Elsa-Eska's eyes had begun to swirl and flash like lightning in a storm.

Aldi moved next to his wife and placed a hand on her back. "Now do you understand why we carry the sadness of our people so close? The Hori have taken much from our people." He said something to Elsa-Eska in their own language, to which she nodded once. He continued, "When we learned about Arkel and Jalamin, we thought the Hori had come here."

"Oh, Elsa-Eska," Jane said, reaching across the table to place a reassuring hand on her arm. "There aren't any Hori here. You're safe with us." She gave Rick a slight nod of the head.

"Jane's right," Rick agreed, moving closer and reaching up to put a hand on Aldi's shoulder. "You don't have anything to worry about here." He hoped he sounded more convincing than he felt. Although he was fairly certain there weren't any Hori on Earth (he was banking on the assumption that the Hori were safely bound to a planet millions of miles away), he could think of a hundred other scenarios just as frightening.

"We know we are safe here," Aldi said. "The Before One has led us to you and Jane."

"Yes," Elsa-Eska said, looking up for the first time. "The Before One has put us in a good place. What happened to Jalamin and Arkel will not happen here."

After a moment, Jane said, "Thank you for telling us. Even though it is painful, it helps us understand. We are so sorry for the sadness you carry for your people."

Rick nodded and squeezed Aldi's shoulder.

The telephone rang.

"Excuse me," Rick said. He picked up the telephone and moved a few steps back from the table. "Hello."

Jane, Aldi, and Elsa-Eska listened with curiosity.

"Jacques," Rick said with his cheery telephone voice. "Hey, what's going on?" There was a long pause as Rick listened. "Uh-huh." More pause. "Uh-huh." More pause. "Oh, man, I'm sorry. You're still coming up though. Uh-huh. Well, you never know. No, the baby hasn't come yet. She's fine. No, I haven't forgotten. Yes, I'll tell you when you get here. I know, I know…I promise, you won't be disappointed." He winked at the three still listening to him from the table. "What time does your flight get in? Uh-huh. Yeah, turbo-prop.

23 seater. No, you're not going to call a cab. I'll come get you. Okay, see you tomorrow. Goodbye."

"Sorry about that," Rick said, setting the telephone back on the table.

"What did he say?" Jane asked.

Rick leaned against the back of the couch and folded his arms across his chest. "They'll be here tomorrow at 3:30."

"Hey, that's when mom gets in. They must be on the same flight."

Rick nodded. "That's good. That means only one trip into town."

"You said you were sorry—what was that about?"

"His meeting was a bust. The guy's super-secure Internet application got hacked."

"Too bad."

"Yeah, well, you know Jacques; always the optimist. He said he had a feeling something better was just around the corner."

Jane raised a knowing eyebrow as Rick smiled at Aldi and Elsa-Eska.

Rick glanced at the television and noticed the football game had resumed. "We can turn this off if you guys want to talk some more." He reached for the remote.

"No, I would like to watch," Aldi replied. "I think I am beginning to understand this game."

The men returned to the couch and Jane returned to her book. Elsa-Eska quietly cleared the table of the twentieth century and set her eyes on the football game from where she sat. She flinched with each play as the line of scrimmage became the scene of one mini battle after another. After one particularly devastating tackle that left a man lying motionless on the field while the rest milled around, Rick's commentary that it was a good clean hit left her bewildered. Then, as the man limped off of the field between two much smaller men, and the crowd erupted in applause, the whole thing seemed even less like a game to her. No one noticed as she got up from the table and moved over to Rick's morning chair. She stared out into the darkness, lost in her thoughts; images of the World War II soldiers flitted through her mind. What disturbed her most were their faces—devoid of all emotion as they carried out their missions of death. They were the same faces she had seen in her dream. They were the faces Jalamin and Arkel had seen just before they died. Were these the Hori of this world?

CHAPTER 26:

THE DAY EVERYTHING CHANGED

Something pulled Rick from the dream realm into the world of the awake. A sound. A disturbance. An intuitive awareness that something was different. The room was still dark, but he sensed movement at the foot of the bed. "Jane? Is that you?" He swept his hand across her side of the bed only to find the still warm indentation of where she had been just a few seconds earlier. "What's going on?" There was a click and everything went white. Rick squinted and shaded his eyes with his hand. "Jane?"

"It's time," Jane gasped. She was doing something over by the dresser.

"Time?" Rick repeated, trying to make sense of it all. He looked at the clock on the bedside table. "It's six o'clock. Time for what?"

"Oo! Oo!" Jane was motionless, hanging on to the edge of the dresser with both hands. Then it was all rapid breathing.

"Oh! It's *that* time!" Rick sprang out of bed, but his feet got twisted up in the blanket; he hit the floor hard. "I'm okay! I'm okay!" he said as he scrambled to his feet. He was instantaneously beside her, steadying her with a hand on her shoulder. He tried to speak, but he couldn't think of anything to say or ask. He shook his head to scatter the last remnants of the sleepiness.

"Get the suitcase," Jane ordered between breaths.

Rick grabbed the pre-packed suitcase from beside the dresser. Funny how the weeks and months leading up to this moment had been so peaceful and orderly, like they had all the time in the world. Now, suitcase in hand, Rick paced around the living room unsure of what to do next.

"Rick!" Jane called from the bedroom.

"Oh, sorry," he said, coming back for her. "Here, let me give you a hand."

"Stop! Breathe. And calm down." Jane's own breathing slowed and she stood up as the pressure from the contraction eased. "First, put some clothes on."

Rick looked down at himself. He was wearing only his boxers and the shoes he had stepped into in the living room. "Oh, gosh." He kicked the shoes off and pulled on a pair of blue jeans. Rummaging through the closet, he called out, "Honey, have you seen my black short-sleeved…?"

Jane rolled her eyes. "Just pick something…oooohhhh." She grabbed the dresser again.

"Oh, right, I'm sorry." He grabbed the first shirt he came to and jammed his arms through the sleeves. "What can I do to help?"

"Just a minute," Jane said through her rapid breathing technique.

"Are you in a lot of pain?"

"No, not pain really. Just a lot of pressure. Actually it feels kind of funny."

"Funny is good. Now what?"

"I guess we better go to the hospital."

"But you aren't due 'till Friday."

Jane chuckled. "I don't think Marissa cares what day it is."

"Who's Marissa?"

Jane shook her head and prayed. "Please, Lord, help my husband get through this."

"Oh," Rick clued in. "It's Marissa now. Are you sure? Last night it was Phoebe. Wasn't it?"

"It was never Phoebe. Why would I want everyone to think we named our daughter after a character on *Friends*?"

"At least everybody knows Phoebe is the cool one."

"No, *you* think Phoebe is the cool one. Everybody likes Rachel. Why are we having this conversation? Let's go!"

They made it to the Jeep without further delay. Jane had another small contraction, but Rick hardly noticed it at all. As they backed out of the driveway, the headlights of the Jeep shone on a tall figure standing on Rick's back deck.

"Aldi," Rick said. "What should we do about Aldi and Elsa-Eska?

Aldi waved and started toward them.

"Oh, honey," Jane replied. "Can't it just be us this time? It might not even be time. I'd hate to get Elsa-Eska up, get all the way into town, and then have the doctor send us back home."

Rick looked at the pleading expression on Jane's face. "Gee, I don't know. It's just that we've never left them here by themselves. I guess they'll understand. You better let me talk. I'll explain it to him." Rick rolled down the window just as Aldi approached the Jeep.

"Rick, Jane," Aldi said. "Where are you going?"

"Jane's having a few contractions," Rick explained. "It might be nothing, but we're going to the hospital just in case."

Aldi smiled warmly and nodded. "This is your happy day." He leaned down and touched his forehead to Rick's. Then he jogged around to Jane's side. When she rolled her window down, he leaned down until their foreheads touched. "We will share your happiness when you return. Goodbye, Jane." At that, he turned and walked back up onto Rick's deck.

"That was close," Jane said. "For a minute there, I thought he was going to jump right in. You know, these Klyvians might be smarter than we give them credit for."

Rick didn't need to look at her to know the expression on her face. He'd seen it enough these past few months to last a lifetime. He jammed the Jeep into first gear and punched it. They had a thirty-minute drive ahead of them. The sooner they got to the hospital the better; not only for Jane, but for him as well.

Rick wheeled the Jeep into the Emergency Room parking lot at 6:45 AM. They were instructed to check in there if they happened to arrive at the hospital before seven o'clock when the main admission area opened. The ER waiting area was empty and there was no one behind the reception desk. A television set mounted close to the ceiling in one corner of the room was tuned to CNN, but the sound was muted.

"That's odd," Rick said, trying to peek in through the window behind the desk. "I don't see anyone."

"Somebody must be here," Jane said.

"How are you feeling?"

"Fine. In fact, I haven't had another contraction since we left the house."

"Huh. Maybe it was a false alarm. Still, we're here. We may as well see a doctor. Do you want to sit down?"

They took two seats closest to the reception desk. Jane yawned and leaned her head against Rick's right shoulder. A few seconds later, restlessness kicked in, triggering an involuntary twitch in Rick's left leg. He yawned, rolled his head from side to side, and rubbed the sleep out of his eyes. Glancing at his watch, he noted the time—6:52 AM, still no signs of life.

Another minute passed. Rick shifted in his chair in an attempt to find a more comfortable position. The twitching in his left leg transferred to his right leg, developing into a rapid up and down jumpiness. The energy from his jumpy leg moved up the right side of his body and into his right shoulder. Jane was just about to drift off to sleep when her head started bobbing up and down, causing a vibration that tickled her nose hairs. She wrinkled up her nose and rubbed it with the back of her hand, but the sensation would not cease. When she finally realized what was the cause of her discomfort, she made a growling sound and twisted in her chair so that she was facing the opposite direction. Now fully awake, she propped her elbow on the armrest and rested her chin in the palm of her hand. From this new position, she was staring directly at the television across the room.

Normally, she would not have paid much attention to the television screen. She rarely ever watched the news, and with the sound off, nothing could be less interesting than a muted talking head. But something was happening. The picture kept switching between the reporter at the news desk and another reporter standing on a city street somewhere. Behind him was a very tall building, the top of which was entirely obscured by thick black smoke. She wondered what building it was. Something about it looked familiar, but she could not place it. It was obviously a skyscraper; and by the looks of the bright blue sky, it had to be somewhere in the east.

Drowsiness was starting to take over, causing each blink of Jane's eyes to last a little longer than the one before. Several minutes elapsed and the images on the television were still the same—the reporter, the building, the smoke, people in the background staring up at the unusual spectacle. Jane closed her eyes for a full minute this time, aware of how good it felt to just let them close. If only she could get the rest of her body in a comfortable position. She must have drifted off to sleep because as the muscles in her neck relaxed, her head rolled to the left just enough for her chin to slip off of her hand. The sudden pitch forward startled her awake and she snapped her head back upright. When she opened her eyes this time, the image on the television was very different. The building was still belching black smoke, but its twin (now she could see it from the different camera angle) was consumed in an enormous ball of fire. She gasped and jumped up out of her chair.

"What's wrong?" Rick asked, startled by the sudden movement.

Jane did not respond. She just stared at the silent mayhem on the television.

"Jane?" Rick asked again. "What is it?" He thought she had another contraction, but when he saw the expression on her face, he followed her gaze toward the television. "What the…" He got up and stood beside her.

"What movie is that?" Rick inquired.

"It's not a movie," Jane replied, her voice trembling. "It's the news. It's…real."

Both of them moved slowly toward the television as if drawn by some unseen force.

"Is that the World Trade Center?" Rick asked, studying the surreal image.

"Rick, what's happening?" Jane reached both arms around his waist and held onto him.

They finished the distance to the television. Rick reached up and fumbled around the edge of the television until he found the volume control. Within a few seconds, they knew as much as anyone else. Twenty minutes earlier an airplane (maybe a commercial airliner) hit the North Tower of the World Trade Center. What was initially believed to have been an accident was now being called an intentional act of terrorism, confirmed by the second strike to the South Tower. The news crews that were sent to cover the "accident" had actually filmed the second strike as it happened. Rick and Jane both gasped as the horrific scene was replayed before their eyes. The second airplane could be easily seen. It was a commercial airliner. It was not an accident.

"I can't believe it," Rick mumbled numbly. "It doesn't look real."

They stared at the television for several minutes in stunned silence. The announcer kept repeating the same information over and over, adding little details and speculations as they trickled in.

"I think I'm going to be sick," Jane finally said. "I'd better sit down."

Rick helped her into the chair directly behind her. He watched the color drain from her face.

"What is it? What's wrong?

"M-m-my mom. She's flying this morning." She brought her hand up to her mouth and her entire body started to tremble.

"She's fine," Rick said, trying to sound confident. "She's okay. Her flight left hours ago and it wasn't anywhere near New York. She's probably in Atlanta waiting for her connection." Rick tried to get his mind to recall her exact flight itinerary, but it would not engage. All he could see was the World Trade Center on fire from the impact of two commercial airliners. "She's fine," he repeated and let Jane bury her face into his chest.

Maybe it's not real, Rick thought to himself. *Maybe it's a mistake or a sick joke or an advertisement for a new disaster movie—anything but this.* He stroked Jane's hair and rocked her back and forth as the images of carnage replayed themselves over and over before his eyes. It was real.

It seemed to them a very long time, but only a few minutes past before the receptionist returned to her post. When she noticed Rick and Jane, she came around the desk and walked over to them. "Can I help you?"

Rick had not seen her approach from behind him. He jumped at her words. "Oh, yes. It's my wife. Um, she had some contractions a little more than an hour ago, and well, uh, it's our first time. So…here we are. Did you see this?" Rick pointed toward the television.

The receptionist, an ER veteran, slipped easily into her professional mode; she nodded at Rick without offering comment and then got Jane's attention. She asked her how she felt and assured her that she had made the right decision to come on in.

The next several minutes were a blur. A nurse and an attendant appeared with a wheelchair. Rick was bombarded with all the routine questions as Jane was being helped into the wheelchair, then they were whisked away to the maternity ward. On the way, they passed another waiting area where a small group of people were huddled around a television set, speaking in quiet murmurs. At the nurses' station in the maternity ward, a television had been wheeled in on a cart. The nurses continued their duties, pausing briefly in front of the television as they moved from one patient to the next. After the nurse and attendant wheeled Jane into one of the examination rooms, they left her with instruction to put on a hospital gown.

Rick helped her into the gown and up onto the examination table. He held her hand and took in the details of their new environment. It was cold and impersonal, and Jane looked nervous. When Rick leaned over to touch his forehead to hers, she managed a weak smile. "It's going to be okay," he said.

Jane nodded. "It's all wrong."

"What do you mean?"

Jane sighed. "Here we are on what's supposed to be the happiest day of our lives, and…*that's* happening. I can't stop thinking of all those people, Rick. They just died. And then there's mom—I don't know where she is. I don't know if she's okay. I'm supposed to be happy, but I can't. I just…I just can't."

"I know, babe. I know." He patted her hand wishing he could think of something to say that would make it all better.

"I wish Elsa-Eska was here."

The thought of Aldi and Elsa-Eska was like a splash of cold water in the face. He knew they were okay at the ranch. New York was almost two thousand miles away. Still, it seemed like they should be together at a time such as this.

They waited a long time, close to thirty minutes, before the door to the examination room opened abruptly. Rick jumped. A young doctor in a cowboy hat stepped into the room and let the door slam behind him. He was carrying Jane's chart, which he examined longer than Rick thought necessary. In fact, everything about this guy was more than necessary. He was younger and better looking than necessary. His cowboy boots were too shiny, and his hat was too big. He looked ridiculous. When he shook Rick's hand, his grip was too firm, and when he tipped his hat to Jane, he looked like a singing telegram actor who had taken his cues from a Saturday afternoon western.

The "kid" introduced himself as Dr. Bridger and said he would attend to Jane until her delivery doctor arrived. When he asked Rick to step out of the room while he examined Jane, Rick hesitated. Although he was very professional, Rick thought he sounded a little too eager. Jane read his mind and gave him one of her looks that said, *I'll be okay, please don't make a scene.* Rick got the message and leaned down to kiss her on the lips, making sure the good doctor saw it. Then, loud enough to guarantee Dr. Bridger would hear him, he told her he would be just outside the door.

Outside the room, Rick could see the portable television. The live images from New York City proved that what they had seen earlier was still happening. Rick could not help but watch. It all still looked staged. He glanced down at his watch—7:45 AM—and then back at the television. The image of the burning towers disappeared, replaced by a grim looking announcer. Rick could not hear what he was saying, but he could tell there had been a development. He took a few steps closer so he could read the words scrolling across the bottom of the screen: *Explosion at the Pentagon.* The words did not register at first. There was no connection between the attack on the World Trade Center and an explosion at the Pentagon. There couldn't be. It had to be a coincidence.

Rick was pulled back into his own little crisis when the door to the examination room opened. Dr. Bridger nearly filled the doorway with his big hat and attitude, but Rick could still see Jane.

"Congratulations, Mr. Blackwell. Looks like today's the day."

"It is?" Rick looked around the big man, half-expecting to see Jane holding their new baby. Realistically, he knew it could not have happened that fast, but the way Dr. Bridger said it…he looked again.

"Yes, sir. She's got a ways to go yet, but I think she'll deliver sometime today. We're going to get her settled in a more comfortable room. Dr. Jenkins will be here in about an hour."

"An hour, that long?"

Dr. Bridger chuckled and put his hand on Rick's shoulder. "Hey, this is the fun part. Get something to eat, watch some television, read a book. You might even want to catch a nap. Once the show starts, you won't have time for any of that."

The doctor left Rick puzzling over what he had just said. What did he mean by *won't have time for any of that?* Was he talking about today or life from here on out? The riddle dissipated at the sight of Jane's glowing smile. New York may as well have been a million miles away.

"Hey, Daddy," Jane said, flashing him that irresistible crooked smile. "Look's like Cassandra will be here soon."

"Cassandra?" Rick thought for a moment. "I was just getting used to Marissa; now it's Cassandra. Would we call her Cassie or Sandra?"

Jane furrowed her eyebrows. "Oo, I don't like either of those."

"Okay then," Rick nodded. "Good thing we've got hours. How do you feel?"

"Great." Jane perked right up. "I don't know what I was so nervous about. So far this is a piece of cake."

"Hmm. Speaking of cake…" Rick looked at his watch. "It's ten 'till eight. How 'bout I get us some breakfast after we get settled into your room?"

"I don't know if I can eat anything this close to delivery. That's okay though. I'm not that hungry. But you should get something."

"Maybe after they move us."

"You know, Dr. Bridger said it will be hours. I was thinking, maybe you should go home and check on Elsa-Eska and Aldi."

"I'm sure they're fine."

"What if they get worried because we're gone so long. We left so unexpectedly. I didn't get to tell Elsa-Eska where we were going."

"Aldi will tell her. Besides, you didn't want to wake her."

"I know. But now I wish we had. Too bad we can't call them."

"I know. I wish we had gotten that phone line installed. I gotta get that done." The thought of another project caused Rick's mind to wander.

"So, are you going?" The way Jane posed the question told Rick that she had already made up his mind.

He didn't like the idea of leaving Jane for an hour, but if he didn't go now, it would be even harder to go later. Besides, it would put Jane's mind at ease to know Elsa-Eska and Aldi were okay and not worrying about her. "Are you sure you don't want me to just bring them back with me?"

Jane considered it. "Naw, I think I'd like it to be just us this time."

"Okay. Well, I guess I'll go then. And I'll get something to eat at home. I probably won't be back for at least an hour and a half."

"Aw," Jane stuck out her bottom lip. "One hour." She reached out and laced her fingers with his.

"Okay. I'll eat while I'm driving."

"Be careful. And don't speed."

"I will. I mean I won't. You know what I mean."

"One more thing. Do you think you could bring my suitcase?"

"Your suitcase?" Rick rubbed his unshaven chin and replayed the events of the morning. "Oh, gosh. I had it, but I must have set it down in the living room. Yes, I'll bring it. Sorry."

"That's okay." Jane smiled, and lifting her chin toward him, she puckered her lips.

Rick leaned over and kissed her.

"I love you," Jane said. "Hurry back."

"I love you, too. Now don't you have that baby while I'm gone." He leaned over and kissed Jane's round belly. "And I'll see you in a little while, Cassandra."

As Rick left the room, Jane stared up at the ceiling. "Cassandra. That's not going to work."

On his way out, Rick saw several doctors and nurses gathered around a television set. There was an odd silence about them. He stopped just in time to watch the South Tower of the World Trade Center collapse in a huge cloud of dirt and debris. It looked so much like the controlled demolitions he had seen on the *Discovery Channel* that it didn't register in his mind that he had just witnessed the alteration of the New York City skyline. Then, the view from street level—the panicked crowd running toward the camera, away from an ominous cloud of dirt and debris—it looked like a scene from a monster movie. CNN kept the feed from the street level camera going until the cloud gobbled it up. Then it jumped back to the clean newsroom where the announcer stared in disbelief at what everyone had just witnessed. This shift between the surreal and the real was just one of several that would roll over the entire nation as the day's events played out.

CHAPTER 27:

NEVER THE SAME

♍

The drive back to the ranch was eerie. Traffic was unusually light for a Tuesday morning, but everything else looked just as it always did. The cattle were making their way out to pasture, the ranchers were already three hours into their daily routines and a school bus carried its load of rowdy kids. Everything was just as it should be, yet the images of the horror happening at that very moment flashed through Rick's mind—the smoke, the flames, the terrified people, the rolling cloud of dirt bearing down on that poor camera man. He shook his head to clear his mind of the carnage, but he couldn't make it go away. The South Tower fell over and over again in his mind. The people kept running. The debris monster kept rolling.

Rick kept turning the radio on and off in an emotional tug-of-war. Part of him wanted to block it out and pretend the attack was not real, but another part of him was compelled to listen, to stay connected to what was happening to his country. Rick was almost to his mile-long driveway when the North Tower fell. The reporter's description of it matched the image that was playing over and over in Rick's mind—the sound of each floor collapsing onto the floor below it; the cascade of debris raining down onto the people in the street below; the rolling monster of debris. Rick drove the rest of the way home on autopilot, instinctively dodging the potholes until he stopped the Jeep in front of his house.

Aldi was still on the back deck where he had been two hours earlier. He had to have heard Rick pull up, but he didn't interrupt his meditation until Rick climbed the steps of the deck and stood beside him.

"Jane is not with you," Aldi observed. "Is she well?"

"Yes, she's fine," Rick replied. He started to tell Aldi about what was happening in New York, but then he thought about all the questions that would surely follow. How could he even begin to explain something to a Klyvian that he didn't understand himself. For the first time since their arrival, Rick wished he had another human to talk to.

"Something is different today," Aldi said.

"What do you mean?"

"The sky is empty." Aldi waved his hand across the expanse.

Rick surveyed the sky in all directions. It was one continuous, unmarked swath of bright blue.

Noticing the uncomprehending look on Rick's face, Aldi explained. "There is always an airplane somewhere in the sky. Now there are none. I think it is the first time I have seen the sky empty like this. Today is different."

Rick looked around again. Then he remembered. About an hour ago, in the midst of all the facts and speculations, he heard the CNN reporter say the FAA had grounded all air traffic nationwide. Ominously, the empty sky in Wyoming served as evidence of the events that were unfolding two thousand miles away.

"Do you know why the sky is empty?" Aldi asked.

As best he could, Rick explained what was happening. Aldi took in the information. Sensing the heaviness in Rick's demeanor, he refrained from asking any questions about it. "So anyway, I've got to get back to the hospital." Rick paused as an idea came to him. "Say, do you think you and Elsa-Eska could stay in our house today?"

Aldi cocked his head questioningly.

"That way I can call you when the baby comes."

Aldi nodded.

"Great. I'll call you when I get back to the hospital and give you the number where you can call us if you need anything. Are you and Elsa-Eska going to be okay while we're gone?"

Aldi smiled and put a hand on Rick's shoulder. "We will be fine. Jane gave Elsa-Eska a new book. I think I will see what makes your computer work."

Rick did a double-take. "My computer?" Then he remembered Aldi telling him how he and Arkel had disassembled the ship's computers to satisfy their curiosity. "Are you serious?"

Aldi laughed. "Don't worry, Rick. I made a joke." He sighed and shook his head. "Human humor, you gotta love it!"

"Gotta love it," Rick agreed with a mock chuckle.

"Are *you* okay, brother?" Aldi said, his expression becoming serious again.

"Yeah, I'm just a little anxious about everything."

"We will be fine here. Tell Jane we will see her soon."

Rick reached up and squeezed Aldi's shoulder, then he turned and went into the house. The suitcase was in the living room, right where he had left it. Scolding himself for his lack of focus, he moved it in front of the door so he would not forget it again, then he went into the kitchen. The close proximity to food set off a wave of hunger, but he could not decide what he wanted. The refrigerator was packed, but offered no quick fix. The cupboard was equally unyielding. The empty coffee pot mocked him. He scolded himself again for his inability to focus his mind. Frustrated, he grabbed two bananas and a half-empty carton of orange juice. Not a great breakfast, but at least it would put something into his stomach. He could get something more substantial later at the hospital cafeteria.

Rick was just about to step out of his house when the blinking light on the answering machine caught his attention. He almost ignored it, but something inside urged him to check it. He punched the play button with the corner of the orange juice carton and listened: *Hello, Janie? This is mom. I'm okay. Listen, honey, in case you haven't seen the news, something terrible is happening. I'm at the airport in Atlanta and I'm safe. They're telling us all flights have been cancelled all across the country. I'll call you later when I know something. Be careful. I love you.*

Rick breathed a sigh of relief. "Thank God." His words surprised him. Why would he thank God when the jury was still out for him? *It's just an expression*, he told himself. Then again, *why* was it an expression? Why not *Thank Zeus* or *Thank Santa Claus* or *Thank Ka-Rel*? Why thank anyone? He pushed these thoughts out of his mind. What did it matter who he thanked? What mattered was Jane's mom was safe, and that would mean one less thing for Jane to worry about.

With the suitcase in one hand and his breakfast in the other, Rick climbed into the Jeep and fired up the engine. He waved to Aldi as he pulled away from the house and switched on the radio:

CNN has just reported they have received confirmation of a fourth incident. A large plane, possibly a Boeing 767, crashed about forty-five minutes ago in western Pennsylvania, about 80 miles from Pittsburgh. That is all we know at this time, but it seems clear that this is part of a coordinated attack on the United States. Other reports are coming in, and I must emphasize that these are not confirmed…there is possibly another hijacked plane or planes heading for Washington DC. I repeat, these reports are not confirmed. We will continue this coverage and bring you the latest details as we receive them. We urge you to stay tuned…

Rick's mind reeled with a flurry of emotions as he wound his way through the minefield of potholes in his driveway: Shock over the fourth attack; profound sadness over the untold loss of life; the feeling of helplessness as he could do nothing but observe; dread at the possibility of further attacks; and finally anger. It was the anger that was the strongest, and yet most frustrating. He was angry that someone would attack so many innocent people with such lethal and indiscriminate destruction, yet he had no idea where or how to direct that anger. By now it was obvious this was a highly sophisticated attack, involving a great deal of resources—both money and people.

His mind drifted from *why* to *whom*. The most recent incident he could think of was the bombing in Oklahoma City. That was a homegrown terrorist group consisting of just a few disgruntled Americans attacking their own government. Devastating, to be sure, but relatively minor compared to the attacks that were happening this morning. In just a couple hours, someone had managed to hijack and crash four commercial airliners, topple two skyscrapers, and knock a hole in the side of the Pentagon; and in the process murder thousands of people.

His analytical mind went to work. TARGETS: Transportation, Finance, Defense—the infrastructure of America. What other targets could be on the list? Utilities? National leadership? Other modes of transportation? SUSPECTS: Who would have the motive and means (not to mention guts) to attack the world's only remaining superpower? It would have to be someone…no, not a someone…a country. But what country could possibly not foresee that such an attack would mean a swift retaliation with even greater loss, if not total annihilation? What country would want to pick a fight they could not possibly win?

Ed Tyler's voice shouted from a dark corner of his mind, *"Commies!"*

No, that's ridiculous. The Russians would never pull something like this. Rick tried to think of other nations who might have the means and motive to attack America. Obviously, there was Iraq—retaliation for the embarrassment of the Gulf War and the fact that George Bush's son was America's new president. Other countries came to mind, but he had to admit he knew so little about current international affairs that none of them really stood out as a realistic possibility. Even Iraq seemed a bit of a stretch. The fact was no country could attack America on this scale without leaving a trail; and once the trail was discovered, it would only be a matter of time before a much more lethal counter-attack would fall upon it. By the time he reached the paved main highway, Rick had pretty much dismissed the likelihood that these attacks were part of any country's foreign policy agenda.

Ed Tyler spoke again from that same dark corner. *"Or aliens."*

Rick laughed at the idea. But then he thought about the Hori and Ed Tyler's mention of bad aliens. *What if…no, that's impossible,* he thought, shaking his head. Then again, just six months ago he would have thought it just as impossible that he would have two aliens living on his ranch. He jammed his foot onto the accelerator and forced his mind to dwell on Jane.

Rick made it back to the hospital in record time, found Jane's room, and knocked on the door.

"Come in," Jane said. Her voice was as clear and cheery as if she were lounging around the house.

Rick entered the room and placed the suitcase on the floor next to the bed. "How are you?" He eyed her, looking for any signs of progress. "Any more contractions?"

"A few. I think they're starting to pick up again. They're more regular, but not very intense. Actually, they feel like little hugs."

"Huh," Rick grunted. "I've always thought labor pains were really bad. Maybe this is as bad as it's going to get."

"Or maybe we just don't know what's coming."

"Ah, the bliss of ignorance. Oh, hey, there was a message from your mom on the answering machine." Jane sat up in anticipation of the news. "She's in Atlanta, but all the flights have been cancelled. She's stuck for who knows how long."

Jane sighed and smiled a half-smile. "At least she's safe. Thank God."

Rick's earlier spontaneous thanks to God flashed through is mind, but he didn't want to go down that road with Jane. "Yeah, it's a good thing she hadn't made her connection. I heard on the radio that planes are landing anywhere they can. At least from Atlanta she can rent a car and get back home if it comes to that."

Jane's expression became grave. "I've been watching the news. I can't believe this is happening. Do you think there will be more?"

Rick shrugged and glanced at the television. There was a non-stop cycle of images from New York, Washington, and Pennsylvania. "I don't know. I would have never imagined both towers getting hit. But now the Pentagon and that plane in Pennsylvania…you know they are saying it might have been heading for the White House. I'm braced for more."

They watched the familiar footage again. The twin towers were falling for the hundredth time, but the result was still the same. Rick and Jane tried and failed to put words to the ache they felt in their stomachs.

Finally, Jane pulled her attention away from the television. "Did you see Aldi and Elsa-Eska?"

"I saw Aldi. They're fine. I asked them to hang out in our house so we could call them later." Rick let out a chuckle of admission. "You know, I don't think they need us as much as we think they do. Elsa-Eska's reading some book you gave her, and Aldi's going to take apart the computer."

Jane's eyebrows shot up in surprise. "Are you serious?"

Rick laughed. "That was my reaction exactly. No, he was just kidding. He's practicing his human humor again."

"I am so glad you got him started on that," Jane said, sounding more like a disapproving mother.

"Maybe he'll give up on it. Or maybe he'll actually start getting funny."

"Oh, whoa!" Jane cradled her stomach and squirmed in the bed.

"What is it? Another contraction?"

"Yeah, that was a big one, and it went all the way around to my back. I think these hugs are getting stronger."

"Did it hurt?"

"No…" Jane assessed the remnant of the sensation. "Not hurt, but it definitely gets your attention."

When he was sure the episode was passed, Rick pulled a chair next to the bed and sat down. "I got your suitcase, but I guess you have to wear their jammies."

Jane frowned. "Yeah, not exactly my style. Kind of drafty in the back, but I suppose they'll be more practical when the time comes."

Rick started to come back with a sarcastic remark, but Jane looked pathetic enough. "So, what do we do now?"

"Just wait. Dr. Jenkins came in while you were gone. She said it could be awhile. May as well make yourself comfortable."

Their attention drifted back up to the television. Jane had seen enough, but she knew Rick would want to keep tabs on what was happening. She compromised by leaving the channel on CNN, but muted the sound. She looked around the room that was made to look homey—comfortable couch, side tables with ornate lamps, framed nature prints on the wall—but it still had that hospital feel to it. She noted the rack of equipment in the corner that she would soon be connected to.

"Can you believe it, Rick," She said. "Today's the day. We're actually going to see our daughter."

"Doesn't seem real, does it?"

"Our lives will never be the same after today."

Rick heard the comment as he watched the people covered in dirt and blood stumbling away from the jagged pile that once was the World Trade Center. He nodded. "You're right. We'll never be the same."

CHAPTER 28:

LOVE AND HONOR

•‖

The hours ticked away slowly. Jane's early morning was catching up with her. She tried to get some sleep, but the contractions were coming regularly. Every fifteen minutes, her "little hugs" woke her up. Dr. Jenkins came in about every hour to check her progress. After the first visit, Rick repositioned his chair so he didn't have to witness the progress checks. Modesty, he learned, was definitely *not* part of childbirth.

By noon, the terrorist attacks, as everyone was now calling them, seemed to have ceased. Every airplane in the country was accounted for and safely on the ground. The president and vice-president were securely hidden away in undisclosed locations. The rescue efforts in New York and Washington continued at a fevered pitch; Pennsylvania was now being called a recovery effort, though there wasn't much left to recover. The nation, it seemed, was beginning to grasp what happened. And the rest of the world was beginning to respond as well. Most condemned the attacks and offered condolences to the grieving nation, but there were a few reports of a different reaction in some parts of the world. There was no shortage of theories as to who was responsible, but already most of the attention was being focused on the Middle East. It wouldn't be long before the shock of the nation turned to outrage. A response would be demanded. One commentator harkened back to the last time America was attacked in 1941, saying a sleeping giant had been awakened.

Just after noon, Dr. Jenkins came in for her routine visit. Jane and the baby progressed to the point that it was time to attach the monitors. Jane was fitted with a fetal heart monitor belt around her stomach and another pulse monitor on her finger. An I.V. line was started to keep her hydrated. When Dr. Jenkins switched on the monitors, two green lines started tracing across the screen. Jane's heart rate was strong and steady, hovering around 65 beats per minute. The line representing the baby's heart rate had slightly less dramatic peaks and valleys, but its beat was much more rapid, around 180. According to Dr. Jenkins, everything was as it should be. Estimated delivery time—hard to tell, but it would be hours rather than minutes. When the doctor left the room, Jane noticed the empathetic look on Rick's face as he assessed Jane's "connectedness."

"It's all part of it," Jane said.

"I know. It just looks so…unnatural. I wonder what Elsa-Eska would think about all this."

"She'd be curious, of course; want to know what everything was for. It's probably a good thing she isn't here. Aldi would be absolutely fascinated by it all."

Rick chuckled at the thought of Aldi trying to make sense of Jane being hooked up to all the equipment. "Yeah, they're better off at home."

"Maybe you'd be better off at home, too."

"What? And miss all this? Not on your life. I'm here for the long haul."

Jane reached for his hand. "I'm glad you're here. I wouldn't want to go through this with anyone else."

"Me, too." Rick leaned over and kissed her forehead. Then his lips curled into a smile. "Hey, I want to try something."

"What?"

Rick leaned over again and kissed Jane full on the lips. She started to giggle, but then responded in kind. With eyes closed, she reached up with her un-connected hand and weaved her fingers into his thick hair. The kiss lingered, becoming more passionate. Without letting up, Rick opened one eye (Jane's eyes remained closed) and looked at the heart monitor. Suddenly, Jane's eyes popped open and she grabbed a fistful of Rick's hair. "Oh!" she said.

"Ow!" Rick replied and pulled his head back. "What was that for?"

"That little hug was a bit stronger."

Rick untangled himself from Jane's grasp and stood upright. "You okay?"

"Yes." Then a questioning look came upon her. "What was that all about?"

Rick rubbed the back of his sore head. "Just seeing how high I could get your heart rate up."

"Rick Blackwell! Here I thought we were having a moment and all you wanted to do was test your…your…romantic prowess."

Rick shrugged and sat back down in his chair.

"Well?" Jane said after a minute, a smile appearing on her lips. "What was it?"

"85." Rick's voice was indifferent like he was talking about the weather.

"Hmm." Jane's eyebrows knit together.

"What?"

"I bet I could get yours up to 95."

"Oh, you do?"

"Easy."

Just then the door opened, and a very young looking nurse poked her head into the room. "Are you okay, Mrs. Blackwell?"

"Yes. Why? Is something wrong?" Jane asked.

"I noticed a spike in your heart rate." The nurse walked over to the bed and made a quick inspection of the monitoring equipment. "How do you feel?"

"Oh, I'm fine."

"You look a little flushed. Are you too warm?"

Rick stared at the television and bit down on his tongue to keep from laughing.

"I'm fine," Jane assured her.

Satisfied that her patient was in no distress, the nurse breathed a sigh of relief. "I probably shouldn't tell you this, but it's my first day. I'm a little nervous."

"That's okay," Jane said. "It's our first day, too."

The nurse looked puzzled at first and then giggled. "Oh, I get it. It's your first day, too. That's funny." She was still giggling as she made her way to the door. "My shift is just about over, but I promise I'll leave you in good hands. Call if you need anything."

"Thank you. We will."

Alone again, Rick stood up. "Too bad she's leaving. We could have had a lot of fun with her. Let's see how fast we can get the next nurse to come check your monitor."

Jane shot him a look. "Rick, you better be nice. We don't want to get a bad reputation on our first day."

"I'll be good." Rick paced around the room, picked up a magazine and dropped it back on the table.

"Why don't you go get something to eat," Jane offered. "You must be hungry. And it will help pass the time."

"I don't want to eat if you can't. That wouldn't be very nice of me." He winked at her.

"Don't be silly. No sense in you starving just because I can't have anything. Besides, I'm really not that hungry. I'd feel better if you got something."

"If you're sure."

"Yes, I'm sure."

"Okay. I won't be long. Say, why don't you call Elsa-Eska? I bet she'd like to talk with you. I told Aldi I'd call him with the number to room in case they need anything."

Jane's face lit up at the idea. "Yeah, I'll do that. That's a good idea. Enjoy."

Rick kissed Jane again, careful to not set off any warning lights at the nurses' station, and stepped out of the room.

The cafeteria was not bad for a hospital. He was hungrier than he thought and ended up eating much quicker than he intended. Knowing Jane would want to talk to Elsa-Eska longer than he had been gone, he decided to go outside for some fresh air. The sky was brilliant blue and cloudless. The absence of airplane contrails was more noticeable since Aldi had pointed it out to him earlier. He wondered how long it had been since the sky over America was completely empty like that. Probably not since his grandparents were young.

When Rick returned to Jane's hospital room, he discovered a different woman sitting up in Jane's bed. There was a strong resemblance to the woman with whom he had shared his life for the last ten years, but it wasn't the same woman—not exactly. The hair was the same, though now it was plastered to her face and neck in random, sweaty strands. The nose was the same, though it was flared a bit. The line of the jaw was the same, but it was set hard and fast. She was staring hard at something on the far wall as if trying to move it by the sheer power of her mind, and her hands were clamped onto the bedrails like the fate of the world depended upon them staying exactly where they were. Her right eye twitched twice and she was panting rapidly.

Rick checked the name on the door. It read: Jane Blackwell. Taking a cautious step into the room, he called out to the woman, "Jane?" The woman turned her head slightly, but kept her eyes fixed on that spot on the far wall. Then, as if someone pulled a plug, she fell back into the pillow and let out a long shaky breath. Her face softened and she looked more like the Jane Rick knew and loved. "Honey, are you okay?"

"Mm-hmm," she replied between the deep breaths she was taking in and letting out through her mouth.

Rick approached the bed and brushed an errant strand of hair back away from her cheek. "What was that?"

"Contraction." Her breathing was starting to approach normalcy.

"That didn't look like the *little hugs* you were having earlier."

"My water broke while you were gone, and the hugs turned into pythons."

"Does the doctor know?" Rick asked anxiously.

Jane nodded. "Dr. Jenkins came in right after it happened. She said it's all part of the process. Things should start happening faster now." She took a deep breath and let it out slowly. "I don't think I'm going to get off as easy as we thought."

"Is there anything I can do?"

"Would you rub my back? It's so tight."

"Sure."

Jane rolled over on her side, and Rick began to massage her back. "Oh, yeah, that's the spot," she mumbled. "Thank you."

Thirty minutes and five strong contractions later, Rick's hands were aching. He wanted to take a break, but seeing the look on Jane's face whenever a contraction hit made him rethink his discomfort. He wasn't about to wimp out with Jane doing all the real work. So he kept on massaging. Jane must have sensed his fatigue. Even in the midst of her labor, she tried to be encouraging by telling him how much he was helping.

By now, another nurse (not the rookie) was popping in every fifteen minutes or so to check on Jane, but they hadn't seen Dr. Jenkins in over an hour. There were two other women ahead of Jane, either of which could deliver at any moment. So they waited—Jane resting between the python attacks, and Rick doing all he could to ease her discomfort and his conscience.

As he massaged, Rick couldn't help but keep his eyes trained on the monitors above Jane's bed. He noticed that Jane's heart rate increased slightly at the beginning of each contraction, so now he could anticipate them just before they hit. He also noticed that the baby's heart rate slowed with each contraction, apparently the result of the stress she was enduring. Rick was always relieved when the contraction ended and both heartbeats returned to normal.

Then came the mother of all contractions. Jane cried out in pain and grabbed the bed rails. Rick intensified his massaging in an attempt to counteract the pain and he watched the numbers on the monitor react as he knew they would. Jane's heart rate spiked, and the baby's waned. The contraction lasted nearly two full minutes, much longer than the others. Jane moaned and writhed. Rick held his breath as if that would somehow help. Finally, the wave passed.

Jane relaxed, but every muscle in her body ached from the tension. As she brought her breathing back under control, Rick felt released to resume his own breathing.

"That was a big one," he said, mopping her forehead with a cool, wet washcloth.

"I don't know how many more of those I can take." She closed her eyes and relished each second before the next contraction.

Out of habit, Rick glanced up at the monitor. Jane's heart rate had returned to normal, but the baby's had not yet rebounded. In fact, it had dropped to 140. Of course, Rick did not know whether this was normal for a fetus, but it was about forty beats per minute less than before. He glanced down at Jane and started to comment about it, but the exhaustion on her face gave him pause. Why add worry to burden, especially if the number started to climb again? When he looked back up at the monitor, his heart sank as the baby's heart rate dropped to 130. It was now lower than he had ever seen it. Rick was just about to say something when the nurse came back into the room. Rick automatically stepped back, making room for the nurse beside the bed.

"What's happening?" Jane asked.

"Just checking, Mrs. Blackwell." There was an edge of concern to her voice that wasn't there the other times she was *just checking*. The baby's heart rate was now 120.

"What is it? What's wrong?" Jane sensed what the nurse was not saying. "Rick, what's happening?"

"I don't know."

"Jane," the nurse said firmly, but in a manner that was supposed to convey control. "Your baby's heart rate is decreasing. It isn't that unusual, but I'm going to call the doctor in just in case."

"In case what?" Jane's voice was shaky.

"Just try to relax. I'll be right back."

As the nurse left the room, Rick slipped back into his place. "Don't worry, babe. I'm sure it's nothing they haven't seen before."

The number on the monitor took another dip—115.

Before Rick could say another word, Dr. Jenkins was in the room. She didn't seem to notice Rick at all. Her entire focus was on Jane, the baby, and the monitor. After several procedures intended to stimulate the baby's heart rate, it rallied back up to 140, dropped back to 130, and leveled off there. The look on Dr. Jenkins's face communicated worry, but her voice was calm and reassuring.

"There's nothing to worry about. You're doing great. Your baby's just getting tired from all the contractions. I'd like you to reconsider the epidural, Jane. I know you said you didn't want one, but I recommend it. You'll be able to relax more and that will help your baby. By the looks of things, I think we've still got a ways to go."

"Dr. Jenkins," Jane said. "Level with me. Is she in danger?"

Dr. Jenkins hesitated and then said, "Her heart rate is lower than we want it to be. I'd like to see it up before the next contraction. I wouldn't say she's in danger, but it's enough for me to be concerned."

The news rolled over Jane in a numbing wave. How could her relatively uneventful pregnancy turn so suddenly? And turn to what? What was enough to concern a doctor who had been through this hundreds of times? What would it take to nudge them over the line from *concern* to *real worry*? Jane was so distracted by these thoughts that she missed the sensation she had come to identify as the precursor to the next contraction.

What came next hit hard and fast, like a freight train. The pythons returned with a vengeance, constricting around Jane's midsection in ever tightening spasms. Jane clenched her teeth and grabbed two fistfuls of sheet. Rick watched the baby's heart rate drop to 110. Dr. Jenkins saw it too and immediately went to work. Rick stepped back, feeling helpless. His own heart began to pound in his chest and he wished there was some way to transfer the excess energy from his heart into the heart of his unborn child.

Then a notion came into his mind: If he could, he would deplete his own heart completely if it would save his child. The thought staggered him. He knew he loved his unborn child, but he also knew that he had not yet bonded with her like Jane had. Was this sudden awareness of self-sacrificing love his first real brush with parenthood? And if it was this strong now, what would it be like once his daughter was born and he could actually see her and interact with her? Would this bond continue to increase over the span of her life? He thought he loved Jane with his whole heart. How was it possible to make room, this much room, for another person? Was it a trade-off? A replacement? Was his daughter taking the place of Jane in his heart?

He looked at Jane struggling to get through the paralyzing contraction and knew beyond all doubt that his love for her had not diminished in the least. Somehow, in a way he could not explain, his capacity to love was expanding. He loved them both, not equally, but completely. The math didn't make sense, but he knew he loved them both with his whole heart.

Then other faces popped unexpectedly into his mind: His mom and dad, his brother, Aldi, Elsa-Eska, even Arkel and Jalamin, whom he had only met that day on the road. It made no sense, but he knew he loved each of them—yes, each in a unique way, but not in degrees or portions. His heart was not a pie that had to be carved up and served out in slices that had to add up to the total of its capacity. The math didn't matter. There was enough love for them all. This moment of clarity shot through his soul like a jolt of electricity. His hands began to shake, his stomach ached, and a few tears leaked out of tear ducts that had been dry for years.

When the contraction ended he was back at Jane's side, wiping her face with the cool cloth and whispering words of encouragement to her. He glanced back up at the monitor. The baby's heart rate was holding at 110, but not on it's own. Dr. Jenkins was still providing the necessary stimulus.

"Rick," Jane said, her voice weak from exhaustion. "I know something's wrong. I feel it now."

"No, no." It was all he could manage to get out.

Jane swallowed and caught her breath. "Please, get Elsa-Eska."

"Honey, I…"

"Rick, please. I need her here."

Rick looked at Dr. Jenkins and saw the concentration on her face, then at the monitor—110, and back to Jane. Her eyes were closed tightly. At first, he thought she was just tired, but then he saw her lips move. Leaning in, he detected the nearly inaudible sound of the Klyvian Song.

"Okay," Rick whispered. "Hold on. We'll be back as soon as we can."

Rick didn't bother telling Dr. Jenkins he was leaving. When he was out of the room, he broke into a full sprint down the hall and out of the building to the Jeep.

Whether it was luck, divine intervention, or the fact that no one was able to leave their television sets, Rick found he was the only one on the road. He pushed the Jeep to its limits, pegging the speedometer on the straights and taking curves at dangerously high speeds. Had a police officer seen him, he would have gotten a lot more than a ticket. He covered the distance back to the ranch in half the usual time. Aldi was already outside when Rick skidded to a stop in front of the house. Rick was about to get out of the Jeep when Elsa-Eska appeared from the house and made her way toward him. They were both dressed in appropriate human clothes. Without need of explanation, Aldi and Elsa-Eska got into the Jeep and buckled their seatbelts.

Seeing the question on Rick's face, Elsa-Eska answered it before he asked. "Jane called and said you were coming to get us." Anticipating the next question, she added, "She and the baby are okay."

Rick pushed his foot down on the accelerator and spun the Jeep around on the dirt driveway.

Very calmly, Aldi said, "Jane said to tell you not to drive like a maniac."

Rick nodded and smiled at how well his wife knew him.

"Rick," Aldi asked. "What is a *maniac*?"

When they entered the maternity ward, everyone stared at Aldi and Elsa-Eska. It was always that way whenever the two Klyvians were in public; first came astonishment at their unusual height and utter beauty, then curiosity as to how anyone so tall could move with such poise. In the last six months, Aldi had put on about thirty pounds of muscle. He was powerfully built, imposing even, yet he moved with the agility of a professional athlete. And Elsa-Eska, who was noticeably pregnant, moved with the elegance of a ballerina. Together, they gave the impression of royalty—confident, yet not ostentatious.

Outside Jane's room, Aldi stopped. "I will wait here. Jane asked for Elsa-Eska."

Rick hesitated, then nodded. "Thanks, brother. I'll come back out in awhile."

When Rick and Elsa-Eska stepped into the room, Jane had just endured the latest contraction. Through her exhaustion, her face lit up at the sight of Elsa-Eska. Dr. Jenkins did a double take when she saw her, but turned her attention immediately back to Jane and the baby. Rick looked at the monitor and noticed the baby's heart rate was hovering just above 100. Jane reached a hand out toward them.

Elsa-Eska looked curiously at all the equipment surrounding Jane and the lines sticking into her, then at Dr. Jenkins. She moved tentatively toward the side of the bed. Rick stayed back.

"It's okay," Jane said. "Dr. Jenkins, this is my sister Elsa. I would like her to stay for the delivery."

Dr. Jenkins looked curiously at Elsa-Eska and then nodded. "As long as she understands that she may have to step aside."

"How do you feel?" Elsa-Eska asked, her eyes soft and compassionate.

"I'm okay, but the baby is having a hard time of it. Dr. Jenkins, would you please explain to Elsa what's happening."

Elsa-Eska tilted her head toward the doctor. Rick took a few steps closer.

"See the monitor there?" Dr. Jenkins gestured with her chin. "That number on the left is the baby's heart rate. It needs to be up around 160 to 180, but as you can see, we can't seem to get it above 110. It's normal for the heart rate to decrease during the contraction, but it's supposed to go back up when the contraction stops. This little one, however, seems to be having a rough day. She can't seem to get her heart rate back up on her own. If it drops below 100, and stays there, the baby will be in distress and, well, we'll have an emergency delivery on our hands."

Apparently, Jane had already been briefed on the situation. Rick, on the other hand, had not heard the term *emergency delivery* until now. He was fairly certain that meant emergency surgery. Elsa-Eska had not heard the term either, but she did not ask for an explanation.

"What can I do?" Elsa-Eska asked.

"Just help Jane stay as comfortable as possible," Dr. Jenkins said. "The baby seems to be stable right now. I'm going to step out and check on my other two moms. I'll be right back." She got up and stood next to Rick. "Mr. Blackwell, they're going to be okay, but I need you to be ready to help us do our job." She leaned in and spoke quietly. "Your wife has refused the epidural against my recommendation. She's holding her own, but I can tell she's weakening. When it's time to deliver, she is going to need all the strength she can muster, and then some. She seems to think her sister will be able to help in some way. If things get dicey, I might ask you to intervene. Can you do that?"

Rick nodded, not completely sure what would constitute *dicey*, but afraid to ask for clarification. "Yes, I can do that."

The doctor nodded and left the room.

"Thank you for coming," Jane said.

Elsa-Eska looked again at all the equipment and then intently at Jane. "I do not know these things Dr. Jenkins says. I do not understand all this. But I will do whatever you ask."

"Just be with me," Jane said. She reached for Elsa-Eska's hand and placed it on her stomach. "When the next contraction comes, you'll know what to do."

Elsa-Eska looked at her questioningly. "You think I know more than I do. Remember, I have never…"

Jane held up her hand. "Just be with me. And when the next contraction comes, you will know."

Elsa-Eska looked back at Rick who simply shrugged, then back to Jane. "Okay."

The contraction came a minute later. Jane closed her eyes and started her rapid breathing technique. Rick watched with dread fear as the heart monitor revealed the affect of the contraction on mother and child. Jane's heart rate spiked and the baby's heart rate began its decline. At first, Elsa-Eska did nothing but watch. A curious look came over her and she looked down at her hand resting on Jane's stomach. Then slowly, but deliberately, she placed her other hand on Jane's stomach and closed her eyes. Her lips began to move in concert with Jane's.

Rick looked quickly up at the monitor. The baby's heart rate dropped to 97. His heart sank. Where there had been a flicker of hope that Elsa-Eska's presence would somehow make a difference, it was now cold and empty. He turned to go look for Dr. Jenkins when movement at the bed caught his attention. Turning back around, he found Elsa-Eska leaning over Jane's bed just above her stomach. He glanced back up at the monitor—holding at 97. Elsa-Eska's head dipped lower until she was touching Jane's stomach with her forehead. He looked back at the monitor. The baby's heart rate bumped up to 98, then 99, then skipped to 103. Five seconds later, it jumped to 105, then 110. Whatever she was doing was working. By the time the contraction ended, Jane's breathing returned to normal, and the baby's heart rate was a hopeful 120.

Elsa-Eska opened her eyes and stood to her full height. She kept one hand on Jane's stomach and caressed Jane's head with the other. "Jane," she said, "was that a contraction?"

"Yes. And you did great." Jane sighed heavily and breathed a prayer of thanks.

Elsa-Eska cocked her head. "What did I do?"

Rick moved next to Elsa-Eska and put his arm around her shoulder. "Just what you always do. You were here."

And so it was for the next hour. Every time a contraction came, Elsa-Eska helped the baby get through it. Jane even said the pain was less intense as long as Elsa-Eska was touching her. By the time Dr. Jenkins returned, the baby's heart rate was holding steady at 150.

"I'm sorry it took me so long," Dr. Jenkins apologized. "Both of my other moms delivered almost at the same time. We've been trying to reach Dr..." The readings on the monitor caused her to stop mid-sentence. "Well, now, it looks like we're doing much better in here." She pulled up her chair and examined Jane's progress. "In fact, you're getting very close to delivery. Let me get my birthing team in here and see if we can bring this little fighter into the world."

A minute later, Dr. Jenkins returned with two nurses. One was pushing a cart equipped with a bassinet and warming lamp. The other wheeled a flat, cloth-covered tray from the corner of the room to the foot of the bed. Dr. Jenkins resumed her position and started issuing instructions. She reminded Rick of a quarterback calling a play just before the ball is snapped. Rick stepped out of the way. Elsa-Eska stayed close to Jane's side.

Rick could no longer see Jane, but he could hear the miracle as it happened. He heard Dr. Jenkins tell Jane it was time to push. There was a volley of encouragement from the nurses. And then a rest. Then another command to push, more encouragement, and rest. Medical chatter filled the interim period between plays, while Elsa-Eska remained silent at her post. At the end of the fourth cycle of this, there was a change in the atmosphere. He heard Jane cry out as she used up her last ounce of strength, and then there was silence. Everyone froze as if to let the newest member of the huddle be heard. Rick caught his breath when he heard the tiniest of whimpers; it sounded like a kitten.

Then, as if on cue, there was a flurry of activity around the bed. One of the nurses stepped toward the receiving bassinet with a small bundle of pink. Seconds later, the tiny whimper turned into a lung-activating cry. Rick caught himself smiling as big as Aldi and found that his tear ducts were working again. Elsa-Eska leaned down, whispered into Jane's ear, kissed her on the cheek, and then stepped back to make room for Rick.

When Rick joined Jane, they were both streaming tears of joy and relief. After all she had been through, Jane was radiating a new beauty that left Rick speechless. Words became wholly inadequate, so he just leaned over and gently touched his forehead to hers. They remained that way until Dr. Jenkins spoke from behind Rick.

"Would you like to meet your daughter?"

Rick stood up and let Dr. Jenkins place the little pink bundle into Jane's arms. Immediately, their eyes connected and the baby's crying seemed to settle back into a soft cooing. Rick gazed upon his wife and new daughter, and all his previous thoughts about undivided love came washing over him again. He had never loved Jane more than he did in that moment, yet there was still room in his heart for another girl.

"Would you like to hold her?" Jane asked, lifting the bundle up to Rick.

Rick gently took her in his arms and instinctively cradled her, swaying slightly from side to side. The baby looked up at him with wide eyes and puckered lips. Her gaze was hypnotic, causing Rick to stop his swaying. Whatever bond was lacking before was instantaneously secured. Rick unconsciously moved to the right and the bright ceiling light above him shone into his daughter's eyes. She squinted and made a face. When Rick moved back to block the light, she opened her eyes again and locked them onto his.

"What's her name?" one of the nurses asked. She was holding a clipboard with three wrist identification bands.

Rick looked at her blankly. "Her name? Uh…Jane, do we have a name yet?"

Jane looked passed him to where Elsa-Eska was standing just a few feet away. "Elsa-Eska, would you like to hold her?"

Elsa-Eska closed the distance between them and allowed Rick to place his bundled daughter into her arms. She beheld her with such love that Rick thought he would cry again. He rubbed his eyes and stepped back to the head of Jane's bed.

"Well," the nurse said impatiently. "I need a name to put on your bracelets."

There was a momentary pause and then Jane answered the question. "Her name is Jalamin. Jalamin Blackwell."

Elsa-Eska looked up at Jane and opened her mouth to speak, but no words came. She closed her mouth and looked back down at Jalamin.

"Jalamin?" the nurse repeated. "That's a new one. Will you spell that?"

Jane spelled it out for her, "J-A-L-A-M-I-N. It's Klyvian."

Rick shot her a look, but she just smiled. The nurse acted as if she hadn't even heard her. When she finished writing the names of mom and dad and baby on the bracelets, she fastened one on Jane's wrist, then Rick's, and finally she attached one onto Jalamin's ankle. "Now do not remove these until you leave the hospital. We've had two other babies today, and one of them is a girl. We don't want to have any mix-ups."

When the two nurses left the room, Dr. Jenkins approached them. "Jane, you had me worried for while, but you did great. And Rick... well, you did great, too." She shook Rick's hand and gave Jane a hug.

"Thank you, Dr. Jenkins, for everything."

Then Dr. Jenkins looked up at Elsa-Eska. "Aunt Elsa, you did good with your sister. You have a very calming way about you. I don't think it would have gone as smoothly without you. Thank you for being here." She peeked into the blanket. "She's beautiful. I'm going to give you all some time. A nurse will be back in a little while to take Jalamin for her assessment. Then we'll get Jane settled in her room so she can get some rest. I'll be back to check on you soon."

The room suddenly became very quiet. Jane and Rick watched Elsa-Eska as she gazed intently upon Jalamin. "Is it okay?" Jane asked.

Elsa-Eska looked at her.

"Is it okay that we named her Jalamin?"

Elsa-Eska nodded and a tear trickled down her cheek. "You have honored my sister. You have honored me. Thank you, Jane."

"Thank *you*. It's the perfect name."

"Oh, no," Rick suddenly said. "I hate to interrupt this moment, but we forgot about Aldi."

As if he had been waiting outside for his cue, Aldi ducked into the room. His smile was bigger than usual. "A lady said I could come in. What did I miss?"

CHAPTER 29:

OLD AND NEW FRIENDS

The days following September 11 were bittersweet at the Blackwell Ranch. The barrier of isolation so cherished by the rugged individualists who dwell in the pioneer regions of the country seemed to come down, and the grief of the nation poured in like floodwaters. Rick and Jane mourned the fallen and honored the heroes right along with the rest of their countrymen; and they shared the outrage that had begun to swell even before the fires from the attacks died away. Aldi and Elsa-Eska had some sense of the magnitude of what had happened. They saw the images on the television and listened intently to Rick's and Jane's interpretation of the news reports. They kept their questions to a minimum, perhaps out of respect or simply because Rick and Jane had almost as many questions themselves. Yet in the midst of it all, there was new life at the ranch. Little Jalamin was the bright spot in an otherwise dark time. Her innocence and purity seemed to shout that evil would not, could not, prevail. She was evidence that the world would go on, changed as it was, and those who mourned now would find reason to smile again.

And there was much smiling at the Blackwell Ranch. Jalamin took center stage. Everything she did, which amounted to a few variations on the common baby themes of sleeping and eating and the other thing, was new, especially to Aldi and Elsa-Eska who had never seen a baby before. Jane secretly wondered how the two Klyvians would respond to the presence of a newborn. Would they be merely curious about her like they were with everything else? Would they want to be with her? Or would they distance themselves to leave Rick and Jane to take care of this high-maintenance newcomer? As it turned out, Aldi and Elsa-Eska were just as captivated by her as were her human parents. They hovered over her like she was their own, *ooing* and *awing* over every expression and movement. And when it came to helping care for Jalamin, they pitched in like it was just one more aspect of the Klyvian way. Aldi, who seemed to never sleep, took the late night shift, allowing Jane to go back to bed immediately after each feeding. By the second night, she was already feeling rested. Elsa-Eska was such a help during the day, it was like having a full-time nanny. With such an abundance of help, Rick was able to avoid diaper duty altogether, which was reason enough in itself for him to smile.

The following Sunday offered the kind of morning that reminded Rick why he loved his Wyoming home so much. The sky was crystal clear, the temperature was a refreshing 52 degrees, and the only sound was that of an intermittent breeze across his massive back yard. Aldi, coming off of his night shift, joined Rick on the back deck.

"Long night?" Rick asked, his voice a little raspy from lack of use.

Aldi pondered the question for a moment before answering. "Slightly longer than the nights before. As the earth revolves around the sun, the tilt of its axis results in changes in the amount of sunlight upon different regions of the planet; the variance is most evident in the extreme northern and southern regions. At this time of the year, this region experiences a decrease in daylight each day until the winter solstice when the daylight will begin to increase again."

Rick took a sip of coffee and offered a slight nod. "*Discovery Channel?*"

Aldi nodded and continued, "The phenomenon is called *axial precession*; Earth wobbles, causing the tilt of its axis to shift between 22 and 24.5 degrees. Of course, we do not notice because it takes 26,000 years to complete one cycle. Currently, the earth is tilted 23.5 degrees."

Rick blinked and set his coffee cup on the deck rail. "Actually, what I meant was did it *seem* like a long night to you, being up with Jalamin and all? We sure appreciate your help, but it must get kind of boring."

"Oh," Aldi nodded in return. Then with a hint of a chuckle, "No. Jalamin is not boring. She is learning many things."

"Oh, yeah? Like what?"

"She does not understand axial precession yet, but she knows the things that are pleasant and the things that are not pleasant. She knows hungry and tired. She knows when she needs a new diaper. She knows all of our voices. She cannot say these things in words yet, but she can communicate."

"Really?" Rick had never considered the learning processes of babies. He always thought of them as fairly passive at this stage with real learning coming much later.

"Oh, yes. She communicates with her face. If you look at her long enough, you can learn what she is feeling by her face."

That last comment stung a little. Rick hadn't seen anything in his daughter's expressions that communicated anything beyond the base emotions of anger and contentment; and even then the specifics were unknowable. Either he wasn't smart enough to understand baby communication or he wasn't spending enough time with his daughter. If the truth be known, he was smart enough to know which was the case.

Aldi continued. "I am teaching her the Song of my people. She likes the part about Jalamin. I have told her much of the one who has the same name." Aldi's smile broadened. "I think Elsa-Eska's sister is very happy to have the same name as your Jalamin. She is honored. We are all honored."

"Yeah, well…" Rick's voice trailed off. He was not awake enough to wrap his mind around axial precession; he didn't like the fact that an alien understood his daughter better than he did; and the way Aldi and Elsa-Eska talked about the deceased Jalamin as if she were still alive bothered him for a reason he could not put his finger on. He looked for a way to shift the conversation to something that didn't make him feel stupid, negligent, or the odd man out of the spiritual club. "Say, isn't it about time to contact the Enterprise?"

"Yes," Aldi nodded.

"Would you mind waiting until later this afternoon?"

Aldi looked at him questioningly.

"Remember my friend I told you about?"

"Jacques Faber."

"That's right. Jacques and his wife will be arriving here today. If it's okay, I would like to show Jacques how your communication works."

"I thought he was not coming. Jane's mother did not come."

"Jane's mom was not far from her home when the planes stopped flying. She was able to rent a car and drive back. She's a little nervous about flying right now, but she might come out in a few months. Jacques and Diane were going to try to get back to their home, but decided to come on up since they were already in Denver. They rented a car. Should be here this afternoon."

Aldi looked up at an airliner flying high overhead. "Do you think more airplanes will fly into buildings again?"

Rick followed his gaze up at the passing jet. "It's hard to say. Actually, it's probably safer to fly now than it has been in years. But a lot of people think there will be more attacks sooner or later."

There was silence again as the two men followed different trains of thought. Aldi watched the airliner, wondering if it would safely reach its destination. Rick mentally rehearsed how he was going to introduce Jacques and Diane to Aldi and Elsa-Eska. When Aldi could no longer see the jet, he shifted his gaze back to Rick.

"I am going to be with Elsa-Eska now."

"Look! There it is." Diane Faber waved a bejeweled hand toward a hand-made sign on the left side of the highway. "Blackwell Ranch."

"Well now," Jacques replied. "Not exactly your name in lights, but it does have a certain charm to it."

"A bit primitive, don't you think?" Diane scoffed, wrinkling her nose.

"*Untamed* is the way Rick describes it."

"Looks more like un*inhabited*."

Jacques slowed the rental car and turned onto the mile long dirt road. Just off to the side of the road, Ed Tyler and Bonko were poking a stick at something on the ground.

"Or un*kempt*," Diane added. "I simply cannot imagine Jane living way out here like this. I would have bet my diamond rings she would have been begging to come back to civilization after just three months."

Jacques didn't respond. After nine years of marriage, he had learned to accept his wife's opinions. Diane had been raised in the comfort of old money and had been sheltered from what her family referred to as *the lower ranks of society.*

Jacques, on the other hand, was only too familiar with the *lower ranks.* It was there, in an impoverished section of Paris, that his entrepreneurial talent was discovered and honed. He worked hard at a variety of ventures, most of which were legal, and managed to get his small family (mother and younger sister) out of the tenements and into a real house in a safer part of the city. Then he set his sights on the next phase of his plan—an American education.

When he came to the United States, his French accent and European deportment caught the attention of Diane Warren, youngest daughter of a fourth-generation Manhattan financier. By the time she discovered Jacques's humble origins, she had already fallen in love with him. *Besides,* she convinced herself, *the lower ranks of France were probably not as low as the lower ranks of America.* And it didn't hurt that Jacques had style, confidence, and an accent that made him sound rich and sophisticated. She never told her parents about Jacques's upbringing; just that he came from an industrious family and was well qualified to provide her with a comfortable life. In truth, the first few years of their marriage were financially difficult, but Diane was able to maintain a convincing front until Jacques's plans started to pay off. Now, as far as she was concerned, everything in her life was back to the way it should be—comfortably wealthy with a high probability of serious money in the not too distant future.

"Say, do you think we should have called from that little town we passed through?" Diane glanced down at her diamond watch. "We're nearly two hours early."

Jacques grinned. "I know. I want to surprise them."

They made their way through the minefield of potholes. Jacques soaked in the atmosphere of the pioneer west while Diane buffed her fingernails. They rounded the last bend in the road, passed the barn, and came to a stop next to Jane's Jeep Cherokee. Jacques switched off the engine and turned toward his wife. "There you have it—civilization at last."

From the passenger seat, Diane assessed the structures that made up the Blackwell Ranch complex. The aged barn they had just passed was now to her left. Directly in front of her was a single story main house. In between, and set slightly back, was a smaller, but apparently newer, guest house. "Quaint."

"I like it," Jacques said as he unbuckled his seatbelt. He reached for the door latch, but did not open the door. He sat immobilized, facing forward, mouth open. Diane, sensing his hesitation, looked to see what had caught his attention. Her eyes popped open wider than seemed possible. The cause of this momentary paralysis was a sight neither of them had expected.

Elsa-Eska had just stepped out of the guest house wearing only her Klyvian robe. She strode gracefully toward the main house not twenty feet away from the stunned Fabers. At the sight of the unfamiliar vehicle, she stopped and turned to investigate. Her waist-length midnight mane caught the breeze and fluttered to the side in luxuriant waves. Diane gasped. Jacques swallowed. Elsa-Eska tilted her head curiously to one side and approached the vehicle to within ten feet. Realizing it was occupied, she smiled and said something they could not hear.

"Rick said they had taken in a couple," Jacques said once he found his voice. "She must be one of them."

"Obviously, we should have called," Diane said.

"Shall we go and make our acquaintance?" Jacques did not wait for an answer. He opened his door and stepped out of the car.

Elsa-Eska closed the distance between them and held out her hand.

She was a good six inches taller than Jacques, so he had to look up to meet her gaze. He took her hand, but did not shake it. "Hello, my name is Jacques," he said, laying his accent on a little thicker than usual.

"Yes, Rick said you were coming. I am Elsa-Eska."

"Elsa-Eska," Jacques repeated musically. "Ah, but of course. A beautiful woman would have such a name. Enchanting. " He waited for her to blush as women usually did when he turned on the charm.

"Your words have an interesting sound," she replied. "And you have hair on your face." She reached out and stroked the Frenchman's meticulously trimmed beard.

It was Jacques who did the blushing, but he enjoyed this odd twist.

Diane, watching the exchange from inside the car, raised her left eyebrow over her narrowing eyes. She steeled herself, got out of the car, and moved next to her husband. She managed a cordial, though chilly, smile and firmly stuck out her hand. "Hello. My name is Diane Faber. I am Jacques' wife." Her gaze swept Elsa-Eska from head to toe and then settled squarely upon her eyes. Though her smile remained intact, the muscles in her jaw tensed as if ready to launch a verbal assault if provoked.

Again, Elsa-Eska was completely unaffected. The invisible vibe Diane was emitting went undetected. "I am Elsa-Eska," she said sweetly. "We are so happy you are here." Noticing Diane's hand, she lifted it to examine the various samples of jewelry. Jane wore only a wedding band, so the opulent display was something new to Elsa-Eska. She offered no comment or indication of envy, as Diane was accustomed to, but simple curiosity. "Come." Elsa-Eska took a step back, drawing Diane with her like a mother coaxing her child. "Jane is this way."

Jacques followed behind them wishing he could read his wife's thoughts. Diane was used to being in control, especially upon first meetings. He knew this beautiful woman, who was obviously immune to the usual intimidation tactics, was something Diane had never encountered. *This should be interesting,* he thought. Watching Diane struggle in her too-high heals in order to keep up with the goddess's stride brought a smile to his lips. *Amusing as well.*

Elsa-Eska did not bother to knock before entering. "Jane," she called out cheerily, "Jacques and his wife, Diane Faber, are here."

Diane flinched at the odd introduction. *Obviously a dig,* she mused. *Perhaps I underestimated her.*

Jane's face lit up at the sight of her old friends. She started to jog across the room, but slowed to a cautious walk, holding her still sore stomach. She greeted them each with a hug. "Diane, Jacques, you're

here. I can't believe it. How was the drive? Not too bad, I hope."
"No, not bad at all," Jacques replied. He kissed Jane on the cheek.
"So, where is the little cherub?"
"I'm sorry," Jane replied. "You just missed her. I just put her down for her nap."
"That's okay, Janie," Diane said, assessing her. "It will give us time to catch up. Now let me look at you." Jane twirled around. "Not bad for just having a baby. You'll have your figure back in no time."
Elsa-Eska puzzled over the comment, but remained silent. She stepped back a few paces, but kept a watchful eye on the new couple.
"I see you've met Elsa," Jane said. The Fabers' early arrival precluded their plans to prepare Jacques and Diane before the big reveal. Now she was thinking fast to come up with a reasonable stall until they could all be together with Rick and Aldi.
"Indeed," Jacques replied. "She provided us with a most enchanting welcome."
Diane shot him a look before forcing a smile. "Yes, she seems very comfortable here at the Blackwell Ranch. Is this considered normal ranching attire?"
Jane read the indignation in Diane's face. Then it occurred to her what had prompted it. She had become so accustomed to seeing Elsa-Eska in her Klyvian robe that she forgot what it must look like to someone seeing her for the first time. "Oh, that," she answered nervously, quickly pulling the quilt from the back of the couch and draping it around Elsa-Eska's shoulders. "It's the whole pregnancy thing. It's just more comfortable this way."
"I see," Diane said, the air of judgment wafting off of her in waves.
"Please, do not make yourself uncomfortable on our account," Jacques said, directing his comments to Elsa-Eska. "This is your home. You should dress as you please."
Diane could see that he was enjoying the situation a little too much. He seemed to derive pleasure in her annoyance. Not to be upstaged, she shifted gears and addressed Elsa-Eska, this time in a more civil tone. "How far along are you, dear?"
"Um, about six months," Jane answered for her. "Due in December."
"Do you know who the father is?" Diane inquired, her smile morphing into a smirk. "I don't see a ring."
Jane knit her eyebrows together, surprised by her friend's brashness.
Jacques folded his arms across his chest. He hated it when his wife played dirty. Embarrassing the poor girl was a cheap shot. Looking down, he braced himself for whatever was to come—an embarrassed retreat, a defensive outburst, tears. *Oh, please, don't let it be tears*, he prayed silently. *Such a beautiful woman should never shed tears of*

sadness.

Elsa-Eska took the question seriously, but missed the insinuation. She beamed as she replied. "Aldi is the father of our child. And he is here."

She had barely gotten the words out when the door swung open. Diane and Jacques reflexively turned toward the door.

"Hey! Hey!" Rick greeted them as he strode across the living room. "I didn't expect you for another two hours." He embraced Jacques in a brotherly bear hug and kissed Diane on the cheek. "If I'd known you were coming this early, I would have been here. Sorry about that."

Jacques and Diane hardly registered Rick's presence; they were distracted by the giant ducking through the doorway behind him.

"I see you've met Elsa," Rick said. "And this is her husband Aldi. Aldi, these are some old friends of ours, Jacques and Diane Faber."

Aldi's infectious grin and easy demeanor immediately put Jacques at ease. Though dwarfed by the seven foot tall Klyvian, the 5'8" Jacques took a confident step forward and offered his hand. "Aldi," he said, "it is a pleasure to meet you."

Aldi tilted his head in curiosity and reached for Jacques's face. Jacques froze as Aldi gently touched his beard. "It is a pleasure to meet you, Jacques Faber." His voice a near perfect imitation of Jacques's French accent.

Jacques looked like he might be offended at first, but then he started to smile and nod like he just caught on to a joke. He laughed loudly and slapped Rick on the back. "Inky, you are the funny one," He said, his accent not nearly as pronounced. He waved his finger in mock reprimand. "I should have suspected you were up to something."

Rick started to laugh along with him and nodded for Jane to respond in kind. Soon everyone except for Diane was laughing, though Jacques was the only one who knew, or thought he knew, what was so funny. Aldi, thinking it was Jacques who made the joke, laughed most enthusiastically. Of course, he would have to get Rick to explain this new human humor to him later. Finally, unable to contain her annoyance any longer, Diane cleared her throat.

"Excuse me, dear," she said as politely as she could muster, "perhaps you should enlighten me as to what you find so amusing."

The laughter tapered off, as everyone else was equally eager to learn what had prompted the outburst.

Jacques stifled his last guffaw and explained. "When I called my old friend a couple weeks ago to congratulate him for his new book, he 'accidentally' mentioned their new residents. When I inquired about them, he became evasive, like he had let something slip. But instead of dropping it altogether, he said he would tell me about it when I came to Denver. Masterfully played, by the way. I can tell you I have been imagining all sorts of bizarre scenarios. Thankfully, none of them have come true...I think." He winked at Rick as if Rick would understand. "Anyway, when we arrive here today, we are greeted by this...this goddess." He gestured toward Elsa-Eska with slight bow of his head. "And then this giant of a man fondles my face and mimics me." He chuckled again. "No offence, my friend, but I prefer the touch of the woman. All strange, very strange indeed. But then I remember." Jacques tapped his finger against his temple. "Inky refers to this place as *the untamed*. I begin to think perhaps this is his clever way of welcoming us into his untamed world; his way of proving to me he has found something here that civilization cannot afford: His own little Shangri-La." He put a hand on Rick's shoulder. "Now that Inky has had his little joke, I fear we will find that it is not so untamed after all. And sadly," Jacques frowned dramatically and shook his head, "we will discover that even the goddess is not who she appears to be. She is beautiful, yes, but human after all." Jacques looked around at the blank faces. "What? Am I mistaken?"

Rick chewed his bottom lip and ran his fingers through his hair. "Well, actually..." He paused. "Actually, I think we should all sit down." He didn't wait for a response, but spun his morning chair around so that it faced the living room and sat in it.

Jane followed his lead and sat down in the easy chair closest to Rick. Elsa-Eska took the other easy chair on the other side of the fireplace, while Aldi pulled a chair from the dining table and placed it next to her. That left the couch open for Jacques and Diane.

"What's this all about?" Diane asked. "Janie? Is Jacques correct? Is this some sort of joke?"

Jane winced. "No. It's not a joke."

"What is it then?" There was a new determination about Diane. "Rick?"

Rick leaned forward with his elbows on his knee and his hands folded underneath he chin. Now that the time had come to present his big idea to Jacques, and especially since they were not able to ease them into meeting Aldi and Elsa-Eska, Rick was not as confident as he had been. He simply couldn't think of how to begin.

"Rick," Jacques said, sensing his friend's unease, "before you begin, let me just say how happy we are to be here. In light of all that's happened this past week, it is a welcome respite to be with you. And let us not forget this joyous occasion. You have a new daughter. So whatever this is about, remember, we are all friends here. You can tell us anything. And if we can help in anyway, we will."

"Oh, for heaven's sake, just tell us!" Diane cut in.

"Okay." Rick nodded as an unforeseen option popped into his brain. "I had this big long speech prepared, but if you will just bear with me." He got up and moved next to Elsa-Eska, leaned over and whispered into her ear. She nodded and Rick returned to his chair. "Rather than tell you myself, I think I'd like them to tell you."

Jacques and Diane turned their attention from Rick to Aldi and Elsa-Eska. Aldi's grin had not faded, but it no longer seemed to them part of the joke. Already they were beginning to sense it was nothing more than an outward expression of his easy character. And Elsa-Eska exuded such an unassuming demeanor that even Diane felt that her judgment was unwarranted. After a pause that seemed more like a breath than a nervous hesitation, Elsa-Eska spoke in a language only a few humans had ever heard. Diane sat back as if jolted by a shock. Jacques leaned forward as if drawn by a magnet.

"What language is that?" he asked, thoroughly intrigued.

"That is the language of our people," Elsa-Eska replied.

"I've never heard anything like it," Diane said.

"Rick asked me to speak to you the words of our people because he thought it might help you understand."

"Understand what?" Diane asked, turning toward Rick. "Rick, what's this about?"

"Elsa-Eska," Rick prompted, "go ahead and tell them."

Diane turned her attention back to Elsa-Eska.

"Aldi and I are not from this world." Her words were as matter-of-fact as if she had said they were from California.

Jacques sat back and stroked his beard, but he kept his eyes fixed upon Elsa-Eska. Diane, however, was somewhat undone. "Jane? You said this wasn't a joke."

"It's not."

"But how…" She fell silent when she felt Jacques' hand upon her arm.

"Please, continue," Jacques said.

For the next fifteen minutes, Elsa-Eska explained to them how she and Aldi came to be in Wyoming at the Blackwell Ranch. She gave a brief explanation of the Mission of Ka-Rel, mentioning that there were others of their kind in other parts of the world; but she left out the deaths of Jalamin and Arkel. She gave a fairly thorough account of their last six months living with Rick and Jane, and when she came to the conclusion of her report, she simply stopped.

All was silent for several minutes. A few times, either Jacques or Diane started to say something, but then fell silent again. Rick and Jane waited nervously for their reaction. Rick recalled his own leap off the edge of belief and prepared himself for someone to faint. By the looks of things, he was guessing it would be Diane. Aldi and Elsa-Eska, of course, were perfectly comfortable with the silence.

It was Diane who finally found the ability to put her thoughts into audible words. "I think I need some fresh air." She got up from the couch and backed away from the group until she reached the door. Then she was gone.

Jane started to go after her, but Jacques stopped her. "She'll be fine," he said. "Besides, where will she go? She's such a city girl, I doubt she'll get further than the rental car."

Whether it was the disruption in the silence or the fact that Diane was no longer present, Jacques seemed to be free from his trance. He asked a question about their ship, which Aldi was eager to answer. Then it was all business. Jacques posed question after question about everything from the ship's propulsion system to how they were able to maintain life support apparently indefinitely. Whatever it was— Elsa-Eska's unidentifiable power of persuasion or Aldi's plausible answers to every space travel conundrum he could think of or a combination of the two—Jacques made the leap to belief with relative ease. To Rick's amazement and relief, Jacques actually began to see the business potential of Klyvian technology without Rick having to introduce the notion.

Now that all of Jacques' questions seemed to be aimed at Aldi, Elsa-Eska excused herself from the conversation. Catching Jane's attention, she got up and moved toward the front door. Jane followed and together they went outside to find Diane. They found her standing next to the rental car, arms folded tightly across her chest, eyes staring blankly out into the distance. Jane motioned for Elsa-Eska to hold back as she approached her.

"Diane? It's me, Jane." She eased up next to her and put her arm around her shoulder. Diane was a statue. "It's a bit of a shock at first, isn't it?" She decided not to mention her own easy acceptance of the truth. "Rick fainted when he first met them." Diane let her eyes flicker toward Jane. Jane took it as a hint she was going in the right direction. "Yeah, he passed out right in the middle of the road. You should have seen the knot on the back of his head." The corner of Diane's mouth twitched with the beginnings of a grin. Jane squeezed Diane's shoulder a little. "I think you're handling this pretty great. It's not everyday you meet someone from another world. In fact, not everyone gets this privilege. It's pretty incredible if you think about it."

Diane turned to look at her. "It is, isn't it?"

"Yeah, it really is."

"Jane?"

"Yes."

"The woman, Elsa-Eska, there's something about her."

"What do you mean?"

Diane sniffed and rubbed her eye. "I don't know…it's hard to explain. When she looks at me, it feels like she's looking right through me. No, it's more like she's looking *into* me. I've never felt so, so vulnerable. Which is ironic since, well, she's the one wearing that skimpy robe."

Jane didn't know how to respond, so she just nodded.

Diane turned to face her again. "What's with that robe anyway? She doesn't even look that pregnant. Does she always dress like that?"

"It's sort of their way," Jane tried to explain. "Apparently clothing is more of a human thing. They wear them for our benefit. And around here where there's nobody but us, I guess the robe is a compromise on our part. Funny, I hardly notice it anymore."

Diane managed a weak chuckle. "Well, I guess if I looked like that…" She didn't finish, but Jane understood. Then she became serious again. "But the way she looks at me, I feel…I feel…I can't explain it, but I don't like it."

"It's okay."

"No, it's not okay. I don't know what it is, but I don't like the way she makes me feel…about myself. And it doesn't have anything to do with looks. Sure, she's amazing. Jacques sure noticed, but I don't even care about that. It's something else." She sniffed again. "She's…she's good. And I'm…not."

"Oh, Diane." Jane gave her another squeeze. "That's not true."

"Yes it is. Janie, I'm not really a nice person."

"Yes you are."

"Well, I'm nice to you, but only because I like you. I'm just not that nice to other people unless *I* want to be. There, I said it. That's the truth. You know, I don't think I've ever said that before."

"That's good, don't you think?"

"I don't know. I suppose." Diane rubbed her eyes again. "But why now? Why here? I tell you, it's that woman. There's something about her. When she looked at me…" Diane sighed. "She must hate me."

"No. Of course she doesn't."

"I think she does."

"Would you like to talk to her?"

Diane didn't respond at first. She just stood there. Then, "She's standing behind us, isn't she?"

"Yup."

"I can't avoid her, can I?"

"Nope."

Diane sighed heavily. "Okay."

Jane turned and motioned for Elsa-Eska to join them. When she came close, Diane sensed her presence before she saw her. She tensed as her defenses started to come up.

Elsa-Eska said nothing to Diane. She made no attempt to confront or console. She simply stood with her. Then, quite unexpectedly, she said, "Jane. I think you should go and check on Jalamin." Then to Diane, "Will you come with me? I want to show you something." She started to walk down the road toward the barn.

Diane met Jane's gaze and then turned to follow Elsa-Eska. Jane watched them until they disappeared around the corner of the barn.

CHAPTER 30:

ACCEPTANCE

When Jane went back inside, she found the men had moved to the dining room table. Aldi and Jacques were deep in conversation about something devoid of any mental handles for her to grasp. Jacques was using such technical jargon that she was sure he was the only one for a hundred miles who knew what he was talking about. Aldi, was listening intently. Though there was no way he could have understood Jacques' terminology, he seemed to be following the general idea. He had drawn something on a sheet of paper to which Jacques was adding his own notes and becoming visibly excited. Rick caught Jane's questioning expression and shrugged. He obviously didn't understand it either. He just sat back and enjoyed the satisfaction that his big idea was no longer an intangible notion in his own mind. It was blossoming before his very eyes. Jacques and Aldi were becoming fast friends, and the fact that they were from two different worlds seemed about as significant as the fact that Jacques and Rick were from different sides of the Atlantic Ocean.

"Where's Diane?" Rick asked as Jane came up behind him and draped her arms over his shoulders.

"She's with Elsa-Eska."

"Which one should I be most concerned about?"

Jane flashed her crooked smile. "Neither. Diane's a little frazzled right now, but she's in good hands. They just need some time together. What's going on in here?"

Rick chuckled and pointed to Aldi. "That one found a new friend." Then he pointed to Jacques. "And that one just hit the lottery."

Jane rested her chin on the top of Rick's head. "What do you mean, *lottery*?"

"I think my big idea might not have been big enough. Jacques has already dropped a few hints about patents. Of course, that's all Greek to Aldi."

Jane's eyebrows drew together and she moved her head next to Rick's so she could whisper into his ear. "You don't think Jacques will take advantage of Aldi, do you?"

"Jacques Faber?" The question caught him by surprise and he spoke louder than he intended. Jacques looked over at him, and Rick had to think fast. "Jacques Faber believes in Klyvians."

Jacques shot him a quizzical look and turned his attention back to Aldi's drawings.

"Shh," Jane shushed in his ear. "Rick, I'm serious. I think we should take this slow. I know Jacques is your friend, *our* friend, but its been five years. People change, you know. He's got to be under a lot of pressure with this new business, and coming off this disappointment in Denver, I can understand how he might see Aldi as, to use your words, a winning lottery ticket."

"Don't worry about it, Jane. Jacques is solid. Besides, would it be so bad if Aldi could help make *our* friend's business a success?"

"No, as long as Aldi understands exactly how he's being used."

"That's a little strong, don't you think?"

"Is it?"

Rick didn't respond. Jane was usually very insightful when it came to people, and he trusted her more than he trusted himself. He considered his two friends. Jacques was a good man, but he was also an ambitious man with a somewhat more "flexible" perspective on the rules of engagement. He had never broken the law, at least not an American law that Rick knew of, but he had pressed them to the limits on several occasions. Rick could not think of a time when Jacques Faber did not get what he wanted. Then there was Aldi. Aldi's goodness was beyond question and he was wise in things that Rick was only just beginning to consider. Still, he was naïve when it came to human ways. Thus far, his time on Earth was under the very protective watch of Rick and Jane. Considering the two men together, Rick had to admit that in this present context, Jacques had the persuasive advantage. It was within the realm of possibility that he could easily manipulate the eager-to-please Klyvian. Rick's thoughts were interrupted by a cry from the nursery.

Jane whispered into his ear, "Aldi trusts you. Be careful." Then she kissed him on the cheek and went to tend to Jalamin.

When he refocused his attention toward the conversation at the table, he heard Aldi say, "Would you like to see it now?"

"See what?" Rick asked.

Jacques answered. "Aldi said he is going to contact his ship. Yes, I would love to see it."

Aldi stood up from the table. "I will get my communicator and meet you on the deck."

When Aldi was gone, Jacques addressed Rick. "This is the most amazing thing I have ever seen. Aldi is exceptional. In thirty minutes he showed me things we could not have imagined in ten years. It's hard to believe he's been here for just six months. His English is better than mine was after two years."

"But you do believe, right?" Rick asked. "You understand he's not human."

The straightforward statement brought Jacques back to the real issue at hand. "Yes, that is what Elsa-Eska said, but they're so much like us. And Aldi's ideas are..."

"Jacques," Rick interrupted, "they *do* seem like us in a lot of ways, and I admit it's easy to forget, but the reality is they are not human. And though they have adapted quite well, they do not think like humans. They have learned to mimic us, but they are not exactly like us."

It was as if Jacques' mind was just now accepting the fact that he had been talking to a being from another world. He had heard the words, but the implications were slow in finding a place to settle. "Was it easy for you at first?" he asked, now ready to deal with his own belief.

"No, it wasn't." Rick reflected to that day on the road that now seemed so much like a dream. "It was unnerving. It changed my entire understanding of reality. And that wasn't easy for me at all. Until I met them, my thoughts about life beyond this world were constructed from scenes from movies —little green men, creatures popping out of your chest, *My Favorite Martian*. But now," Rick shrugged, "I'm a lot more open to things. Can I tell you something?"

"Anything."

"They've actually got me thinking about God."

Jacques gave him a slight shake of the head. "I'm not following you. What do they have to do with religion?"

"Not religion," Rick replied. "God. You know, the Supreme Being. The jury's still out for me, but Jane is convinced that God is the same Being they refer to as the Before One."

"Hmm." Now Jacques was nodding. "Interesting proposition. I wonder what would happen if the world found out about them. We usually think of this sort of thing in the realm of science, but there are religious implications. How would the religions of the world respond?"

"Believe me, I've thought about that a lot. It makes me shudder."

"Lucky for Aldi and Elsa-Eska they landed out here in the middle of nowhere. Or maybe it was divine providence."

Rick eyed his old friend. "I didn't think you went for that sort of thing."

"I'm not saying I do," Jacques agreed. "Then again, yesterday I didn't believe in extra-terrestrial intelligent life either."

"So what? Now you're a man of faith?"

Jacques tilted his head in consideration. "You're asking me to believe you have two aliens living with you."

"Yes, but you've seen them with your own eyes."

"True, I have seen them, but the claim that they are from another world has not yet been proven. This could still be an elaborate hoax. You could be lying. They could be in on the hoax or they could be insane."

"But you know me," Rick said in defense.

Jacques smiled and nodded. "Yes. And that's why I'm willing to believe something that is at first glance unbelievable. At the moment, I trust you more than I trust my own inclinations. If that is faith, then today I am a man of faith."

Rick noticed Aldi standing outside on the deck. He was ready to change the subject, so he gestured toward the window. "Aldi's ready. Come on, you're going to like this."

As the three men made their way across Rick's massive back yard to the little rise in the land, Rick explained to Jacques how the Enterprise stayed concealed behind the moon, coming out once a month for communications with the landing parties. Hearing himself talk about such things to another human besides Jane, it occurred to him how fantastic is sounded. He decided to let Aldi explain the rest.

When they got to the spot Aldi had found provided the best transmission and reception, he stopped to power up his communication device. Jacques watched with keen interested, noting the design of the case, the lighted symbols upon which Aldi's fingers danced, and the liquid black surface. He looked back at Rick, grinning with mounting excitement. The sound of radio static drew his attention back to the device. Finally, after several adjustments, Aldi withdrew his hand and a three-dimensional image began to materialize above the shiny surface.

Jacques gasped at the sight and uttered under his breath, "Three dimensional display. Amazing."

The figure was that of a woman. She was only six inches tall, but the resemblance to the real life Klyvian was unmistakable. In fact, she looked so much like Elsa-Eska that even Rick did a double take. The high resolution of the image rendered her in near perfect detail. Even the expression of recognition upon her face, as Aldi's image materialized on her end of the connection, was clearly visible.

Aldi and the woman spoke for several minutes in Klyvian. Once again, hearing the Klyvian language spoken at such length, Rick noticed a musical quality to it. It had a cadence and melody to it that made Rick believe a musician might actually be able to play it, perhaps on a violin or a cello. It was hypnotic. Rick had to shake his head once to keep from falling into a sort of daydream trance.

Several hundred miles away, in a tax-funded installation that did not officially exist, two young men sat before an array of computers and sophisticated listening equipment. The events of September 11 brought a new sobriety to their work and the two men were much more attentive to their task than they had been a month earlier.

"Dave," the young man named Jim said. "Check out sector two at twenty-one centimeters bandwidth. I think your mystery signal is back."

Dave did not respond. He was monitoring a spy satellite over a suspected terrorist training camp in Afghanistan. Jim tossed a pencil, hitting Dave on the arm.

"What?" he said angrily, lifting one side of his earphones back away from his ear.

"That signal you've been playing with…your new moon signal… it's back."

Dave pulled his headphones all the way off. "New moon?" Then it registered. "Oh! Put it on speaker." He pulled last month's log from the shelf above him and flipped through the pages. "Where's it coming from? Can you tell?"

Jim read the screen in front of him. "Definitely North America. Pacific Northwest. Looks like Wyoming."

"Date. What's today's date."

"September 16."

"Ha! You owe me a hundred bucks," Dave flipped the log book onto the desk in triumph.

Jim held up a finger. "Hold on a minute." He rolled back in his chair to the rack of equipment behind him and fiddled with the controls.

"What are you doing?" Dave asked.

"Remember I told you the signal was massive?"

"Yeah."

"I'm routing the signal to that new archive vault we just got. Maybe I can capture enough to get something."

Dave watched as his partner rolled back to his control panel and click through several commands on his computer. "Well?"

Jim grinned. "We're capturing something, but I don't know if we're going to be able to read any of it. I've never seen a signal structured like this. I think its audio and video, but there's something odd about it."

"Like what?"

Jim's grin morphed to disbelief. "It's layered. If it *is* video, we'd need a truckload of monitors to show it all. Even then, I doubt it would make much sense. Look at this." He pointed to the monitor in front of him. "This is one slice."

Dave rolled his chair over to Jim to get a better look. "What is that?"

"No idea." Jim turned his head to see the image from different angles. "Could be anything."

"What do you mean by *slice*?" Dave asked.

"It's a layer, just one out of thousands," Jim replied.

Dave leaned back in his chair. "Like an MRI."

"What do you mean?"

"Magnet Resonance Imaging," Dave explained. "Haven't you ever had an MRI?"

"No."

"It's like an X-ray, but three dimensional."

Jim turned toward Dave, nodding. "That's what it is. This thing is three dimensional."

"Great," Dave said. "Now all we need is a 3-D monitor to show it."

"Is there such a thing?" Jim asked.

Dave shook his head and chuckled. "Not that I know of. Not yet anyway."

The woman on the display surface bowed her head slightly and stepped into nothingness, disappearing from view. She was replaced by a figure Rick recognized as the man he had seen the previous month—Aldi's father. Aldi and his father spoke only for a minute before he, too, with a nod of the head, stepped out of view. Another woman whom Rick did not recognize stepped into view. She and Aldi spoke briefly and then she was gone. Aldi touched a symbol on the side of the device and the transmission ended.

"That's amazing," Jacques said. "The image was as clear as you and I standing here. I would love to see the schematic if you've got one."

"Schematic?" Aldi repeated.

"It's a drawing," Rick offered. "It shows what your communicator looks like on the inside."

"Why do you need a drawing," Aldi asked. "We have the real thing here. Would you like to see the inside?"

"Actually, I wouldn't know what I was looking at. But I'd sure like to let one of my technicians have a look at it. Is that possible?"

Rick stepped between them. "We can talk about that later. Let's head back to the house. I'm sure Diane and Elsa-Eska will be back soon, and you all haven't even seen the baby."

When they got back to the house, they found the girls sitting in the living room. Diane and Elsa-Eska were sitting close to each other on the couch, while Jane sat curled up in one of the easy chairs. Diane looked like a different woman; she was holding Jalamin and chatting with Elsa-Eska like they were old friends. Jacques knelt down on the floor next to his wife to get a good look at the baby. Rick motioned for Aldi to follow him into the kitchen. "Aldi and I will get some drinks. You all just relax."

Inside the kitchen, Rick put together a tray of glasses and grabbed a pitcher of tea from the refrigerator. "So, what's the news from the Enterprise?" he asked.

"Mallia has given birth to her baby."

Rick thought for a moment. "Mallia and Kai-Tai are in Ireland?"

"Yes. They have a son. He is the first Klyvian to be born on Earth."

"Wow, that's great." Rick wondered about his and Jane's counterparts in Ireland. Were they as protective of Mallia and Kai-Tai as he and Jane were of Aldi and Elsa-Eska? Then it occurred to him how few humans were aware of the incredible events taking place. The earth had just become the home world of a being whose heritage originated on another planet.

"Yes, it is very good," Aldi agreed.

"Say, I recognized your father. Was that Elsa-Eska's mother you were talking to?"

Aldi nodded. "And the other was the mother of Mallia."

"We should have waited for Elsa-Eska. I bet she would have liked to talk to her mom."

"They will speak tonight."

"Oh, I didn't realize you were going to talk to them again so soon."

"Elsa-Eska and her mother will speak for a very long time."

Rick grinned at this unexpected similarity between Klyvians and humans. "I know what you mean. Jane and her mom can talk for hours. It's going to be hard for Elsa-Eska when the Enterprise leaves, isn't it?"

"Yes, we will miss our families, but that is the way of the mission. I am glad we have our family here."

"Me, too."

Back in the living room, Jalamin was casting her spell upon the Fabers. Jacques was holding her and rocking her back and forth.

274   *Michael E. Gunter*

He was standing next to the couch close to Elsa-Eska. "Rick, your daughter is beautiful; just like her mother."

"Thank you," Rick replied. "I must agree."

"Jalamin is a most interesting name. Where does it come from?" In the space of Rick's hesitation, Elsa-Eska spoke up. "Jalamin is the name of my sister."

"Oh, you have a sister," Diane said. "Is she part of your mission?" Jane and Rick exchanged glances, feeling the heaviness of the question.

Elsa-Eska took a deep breath and it looked as if she might defer the question to Aldi. But she collected herself and continued. "Jalamin and Arkel were in Iraq. They were killed."

A silence fell upon the gathering. Jacques continued to gently rock Jalamin, though his mind was trying to absorb what she had just said. Diane looked down at the floor, embarrassed for having broached what was now obviously a painful subject. Rick and Jane both tried to think of something tactful to say. Only Jalamin remained unaffected. She simply yawned and settled deeper into Jacques' arms.

Elsa-Eska, sensing the change in mood, placed a reassuring hand on Diane's arm. "It's okay. Jane honors my sister with her child. Jalamin is pleased to share her name with this little one." She reached up and gave little Jalamin's foot a squeeze. At her touch, the baby squealed happily.

The rest of the afternoon was surprisingly normal. Rick and Jane described their life in the untamed for Jacques and Diane. Jacques found it fascinating, but Diane thought it a bit over romanticized. She dropped several hints, some not so subtle, that she could never live in such a rural environment. This was partly to nix any notions Jacques might be entertaining about having his own midlife wilderness adventure and partly because that's just the way Diane was. In turn, Jacques filled in the details about his new business venture. Rick and Jane both reciprocated with a fair amount of questions, while Diane's body posture made it clear she had no interest in such tedious affairs.

When the conversation finally got back around to Aldi and Elsa-Eska, Diane perked up considerably. Jacques' questions were almost entirely of a technical nature, while Diane's were decidedly more personal. She asked about Aldi's and Elsa-Eska's families, avoiding any further mention of Jalamin, and she seemed especially interested in their impressions of life on Earth. She expressed a few times how she would love to show them the more civilized side of America, doing her best to give them an idea of her life in the city.

Aldi and Elsa-Eska were gracious, as was their nature, but by early evening Elsa-Eska was getting tired. Without the usual tactical maneuverings that are part of human social protocol, Elsa-Eska unexpectedly stood up and announced she was going back to her home.

"Must you leave so soon?" Diane asked.

Elsa-Eska smiled unapologetically and said, "I am tired and I wish to be alone with my Aldi."

Aldi looked like the kid who had just been chosen first to be on the cool team. His smile broadened as he stood.

"Oh, well, okay," said Diane. "If you must."

Elsa-Eska reached for Diane's hand and pulled her up to her feet. "Goodnight, Diane. I look forward to being with you tomorrow." With that she leaned over and touched her forehead to Diane's.

Diane started to pull back, but had nowhere to go as Elsa-Eska had her by both hands and was drawing her close to her. When their foreheads touched, Diane felt a warm sensation pulse through her body. She gasped. When Aldi approached her, Diane's eyes widened. She was still not sure what to make of the big man. As their foreheads touched, she felt the same warm sensation and felt her heart flutter. She remained speechless.

Jacques thought he was prepared as Elsa-Eska and Aldi turned toward him.

"Jacques," Elsa-Eska said, "we will speak more tomorrow. I wish to hear about your home in France." She leaned down, touching her forehead to his. He felt his knees go weak.

Aldi caught him by the arm and lifted him back up as Elsa-Eska stepped back. Instead of the forehead touch, Aldi embraced Jacques in a manly bear hug like he had seen Rick do earlier. "I am glad to meet you Jacques. Tomorrow we will speak again. Goodnight, friend."

Jacques half-fell onto the couch next to Diane, "Tomorrow indeed."

CHAPTER 31:

DEAL

⤳

"I must say," Jacques said after Aldi and Elsa-Eska excused themselves to their own house, "I am impressed with the company you've been keeping out here. I'm glad you didn't try to tell me about this over the telephone. I don't know that I would have believed you, and I may not have come. But as it turns out, our going to Denver was not a waste of time after all. It put us here. I do believe this Klyvian technology could change the whole game, and Saber Technologies will be right on the cutting edge. I could spend the rest of my life on just what Aldi showed me today."

Jane squeezed Rick's hand and gave him a coaxing look.

"Yeah, about that," Rick said. "We should really think this through before we change the world."

"Oh, sure. Patents will have to be filed; there will be many tests to run; we'll have to figure out how to make this stuff compatible with human technology. It could take a year or longer before we get the first piece into production."

"Actually, I was thinking more about Aldi. He's still pretty naïve about the ways of our people." Jane stifled a giggle as Rick's choice of words sounded so Klyvian. He continued, "Aldi is eager to please. He'll give you anything you ask. I just want to make sure he…"

"Say no more," Jacques cut in. "You don't need to worry about that. I personally guarantee he will be generously compensated. He's going to be a wealthy man."

"That's what I'm talking about. Aldi has no concept of wealth. Apparently, it's not important to them."

"You don't say."

"Jacques," Rick said, a firmness creeping into his voice, "you and I have known each other for a long time. I do trust your intentions, but I have to say I'm more than a little concerned."

"Rick," Jacques replied, countering with a lilt of levity, "*you* invited me here. This was *your* idea."

"I know it was my idea, and now I'm saying we need to proceed with caution." Rick weighed his next words carefully. "I won't let anyone take advantage of them."

Jacques smiled innocently and held his hands up in defense—a technique Rick had seen numerous times in the corporate world. "You've always been loyal to your *friends*. I appreciate that. Really, I do. In fact, it's *our* friendship that brought us up here when I should have been heading back home. I didn't mention this before, but there are rumors floating around that the government is already fishing for new contracts. In case you didn't know, we just went to war. Technology, Rick, technology is going to give us the edge in that war. My partners are begging me to get back home before our competitors get their foot in ahead of ours. Do you know what I told them?"

Rick shook his head.

"I told them I was going to spend some time with my friends and celebrate the birth of their first born child because this is what's important in life." He slowly shook his head. "If those attacks last week didn't make that point clear..." He didn't finish his thought. He didn't need to.

Rick tried to discern how much of this display was genuine and how much was business strategy.

Jacques played his final card. "I won't let anyone take advantage of Aldi. And that's a friend's promise."

Rick had to hand it to him, Jacques was convincing. He decided to play along. "Okay. We'll see how this plays out, but I want to make a request."

"Name it."

"Jane and I want to represent Aldi. Whatever arrangements you make with him, you run them by us."

Jacques considered the request. "Deal," he said with a nod. "I wouldn't want it any other way." Then a smile broke upon his face. "You and me, together again. Just like old times, eh, Inky?" He stuck out his hand.

Rick shook it.

"Jane," Jacques said, offering his hand to her. "Are you in agreement?"

Jane took his hand warily and gave it a shake. "Yes."

"You know," Jacques said, "this might actually solve a problem."

"What problem?"

"This arrangement is unprecedented. Given Aldi's circumstances, it's going to be a bit of a trick to make this work on paper. He has no identity, no social security number, no past that can be checked. I'm just not sure how my investors or my partners will react to my hiring someone so…unidentifiable. But if we ran everything through you, put your name on the page…" Jacques chuckled at the oddity of it. "Well, at least you're human."

"Yeah," Rick mused aloud, "at least that."

"Well, then," Jacques said, clapping his hands together once. "Shall we toast our new partnership? Have you got anything to drink out here?"

Diane, who had been only half-listening to the conversation, perked up at the mention of a drink. "Yes, yes, let's have a drink. It's about that time, I'd say."

Jacques leaned over and whispered to Rick, "Actually, its always about that time for Diane."

CHAPTER 32:

FOR THE GOOD OF THE MISSION

○≃

It started out as one of those perfect dreams; the kind that, if it were possible to record and replay dreams, would have been saved in a "Favorites" folder for easy and frequent access. They were on a cruise ship, just Rick and Jane, reclining in lounge chairs on the main deck. The air was warm and heavy, but the breeze from the ocean made it pleasant. Jane was stunning, her bikinied body trim and tan, and her hair nearly as long as Elsa-Eska's. He could not take his eyes from her, nor she from him. They were talking and laughing and sipping tropical drinks that seemed to always be freshly poured. It was one of those perfect dreams.

Then, something about the scene felt wrong. Something was missing. He looked around, but could not remember what it was that should have been there, but wasn't. He tried to focus his attention back to Jane, but that something was pulling hard. Then it came to him—Jalamin. Where was Jalamin? Panic ensued as the absence of his little girl brought a cloud of terror over him. He tried to stand, but it was as if he had been tied to the chair. He tried to tell Jane, but he couldn't make his lips work right.

Then he saw her. Jalamin—a future Jalamin of maybe three or four years old—was climbing up onto the rail of the ship. She looked at him, smiled and waved, and put one foot up on the rail like she was going to stand on it. He tried to scream, but his head felt like it was in a soundproof box. Jalamin stood slowly on the rail like a tightrope walker; arms out for balance, one foot directly in front of the other. She looked back at him, flashed the mischievous crooked grin she had inherited from her mother, and began to walk backward along the rail. It looked so natural, like she had done it a hundred times, that Rick felt the panic begin to wane. But just as he was starting to relax, he saw that she was getting close to a bend in the rail. He tried to call out to her again, but the box silenced him. He looked to Jane only to find that her eyes were closed. When he looked back toward the rail, Jalamin was gone.

Terror ripped through his body enough to release the bonds of the deck chair. Free from his prison, he sprinted across the deck and dove over the rail. It was a long way down to the water, and he hung in the air for an impossible length of time. Just before he hit the water, he found that he was facing up toward the rail of the ship. There he saw Jalamin, now a baby again, safe in Jane's arms. Aldi and Elsa-Eska were standing with them. They were all enjoying the view, completely out of harm's way and completely unaware of him.

The next thing he knew, he was under the water. The light from the sun dimmed and the bottom of the ship became smaller as he sank deeper into the sea. Down he went as if being pulled by something. He could not remember how to swim. The pressure increased rapidly and his ears began to ache. His chest felt like it was being crushed by iron bands. His breath now depleted, he felt his body begin to convulse. He knew it was the end.

By now, the sea around him was very dark; watery shadows moved in slow motion. He noticed a light of some kind coming up from the depths. It occurred to him that maybe he was already dead and the light that was coming toward him was the light he had heard about in accounts of near-death experiences. But he didn't feel dead, at least not yet. As the light drew nearer, Rick could see that it was actually two objects—two golden discs bobbing in the darkness. Was this the last thing he would see of this life? Or was it the first thing he was seeing of the next? All of this took place in a matter of only a few seconds, though in the dream realm it seemed like a very long time. Then he reached the end of himself. He could no longer fight his body's impulse to breath in. He hoped it would be quick and painless. Forcing one last image of Jane and Jalamin to appear in his mind's eye, he gave up the fight.

Rick allowed his lungs to inhale, but instead of a fatal rush of seawater, there was air ; not fresh air from above, but thick, heavy, liquid air. Somehow, he was still alive, or was this death? With his senses renewed, he reassessed his surroundings. He was still in the water, still in the darkness, still in sight of the two glowing discs. Tentatively, he took a second half-breath, then a third, this one nearly full. The relief was almost more than he could contain and he laughed out loud. Wonder of wonders; he wasn't dead!

So overjoyed was he to still be alive that Rick almost forgot about the ship. After a few more deep breaths of this underwater air, he turned in the direction he thought he needed to go and started swimming. Disoriented by the darkness, he swam straight into something hard. The impact to his shoulder spun him around and he could see that the two glowing discs were now very close behind him.

"Rick," a man's voice said.

Rick turned toward the voice and felt a warm breeze upon his face.

"Rick," the voice said again.

He breathed in and detected the distinct aroma of coffee.

"Rick," the voice said a third time, and whatever he had encountered with his shoulder struck him again. The coffee smell was much stronger this time.

The dream realm dissolved from around him, and Rick found himself back in his own warm, dry reality. He forced his eyes open. In the dim light that spilled in from the hallway he could see Aldi's smiling face just inches from his own and he could feel Aldi's big hand heavy upon his shoulder. He recognized at first whiff that Aldi must have drunk a full pot of *Fred and Lulu's Roguish Mountain Blend*. "Aldi?" Then he noticed the two glowing discs hovering above and just to the side of Aldi. "Elsa-Eska?" He pulled himself up on his elbows. "What is it? What's wrong?"

By now, Jane was being pulled from her own dream realm.

"It is time," Aldi said, not bothering to keep his voice low.

"Time? Time for what?" Rick asked, still trying to get his bearings.

"Aldi? Is that you?" Jane reached over and turned on her bedside lamp. She and Rick both squinted in the sudden burst of light. "What's going on?"

"It is time for our child to be born," Aldi said, his voice was alive with excitement, but there was no panic to it. "I am sorry to wake you, but can you take Jalamin for me?"

"Oh, right, of course," Rick said, still not grasping what Aldi was saying. He moved into a sitting position on the side of the bed and took Jalamin from him. She was almost asleep and quickly snuggled into Rick's arms.

"It's time?! Now?!" Jane leapt out of bed and came around to where Elsa-Eska was standing. She appeared to be very relaxed, though her eyes blazed brightly.

Rick's eyes widened at the sight of her. "Your baby's coming now?" He stood up.

"Yes," Aldi replied.

"But I thought you weren't due for another three months," Jane pointed out. "Are you sure?"

"Yes, I am sure."

"What do we do?" Rick asked excitedly. "Do you need anything?

Can I help?"

Aldi placed a hand on Rick's shoulder. "No, brother. Stay with Jane and Jalamin." Aldi gently guided Rick to sit back down on the bed.

"Would you like me to be with you?" Jane offered.

Elsa-Eska shook her head. "Thank you, but no. This is for Aldi."

"Okay. But if you need anything, we're right here."

Aldi and Elsa-Eska turned to leave.

"Is everything okay?" Jacques Faber was standing in the doorway. "I was on my way to the bathroom and heard voices."

"Our child will be born tonight," Aldi said.

Jacques blinked. "Now?" He looked at Elsa-Eska and stepped back at the sight of her blazing eyes. Then he looked to Rick and Jane for an explanation. "I thought she wasn't due until December."

Rick and Jane shrugged in unison and Jane said, "Klyvian."

Jacques nodded. "Shouldn't someone take her to the hospital?"

"No," Elsa-Eska said emphatically. "Our child will be born here."

Jacques thought for a moment. "Elsa-Eska, dear, is your baby coming immediately or do we have some time?"

"It will be soon," she replied. She glanced out the window at the still dark night. "Maybe before the sky becomes light."

"Do you mind waiting here while I have a word with Rick?"

"I can wait," she said.

"Rick?" Jacques gestured with a nod of the head.

"Excuse me." Rick handed Jalamin to Jane and followed Jacques into the living room. "What's up?"

Jacques paced the room, stroking his beard. "Why does Elsa-Eska not want to go to the hospital?"

"I'm not really sure. She's been opposed to the idea ever since we suggested she see Jane's doctor."

"Do you think you can persuade her?"

"I doubt it. Why?"

"Documentation."

"Come again?"

"Identification," Jacques restated, slipping into business mode. "Think it through. Aldi and Elsa-Eska have no identification. Like I said last night, they are unidentifiable. God forbid anything should happen, but what if they encountered a police officer? What if anyone, for that matter, got suspicious and started checking them out? The fact that they have no identification could become a problem."

"I have considered this, but what does it have to do with Elsa-Eska going to the hospital? Wouldn't that be putting her in just such a situation?"

"Yes, it would," Jacques agreed. "But it might be worth the risk. If she can give birth in a hospital, her baby will get a birth certificate and a social security number—real identification. And there will be an official hospital record of it. Thanks to the Constitution, this child will be more of an American citizen than I am." Jacques shrugged. "You tell me, wouldn't a little risk now be worth it in the long run when the child wants to go to school, get a driver's license, or get a job? Not only that, her documentation could prove beneficial to our partnership."

Rick couldn't argue with Jacques's logic. "You're right. Real identification would make life here a lot easier for her. But how do we manage the risk part? Won't they need identification to check in at the hospital?"

Jacques grinned innocently. "It's the middle of the night. In all the excitement, we forgot it. I don't mean this to be an insult, but I suspect a small town hospital might be a little more relaxed when it comes to protocol. If Aldi and Elsa-Eska will let me handle this part, I believe I can get us through it."

Rick considered Jacques' scheme. "I don't know. I agree with everything you've said, and I have no doubt about your persuasive talents, but I don't know if I can get Elsa-Eska to go along with it. For the most part, they are pretty compliant, but she hasn't budged on the hospital thing since we brought it up a couple of weeks ago. Apparently, childbirth is a sacred act for them."

"What about Aldi?" Jacques suggested. "He seems like a reasonable guy. If you can get him to see the logic of it, he might be able to get Elsa-Eska to go along."

Rick suspected Jacques might be right about Aldi, but he didn't like the idea of using him to persuade Elsa-Eska to do something against her will. Still, authentic legal identification was a tempting prize. Finally, the practical overruled the principle. "Let me see what I can do."

Somewhere between the living room and the bedroom, Rick's conscience worked him over. He was fairly certain he could get Aldi to see the situation in light of the benefits it would bring to the mission, but he could not stand the thought of doing it behind Elsa-Eska's back. When he started to ask Aldi to join him and Jacques back in the living room, he heard himself extend the invitation to both of them. Jacques gave him a look, but he did not protest. The next thing Rick knew, the entire house was awake and gathered in the living room; even Diane had come out to see what was happening.

Rick explained the plan just as Jacques had laid it out to him. Everyone listened. Jane and Diane nodded their understanding and agreement when he came to the part about the documentation.

Jacques watched Elsa-Eska closely, trying to get a read on her. Aldi and Elsa-Eska listened as well, though it was not clear how much they understood. Aldi's expression gave a hint of hope when Rick explained how the documentation would help their child carry on the mission, but Elsa-Eska remained unreadable. At the last moment, Rick decided against mentioning the possible benefits to the arrangement with Jacques. Then he waited. He had made his case. Now it was up to Aldi and Elsa-Eska.

The two Klyvians conversed in their own language for a long time. It wasn't that they were trying to be secretive. Rather, it was just easier for them to discuss such a weighty issue in their own tongue. Jacques and Diane listened with great interest at the sound of the unfamiliar language. There was no way any of the humans could tell what was being said. They tried to read the expressions and decipher the tone of the conversation, but they could make no sense of it. For all they knew, the two Klyvians could have been chatting about the folks back home or planning an invasion of Earth. Finally, after about ten minutes, Elsa-Eska spoke directly to Jacques.

"We understand the words our brother Rick has spoken. We understand this *identification* is a good thing in the ways of humans, but it is not the way of our people." She paused as if trying to decide how best to say in English what she was thinking in Klyvian. "Many of our ways do not fit in your world and many of your ways do not fit us. It comes into my mind that some of our ways can be put away so we can live with humans. This is for the good of the mission. But it is strong in my mind that some of our ways cannot be put away, not even for the mission. It is strong in my heart and in the heart of my Aldi to welcome our child alone, in the way of our people. But my Aldi believes this is one of the ways we should put away for the mission. My Aldi is of the true...I mean, Aldi is wise in the truth." Elsa-Eska got up from the couch and walked over to Jacques with her hands extended. She lifted him to his feet, held his hands tightly in her own, and fixed her eyes upon his. "I do not know you, Jacques Faber. You are different from the other humans we know. If these words had come from you only, I would not put away what is in my heart for them. But my Aldi and I trust our brother Rick. We will do this because he believes it to be the best way."

Jacques was not used to being addressed so bluntly. The intensity of her gaze made him uncomfortable. He wanted to avert his eyes, but he dare not for it was his way to remain in control, to maintain the upper hand. Elsa-Eska's eyes flared brightly, and for an instant Jacques was scared. It was not a fear of danger or injury, but a fear that comes from being exposed. Like all men, especially those who cast their lot into the arena of ambition in order to succeed, Jacques had secrets. He had done things—things he believed were necessary to advance his career; things he believed were justified by the fact that so many others had done them and were hailed as brilliant and admirable; things he believed were simply part of the game. And like all men who have secrets, he understood the nature of them and why such things must remain hidden. And so he buried them deep, so deep that not even he would have to acknowledge what he had done. But here, under the spotlight of those eyes, those curious eyes, he felt vulnerable. It was as if she could see right into his soul and read every detail of his past like words on a page of a book. It was all he could do to maintain his façade for the others, but he knew it was too late to bluff Elsa-Eska. She had penetrated his defenses, and though he didn't know how much of him she could understand (he hoped her inexperience with humans would render her unable to fully grasp the darkest of his deeds), it was obvious she understood enough to justify her mistrust of him.

When Elsa-Eska let go of Jacques's hands, he quickly sat back down in his chair. The encounter left him weak, and he wondered if the others had noticed. He was relieved that everyone's attention seemed to be upon Elsa-Eska. He was not at all surprised by this, as he himself found it impossible to fix his attention anywhere else whenever she was present.

Elsa-Eska took Aldi by the hand and started for the door. "We will be ready to go to the hospital in a few minutes. I would like Jane to be with me. Diane will stay here with Jalamin. Rick, you may bring Jacques Faber if you think it is the best way."

"Jane, dear," Diane said after Aldi and Elsa-Eska had gone. "Don't you worry about Jalamin. She'll be in good hands."

"Are you sure?" Jane asked. She had never once heard Diane speak positively of children. She wondered how she would do with a baby—her baby—all by herself.

"Of course," Diane replied. There was an uncharacteristic softness to her that Jane had never seen before. "Really, Janie, we'll be fine. Go with Elsa-Eska. She wants you." Then Diane smiled. "And she trusts me."

"Okay." Jane beheld her old friend in a new light. "Thank you. Let's go back to the nursery. I'll show you how everything works."

Diane put her hand on Jacques' knee. When their eyes met she raised her eyebrows and chuckled softly.

"What?" Jacques asked.

"She's not as naïve as you thought, is she?"

Jacques scowled.

"I like her." With that, she got up and followed Jane to the nursery, leaving Rick and Jacques alone in the living room.

"Well?" Jacques asked after a minute. "Am I going with you?"

"Do you still want to?"

Jacques nodded. "Yes."

"Hey, don't let it bother you. She's flashed those eyes at me, too."

"Does she do that a lot?"

"No, not a lot. Like I said, they're pretty compliant about most things, but I guess some things hit a nerve. I don't think we fully appreciate what it's like for them, trying to fit in here with us. It must be hard."

"Can they read minds?" Jacques queried.

"It seems like it, but Aldi told me they can't. It's more like intuition. I think they can somehow read emotions."

Jacques nodded as he considered what he had just experienced with Elsa-Eska. "What about intent?"

"What do you mean?"

"Do you think they can spot a fraud?"

Rick pondered the question. "I'll put it this way: They learn quickly and they remember everything. When they first got here, they took everything we said at face value without question. We could have told them anything and they would have believed us. But now that they've been around us so much, I don't think much gets by them. They don't do it as much anymore, but they used to point out every contradiction they saw in us. I never knew how inconsistent I was."

"Sounds irritating."

"Believe me, it was at first. But you see, even with that, they seemed to sense how it made us feel. I have to believe they learned how to differentiate between common human inconsistency and a real contradiction. Now they only point out the major contradictions and let the minor inconsistencies go. I'd say that once they get to know someone, it would be nearly impossible for them to be deceived."

"That's good to know."

Jane and Diane came back into the living room. Diane was holding Jalamin and actually looked like she was enjoying it. Jacques took notice of her and smiled at this new side of his wife.

"Are you going like that?" Jane asked.

Rick looked down at himself and noticed he was still wearing his boxers and t-shirt. Jane tossed a pair of jeans to him and grabbed her coat from the hook by the door. "We better get going."

CHAPTER 33:

NATURAL BORN CITIZEN

Xo

The ride into Riverton seemed more like a leisurely drive in the country than a middle-of-the-night dash to the hospital with an expectant mother. Elsa-Eska and Aldi had recently learned about speed limits and insisted Rick observe them. Elsa-Eska did not seem to be in any kind of distress, so Rick acquiesced. Aldi took his usual place in the front with Rick, forcing Jacques to squeeze into the back with Jane and Elsa-Eska. Jane sat between them. The conversation was light, and Aldi took the opportunity to pepper Jacques with questions about his company. Elsa-Eska remained quiet, but Jacques was aware that she was listening to him intently.

Rick's words echoed in Jacques' mind: *They learn quickly and they remember everything.* Jacques knew good advice when he heard it. Even though Rick's words were not offered as such, he took them as a useful insight into his newest venture. He decided to suspend his usual approach of *disarm with charm / dominate with confidence.* Instead, he gave Aldi (and Elsa-Eska) straightforward answers. Besides, he knew Elsa-Eska was immune to his charm, and her presence had all but shattered his confidence. Aldi, on the other hand, suddenly became a mystery to him. Initially, he had thought of the big man as a naïve, happy-go-lucky sort of chap whom he could easily manipulate. But after his encounter with the man's wife, he realized he might have underestimated him as well. Now he suspected there was much more to Aldi than his infectious smile and eager countenance.

By the time they reached the hospital, Jacques had pretty much revealed his entire strategy for making Saber Technologies the preeminent force in shaping the technological landscape of the 21'st Century. Such talk would have impressed anyone with a stake in the technology game, but the genius of his plan seemed to be lost on this audience. Aldi was much more interested in how Klyvian technology could interface with human technology and how the two together could be better than either one by itself. Whenever Jacques interjected promises of monetary compensation and notoriety to reinforce Aldi's involvement (which Jacques seemed almost compelled to do as it was part of his business nature), Aldi would counter by saying something completely unrelated. In spite of Rick's warning that such human motivations meant nothing to Klyvians, Jacques found it nearly impossible to accept it as the truth. He was even beginning to imagine Aldi's naïveté as a clever ruse to throw him off his game. Consequently, Jacques expended a lot of mental energy defending against strategies that simply did not exist. The conversation ended abruptly when Elsa-Eska announced that they should find a place for her quickly as the baby was coming soon.

To Rick's relief, the emergency waiting area was deserted, and the attendant at the desk had a pleasant look about her. Having just been through the drill only a week earlier, he knew exactly what was needed in order to process Elsa-Eska to the maternity ward. He quickly completed the front side of the first page of the admittance forms, filling in the unanswerable questions with illegible scribbles. In a matter of minutes, Elsa-Eska was being wheeled through the empty halls of the hospital with her entourage trailing behind. Rick was thankful for the lateness of the hour, for they were able to avoid unwanted attention.

"That was the easy part," Rick whispered to Jacques. "The maternity ward will be different. Let's see if we can get Elsa-Eska into a room before we deal with the business end of it."

"I agree," Jacques replied.

Entering the maternity ward was like entering a different world. Babies, it seemed, preferred to enter the world in the middle of the night. There were three other women in various stages of labor, and just like the day Jalamin was born, there was only one doctor on duty to juggle them all. The nurses' station was a flurry of activity and no one seemed to notice them when they entered. The orderly who was pushing Elsa-Eska's wheelchair seemed reluctant to upset the delicate balance by adding another patient. When the unit clerk finally did acknowledge them, she made no effort to hide her annoyance. Ignoring Elsa-Eska, she glowered at the orderly. "Papers," she barked.

The orderly handed over the admittance forms and stepped back behind the wheelchair. Rick, who was standing closest, noticed that the orderly avoided eye contact with the clerk.

The clerk scanned the first page, flipped through the others, and shook her head. "Unacceptable."

The poor kid looked like he had just been called into the principal's office. Seeing the kid's anxiety, Rick stepped up to the desk.

"I'm sorry, ma'am," he said, trying to look apologetic. "It's not this young man's fault. It's mine. We're about to have a baby here and we're all a little flustered. Couldn't we do the paper work later?"

The unit clerk looked at the patient over the top of her reading glasses. "How close are your contractions?"

"Contractions?" Elsa-Eska repeated. She looked like someone on the second day of a week long vacation.

Jane quickly stepped up to the desk next to Rick. "They're close."

The clerk looked at Jane with an annoyance that seemed to be permanently etched into her face. She placed the forms on the desk and slid them toward Rick. "We cannot admit her without the completed forms. It will only take a few minutes. Obviously, she's in no hurry."

Rick was about to make another play when he was interrupted by a friendly voice.

"Mrs. Blackwell?" A nurse had just stepped out of the room closest to the nurses' station. "Hi! Remember me?" It was the new nurse Rick and Jane had met the week before.

"Oh, hello, Jennifer," Jane replied, glancing at the nurse's name tag. "Of course, I remember you. How are you?"

"I'm still here. So, what brings you in tonight?" Her smile morphed into a look of concern. "Are you okay? Is your baby well?"

"We're fine," Jane said. "This is my sister. She's visiting from out of town and, well, babies come when they want to."

"I know," Jennifer said as if it was the most amazing revelation. "They really do."

The clerk leaned back in her chair and folded her arms across her chest.

"Well, I'm here all night," Jennifer continued. "I guess we'll be spending it together. Let me know if you need anything."

"Actually," Jane said, turning her back to the clerk. She spoke in a low voice. "Do you think there's any way you could get my sister into a room now?"

Jennifer glanced over at the unit clerk. "Gee, I don't know."

Jane leaned closer and whispered into her ear.

Jennifer nearly melted with compassion. Kneeling next to Elsa-Eska, she placed a reassuring hand on her arm. "Can you hold on for just a minute? I'm going to check on something. I'll be right back." Avoiding the glare from the clerk, she disappeared down the hall.

There was the sound of a throat being cleared followed by a tap, tap, tap. The clerk was staring hard at Rick and tapping her pen on the admittance forms. It was like a scene from an old western movie. On one side of the desk was Sheriff Clerk. On the other was the notorious Rick Blackwell and his sidekick Calamity Jane. They eyed each other, waiting for just the right moment to draw. In the grand scheme of things, the point of contention was rather trivial— admittance forms could be filled out later. But Jane had crossed the line by bringing a nurse into the matter. The way the clerk saw it, these people were challenging her authority. Now it was a matter of principle.

Two minutes later, Jennifer returned, accompanied by none other than the doctor on duty. The unit clerk sat up straight and tried to find her professional face.

"Jane," Dr. Jenkins said, "it's so good to see you. Jennifer tells me you are here with your sister." She looked beyond Rick and Jane to where Elsa-Eska was sitting patiently in her wheelchair. "Oh, yes, I remember. Elsa, right?" She spoke directly to Elsa-Eska. "You left quite an impression on my staff last week, the way you helped your sister. And now it's your turn. I didn't realize you were so far along. Don't worry, everything's going to be just fine. Jennifer will help you get settled. I'll be in shortly." Then she turned toward the orderly. "We can take her from here."

The orderly took advantage of the opportunity and made a hasty exit.

"Jen, take her to number three and get her prepped. I've got to get back to Mrs. Johnson. I'll be in as soon as I can."

Jennifer wheeled Elsa-Eska to Delivery Room #3. Aldi followed close behind.

"Thank you, Dr. Jenkins," Jane said. She winked at Rick and headed for number three.

"Excuse me, doctor," the unit clerk said as Dr. Jenkins turned to go back to her waiting patient. "She hasn't been properly processed. Her admittance forms are incomplete."

"Noted," Dr. Jenkins said without slowing.

Rick smiled innocently and took the admittance forms from the desk. "I'll just fill these out over here." He felt the stare of the unit clerk boring into his back as he and Jacques made their way to the waiting area.

"It wasn't the cleanest execution," Jacques noted. "But we're in. It's a good thing that nurse remembered Jane. What do you suppose she told her?"

Rick shrugged. "I don't know and I don't know if I want to know."

In Delivery Room #3, Nurse Jennifer locked the wheels of Elsa-Eska's wheelchair. "The bathroom is right over there. Do you need any help?"

"No, thank you," Elsa-Eska replied. "I am familiar with the bathroom. We have one at the house."

"Thank you, Jennifer," Jane cut in. "You've been a tremendous help, but I'm sure you've got other patients to attend to. I can take it from here."

Jennifer hesitated. "Is she okay?"

"Yes, yes, she's fine. She just needs to, you know." Jane nodded toward the bathroom.

Jennifer nodded. "Okay, then. I'll be close if you need me. There's a gown for her on the bed."

"Okay, thank you." Jane closed the door and breathed a sigh of relief. "Whew, alone at last. What do you want me to do?"

"There is nothing, Jane," Elsa-Eska said. "When it is time, Aldi will know."

"How long do you think it will be?" Jane asked.

"Soon."

Jane looked anxious. *Soon* to a Klyvian did not mean the same thing as *soon* to a human. "I don't mean to rush, but we won't be alone for long. Somebody will be in any minute to check on you."

"Then there is something you can do," Aldi said.

"What's that?"

"Give us this time alone."

Jane beheld her two friends. They were so calm, as if they didn't have a worry in the world. She wished she felt the same. "I'll see what I can do." She stepped out into the hallway and closed the door behind her.

Jennifer saw Jane and asked, "Is everything okay?"

"Yes, fine."

"Good, I need to take her vitals. May I go in?"

"No. Um, not yet," Jane stalled. "They, uh, they need a little more time."

Jennifer took a step closer. "Are you sure she's okay?"

"Yes."

"What about you? You seem anxious."

"I guess I am a little nervous, this being her first and all."

Jennifer smiled sympathetically. "That's understandable." She hesitated, then said, "Mrs. Blackwell, I hope I'm not out of line here, but are you sure your sister is ready to deliver?"

The question caught Jane by surprise. "She's says she is."

"Pardon me for saying, but she doesn't seem...I mean, she doesn't look ready to deliver. I know this is only my first week here, but…" She hesitated again and then said, "I'm sorry, Mrs. Blackwell. I shouldn't have said anything. Please don't say anything to your sister."

"That's okay," Jane said, thankful that Jennifer's inexperience had given her a way to avoid her astute observation. "I promise I won't say a word."

Just then, another nurse appeared from around the corner. "Jennifer, Dr. Jenkins needs you in six. Mrs. Johnson is ready to deliver."

"Excuse me," Jennifer said. "I may be awhile. If you need anything, just grab one of the other nurses."

"I'm sure we'll be fine." After Jennifer had gone, she added, "Take all the time you need."

Just then, Rick rounded the corner. "There you are. How is she?"

"Fine, I guess. I'm trying to buy them some time. Fortunately, one of the other women is delivering right now, so Dr. Jenkins and Jennifer will be occupied for a while. But it's only a matter of time before they're going to want to see Elsa-Eska. I don't know how long I can stall them."

Rick chuckled.

"What's so funny?"

"Did you ever imagine in your wildest dreams that we'd be standing guard so visitors from another planet can give birth to their baby?"

"No."

Rick sighed. "It kind of messes with your head when you think about it. Everything they do is so incredibly amazing, yet we're the only ones who know about it."

"Yeah, well, let's just hope we can keep it that way. How's the paper work coming? Are you finished?"

"Almost. I had to make up just about everything on it—birth date, medical history. But there's one thing we need to talk to them about. They need a last name."

"What about Eska?" Jane suggested. "Elsa-Eska. Aldi Eska. Sounds good to me."

"I thought of that, too. But Jacques thinks it should be more common— something that wouldn't attract attention. I think we should ask Aldi and Elsa-Eska. After all, they're the ones who will have to live with it."

Jane looked at the door. "I don't think this is the time to ask them."

"You're probably right. Say, do you think you could come with me for a minute? There are a few female questions I'd feel better if you made up the answers to."

Jane bit her bottom lip. "What if someone comes? I should stay here and guard the door."

"It'll only take a few minutes. Besides, I could see the room where Dr. Jenkins and Jennifer are. If they come out, you can head them off."

Jane thought for a moment and then nodded. "I guess it will be okay."

Back in the waiting area, Jacques was going over the admittance form again. At the sight of Rick and Jane, he set it on the table and stood to greet them. "How is she?"

"Fine," Jane said with a shrug. "I guess there's nothing to do but wait…and keep everyone out of their room. They're convinced they don't need any help."

"Maybe they don't," Jacques suggested. "Who are we to assume they would conform to our cultural norms? It wasn't that long ago that our ancestors delivered their children at home without any medical assistance. Perhaps they have not yet evolved to the point of dependency like we have."

Jane put her hands on her hips. "Hey! New mom standing right here," she said teasingly.

"I'm just saying…"

"I know what you're saying," she interrupted.

"All I am suggesting is that we should trust them to know what they are doing."

"I know. You're probably right." She pointed to the admittance form on the table. "How is this little venture going? Rick said there are some questions you guys want me to lie about…I mean answer." She winked at Rick.

The three sat down and Jacques handed the form to her. "There are just a few on the back." He pointed to the spot. "Have you noticed that our two Klyvian friends have the same initials as Adam and Eve."

Jane looked up from her task. "I beg your pardon."

"Like in the Bible," Jacques replied. "Adam and Eve, A and E, Aldi and Elsa-Eska. They have the same initials."

Rick cocked his head. "I never though about it, but what's your point?"

"It's an interesting coincidence, don't you think? According to the Bible, Adam and Eve were the first humans on Earth. Aldi and Elsa-Eska are the first Klyvians on Earth."

"I don't get it," Rick admitted.

Jacques chuckled. "Imagine that, it took an atheist to notice the similarities between the myth of the Bible and the reality living right under your noses."

"What similarities?" Rick and Jane asked in unison.

"The clothing-optional thing for one—which, I must say, I'm perfectly fine with. Then there's a certain naïveté about them—not exactly ignorance, for they have learned an extraordinary amount about us in a relatively short amount of time. It's quite obvious they possess an advanced intelligence, likely much more advanced than our own. No, it's more like innocence. Yes, that's it. They seem innocent to me, completely unstained by the corruption and cynicism of our world." Jacques nodded at his assessment. "*And they were both naked, yet they were not ashamed.* That's in the Bible, in case you didn't know."

The look on Rick's face betrayed his lack of Bible knowledge. His perception of Adam and Eve came from a few references in movies and a BBQ restaurant he used to frequent called *Adam's Ribs*—the cover of the menu had a caricature sketch of Adam and Eve wearing BBQ bibs. And there was something else about an apple, but he didn't know the story behind that.

Jane dropped the admittance form onto the table and got up from her chair. "Excuse me," she said and made a hasty exit.

Rick watched her disappear around the corner and turned back to Jacques. "So, now you're reading the Bible. It has been awhile hasn't it?"

Jacques shrugged. "I am at that age when a man begins to evaluate his life. I'm open to more than I used to be. An associate of mine got me to look at the Bible. He said it offered some interesting insights into human nature. I was skeptical at first, of course, but he was right. I swear some of the stories could have been written about people I deal with everyday. You know, as a writer, you might want to look at it yourself. Who knows? It might provide some ideas for characters in your next book."

Jane knocked lightly on the door of Delivery Room #3. Almost immediately, the door opened and Aldi's smiling face greeted her.

"Jane, come in." He stepped back and allowed her to enter the room.

The room was dimly lit, but she could see Elsa-Eska sitting on the side of the bed holding something small in her arms. Even from that distance, Jane noticed the radiance about her. A soft glow shimmered as golden flecks swirled in the irises of her eyes. Jane thought she was even more beautiful than usual.

"Is that…" An unexpected wave of emotion caught her breath.

"Come and see," Aldi offered. Taking her by the hand, he led her to the bed.

Jane gasped at her first sight of the tiny infant in Elsa-Eska's arms. It was much smaller than she expected, about half the size of her own Jalamin, and lying perfectly still. Jane immediately thought the baby might have been delivered prematurely; she feared the worst. "Are you okay?" Jane whispered. "Is your baby okay?"

"Yes." Elsa-Eska made no attempt to quiet her own voice. "We are both well."

At the sound of Elsa-Eska's voice, the baby stirred. It extended its tiny arm and grabbed a fist-full of Elsa-Eska's hair.

Jane sighed in relief. But still, the child was so small. "A girl, right?"

"Yes," Aldi confirmed. "She is as we were told. Jalamin will be very happy to see someone her size."

Jane looked at Aldi. She still couldn't tell if he was being serious or trying to develop his sense of human humor. There was always something odd about the way he spoke of Jalamin – like he really could communicate with her. Jane pushed her suspicion aside and turned her attention back to the baby girl. "Have you decided on a name?"

"Her name is Suraeka," Elsa-Eska replied. "But she will be called Sara. I read that name in the book you gave to me."

"Both names are beautiful," Jane said, still in a whisper, "just like her."

Elsa-Eska smiled. "We thought she should have a human name as well. Would you like to hold her?"

"Oh, yes." Jane held out her arms and allowed Elsa-Eska to place the blanketed bundle in them.

Sara held tightly to the strand of Elsa-Eska's hair as if it was her lifeline to her mother. Gently, Elsa-Eska opened the tiny fist, freeing the strand of hair. Keeping her eyes tightly closed, Sara frowned, stuck out her bottom lip, and reached up with her other hand until she found the edge of Jane's blouse. Satisfied to have another security hold, she returned to her peaceful slumber.

"She's so tiny," Jane said, "but she's perfect." She looked closely at the delicate features of the tiny face. Except for being so small, there was nothing unusual about them at all. Her skin was olive colored, just like her parents', and her eyebrows and lashes were black. The wisps of hair on the top of her head were dark, almost black. Jane studied the little face more closely, looking for traces of her parents. Sara yawned, and her lips relaxed into what appeared to be grin. "Oh, look at that. Aldi, she has your smile."

Aldi peaked over the edge of the blanket and smiled as broadly as Jane had ever seen him.

"And I think she has your nose, Elsa-Eska."

At the sound of Jane's voice, Sara opened her eyes and looked directly at her.

Jane gasped. "She definitely has your eyes."

Sara's eyes sparkled with tiny golden flecks swirling luminously in their soft dark brown irises. Then, as calmly as if she were in her own mother's arms, she closed her eyes and drifted back to sleep.

CHAPTER 34:

SOME KIND OF INVASION

"Hey," Jane said as she stepped out onto the back deck. She was carrying Jalamin wrapped in a blanket like a human burrito. "We've been waiting for you to say goodnight."

Rick drew them in close to his side. He looked down at his daughter and tried to find the look of awareness that Aldi kept talking about. He didn't see it.

"Deep in thought?" Jane asked.

"Uh-huh. Just thinking about how much the world has changed in the last few weeks."

"I know. Diane called and said the airport in Denver looked like a militarized zone. There were soldiers in full combat gear with machine guns and everything. They won't even let you go to the gate unless you've got a ticket."

"At least they got home safely," Rick offered. "I know Jacques was eager to get back to work."

"Diane said the plane was nearly empty and everybody was so nice."

"I wonder how long that will last."

"What? The empty planes or people being nice?"

"Neither. I wonder how long Diane will notice anything but herself."

"Rick! I think Diane really had a life-changing experience while she was here. Elsa-Eska had quite an impact on her. In fact, she called to make sure she and Sara were doing okay."

"I'm sorry. That was mean." Rick paused, then redirected. "Actually, that's what I was thinking about. You're right, the world *does* seem different since the attacks. But the world has changed in another way. Our planet is now the home world for an intelligent creature who isn't human. Two, actually. Aldi said Mallia had her baby in Ireland—a boy. Just think; Aldi's and Elsa-Eska's baby is just as much an American citizen as our baby." Rick and Jane looked toward the newly constructed house. Through the window, they could see Aldi standing with Sara in his arms. "I wonder what it will be like for her," Rick mused out loud. "A Klyvian born and raised among humans."

Jane considered the idea for several seconds. Finally, she said, "It is the mission."

Rick chuckled, then replied, "You speak the true."

"You know, Rick," Jane said, "Diane isn't the only one who's had a life changing-experience. We all have. And what will it be like for Jalamin—a human born and raised among Klyvians."

Rick nodded as he considered Jane's perspective. He looked down at Jalamin again and found her staring up at him. He smiled and it seemed to him that she smiled in return. Maybe Aldi was right. Maybe Jalamin really did understand him. Maybe she was trying to communicate just now. Rick was about to comment about it when…

"Oops," Jane said. "I think somebody needs a new diaper. We'll see you when you come in."

Alone again, Rick looked up at the tiny sliver of the moon. "Well, Children of Ka-Rel, looks like your mission is proceeding. Hey, this wouldn't be some kind of invasion now, would it?" He chuckled at his own joke and glanced back at the new house. Through the window, he could see that Elsa-Eska had joined Aldi. They were standing forehead to forehead with little Sara in between them. It looked like they might be dancing. He watched them for a long time, allowing snapshots of the last six months to drift randomly through this mind. Just six months, yet so much had happened. So much had changed. Rick could hardly remember what his life was like prior to that day on the road when he first met them. One day, there was no such thing as space aliens, and the next day they dropped into his life and altered it forever. Unannounced, uninvited, with no resistance of any kind, they just came to him. No fight. No threat. No clever deception. They simply took him. In a way, Rick Blackwell had been abducted by aliens. He marveled over the notion that he, the skeptic, had experienced for real what so many had fabricated because they wanted so badly to believe.

Rick looked back up at the moon, at what only a he and a few others knew was just beyond the moon, and lifted his hands. "If this *is* some kind of invasion, I surrender."

PART IV

MAN OF TROUBLE

CHAPTER 35:

TRACKERS

Δ

"Are you sure this is the right way?" Jim Calvani asked from the driver's seat of his 1999 Honda Accord.

His passenger and friend, David Phelps, looked up from the hand-drawn map balanced on his leg. "These are the directions your dad gave us." Paper-clipped to the edge of the map was a smaller scrap of paper with handwritten notations. "You do realize this isn't a real map."

"I know," Jim conceded.

"This road isn't even on the map I bought at that gas station a hundred miles back." That map had been tossed into the back seat an hour earlier when they turned onto a road that did not officially exist. "I hope this isn't a wild goose chase."

Jim frowned and gripped the steering wheel tighter. "Don't forget whose idea this was."

"Yeah, but you know the guy."

"I never said I *know* him," Jim corrected. "I said I *met* him once. My dad knows him."

"I still can't believe you never mentioned it until now."

"I never had a reason until now."

Dave stared out the window for a moment thinking of the reason. "You really think he'll be there?"

"He said he would be. By the way, thanks for volunteering my services for this little adventure. You know, I think my dad likes you more than he likes me."

"Probably," Dave said jokingly. "Say, you don't think we'll get busted for this, do you? We did take government property out of a government facility without asking."

Jim shrugged. "I wouldn't worry about it. We're only *borrowing* it.

We'll have it back before anyone notices."

That was the part of the plan Dave did not like. He quickly changed the subject. "Tell me about him. What's he like? I've read a few of his essays— boring, but the implications are intriguing."

"Why are you so interested in that stuff? Don't tell me you actually believe in aliens."

Dave didn't reply.

Jim looked over at his friend. "Do you?" He gasped. "You do. You're not gonna get all *X-Files* on me, are you?"

"It's not like that," Dave shot back. He knew his friend was only joking, but the accusation stung all the same. "I've just always liked to think there might be someone else out there—you know, like we weren't alone in the universe."

"Huh, you think you know someone." Jim drummed his fingers on the steering wheel.

"Well?" Dave said after a minute of silence. "Are you going to tell me about him or not?"

"It was a long time ago," Jim replied, his smirky smile flattening into a thin line. "I was just a kid. I don't remember much about him."

"Oh, come on. You gotta remember something. Was he cool?"

Jim laughed. "That's not the word that comes to mind when I think of Carl Drake."

"Hah! You do remember. I knew it."

Jim gave his friend a sideways glance. "You tricked me. You knew he wasn't cool."

"It's not rocket science…well, actually it kind of is." Dave laughed at his own joke. "Come on, the guy worked for SETI. I doubt the girls were knocking down the door of their little listening hut."

"You really want to know about the legendary Carl Drake."

"Yeah, I do."

"Okay, I'll tell you about him. But first, I want to be clear about something. I don't believe in any of this stuff—none of it. Understand?"

"Yeah, sure, whatever you say."

Jim thought for a moment, calling up the old memories. "Like I said, I was just a kid—fourteen, maybe fifteen. My dad took me and a friend of mine out to dinner one night, and we met two friends of his. Dad introduced one of them as The Doctor and the other one as Carl Drake. I'd never heard him mention either one before that night, but that was nothing unusual. Anyway, The Doctor hardly said anything the entire evening. It was all Drake. The guy never shut up. It was one story after another. He was kind of like that obnoxious kid in school who knows everything and wants everyone to know that he knows it."

Dave nodded. He knew the type. "What'd he talk about?"

"Crazy stuff. He was really into crystals and pyramids, things like that. He was all excited about this energy helmet he made that helped him stay awake so he could drive all night."

"Really?"

Jim chuckled. "Yeah, really. I'm telling you, the guy was nuts."

"Did he talk about SETI?"

"Not at the restaurant. He waited until we got to his house."

"You went to Carl Drake's house?"

"Yes."

"What was it like?"

"It was a house. From the outside, it wasn't all that impressive. But inside…" Jim laughed again.

"What?" Dave asked, sensing the good stuff was about to come. "What was inside?"

"That's the weird part," Jim explained. "There were pyramids everywhere, but they weren't just decoration. He said there was something about the shape; it was like a receptor for energy. He claimed this energy could be harnessed and used for all sorts of things; health, dream enhancement, clarity of thought. I remember there was a pyramid over a bowl of bananas on the kitchen table. He said they'd been there for weeks. There was a pyramid over the dog dish and even one over the dog's bed. I didn't see it, but he said he had a big one over his own bed. He claimed it helped him remember his dreams. Oh, and he had this basket of forks and spoons that were all twisted up. He said the pyramids gave him the power to bend metal with his mind."

Dave's eyebrows arched. "Wow, that's pretty wild."

"Yeah, but it gets better. He had this room…just a square room with nothing in it but a giant pyramid. He must have constructed it to fit because the base of it ran tight up against the walls and the apex stuck into the center of the ceiling. And the walls were covered with maps of the world. On one of them he had drawn lines along the west coast of the U.S. and labeled them with dates when California was supposed to slide into the ocean. I guess it was his channeling room where he got in touch with the universe."

"Did you go in?"

Jim hesitated like he didn't want to talk about it. But then he admitted, "Yeah, I went in."

"What happened?"

Jim didn't respond.

"Come on, Jim. I won't tell anyone."

"Okay," he said after a moment. "I felt something. It was like a tingling sensation."

"Really?"

Jim stared hard at the road in front of him, avoiding Dave's gaze. "Remember, I was just a kid. I was impressionable. I wanted to feel something. I'm sure it was nothing more than my imagination."

Dave turned his attention to the road ahead. "Yeah, I'm sure that's all it was. When did he talk about SETI?"

"Actually, he only mentioned it. He was kind of teed off about something; funding or management or something like that."

"Oh," Dave said, disappointed.

"He did tell us about this guy—a retired Air Force pilot, I think—who claimed he'd had a series of encounters with aliens over a period of several years."

The look on Dave's face was a mixture of skepticism and intrigue.

Jim continued. "Yeah, he said they were from the Pleiades, and had come to observe our planet. They said we were doing okay, but that we needed to be careful or we might destroy ourselves. Oh, and get this—all their pilots were women. Apparently, the males were so aggressive they would blow our aircraft right out of the sky."

"Okay." Dave nodded. "So, Carl Drake is a little out there. Tell me again why I thought this was such a great idea."

Jim answered in a droning monotone: "Because Carl Drake is the foremost radio astronomer in the country, he's been with SETI since the '70s, and he's heard and catalogued every signal collected by the most sophisticated radio telescopes scattered all over the world. He practically wrote the book on discovery and response protocol for SETI, and he was the lead consultant for the verification software used by every accredited listening outpost."

"Wow, Jim, you sound exactly like your dad."

"I should." Jim's normal voice returned. "My dad's been rattling that stuff off ever since they spoke on the phone last month." He shook his head. "It's weird. My dad hasn't mentioned Carl Drake in ten years, and now it's like he's best friends with a celebrity. You'd think he knew the Pope."

Dave chuckled.

"But I will say this," Jim added. "There's a good chance we'll get to the bottom of this mystery signal. Drake may be weird, but he knows his stuff. And he's meeting with us off the record."

Dave crossed his arms.

Jim knew exactly what his friend was thinking. He cleared his throat and donned his best imitation of their unit director. "Mr. Phelps, need I remind you of the seriousness of your duties. This installation does not exist to indulge your conspiracy theories or contact alien life forms. We are at war, Mr. Phelps. Forget about your little ET signal and put your ears on those terrorist training camps. Have I made myself clear?"

Dave waved his hand in surrender. "Okay, okay, I got it. You're good at impersonations. Have you ever thought about taking this act on the road?"

Jim chuckled. "I'm already here. Hey, did you see that sign we just passed? It said: CAUTION: EXPLOSIVE LADEN VEHICLES. What do you suppose that means?"

"Hey, that's on this note." Dave scanned down the scrap of paper clipped to the hand-drawn map. "There it is. It says turn left at the next dirt road."

Dave was immediately pinned to the passenger door as Jim whipped the car off the highway and onto the unmarked dirt road.

"Whew! A bit more warning next time," Jim said. "Now what?"

Dave righted himself in his seat, shot Jim a look, and turned back to the note. "Drive about nine miles and take a left at the boot. That's what it says, *left at the boot*. Then go another five miles and you should see the dish. It should be right there."

Nine miles later, they came to a wood post with a cowboy boot bolted onto its side. Five miles later, the giant dish of the radio telescope came into view. The road ended at a small steel structure about the size of a double car garage. Parked next to the structure was a dark green 1965 Ford Mustang convertible. Its white interior glistened in the sun.

Jim parked his Honda next to the Mustang and turned off the engine. Both men stared in wonder at the machine. Except for the fine coating of dust from the dirt road, the Mustang looked like it could have just rolled out of the factory.

"I think Carl Drake's cool factor just jumped up a few points," said Jim.

Just then, the door to the structure opened. A short man with leg braces and crutches hobbled out.

"Uh," Jim said. "That's not him."

"What do you mean, that's not him?"

"That's not the man I remember as Carl Drake."

Dave suddenly became nervous. "Let's go. We don't need to be here."

"No, wait a minute," Jim said, opening his door. "That's the other guy."

"What other guy?"

"The guy from the night I met Drake—The Doctor. I remember

the leg braces." Jim got out of the car and walked toward the man.

"Jimmy Calvani?" the man called out.

"It's Jim," he answered, stopping about halfway between his car and the man.

"Sorry 'bout that. The last time I saw you, you were Jimmy."

"We've come to see Carl Drake. Is he here?"

The man cocked his head. "I'm Carl."

"But I thought…" Jim stammered. "I thought you were The Doctor."

"Doctor?" Drake repeated. "Nope. Just Carl."

Jim closed the distance between them. "That night we met at the restaurant, I could have sworn my dad introduced you as *The Doctor*. And the other man—that big guy—I thought he was Carl Drake."

Drake thought for a moment. "You thought *I* was *The Doctor?*" He started to chuckle and then burst into full laughter. "Boy, if you thought you were coming to see The Doctor, you'd be just as crazy as he was."

Realizing his mistake, Jim laughed along with Drake. He was embarrassed, but also relieved.

"The Doctor!" Drake said through his laughter. "That guy was a lunatic. You know, he actually believed in all that pyramid nonsense. Man, I haven't thought of ol' Doc since…" Drake became serious. "Well, since he died."

"I'm sorry," Jim replied.

Drake shook his head. "Actually, I didn't know him all that well. I was going through a bit of a rough spell, and Doc let me stay with him for a while. He was more like a friend of a friend, if you know what I mean. But yeah, he died about five years ago. Food poisoning, I think; rotten bananas." Drake nodded toward the Honda. "Is your friend gonna stay in the car, or do you boys want to come in?"

Jim waved for Dave to come in, and then he pointed at the Mustang. "You sure have a sweet ride, Mr. Drake. Is it a '65?"

"Sure is," Drake replied. "Bought 'er brand new. She's the only car I've ever owned. Please, call me Carl."

"You've sure kept it in good condition. Is that the original upholstery?"

"She's all original. My philosophy, if you care to hear it, is you give enough care to something, it should last as long as you want it to. Works that way with a lot of things. Of course, with people, you gotta both want it." With that, Carl disappeared into the building.

Jim digested the older man's philosophy, wondering what stories made up its history. When Dave joined him with the *borrowed* equipment he had retrieved from the trunk of Jim's car, they went inside, closing the door behind them.

The sign on the door read:

SETI LISTENING OUTPOST ELVIS – NO TRESPASSING.

The inside of the building was small, but comfortable. In one regard, it was a lot like the listening outpost Dave and Jim occupied. The walls were lined with racks of electronic equipment, most of which was identifiable, though some of it looked old enough to be in a museum. And there was a control panel that could have been a prototype for the one they used to spy on terrorists. In another regard, it was very different from their outpost. One of the antiques was a functioning 8-Track player. A live version of Deep Purple's "Child in Time" was playing from speakers hidden somewhere amongst the racks of equipment, and the heavy smell of incense hung in the air. Dave thought it was incense; Jim suspected it might be something else.

"I'd give you the formal tour," Carl said, waving his crutch in a wide arc around the room, "but from what your dad tells me, you boys probably know a lot more about this stuff than I do." Then seeing the question form in Dave's eyes, he added, "I was never interested in the hardware side of SETI. My specialty was operations and analysis. Unless you guys want to have a look around, let's get down to business." He fixed his eyes upon the digital archive unit Dave had placed on the table in the center of the room. "So, that's where you keep this *new moon* signal, eh? Nothing like a mysterious black box to set the mood."

"Yes, sir," Dave replied. "If we could just connect to your server, it shouldn't take more than a few minutes."

"Go right ahead," Carl offered, stepping over to a tattered old sofa. "Let me know when you're ready. By the way, I took the liberty of aligning our dish to the moon in case your signal reappears."

Dave and Jim both looked up from their work.

"That is why we met here on this date, isn't it?" Carl asked. "October 16."

"Oh, yeah, right," Jim replied. "I wasn't thinking."

Carl leaned his crutches against the wall, unlocked his leg braces, and dropped onto the sofa. "I'll just wait over here."

Ten minutes later, the digital archive unit was connected and feeding its payload of information into the SETI computer system. Several monitors displayed the information in what appeared as random blips on their screens. The system speakers had been muted, so there was no audio for what was being displayed on the monitors.

Carl lifted himself up from the sofa and hobbled over to the control desk, taking one of the chairs. "Well, well, let's see what you've got here." Carl studied the lines, dots, and characters for several minutes. He made several adjustments to the equipment and typed a few commands into the computer, but the images on the screens remained undecipherable.

Dave and Jim looked at each other and then back at Carl. "What are you doing?" Jim finally asked.

"I'm listening to your signal," Carl replied.

Jim scratched the side of his face. "Uh, excuse me for sounding stupid, but I don't hear anything. Don't you want to turn the speakers on?"

"Not yet," Carl said. "I like this song."

Jim looked at Dave and held his hands up. Dave shrugged in response.

After another minute, Carl turned around to face them. "You boys look like someone just told you there's no Santa Claus. I'm sorry to be the one to break it to you, but we don't sit around out here and listen to the music of the cosmos in hopes of picking up some alien broadcast of their evening news. It's one thing to point a satellite down at a known target in the Middle East and eavesdrop on our enemies. It's a whole different ball game when you direct your attention up into the heavens. The universe is huge. Back when SETI first began, we actually did put on the headphones and scan one channel at a time. But it didn't take long to realize the futility of that. Fortunately for us, computer technology was revving up about the same time we were. Now, instead of me monitoring one channel at a time, our computers scan tens of millions of channels simultaneously; and they don't get bored or tired."

"How would you know if you ever got a hit?" Dave asked, intrigued by this new understanding of the operations of SETI.

"We've got software that looks for anomalies, repetitions, anything too organized to be natural. When the computer finds a signal that matches certain parameters, it flags it and notifies us. This way we are able to scan much larger portions of the sky, but still we are only listening to a very small fraction of it at any given time."

"That's very interesting," Dave said.

"What do you think about our signal?" Jim asked, pointing to the monitor next to Carl.

"It's definitely a signal," Carl replied. "A strong one, too. But I can't tell you what it is."

"You can't?" Dave protested. "Then why did we drive all the way out here? I thought you were the expert on this sort of thing."

"Yeah," Jim added, "why were you so eager for us to meet you out here?"

Carl let the questions hang in the air before answering. "There are two things about your signal that raises flags, neither of which have anything to do with what I see on that screen. First, the location; you say this signal is a two-way between the earth and the moon. That's not all that unusual since we sometimes bounce signals off reflectors left on the moon's surface in order to measure the distance between here and there. But the last time I checked, there weren't any humans on the moon. So actual information transmission would be highly anomalous. Second, the time of the occurrences; you say this signal appears only when the moon enters its new moon phase. Frankly, I don't know what to make of that. But it's just the kind of thing that gets my attention." He let his analysis sink in before continuing. "I hate to disappoint you, but your signal is unreadable. There's definitely something there, but whatever it is, it's not compatible with our play-back equipment."

"In other words, this was all just a waste of time." Jim sighed and shook his head.

"On the contrary," Carl said. If he was the least bit disappointed, he didn't show it. In fact, there was a hint of excitement about him.

"Am I missing something?" Dave asked.

Carl looked like he was about to follow one train of thought, but suddenly switched tracks. "Our meeting is on this particular date for a reason. And, again, I have aligned our dish to the moon's position."

"I'm sorry, Carl," Jim said. "I'm still not following you. If you were going to listen for the signal anyway, why bother bringing us out here?"

"Verification," Carl said. "You possess the original signal, which you say has occurred several times whenever the moon is in a certain phase. If it shows up again, and we positively match its signature to what you've recorded, then that verifies we have the same signal. And, with our radio telescope we can listen, and I mean really listen, to see if there are any ghosts."

"Ghosts?" Dave repeated. "What's that?"

"A ghost is another signal that might have gone unnoticed by your equipment. Suppose there is something on the moon that is receiving and transmitting loads of information. Whatever it is might be unintentionally broadcasting another signal. It could be a piece of machinery or some kind of mechanism with a distinct signature all its own. I know it's a long shot, but it just might make a difference."

"Okay," Jim said, a little more hopeful that this was not a complete waste of time. "What do we do now?"

"We wait."

Nearly two hours passed without a blip, bell, or siren. Twice Dave and Jim had to excuse themselves for some fresh air and escape the confines of the time capsule from the '60s. Carl, however, seemed right at home. After one particularly long period of mind-numbing silence, Carl slowly got up from the couch and hobbled his way over to the control panel. Without announcement or explanation, he switched off the 8-Track and switched on the audio feed from the radio telescope. A strange warbling sound emanated from a speaker mounted on the wall above the control panel.

"That's it," Dave said excitedly, springing up from his chair. "That's our signal!"

"What do you make of it?" Jim enquired.

"Not sure. Give me a minute." Carl went to work, his fingers flying over the controls on the equipment surrounding him. One video monitor depicted a pulsating sound wave graphic, and another plotted coordinates on a digital representation of the earth. After about a minute, he began rattling off what the equipment told him. "Man, there's a boatload of information here. It's definitely the same signal. The signature is identical. And you were right; it's two-way. Points of origin are geo- and lunar-based." Carl grabbed the mouse in front of the main computer and clicked open a dialogue box.

"What are you doing?" Jim asked.

"Response protocol. I'm sending a real-time data stream to several of our sister outposts around the world. I need to see if anyone else is getting this."

Within seconds, the replies came back. The Arecibo station in Puerto Rico was the first to respond. They were getting a strong signal, confirming Carl's observation. Then came Green Bank Observatory in West Virginia—also a confirmation. The Westerbork Station in Groningen, Netherlands responded next, followed by ATCA (Australian Telescope Compact Array). Carl typed messages to all four stations, requesting them to continue monitoring.

"You're not going to believe this," he said. "This isn't an isolated event. Puerto Rico and West Virginia confirm your signal; they're saying it's coming from the Pacific Northwest. Westerbork is saying they intercepted an identical signal yesterday coming from Ireland. ATCA says they've been monitoring the same signal in their own neighborhood for months; the latest occurrence was yesterday. Guys, we've got at least three unidentifiable transmissions from three different locations on the earth—all to the moon."

"What does that mean?" Dave asked.

"I don't know. If there is lunar activity, I can understand the U.S., but Ireland and Australia? It doesn't make any sense."

"What about that ghost thing you mentioned?" Jim asked.

Carl nodded and went to work again, typing commands into his computer and adjusting the knobs on the audio equipment. "Look here." He pointed to one of the monitors. "This is the main signal. As you can see, it has multiple layers of information."

Jim smiled smugly. "I knew that."

Carl continued. "Now watch this. You can tell by the oscillations that these frequencies contain the information being transmitted. Whatever it is—sound, video, or whatever—it doesn't come across as a pure, uninterrupted signal. But this one here—look at how steady it is. It's perfectly uniform." Using the mouse, Carl selected several frequencies and muted them. "Now if we mute these frequencies, this is what we have left."

The sound coming from the speaker changed from the strange warbling sound to a very low and dull *whump, whump, whump.*

"That, gentlemen, is our ghost. You couldn't hear it for all the other noise, but it's always been there."

"Okay, so what is that?" Jim asked.

Carl sat back and laced his fingers together behind his head. "I've been listening to this stuff for thirty years. I've heard everything from airplanes to electric garage doors. Now I've never heard this exact signal, but I can tell you what it reminds me of." A smile crept onto his lips.

"Go on," Dave urged.

"It sounds an awful lot like an engine."

"An engine for what?" Jim asked.

"Well, given that it's coming from the vicinity of the moon, I can pretty much eliminate trucks and motorcycles. It's a ship."

"A ship," Jim echoed. "You mean a…a…a *space*ship?"

"It ain't no cruise ship. Of course, it's a spaceship. Lunar orbiter, space shuttle, whatever you want to call it, that is some kind of spacecraft."

"Wait. Just hold on." Jim paced around in a circle. "Are you telling me there's a spaceship orbiting the moon communicating with someone in the America, Ireland, and Australia, and we don't know about it? That's not possible. If we sent a ship to the moon, don't you think it would have been on the news? Don't you think somebody would have sent us a memo? We work for the government."

"You assume it's one of ours," Carl noted.

"Whose else could it be?"

Carl sat back in his chair, grinning.

"Oh, come on!" Jim exclaimed. "You don't expect me to believe… you can't seriously be suggesting…" Jim rubbed his face in his hands.

"Are you telling me that's a UFO?"

Carl chuckled. "If it's in the vicinity of the moon, it had to *fly* there. And at the moment it is *unidentified*. By definition it is a UFO."

"Don't get technical with me," Jim said. "Are you saying that's a spacecraft from a planet that is *not* Earth?"

Dave, who had been listening intently to all that was being said, spoke up. "Carl, you started to say something earlier—something about not being able to read the signal with your equipment. What were you thinking?"

Carl shrugged. "I'm not saying your signal is from aliens, but suppose it is. What are the chances of even our most advanced technology being able to actually read a signal of alien origin?"

The look on Dave's and Jim's faces suggested they had never considered this before.

"You didn't think we'd actually be able to decipher an alien signal." Carl laughed out loud. "What did you think? That we'd be able to translate their language? Communicate with them? If you thought that, you've been watching too many movies. The very best we can hope for is a signal that would suggest the existence of extraterrestrial intelligent life. I don't know anyone in the scientific community who believes we will ever actually communicate with an alien—not in our lifetime, anyway."

Dave and Jim were stunned by this honest assessment of the limitations of SETI's work. "But what about this?" Dave pointed to the monitor. "Doesn't this prove something?"

Carl shrugged. "All I know is that it proves activity in the vicinity of the moon. Highly unusual? Yes. Conspiratorial? Likely. Alien?" Carl didn't give an answer to that question.

"What if it *is* alien?" Dave queried. "It could validate everything you've been doing here."

"*Used* to do here," Carl corrected. "I don't work for SETI anymore."

"You don't?" Jim asked. "Then how did we get in here? Never mind, I don't want to know."

"Still," Dave continued his train of thought, "it could be the final word on your life's work. Wouldn't you like to silence all those who have doubted the legitimacy of your work? Wouldn't you like to take this signal and shove it right into their faces? Wouldn't you like to prove yourself?"

"You have no idea," Carl admitted. "Do you know what it's like to believe in something with all your heart, to dedicate your life to finding it, and after thirty years have absolutely nothing to show for it? That's right, I've spent my entire life searching for just a speck of evidence that intelligent life is out there—it's all I've ever wanted.

I'm almost sixty years old, and have no more proof now than when I was an idealistic young fool. If I've learned anything in the last thirty years, it's how to be patient. I'll admit, you two have stumbled onto something. Something big. But I am not about to jump to the conclusion that it's what I want it to be. I've already been down that road. I won't get burned again."

An uncomfortable silence fell upon them.

"So, what do we do now?" Dave asked.

"Well, there's not much you can do today. But on…" Carl flipped the page on the lunar desk calendar. "November 14 you could go to…" He punched in a command and read the data that popped up. "43.30 degrees north, 107.96 degrees west and find out who's talking to the moon. But if you do, I suggest you use caution. There's a good chance that whoever it is doesn't want anybody to know about them. Looks like they're in…" Carl clicked on a button labeled *map* and a map of the United States popped up on the screen. An image of a little flag blinked on and off in the upper left-hand quadrant of the screen. "Central Wyoming. Middle of nowhere."

"You'll come with us, won't you Carl?"

Carl shook his head. "Sorry." He paused and then added, "But if you find anything, I'd appreciate it if you called me. You have my number."

"Whoa," Jim said, his hands up in front of him. "I am not driving all the way to Wyoming to get tangled up in something we're not supposed to know. If the government wants my help, they can ask me. I'll be at my post."

Dave knew his friend well enough to know his mind was made up. And by the looks of Carl Drake, he was quite sure the old man would be of no further help.

CHAPTER 36:

A STORM IS COMING

. . .
. .

Good Wednesday morning. It's 6:00 in the Big Sky country, the fourteenth day of November, 2001. Can you believe it? Thanksgiving is just about a week away. If you're a turkey, you might want to start making plans to get out of town. (Gobble, Gobble sound effect). Seriously though, if you're a human and you're getting ready for work, you might want to warm up your truck. Temperatures dipped to a frosty twenty-eight degrees last night. I had to scrape the ice off my windows this morning. But don't worry, it's going to be a beautiful, sunny day today with temperatures soaring to about fifty-five by this afternoon. Speaking of weather, have you seen the storms stacking up off the coast of California? Looks like winter's coming in with a vengeance. The National Weather Center has issued a major winter storm warning for the entire northwest. According to our weather models here at the station on the campus of Central Wyoming College, we should be seeing the first traces of snow by late tomorrow night. We're also looking at a major dip in the jet stream, which will bring that frigid arctic air right down on top of us. We could be looking at six or seven days of freezing temperatures; and those are the highs, my friends. So, take advantage of today and tomorrow, check your food stocks, bring in some extra wood, and above all find somebody you love to stay warm with. If you're out there, Sarah Conner, keep a sharp eye because...a storm is coming. (Cue music: "Riding the Storm Out" by REO Speedwagon).

Rick groaned as he hit the snooze button on his bedside clock radio. "Did you hear that, Jane?"

"Mm-hmm." Jane snuggled closer to his side.

"I was planning on going into town tomorrow, but I can go today. If you make a list, I'll go to the grocery store."

Jane yawned and stretched. "Did he really say six or seven days?"

"Yeah. I was watching the Weather Channel last night. There are at least three storms coming in. I didn't realize they would get here by tomorrow."

"I better go with you then. I'm going to have to do all the shopping for Thanksgiving."

"Oh," Rick sighed. "Maybe I can drop you off at the grocery store while I run a few errands. Do you think Aldi and Elsa-Eska would mind watching Jalamin for us?"

"Or we could all go."

"Really? You want *all of us* to go Thanksgiving shopping right before a major storm? You do realize we won't be the only ones trying to get a jump on the crowds, don't you?"

"Oh, come on. It'll be fun. Besides, if we're all going to be cooped up here for a week, it will do us all some good to get out for the day."

"For the day?" Rick complained. "I was hoping for more of a fast attack strategy. You know, get in, grab it, and get out. You're talking full-scale invasion with diaper bags and everything."

"I tell you what," Jane said. "Elsa-Eska and I will do the food shopping and keep the girls with us, and you and Aldi can run your errands. Then we can go to The Bull for lunch. We'll put the frozen stuff in the cooler; it'll be fine."

"The Bull?" Rick's mouth began to water. "They serve meat there. Oh, what I'd give for one of their buffalo burgers." He could picture the thick, juicy goodness.

"Oh, yeah," Jane replied. "We better go to the Golden Corral instead. They've got a good salad and veggie bar. Good thinking."

"Yeah, good thinking." In Rick's mind, the buffalo burger grew legs and ran off into the woods, leaving him surrounded by a pile of wilted lettuce and shriveled tomatoes. "That's just great," he mumbled to himself.

Out in the living room, Rick found Aldi sitting on the couch with both girls, one in each arm. Their eyes were transfixed upon Aldi's face as he was speaking to them in a low soothing voice. When Rick got close enough, he discovered Aldi was speaking in Klyvian.

"Good morning, Aldi," Rick said.

"Good morning."

The two girls glanced over at Rick, but quickly turned their gaze back to Aldi.

"What are you doing, telling them Klyvian children's stories?"

"I am teaching them the Song of our People."

"Oh, that's nice," replied Rick. "Want some coffee?"

"Yes, please."

As Rick turned to go into the kitchen, he could hear Aldi resume the Klyvian Song. Waiting for the coffee to brew, he thought about how much things had changed since their arrival. When he first heard the Song, he wanted so badly to understand it. He even tried to learn some of the Klyvian language along with Jane, but after a few lessons, he gave up. Now, the Song seemed to him little more than a children's song. After the coffee maker burped out the last few drips, Rick filled two cups and joined Aldi back in the living room.

"Thank you, Rick," Aldi said and took a sip. "Mm, this is good."

"Glad you like it," Rick said. "It's a new one from my Coffee of the Month Club. It's called *Ibu Brew*. It's from Indonesia."

The two men sipped their coffee in silence while the girls squiggled and squirmed playfully on the blanket where Aldi had laid them. Sara had a hold of Jalamin's hand, trying to get her thumb into her mouth.

"Say Aldi," Rick said, "we heard on the radio that there's a large storm coming in tomorrow night. Jane and I need to go into town to buy food, and I have a few other things to take care of. We thought it would be good if we all went. Do you think Elsa-Eska would be up for a day in town?"

"We cannot go," Aldi said. "It is time to speak to the Enterprise."

"Oh, I didn't realize it was time again." In Rick's mind, he heard the sound of a lone buffalo burger running toward him. His mouth began to water. "Well, we'll probably be back sometime after lunch."

CHAPTER 37:

ROADSIDE ASSISTANCE

Word of the coming storm had spread fast. The grocery store was packed by the time Rick and Jane arrived, and the stock on the shelves was already thin. Rick decided to stay with Jane, partly to keep Jalamin occupied while Jane hurried through her list, and partly because Jane consented to lunch at The Bull afterward. Enduring a crowded grocery store was a small price to pay for meat. And it was worth it. Rick savored every bite of his buffalo burger—his first in over eight months. Even Jane, who had adjusted easily to their Klyvian-friendly vegetarian diet, admitted that her chicken sandwich hit the spot. Still, she said she felt like a kid sneaking candy behind her parent's back.

"I'm sorry you didn't get to do everything you wanted today," Jane said as they drove out of town. "What was it anyway?"

Rick hesitated, trying to keep his face expressionless. "Oh, nothing. Just a few things I needed to take care of."

Jane had seen the expressionless expression before. She knew it meant he was up to something. "Oh, come on. Tell me," she begged teasingly.

"No."

"Why not?"

"Because."

"Because why?"

Rick shook his head. "Janie, Janie, Janie. You are such a kid. And kids should know not to ask questions this time of year."

Jane gasped and her eyes grew wider. "You mean…?"

"Yep." Rick nodded and allowed a smile to form on his lips.

Jane clapped her hands and twisted around so she could see Jalamin in her car seat. "Daddy's buying Christmas presents."

Halfway between Riverton and the Blackwell Ranch, Jane's Jeep coasted to a stop on the shoulder of the highway.

"What's wrong?" Jane asked.

"I don't know," Rick replied. "The engine just cut off."

"Are we out of gas?"

"No. There's still a half a tank." Rick pulled the hood release and got out of the Jeep. He went around to the front and lifted the hood.

Jane sighed. Rick knew about as much about automotive repair as she did, which was nothing. Five seconds later, Rick got back into the Jeep. Jane looked at him, doing her best to hide her amusement. "What did you find?"

Rick nodded. "The engine's still in there."

"What now?"

Rick shrugged and set his hands back on the steering wheel. "We have got to get one of those cell phones."

A knock on Jane's window startled her. She turned to see a young man smiling in at her—he looked to be in his late-twenties, maybe thirty with sandy blond hair, blue eyes. He was dressed in hiking gear and had a large pack on his back. Stepping back, he made a motion for Jane to roll down her window.

"Hold on," Rick said. He got out of the Jeep and walked around to the other side.

"You folks need some help?" the man asked.

Rick sized him up. It wasn't all that unusual to see people hiking through the area. The man was certainly dressed for it. "You know anything about cars?"

"A little. What happened?"

"I don't know," Rick replied. "It just died."

"Mind if I take a look?"

Rick made one more inspection of the man. He seemed okay. "I'd appreciate it."

The man approached Rick and stuck out his hand. "My name's William."

"I'm Rick." He shook William's hand. It was a firm handshake, the kind that communicated confidence, but not overly firm like a man with something to prove. The two men stood there for a moment, hands and eyes locked. There was something about him, Rick couldn't put his finger on it, but he knew he liked the man.

"Good to meet you," William said, pulling off his backpack and setting it on the ground. "Now let's see if we can raise the dead." He approached the patient and began his examination.

"Where you heading?" Rick asked, more to make conversation than gain information.

"West."

"How far?"

"Not sure. Guess I'll know when I get there."

"Just passing through then?"

William looked Rick in the eye. "Aren't we all?" He winked and turned back to engine. "I'm not trying to be evasive. It's just that I'm not really sure where I'll end up. I just got out of a bad situation and I'm out here trying to make sense of it. Know what I mean?"

"Actually, I know exactly what you mean."

"Strange how life is."

"How's that?"

"Just last month, I was sitting in a nice office, pulling down six figures. Lots of friends. Pretty girlfriend. Then one day I woke up with a question in my head." He paused just enough to make sure Rick was really listening. "You want to know what it was?"

"Yeah, sure."

"Is this all there is?" He paused again. "Man, I had it all, but it just hit me that there's got to be something else besides money and good times. You ever asked yourself that question, Rick?"

Rick nodded.

William continued. "So I cashed in and checked out. I know that sounds irresponsible. At least it does to my parents. But I have to tell you, I was about to suffocate." He took a deep breath and let it out, savoring it like the aroma of a rose. "I feel so much better now. I can breathe again."

"Huh," Rick said. "That was me about five years ago. We lived on the east coast before moving out here."

William made eye contact again. "Well, my fellow escapee, maybe you can enlighten me about something."

"What's that?"

"There's something about this place I can't quite identify." He took a long look at the wide-open space that surrounded them. "I feel small here, vulnerable, like the land could swallow me up. Yet it doesn't scare me."

Rick nodded. "I know what you mean. I have that same sensation."

"I want to call it something, but I can't quite think of it. *Wild* almost gets it, but not quite."

"What about *untamed*?" Rick offered.

William flashed a big toothy smile and nodded. "That's it. *Untamed.* That's what it is." William lowered the hood of the Jeep. "Let's see if that got it."

"Really?" Rick looked doubtful. It didn't seem to him that William had done anything under the hood but look. "Okay." He stepped around to the driver's side and got back into the Jeep.

"Who's that?" Jane asked.

"Just some guy. His name's William."

"Was he able to fix it?"

"We'll see." Rick turned the key, and the engine started immediately. Rick looked at Jane. "I guess he did."

Jane rummaged through her pursue and pulled out a twenty dollar bill. "Here. Give this to him."

"Good idea." Rick took the twenty and got back out of the Jeep.

William was putting on his backpack. "Good as new, eh?"

"Yeah. Thanks a lot. You really saved us. Here, take this." He offered William the money.

"Oh, no," William protested, waving his hands in front of himself. "Really, I don't need it. I'm set." He took a step toward Rick and stuck out his hand. "Just one escapee helping another."

Rick shook William's hand. "There must be some way we can express our appreciation. You really helped us out."

William looked like he wanted to say something, but hesitated. "You already did. You gave me the word. Here's to the *untamed*."

"If you're sure. Thank you, thank you very much."

William turned and started walking down the road.

Rick got back into the Jeep and handed the twenty back to Jane. "He wouldn't take it."

"Where's he going?" Jane enquired. "It'll be dark soon. Where's he going to stay?"

"I don't know."

"We can't just leave him out here. He'll freeze to death." Jane thought for a moment. "He could stay in Burt's place, just for tonight. I doubt Burt would mind."

"You sure about that?"

"I think so. He seems like a nice enough guy. After all, he sure got us out of a spot. Ask him."

Rick pulled the Jeep up next to William and slowed to match his walking pace. Jane rolled down her window. "Hello, William? Hi. Thank you so much for your help."

"Your quite welcome, ma'am," William said, still walking.

"Say, we were just noticing it's getting kind of late in the day. Do you have a place to stay tonight?"

William spread his arms out wide. "You're lookin' at it. Out here in the untamed. Eh, Rick?"

"You do realize how cold it gets out here, don't you?"

"I'll be alright. I've got a polar-rated sleeping bag."

Jane shuddered at the thought of spending an entire night alone out in the desert. "We've got a place not far from here. Why don't you let us give you a good meal and warm place to sleep?"

"Thank you, but I don't want to impose."

"Actually, we own a ranch with a vacant guest house. You could stay there; have all the privacy you want. What do you say?"

William walked several more steps. "You sure I won't be any trouble?"

"No, no trouble at all. Come on, get in."

William stopped and turned toward the Jeep. "A warm bed would feel pretty good. Okay, I accept."

Rick got out of the Jeep and opened the rear hatch. "You can put your pack in here."

William slipped his backpack off and stowed it in the back of the Jeep. Then he climbed into the back seat behind Rick. "What a beautiful baby. Must be a girl. She looks just like you, Jane."

CHAPTER 38:

COLD

`∂`

"Jalamin," the stranger said. "That's an interesting name. I don't believe I've ever heard that one before."

"It's…" Jane caught herself mid-thought. "It's, uh, Russian."

Rick gave her a sideways glance.

"Where did you hear it?" William asked.

Jane hesitated, looking at Rick for some assistance. He kept his eyes fixed ahead, but gave a slight shake of his head. "A friend," she finally replied.

Rick glanced into his rearview mirror. He was starting to have second thoughts about picking up the stranger. *What was I thinking? I never pick up hitchhikers, especially with Jane and Jalamin in the car. What if this guy's a mugger or an escaped convict or a serial killer?* Then he thought of Aldi and Elsa-Eska. *What if he's some kind of X-Files FBI agent? What if the government somehow figured out Aldi and Elsa-Eska are here and they sent this guy to catch them?* He looked into the mirror again and saw William staring blankly out the window. *Naw, he's probably just a guy like me trying to get a handle on life.* Rick tried to concentrate on his last thought in hopes that it would dispel the others.

William's voice cut into Rick's concentration. "I can't tell you how much I appreciate your kindness. You know, most folks don't like to pick up strangers. It's a shame how hard it is to trust people these days. I was a little nervous about accepting your offer. I mean, you guys aren't going to rob me, are you?" He spoke these last words with a chuckle in his voice.

Rick and Jane joined in with nervous laughter of their own. "Of course not," Jane said.

"No, of course not," Rick echoed. "But watch out for Jalamin. She might steal your heart."

William chuckled, more easily this time. "I'll bet she could."

The levity succeeded in putting Rick's mind at ease. *A bad guy wouldn't joke around like that, would he?* Still, the sooner William was on his way, the better he would feel.

Rick stopped the Jeep at the first structure they came to on the dirt road leading onto the Blackwell Ranch. "Here it is. Jane, if you want to drive on to the house, I'll help William get settled and walk the rest of the way."

Jane's forehead creased with concern. "No, we'll wait for you. Jalamin's asleep anyway. Take your time."

"Okay."

"Thanks again, ma'am," William said as he opened his door. "I wish there were more people like you folks in this world."

Jane smiled. "You're welcome, William. And may God bless you on your way."

The temperature inside the guest house was about the same as outside. Rick flipped on the light switch and adjusted the thermostat. "It shouldn't take long to warm up in here. There's some wood out back if you want to make a fire."

"Thank you, Rick." William looked around at the cozy quarters. "Not a bad place."

"Our ranch manager stays here during the summer. He heads south when the weather turns cold. Feel free to make yourself at home. There's a bed in the back, and a bathroom. The TV works, though we don't get very good reception out here." Rick looked toward the small kitchen and noticed there was a pot left on the stove. "Uh, I don't think there's any food left in the kitchen. But if there is, I wouldn't eat it. I'll bring something to you later."

"No, that's alright," William protested. "I've got food in my pack."

"How 'bout some coffee?"

"Thanks, but really, I'll be fine."

"Okay then." Rick took one last look around the place. "Sleep well and stay as late as you like tomorrow."

"Thank you, Rick." William extended his hand. "Your kindness is more than I could have hoped for."

Rick shook William's hand. "Just one escapee helping another."

"Here's to the untamed."

"The untamed."

Aldi came out to greet Rick and Jane as they pulled up in front of the main house. "Hello," he called out as soon as Rick and Jane got out of the Jeep. "Did you have a good day in town?"

"Yes, it was very nice," Jane said. She slung the diaper bag over her shoulder and gently hoisted the sleeping Jalamin out of her car seat. "I'm going to take Jalamin in. Rick, do you mind if I leave the groceries to you?"

"Not at all." He opened the back hatch of the Jeep.

"I'll help." Aldi grabbed two bags.

"What's the latest news from the Enterprise?" Rick asked, grabbing two bags of his own.

"My father says they are preparing to leave."

"What's the hurry?" Rick asked. "I thought they weren't leaving until January."

"There is no need to stay. All of the teams are in place. They must continue the mission."

"When are they leaving?"

"We will speak once more when the moon is hidden again."

"That soon?" Rick considered the schedule revision. "I bet it'll be hard for you to not have them just right up there."

"*Hard*?" Aldi mused.

"Difficult," Rick offered. "Now, you can at least see where your family is. And if you need anything, you can make contact. It just seems to me that you might feel stranded here after they're gone. Didn't you say you don't know when they'll come back?"

"Yes, I did say that," Aldi replied. "I also said that our family here will help us not miss so much our family there."

After three trips each, Rick and Aldi brought the last of the groceries in. Jane was already putting the items away.

"Where's Elsa-Eska?" she asked.

"She is with Sara," Aldi replied. "They are both asleep."

"Is she not feeling well?" Jane remembered that when they first arrived Elsa-Eska had slept a lot, but that was only until she became acclimated to the earth's environment. Jane could not recall the last time Elsa-Eska had napped during the day.

"It's the cold," Aldi explained. "She will be fine when it gets warm again."

Rick and Jane exchanged glances.

"Uh, Aldi," Rick said. "I hate to tell you this, but it's going to get a lot colder. And the warm weather won't return for about five or six months."

A look of concern came over Aldi. "How much colder?"

"You know how it felt this morning before the sunrise?"

"Yes. It was very cold."

"That was about thirty degrees. There will be many days when you'll be wishing it was that warm."

Aldi considered Rick's words, but he had no point of reference for what Rick was trying to explain.

"It's called seasonal change," Rick explained further. "It has something to do with the way the earth is tilted and its position in relation to the sun."

"I understand axial precession. That is why there is less sunlight now than before."

"That's right. And with less sunlight on this part of the earth, the weather gets colder."

"I understand," Aldi said, but the look of concern did not leave his face.

"What is it, Aldi?" Jane asked.

"I do not know how it will be for Elsa-Eska. The air is cold to me, but I am able to stay in it. The cold causes Elsa-Eska to shake like this." Aldi imitated the way he had seen Elsa-Eska shiver. "And it causes her to have pain in her head. It was like that today when the air was not very cold. I do not know how it will be for her when it gets as cold as the night air. She will not be well in that cold."

"And it will get even colder than that," Rick said. "Much colder."

A silence fell upon the three as they considered this new challenge. Finally, Jane spoke. "Maybe she'll get used to it. Until then, we'll just have to keep her inside where it's warm."

That evening, dinner was served at Aldi's and Elsa-Eska's home. Jane created a culinary masterpiece fit for the kings and queens of Klyv, or at least the only Klyvian king and queen they knew: Homemade vegetable soup, meatless quesadilla rolls, and two loaves of French bread. She also brought a pitcher of sweet iced tea, and apple cobbler for dessert.

Although the inside of the their home was quite warm to Rick and Jane, Elsa-Eska shivered under the thick quilt she kept wrapped around herself. She sneezed several times when Rick and Jane and Jalamin arrived, and she moved slowly as if her entire body ached.

"We're so sorry you're not feeling well," Jane said, setting Jalamin's carrier on the floor next to Sara's. The two girls gurgled and cooed when they saw each other.

"Thank you, Jane, for bringing dinner here," Elsa-Eska said.

"It's no problem at all." Jane approached Elsa-Eska and felt her forehead with the back of her hand. "Hmm, you feel warm to me. I wonder if you've caught a cold."

"Yes," Elsa-Eska agreed. "There is much cold. Aldi says it will get even colder."

Rick tried to hide his amusement. Even after all this time and all their progress, Aldi and Elsa-Eska still took human phrases literally. "You're right, it is cold outside," Jane explained. "But *a cold* is something different. It's when you don't feel well on the inside. It's what we call being sick. Haven't you ever been sick before?"

Elsa-Eska shook her head. "I have felt like this only when we first arrived here."

"I see." It made sense to Jane. Given the vacuum of space and the containment of the space ship, it would have been impossible for them to have been exposed to any germ that didn't come onboard with the original crew.

After dinner, Elsa-Eska looked as if she would fall asleep at any moment. Aldi agreed to let Jane take both girls for the night so he could tend to her. So with both girls in tow, Rick and Jane said goodnight and left Aldi and Elsa-Eska alone.

Back in their own house, Rick helped Jane get the girls situated, which meant getting their pajamas on and putting them down in the playpen in the living room. The girls were both wide awake and intent on an evening of play. Once they were settled, and Rick was free from his responsibilities, he started thinking more about William.

"Say, I think I'll take some of this soup down to William. He said he had food in his pack, but I doubt it's as good as this."

"You think that's a good idea?" Jane asked. There was a note of anxiety in her voice.

"Sure," Rick replied. "I just keep thinking of the poor guy all alone with nothing to eat but a pack of crackers. And here we are all fat and happy with all this left-over soup and cobbler."

"You do have a point."

Rick could always count on Jane's compassion over-riding her caution. Still, he didn't want her to worry. "If I'm not back in thirty minutes, just call. It'll give me a good excuse to leave."

Jane poked her bottom lip out in a mock pout. "Promise me you'll be careful."

"I promise."

"And you'll come back before I have to call?" Her pout morphed into her crooked grin.

Rick smiled and shook his head. He was a sucker for Jane's crooked grin. "Okay, I'll make it quick."

"Promise?"

"Promise."

Jane reached her arms around his neck and pulled him in for a toe-curling kiss. After several long, passionate moments, he came up for air. "Whoa! What was that for?"

"Incentive."

CHAPTER 39:

SWAPPING STORIES

$\int\approx$

When Rick arrived at Coop's house, he found the place dark. Seeing no sign of movement, he wondered if William might be asleep. He was about to abort his mission of good will and return to Jane when the door opened.

"Rick?" a voice called out in the dark. "Is that you?"

"Yeah, it's me."

"I thought I heard something. Come in."

Rick stepped into the darkened house and closed the door behind him. "Mind if I turn on a light?"

"Not at all."

Rick flipped the light switch and a lamp in the corner came on. "I thought you might be asleep."

"No. Just enjoying the accommodations."

Rick noticed William's backpack on the floor where he had last seen it. It didn't look like the man had done anything in the room since Rick left him. "I don't want to disturb you. I just thought you might like some hot soup."

William closed his eyes and inhaled deeply. "Let me guess—vegetable, no meat?"

"Hey, that's right. Sorry about the no meat. We're kind of on this vegetarian thing. But it is hot and there's plenty of it."

"Thanks." William fixed his eyes upon his host. "I could use a hot meal…and the company if you can stay."

An image of Jane with her crooked smile flashed through Rick's mind. He wanted to hurry back to her, but he didn't want to be rude to his guest. "I can stay for a few minutes."

"You're thinking of that pretty wife of yours."

"That obvious, eh?"

"I know I would be. Besides, I'm pretty good at reading people. That's why I accepted your offer to stay here tonight. I can tell you're good people."

Rick blushed at the compliment. "Well, uh, here's the soup. It's best when it's hot."

William accepted the container and sat down in one of the chairs. Rick took the only other chair in the room.

"Mm, fantastic. I'd forgotten how good real food can taste. My compliments to the chef."

"Has it been awhile?"

"A few weeks."

"If you don't mind my asking," Rick said, "where'd you escape from?"

"Escape?" William asked quizzically, then he caught the reference. "Oh, right. I escaped from New York."

"Wow! You walked all the way here from New York?"

William shook his head and swallowed another large mouthful of soup. "Not walked, rode. I sort of stumbled upon an all-access pass." He nodded toward his backpack. Plastered across the back were two large decals—an American flag at the top and beneath it an I♥NY bumper sticker. "Ever since the attacks, these have taken on a whole new meaning. Patriotism is making a comeback."

"Were you in the city on September 11?"

William nodded and took another bite of soup. "I saw the second plane hit and watched the towers fall. Never seen anything like it in my life."

Rick recalled the horrific images he had seen on the television. He remained silent as if out of respect.

William continued. "Actually, that was the day I started planning my escape. I knew a lot of people who worked in the World Trade Center. We were all chasing the same dream, but on that day everything changed. Watching my friends die sort of opened my eyes, and I realized that what I thought was so important really wasn't."

Rick found himself being drawn into William's story. Though the catalyst was different, the result was the same as what he had experienced years before when he was dreaming about his own escape from the rat race.

"I didn't leave right away. I just kept going through the motions. Like everybody else, I was trying to find meaning in it all and regain a sense of normalcy. But there wasn't any. No meaning. No normalcy." He paused and then, "Rick, can I ask you something?"

"Sure."

"What would you do if you suddenly realized that something you believed in your entire life wasn't true?"

The question tapped into Rick's own experience of the last eight months. He flashed on Aldi and Elsa-Eska and how their existence had completely altered his worldview. He remembered his futile resistance that day on the road; how he fought to preserve the belief he had held his entire life. Then he remembered how it felt to finally let go and accept his new reality. He recalled how his fear of the unknown had been turned to joy of discovering the truth.

"Have you ever had that experience?" William asked when Rick did not answer. His gaze upon Rick was intense as if Rick's response would provide a clue to his own quest.

"Actually, I have," Rick replied slowly.

"How did you deal with it?"

"I resisted at first. I didn't want to believe it, but it's hard to ignore the truth when they're staring you in the face."

"And they helped you believe something you previously thought was impossible?"

Something in Rick's gut told him to be careful. "Yes. Why do you ask?"

The intensity in William's eyes softened at once, and his disarming smile returned. "I'm interested because I find myself in just such a mental dilemma, but from a different angle. For you, it sounds like the impossible turned out to be true. For me, something I thought was true turned out to be false."

"Oh yeah? What was it?"

"Life," William replied. "Actually, the motivation of life. I used to believe it was all about the hunt. Money, women, fame—all the stuff of success—that was the prize. You either win it or you die. That was life to me, just one long drawn out game. I was pretty good at it, too."

Rick nodded his understanding.

"There's got to be more to it than that, Rick. I mean everybody dies in the end, right? Even the winners. So why do we get so caught up in the game?"

"I guess we don't know any better," Rick offered. "When everyone around us is living that way, we just sort of get sucked into it. I know exactly what you're saying. I was there myself."

"But you broke free," William pointed out. "You did it. You got out. Look where you are now. You saw the machine for what it is and you took back your life."

Rick chuckled. "I don't think it was quite as dramatic as all that. Truth is, we got lucky. A friend of mine got us in on the front end of the dot com wave, we made some money, and we cashed out before it crested. We made enough to buy this ranch and have the kind of life we wanted. I get to write, and Jane teaches at the college in town. We're not rich, but..."

"But you live on your terms," William said, completing Rick's sentence for him. "That's what I'm talking about. Out here, you don't have to live up to anyone's expectations but your own. That's freedom. I know a lot of people who say they're free, but they aren't. They have many masters—bosses who dole out choice projects and fat paychecks like drugs, colleagues who are gunning for the next promotion, the neighbor with the big boat in his driveway. Even their kids add another layer of expectations because they're caught up in their own version of the game. Man, I know so many miserable people who would love to live like you do, but they can't break the addiction."

"It looks like you did," Rick pointed out.

"That's right, I did. But it's been tough. Obscurity is a frightening prospect."

Obscurity. The word caught Rick by surprise. It sounded so demeaning, so humbling, so lonely—almost like death. He had never thought of his Wyoming adventure in those terms before, but there was a ring of truth to them. It wasn't long after he and Jane moved to the ranch that Rick discovered how small and insignificant he felt in the bigness of the land and sky. He also learned how vulnerable humans were to the elements of the untamed. Many times he was aware that he could disappear and no one would notice for a very long time. These things were unnerving in the beginning, but he learned to appreciate them. They gave him a different perspective on life. They taught him that there was indeed something much bigger than himself. In time, he found himself attracted to the very ideas that at first frightened him. *Obscure*—is that what he had become? *Obscurity*—is that the kind of life he wanted? Rick was staring at nothing, lost in his thoughts.

"Hey, Rick, you still here?" William waved his hand in front of Rick's eyes.

"Oh, sorry," Rick said, coming back from his mental excursion. "I was just thinking about what you said. This kind of life does take some getting used to. But if I can do it, anybody can."

"You really think so? I've been away from civilization for nearly a month. I think I might be going through withdrawals. Just this morning I was considering going back to New York to try to get my old job back."

Rick hoped he hadn't spoken too soon. He wanted to be encouraging, but he didn't want to encourage the wrong thing. What did he really know about this man? What if he wasn't cut out for this kind of life? Rick and Jane had moved to Wyoming with a plan and a healthy bank account; even then there had been challenges. Maybe William should go back to his old job. "Then again…"

"But now," William continued, "I feel better about being here. Meeting you and knowing you made it—you've inspired me."

"I have?"

"Sure. If I'm going to make a clean start I should just do it. I'm young. I've got no attachments. My back is strong and I don't mind getting my hands dirty. I'm sure I can get a job somewhere."

An idea began to form in Rick's mind. Rick and Aldi had done their best to continue the routine tasks around the ranch, but even a semi-working ranch had more work than two men could do by themselves. There were already indications that the Blackwell Ranch was suffering from neglect. They could sure use the help. Maybe it wasn't happenstance that the Jeep stalled where it did, and William was able to get it started.

"You know," William added, "maybe our meeting wasn't happenstance."

Rick did a double-take. "Huh, I was just thinking that very thing. Weird, eh?"

William shrugged and grinned. "Yeah, weird. So, what was your big revelation?"

"My what?"

"The thing you now believe. What was it?"

Rick was just about to make up a lie when the telephone rang. *Saved by the bell.* He scrambled to answer the phone before the next ring. "Hello…uh, huh…just talking…yes, he's eating it now…okay, I'm on my way…goodbye."

"Your wife wants you to come back to her," William said.

"Yeah, I told her I wouldn't be long."

"I guess you better go. Please tell her I loved the soup. Best I've ever had."

"I will."

"And thanks for the company, Rick. I truly enjoy talking to you. Maybe we can talk some more tomorrow before I head out."

"I'd like that." Rick got up and made his way to the door, then stopped. "Say, I can take you over the pass into Jackson, if that's where you're going."

"You've already done so much. I really don't want to impose upon your kindness."

"I can't let you just head out on foot. Besides, there's a storm coming in tomorrow evening. You don't want to be caught out in it."

William shuddered at the thought. "I can't argue with that. If you don't mind, I'd appreciate the ride. I guess I can get a hotel room in Jackson and wait out the storm there."

"Good," Rick said. "We'll want to get an early start. How 'bout I pick you up at seven and we grab some breakfast in DuBoise? It's about halfway."

"That sounds great. But it will be my treat. I insist."

Rick nodded. "Alright. Your treat."

"Don't forget to thank Jane for the soup."

"I won't." Rick opened the door. "See you in the morning."

CHAPTER 40:

INTO THE STORM

I

The next morning, Rick found Aldi standing out on his back deck watching the ominous clouds spilling over the mountains to the west. The sun had just risen behind him, but the day already seemed to have been claimed by the dread of the coming storm.

"Good morning, Rick," Aldi said. "The storm is coming sooner than tonight."

"It sure looks that way," Rick agreed. A sense of unease crept over him as he thought about the day's trip to Jackson. On a clear day, it was about an eight-hour drive roundtrip. By the looks of the sky, it was almost certain he would encounter bad weather on the way home if not sooner. "How is Elsa-Eska feeling this morning?"

"Better," Aldi replied. "She slept most of the night. How are the girls?"

"Great. Jalamin slept the whole night, and Sara woke up only once."

Aldi smiled. "That is good. Thank you for keeping Sara with you."

"No problem. I think they're getting old enough for us all to start sleeping normally again."

The two men turned their attention back toward the approaching storm. Aldi shivered and rubbed his hands together. "I can feel the air getting colder," he said. "I am concerned for Elsa-Eska. Even inside, she is not warm."

"Hey, I think we might still have an electric blanket," Rick said. "I'll ask Jane to get it for you."

"What is an electric blanket?" Aldi asked.

"It's a blanket that you can plug into the electric socket and it gets very warm."

Aldi nodded, seeming to understand.

"Say, Aldi," Rick said. "I'm going to be gone most of the day. Maybe you and Elsa-Eska and Sara should spend the day over here with Jane and Jalamin."

"Where are you going?"

"I have to drive to Jackson. It's on the other side of the mountains." Rick nodded toward the west.

A look of concern came over Aldi. "I do not see the mountains."

Sure enough, in the few minutes they had been standing there, the mountains had become completely obscured by the dark storm clouds. Rick checked his watch. It was 6:30.

"Rick," Aldi said, looking over Rick's shoulder. "There is a man."

Rick turned around and saw William walking toward them on the road just in front of the barn. He was wearing his backpack.

"Rick!" William called out and jogged the last fifty yards to the deck. He stopped short of climbing the steps. Now that he was close enough to get a good look at Aldi, his face showed his surprise. "Oh, I didn't realize there were others here."

Rick moved to the edge of the steps. "This is my brother, Al." He turned back toward Aldi. "Al, this is William. He's, um, just passing through the area and stayed in Coop's house last night."

"Good to meet you, Al," William said with a wave and a nod.

Aldi moved next to Rick and looked curiously at the man, but did not speak. This struck Rick as odd—Aldi was always so eager to meet another human—but he took advantage of Aldi's silence to take control of the situation.

"That storm is moving in faster than I thought. We better get on the road."

"I was just coming to talk to you about that." William put his foot on the bottom step. "Do you still think that's a good idea?"

From the corner of his eye, Rick noticed Aldi stiffen and take a step backward. "Oh, sure, but we better get going. Go ahead and put your pack in the Jeep. I'll be there in a minute."

William hesitated and looked at the storm clouds in the west. "I don't know, Rick. It's looking pretty bad. I'd hate to get stranded somewhere. Maybe we better come up with a Plan B."

"No, we'll be fine." Rick insisted, sounding more confident than he felt. "Wait for me in the Jeep. I'm just going to go inside to tell Jane we're leaving."

William took several steps backward away from the deck. He turned to walk toward the Jeep, but kept his attention focused on Rick and Aldi. Rick took Aldi by the arm and tried to pull him into the house. Aldi resisted at first as if he didn't want to let William out of his sight. Finally, he relented and followed Rick into the house.

"What was that about?" Rick asked, "What's wrong?"

"Who is that man?"

"Just a guy we met yesterday. He helped us with the Jeep, it was getting late, and we let him stay the night. That's called *human kindness*. Why did you…"

"Where did he come from?" Aldi interrupted abruptly. There was an uncharacteristic edge to his demeanor.

"He's from New York. Why did…" Rick interrupted himself when he saw Jane appear from the kitchen. She was holding Sara in her arms. The baby cooed happily at the sight of her father and reached a hand toward him.

"I thought I heard you guys," Jane said. "Good morning, Aldi."

Aldi's expression softened. "Good morning, Jane." He took Sara into his arms and touched his forehead to hers.

"What's going on?" Jane asked.

"I was just about to leave with William and…" Rick started to comment on Aldi's strange behavior, but changed his mind. "Do we still have that electric blanket?"

"Yes."

"Would you please get it for Elsa-Eska? I think she should spend the day here with you. I need to go."

Jane sensed the tension in the room. "Is something wrong?"

"No," he replied sharply. "I just need to get going before that storm gets too bad."

"You should not go with that man," Aldi said firmly.

Rick ignored the comment and kissed Jane on the cheek. "I hope to be back before dark. Bye, babe."

Rick was out the door before Jane or Aldi could offer another protest. Jane walked to the window in time to see the Jeep pull away from the house.

"What was that about?" Jane demanded as she turned away from the window.

"Rick should not be with that man," Aldi answered.

"Why?"

Before Aldi could answer, the front door opened and Elsa-Eska walked in. "Who is that man with Rick?"

"Whoa!" William said, looking back toward the house. "Who is that?"

"That's Al's wife."

"Do they live in that house next to yours?"

"Yes," Rick nodded.

William let out a curious snort.

"What?" Rick asked.

William shook his head and chuckled. "Man, that is one good looking woman."

Rick shot him a sideways glance and stepped down on the accelerator.

Back in the house, Aldi said something in Klyvian that brought a look of concern to Elsa-Eska's face. Jane recognized only a few words, but they made no sense to her. When Elsa-Eska took Sara into her arms and held her tightly, Jane understood the motherly instinct to protect her child.

"What's going on?" Jane asked. "English, please."

"That man," Aldi said. "He is not like other humans."

"In what way?" Jane asked. "I heard you say something about fear. I don't think there's anything to be afraid of."

Aldi put his arm around Elsa-Eska and led her to the couch. Jane moved tentatively toward the chair and sat down. "What is it, Aldi?"

"We have no fear of the man," Aldi replied. "And he has no fear of us."

"I don't understand," Jane said.

"The man has no fear at all."

Jane tried to process what Aldi was saying, but it meant nothing to her.

"Jane," Aldi said. "I know my brother very well. Rick does not appear to be afraid of the storm, but he is. He tries to hide his fear, but I could feel it. The man tries to show fear of the storm, but he is not afraid."

"Are you sure?" Jane asked.

"Yes."

"What *did* you sense in him?"

Aldi thought for a moment. "I do not know the human word, but I think it is what humans feel when they have war; not the fear, but what they feel for their enemy. Do you know the word for that?"

Jane nodded. "Yes. It's called *hatred.*"

By the time Rick and William arrived in DuBoise, about two hours down the road, they were seeing the first flakes of snow falling innocently onto the windshield and disappearing upon impact. They stopped at the Cowboy Café in hopes of getting a quick breakfast before tackling what would probably be a treacherous drive over

Togwotee Pass (elevation 9658 feet). So far, the journey had been uneventful and the conversation was only mildly interesting. Mostly, William asked Rick a lot of questions about his adjustment from life in the city to life on the ranch. Oddly, but much to Rick's relief, William did not ask about the other residents of the Blackwell Ranch. Only after they had begun to eat did the conversation shift abruptly toward the subject Rick most wanted to avoid.

"Mm, this tastes so good," William said around a mouthful of very rare breakfast steak. "And these eggs are fantastic."

Rick wondered how William was able to taste his breakfast for the speed at which he ate it. The sight of the barely cooked steak made him queasy so that even his own extra-crispy bacon lost its appeal.

"Tell me about your brother and his wife," William said casually as he sopped the blood from his plate with a piece of toast and crammed the entire slice into his mouth.

Rick pushed his own plate away, his appetite gone. "There's really not that much to tell."

"How long have they lived there with you?"

"Not quite a year. Would you like something else to eat?" Rick asked in hopes of steering the conversation in another direction. He didn't want to watch William devour another animal, but even that would have been better than having to tiptoe around the subject of Aldi and Elsa-Eska.

"No, thank you. I'm done," William wiped his mouth with his napkin and laid it on the spotless plate. "Where did they live before they moved out here?"

"California," Rick lied. It was the first thing that came to his mind and he hoped William would not ask where in California.

"Wow, that must have been quite a change for them."

"Yes, it sure has," Rick said. *You have no idea*, he thought.

"They don't really seem to fit out here in the untamed," William noted.

"How's that?"

"Actually, I was thinking more about your brother's wife. She looks like a city girl to me. It's a shame to keep a good looking woman like that hidden away."

Rick was starting to get uncomfortable. "Hey, we better get back on the road." He got up from the table and made his way to the cashier.

"Unless there's a good story behind it," William said, following closely behind.

"What do mean by *good story*?"

"She just looks like someone who would have a good story, that's all."

The cashier greeted the two men with a friendly smile and asked if they enjoyed their meal. Rick said they did and waited for William to pay the bill. William seemed to have forgotten his offer to buy breakfast, so Rick pulled out his wallet and gave the cashier a twenty. She thanked them for coming in and then said something about a storm advisory she had just heard on the radio.

Back in the Jeep, William continued to press. "What's her name?"

"I think I'd rather talk about something else."

William chuckled. "That confirms it. People always try to change the subject when there's a good story."

Rick set his jaw and gripped the steering wheel. He could feel William's gaze upon him, but he kept his own eyes trained on the road in front of them. The snow was now falling steadily and sticking on the shoulders of the road.

"Question is," William said analytically, "does *her* story have anything to do with *your* story."

Rick had heard enough. He turned on William. "Now what's that supposed to mean?"

William chuckled again. "Defensive, too."

Rick struggled to regain his composure. "You have no idea who any of us are. I really think we need to change the subject."

For the next several miles, Rick concentrated on the road that was starting to show signs of snow accumulation. William stared quietly out the side window. After about ten minutes, he turned toward Rick, his expression a mixture of amusement and smugness. "I don't think *you* have any idea who they are."

CHAPTER 41:

OTHER VOICES

≈̇

The snow was falling steadily upon the Blackwell Ranch and getting heavier by the hour. Already the overall appearance of the ranch had been transformed from its various shades of dirty brown to a pristine white. Even the aged barn looked younger under its new blanket. The storm clouds that conquered the mountains of the Wind River Range earlier that morning marched steadily across the desert plains, bringing with them all the beauty and danger of winter. They hung low over the land, stealing the brightness of the day and casting the entire valley in dull grays.

It was cold, bitter cold, the kind of cold that could shake even the most adaptable inhabitants of *the untamed*. Anything with warm blood in its veins, be it animal or human, had long since found shelter in holes and homes. Now the outdoors played host to the mournful wind that blew the snow around like lost souls looking for a place to rest.

There in the midst of the storm that had arrived twelve hours ahead of schedule, a tiny oasis sustained the lives of five who would not have survived long without it. Inside the Blackwell home there was warmth and food and drink enough to last three such storms. The warm glow and crackle of the fire in the hearth, the aroma of freshly made coffee and muffins, and the sounds of soft jazz from the stereo gave the look and smell and feel of home. But the ambiance was tainted by the absence of one who should have been home, but was out there somewhere in the storm.

Jane wandered back to the front window and peered hopefully into the steely gray of late afternoon. She longed to see the headlights of the Jeep that would mean Rick had found his way home. But all she could see was an open and empty expanse; the snow had filled in the deviations in the land that marked the road down which Rick and the stranger disappeared early that morning.

"Jane," Aldi said from the couch where Elsa-Eska lay huddled next to him. "Tell me more about *Giving Thanks Day*." Rick had already recited the history and tradition of Thanksgiving to them, but Aldi thought a conversation might help distract Jane from her worry.

Jane returned from her window-watch and curled up in the chair closest to the fireplace. "I'm sorry, Aldi, but I don't feel much like a history lesson right now."

"You have worry for Rick," Aldi observed.

"Yes," Jane nodded. "But I don't know what worries me most—where he is or who he's with."

Elsa-Eska shivered beneath the electric blanket and let out a discomforting moan.

Jane frowned and looked upon her with concern. "She still can't get warm?"

Aldi shook his head.

"At least she's getting some sleep," Jane noted.

"She is not asleep," Aldi replied. "Elsa-Eska sings to the Before One."

Jane looked more closely and saw that Elsa-Eska's lips were moving as if she were whispering, but there was no sound. She wondered if this was some sort of Klyvian prayer or meditation. Perhaps Elsa-Eska was asking the Before One to bring her warmth or comfort.

"We should sing with her," Aldi said. He closed his eyes and let his head lean back against the couch.

Jane closed her eyes and bowed her head. Before, when she sang with Aldi and Elsa-Eska, it had just happened on its own. She never tried to join the Song by her own volition. She concentrated and began to pray for Elsa-Eska in the only way she knew—with human words. She prayed that Elsa-Eska would be able to get warm and that she would not be getting sick. She asked God to protect and sustain her and give her body strength to endure the cold.

A full minute passed. Jane neither heard nor felt anything different. Opening one eye, she saw that Elsa-Eska and Aldi had not moved. Elsa-Eska appeared to be asleep, and Aldi was now moving his lips. Still, there was no audible Song.

Jane closed her eye and tried to pray again. After offering the same prayer twice more, she stopped trying to form her thoughts into words. Instead, she quieted her mind and listened. Another minute passed and then two more. Still nothing.

Then she became aware. It wasn't like a new thought emerging from nothing, but rather the awareness that it had been there the whole time. She remained still and let it grow until it became like a presence so strong that she had to fight the urge to open her eyes to see who entered the room. Then, as if someone changed the channel or un-muted the volume, the Song came upon her in a new way. Before, when she heard the Song, she did not realize she had been singing along with it until afterward. This time, she was fully alert to what was happening; she heard the Song clearly in her mind, and her lips formed the words as if they were her own. She could recognize them as Klyvian, but there was a difference from when she heard them spoken by Aldi and Elsa-Eska. It was as if they somehow existed unbound by linear time. Many words rang simultaneously, but they did not create a cacophony of confusion. Instead, they were like a symphony of many different instruments played beautifully in concert. Jane was surprised to find that she was able to hear them all at once as well as individually, sort of like listening to a choir and also being able to pick out the individual voices.

As Jane continued to listen to the Song within her, its meaning became clear. She was not hearing the Song in English, nor was she translating the Klyvian words into English. She was able to understand them in their original language. *How* this was happening, she had no explanation. *That* it was happening, she had no doubt. Somehow, she was able to understand the Song in its native Klyvian as clearly as if it were an English song on the radio.

Listening further, Jane heard the now familiar story of how the Before One created, cared for, and guided Klyvians for generations. But woven into the ancient text were references to people and things not Klyvian. Jane was surprised to hear her own name and the name of her husband. Having become so involved in the Mission of Ka-Rel, they were among the first humans to be written into the Song. Jane wondered how many others had been so highly honored.

Suddenly, the truth of the singing dawned on her. Elsa-Eska was not singing to the Before One for herself. She was singing on behalf of Rick. It was now apparent that the three of them had become united in the Klyvian Song as a prayer for Rick's deliverance. But deliverance from what? Certainly, there was mention of the storm, but most of Elsa-Eska's and Aldi's supplication was made in reference to the stranger.

Jane stopped singing when she became aware of other voices that were different from those of Aldi's, Elsa-Eska's, and her own. She couldn't tell for sure, but she suspected they had been singing along with them since the very beginning. The choir of voices became louder and louder until they filled Jane's mind completely. Then, as if someone flipped a switch, the voices were silenced. Jane gasped at the suddenness of the silence and opened her eyes.

"Jane, are you okay?" Elsa-Eska asked. She was sitting up, but still very close to Aldi's side.

Jane took a moment to collect herself. She could still feel her heart beating rapidly and her hands trembling. She took a deep breath and blew it out through her mouth. "The Song," she said. "I could hear it."

"Yes," Elsa-Eska said. "The Song is in you."

"But it was different this time."

"How?" Aldi asked.

"I could hear voices. At first, it was just the three of us, but then I heard others."

Elsa-Eska smiled. "Our people."

Jane looked perplexed. "Your people? I don't understand."

"The Song," Elsa-Eska explained, "is very old. It has always been and always will be. It is a part of us. What you heard are the voices of all who sing, from the before time to this time."

"Amazing," Jane whispered.

"It is good that you hear them," Elsa-Eska continued. "It will remind you that you are never alone."

Jane's eyes widened as a thought occurred to her. "Was I hearing the actual voices of other Klyvians?"

"Yes," Elsa-Eska and Aldi said in unison.

"Klyvians on…on Klyv?"

"And more," Elsa-Eska said. "The voices of our fathers and mothers who have passed are there also. We can hear the voices of Jalamin and Arkel."

Jane was stunned by this new revelation. Aldi and Elsa-Eska had never mentioned this aspect of the Song. She probably would not have been able to understand it if they had.

CHAPTER 42:

THE COLLECTOR

~⋏⋋

"Did you hear what I said?" William asked.

Rick had heard, but he was too stunned to respond. He just kept driving, wondering if he had even heard the man correctly.

"Let me put it another way." William's tone softened and his demeanor changed from accuser to confidant. "The man and woman are not who they appear to be. Al isn't your brother, is he?"

Rick felt his forehead tingle as perspiration began to form on his brow. He swallowed and tried to sound convincing. "Of course he is." He concentrated hard on how he and Aldi referred to each other as brothers in hopes of avoiding the tale-tell signs that he was technically lying.

William rubbed his hand across his chin. "I see." He then folded his arms across his chest and settled his gaze upon Rick.

Whether it was because William didn't know what to say next or he was using some kind of psychological tactic meant to wear him down, Rick couldn't tell. After a full minute, Rick decided it was a tactic because it was working. Trying to get a read on the man was futile. William's expression held no clue as to what he was thinking. It was like watching someone watch television, and Rick was the television. Finally, he could take it no longer. "Why don't you cut the mind game and just say whatever it is you think you know?"

"Very well, but I must warn you this might be difficult to hear." A hint of a grin appeared on William's lips. "You'll no doubt resist at first. You won't want to believe it, but it'll be hard to ignore the truth when they're staring you in the face."

Rick did a double take as he recognized these words as his own from the night before.

"The truth is," William continued, "I know who Al and his wife are. I know they aren't…well, there's just no other way to say it…they aren't human." He paused to get Rick's reaction. Rick gave none – he just kept his eyes fixed on the snow-covered road ahead. "I'll take your lack of surprise as confirmation. Now where do we go from here? That's the question, isn't it? Now that the cat's out of the bag, so to speak, what next?"

Rick weighed his options: Deny it, play dumb, or play along and see what the man wants. It was too late for denial and he was never good at playing dumb. That left him only one option. Rick decided to forgo the admission and get right to the part about which he was most concerned. "What do you want?"

William chuckled. "A bottom line guy. No doubt a characteristic left over from your former life in the corporate world. I can respect that. What I want is what's best for everyone."

Rick sensed William was stalling. But why? Now that the cat was out of the bag, why not just get right to it? Then, from a dark corner of his mind, a fourth option began to materialize. Rick glanced over at William and made a quick assessment of the man's physical condition. He looked to be a few years younger than Rick and obviously in good shape, but Rick had the size advantage and he was in control of the vehicle. If he could capitalize on the element of surprise, he stood a fairly good chance of over-powering the man. Rick shuddered at the dark thought. How far could he take this scenario? No, he wouldn't actually have to kill the man or even injure him. All he would have to do is get him out of the Jeep. He could then easily get back to the ranch, pack everything they would need, and disappear. Yes, running was certainly a viable option.

"And what *is* best for everyone?" Rick asked, looking for an opportunity to employ the fourth option.

"The truth," William said. "That's always a good place to start."

"That's what you want, to get the truth out about them?" Rick felt a sense of relief. "I thought you were a government agent. You're just a reporter." The fourth option retreated back to its dark corner. A reporter, he could handle. "Who do you work for?"

"You thought I was a government agent?" William laughed out loud. "That's a good one."

Rick couldn't help but laugh along with him. "Yeah, for a minute you had me going."

They laughed some more. Between guffaws, William said, "And you seriously thought you could take me out?"

Rick stopped laughing. How did William know what he had been thinking?

"Oh, man, that would have been something." William's own

laughter subsided to a sporadic chuckle. "It's a good thing you didn't try. It wouldn't have worked." He took a deep breath and let it out loudly. "No, my friend, I am not a government agent. I'm not a reporter either. Why don't you ask me how I know who they are?"

Whatever control of the situation Rick thought he had quickly disappeared. He was back to the third option. Play along. "All right, how do you know?"

"This is the part you're going to find difficult at first." He shook his head and chuckled again. "I've never been able to find just the right way to say it. Oh, well. I'm not human either."

Rick's mind fought hard to process what he heard. *Not human.* Rick mumbled the only thing he could think of. "Are you Klyvian?"

"Yes."

"But how...I mean, when..." Rick could not get his thoughts into words.

"I know it's a bit of a shock. Aldi could hardly believe it himself. Did you see the look on his face when he saw me?"

Rick tried to remember the morning's meeting. Aldi did behave strangely.

"I'm sorry I didn't get to meet Elsa-Eska. That would have been interesting."

Rick stiffened at the mention of her. *He knows their names. He knows them. He's one of them.* "You lied to me," Rick said as the fragments of their conversations came back to him. "All that talk about discovering there was more to life than work, coming out here to figure it all out...it was all a lie. Were you even in New York?"

William held his hands up in defense. "I'm sorry, Rick. I hated to do it, but I had no choice. I had to act fast and I didn't know what kind of human you would be and I..."

"Whoa, whoa, slow down," Rick interrupted. "I have to get my head around this."

"Of course. Take all the time you need."

They drove in silence for several minutes as Rick tried to comprehend what was happening. Finally, he asked, "What's your real name?"

"Kozum-Al."

"How did you get here?"

"We came on a ship, of course, like the others."

"But not *their* ship?"

"No," Kozum-Al said. "I'm afraid we would not have been welcome on their ship. They do not know we are here."

"How many of you are there?"

"Ten, including myself."

"When did you arrive?"

"Almost six earth-months ago."

"Where is your ship now?"

"Africa."

"Where are the rest of your group now?"

"Various places."

"Are any of them close by?"

"No. We are able to cover more area alone."

William, or rather Kozum-Al, answered Rick's barrage of questions without hesitation. In Rick's experience, this was a plus. He was about half-convinced this Klyvian was telling the truth. Now for the other half. "Okay, Kozum-Al, I'm ready to hear it. Why are you here?"

"First, I must ask you to forgive my deception. It is against our nature to speak the untrue. I will not do it again."

Rick recognized for the first time a hint of the manner in which Aldi and Elsa-Eska spoke, but he was still wary of the man. "I'll think about it while you explain what's going on."

Kozum-Al nodded respectfully. "How much did Aldi tell you about our people?"

"They told us quite a lot," Rick replied.

"Did he tell you about the Time of Trouble and the Great Rebellion?"

"Yes."

"Then you know of the Raphim?"

"Yes."

"Did Aldi tell you how the Raphim came to be, and how they tried to destroy the true Klyv?"

"Yes."

Kozum-Al nodded. "All that is true. Did Aldi tell you he was true Klyv?"

"Yes."

"I suspected he would. Aldi is a very clever man."

Rick eyed Kozum-Al. "Why do you keep referring to Aldi as if he would be the only one to tell us these things? Actually, Elsa-Eska told us as much, if not more."

"She did? Aldi is a very clever man. Rick, you must understand that Aldi speaks both the true and the untrue, and it is difficult to know the difference."

"I thought it was against your nature to lie."

"It is for true Klyv, but not for the Raphim."

"Now wait just a minute," Rick said, his anger mounting. "Are you telling me Aldi is…" He couldn't bring himself to say it.

"Yes, Aldi is Raphim." The look on Kozum-Al's face was one of regret rather than contempt.

"I don't believe it." Rick felt his loyalty toward Aldi come to bear. "That can't be true."

Kozum-Al's face had a pained look. "It is as I said, you do not want to believe. But I assure you I speak the true. Rick, I know you must be very confused. You do not have enough experience with our kind to know the difference between true Klyv and Raphim."

Rick thought about this last statement. He had to admit he had been so willing to accept everything Aldi said as the truth that he never considered an alternative. "What about Elsa-Eska?"

Kozum-Al managed a weak smile. "Elsa-Eska is true Klyv, but she speaks only what Aldi tells her to speak."

"What do you mean?"

"Please stop the vehicle."

"Stop? Why?"

"What I am about to tell you will most likely alter our course."

Rick felt sick to his stomach. The weight of indecision bore down upon him. His instincts told him to press on, to get Kozum-Al as far away from Aldi and Elsa-Eska as he could, to even sacrifice himself for them if it came to that. But a small part of his reasoning insisted on complying.

They were nearing the top of the pass where Rick knew there was an inn and restaurant. When they arrived at it, he pulled the Jeep into the parking lot, but left the engine running. He turned in his seat to face the man seated next to him. "Alright, go on."

Kozum-Al nodded again, but this time it seemed to Rick more like a bow. "Your friend Aldi is not the man you believe him to be."

"You've already said that."

"Aldi is what my people call a *collector*."

"A collector?"

"Yes, he collects…mates."

Rick blinked in surprise. "Aldi, a ladies man? You must have the wrong guy. Aldi loves Elsa-Eska."

"I am sure he does. He loves them all. But Elsa-Eska is his favorite."

Rick pinched the bridge of his nose. "I'm sorry. I just don't see it. I've never met a better man than Aldi. He couldn't be a…a collector."

Kozum-Al seemed to mirror Rick's emotional pain. "It is hard to understand. Aldi is a very clever man. He has a way about him that is hard to resist. That is how he acquires his collection."

"But what about Elsa-Eska? She loves him."

"No." Kozum-Al shook his head. "She only appears to love him because that is what he requires of her. She fears him."

Rick switched the engine off and sat back in his seat. That last statement fell hard upon him like an unbearable load. He tried to survey the last eight months for any indication that Elsa-Eska had been acting under duress. Try as he may, he could not think of a single instance that would substantiate Kozum-Al's outrageous claim. Then again, he was judging everything by human logic. Was human logic a reasonable standard by which to judge Klyvian or Raphim behavior? What if Aldi really was this clever monster and Elsa-Eska his frightened pet? Would he and Jane even be able to see it?

"Rick," Kozum-Al said after several minutes. "I doubt you will find evidence of what I have told you. Aldi has been doing this for a long time. He is very good at…what is the human word? Oh, yes, manipulation. But I do have one piece of evidence, if you will consider it."

Rick just nodded.

"Look at me."

Rick had been staring straight ahead at the snow falling onto the windshield. When he turned to look at Kozum-Al, he gasped. The dark irises of Kozum-Al's eyes were alive with tiny golden flecks flickering and swirling like the wind-blown snow outside.

Kozum-Al let Rick gaze upon him for a moment before he spoke. "You see? It is this way with all true Klyv. Not with the Raphim."

Rick was amazed to see within this stranger the phenomenon he had come to associate with Elsa-Eska. He had been led to believe it was a characteristic unique to the female members of Elsa-Eska's family. Now that he saw it in the eyes of another who claimed to be true Klyv, it made sense that it would be a trait shared by an entire species. That, plus the fact that Aldi's eyes did not glow, provided more convincing evidence that Kozum-Al might be telling the truth.

"Okay," Rick said, "I'm not saying I believe you, but let's just suppose what you're telling me is the truth…"

Kozum-Al nodded.

"…and Aldi is a Raphim collector. What's his agenda? What's he after?"

"I am surprised you do not yet see it," Kozum-Al replied. "Why would a collector of books wander into a new bookstore? Why would a collector of sea shells stroll along the beach?"

"You've got to be kidding," Rick retorted.

"I am not. Aldi is seeking to add to his collection. He wants your wife."

Rick had no response. He wanted to refute the ridiculous notion that his best friend was making a play for his wife, but his mind became flooded with snapshots of Aldi and Jane together over the last several months. Private conversations and walks around the ranch that had once been unquestionably innocent in Rick's mind suddenly became suspect. It was no secret that Jane liked to talk to Aldi (and presumably Elsa-Eska) about God, but now he wondered if that might have all been a smoke screen. God was the one subject that almost always caused Rick to find something else to do. What if Aldi used it to get rid of him so he could spend time alone with Jane? And then there were Elsa-Eska's questionable health issues. Was she really suffering from fatigue and cold, or was she making excuses in order to get away from Aldi for a while? Or were these conditions inflicted upon her by Aldi to keep her under his control? Was Elsa-Eska's need for sleep a convenient way for Aldi to spend time with Jane? Rick felt his stomach churn at such thoughts.

"Take all the time you need," Kozum-Al said calmly. "I know this is a lot to process."

Rick let his head fall into his hands so he could massage his aching temples. More images flashed through his mind. Recollections of conversations took on entirely new meanings. An image of Aldi materialized in his mind; his characteristic smile morphed into a sinister smirk. Then he pictured Jane; she looked naïve and vulnerable.

Kozum-Al spoke again, his voice tinted with urgency. "Your wife is in danger. He will have her unless you stop him."

Rick now thought of Elsa-Eska; her innocent gaze became a plea for help.

"You could even save Elsa-Eska," Kozum-Al said. "She will leave him if she believes someone could protect her from him."

The images in Rick's mind became even more vivid. He could see Jalamin and Sara lying next to each other in Sara's crib.

Kozum-Al's voice was closer now, a mere whisper. "Some of Aldi's collection came into his possession as young children."

Rick flinched at this last statement. The confusion he felt began to dissipate, replaced by a mounting rage. Like a fire in his gut, he felt the anger build. His fingers ceased their gentle massage of his temples as his fists became clenched. His stammered breathing evened out into measured inhale/exhale repetitions through his nose. The muscles in his jaws twitched as his teeth ground together.

"Rick, my friend," Kozum-Al spoke softly, hypnotically. "See the true. Accept it. Embrace it."

Rick sat up straight in his seat and grabbed the steering wheel. "What else can you tell me?"

"If he follows his normal pattern, he will leave soon. Has he said anything about wanting to go somewhere else?"

Rick thought for a moment. "His ship. He's been communicating with his ship. He said they are planning on leaving Earth's orbit in a few weeks."

"He plans to be on that ship with your wife and child."

Rick put his hands on the steering wheel and looked at Kozum-Al. "Do you have a plan?"

"Oh, yes. I have dealt with his kind before. Take us back to your ranch, and I will help you save your family. And Elsa-Eska, too.

In spite of the near blizzard conditions, Rick pushed the accelerator all the way to the floor. The Jeep spun around in the parking lot, missing two other vehicles by mere inches. He fishtailed out onto the road and pointed the Jeep toward home.

Kozum-Al held on tightly to the door handle, but showed no concern over Rick's dangerously aggressive driving. The glowing flecks of gold in his eyes diminished until the once liquid irises grew cold and lifeless. Leaning his head back against the headrest, he took a deep breath and let it out slowly. He was fatigued, but satisfied with the progress of his mission.

CHAPTER 43:

HELP

∘⦂

"Can...make...warmer?"

It had been nearly an hour since Elsa-Eska last spoke. Jane assumed she was asleep. The intermittent shiver from beneath the blanket that covered her tightly curled body was now a constant shudder. Every muscle was tensed in an effort to retain body heat. Her brief request through chattering teeth was made with great effort. Now her breathing was a rapid, shallow cadence accompanied by a low moaning, emanating from deep within.

Aldi glanced down at his wife and then at Jane. The look on his face was one of concern, but also helplessness.

Jane set her book on the coffee table and moved to the couch. She placed her hand on Elsa-Eska's forehead expecting to detect a fever; instead, she found her skin cool to the touch. For no apparent reason, Elsa-Eska's body was losing heat.

"Aldi," Jane said, trying not to sound alarmed. "She's very cool. What can we do?"

Aldi shook his head, unable to provide an answer.

"I don't suppose you've ever seen this happen before."

Aldi shook his head again. "When we first arrived, the cold affected her more than me, but it was not like this."

Jane glanced around the room hoping something would spark an idea. The fire in the hearth was doing its job; they could move Elsa-Eska closer. There were more quilts in the closet; they could pile another one on top of her. There was plenty of food in the kitchen. Maybe some hot soup or coffee would help. The last thought gave her an idea. "What about chippick? I know it's more of an energy booster, but it might help some."

Aldi shook his head. "It is all gone."

Reluctantly, Jane conceded to herself that she had come to the end of her ability to help her friends. "Aldi, will you pray with me?"

Aldi made no reply. He just bowed his head and started to gently rock back and forth. When Jane noticed his lips were moving, she knew he had begun to sing the Song. Jane closed her eyes and offered a prayer for Elsa-Eska in her own language.

After about a minute, Jane sensed a change in the room. It was nothing she could put her finger on, just a feeling. Believing the change might be in response to her prayer, she opened one eye to see if Elsa-Eska had stopped shivering. What she found was not what she'd hoped for. Not only was Elsa-Eska still shivering, but now the room was dark, lit only by the dying fire in the fireplace. She also noticed that the music from the stereo had ceased.

"Aldi," Jane whispered. "I don't want to alarm you, but I think we might have a problem."

Aldi opened his eyes and looked around the darkened room.

"We've lost power," Jane whispered. "I'm afraid it's going to get cold in here."

They both looked down at Elsa-Eska and shared the same concern.

"We may have to…" Jane started to suggest something, but was cut off mid-sentence by a flash of light from outside. Suddenly, the entire room was lit up brighter than it had been before the power outage. "Rick?" Jane jumped up from the couch and ran to the window.

Jane couldn't make sense of the scene outside. Through the heavily falling snow she could identify two sets of headlights—one set in the normal position, apparently on high-beam; and a second brighter set high above the first. It definitely was not her Jeep Cherokee, which meant it was definitely not Rick. Her heart sank a bit at the realization. But who could it be out on a night like this? And what could they want?

Before any of them could react, a knock sounded at the front door. Jane glanced back at Aldi and then moved to the door. She peeked through the peephole, but could see nothing but the blinding light from the vehicle outside. The knock sounded again. Jane quickly slid the deadbolt into the lock position and backed away from the door.

"I don't know what to do," she said.

"Why don't you open the door?" Aldi asked.

"I can't see who it is. What if it's…" Jane didn't want to say what she was thinking.

The knock sounded again—louder and with greater urgency. Jane jumped.

Aldi looked at her questioningly. "It could be help."

Just then a muffled voice could be heard from outside. "Kevin? You in there? It's me, Ed."

Jane sighed as relief replaced her fear. "Oh, it's just Ed." She unlocked the door and opened it. "Ed Tyler, what are you doing here?"

As Ed pushed his way into the house, Jane was surprised when a second figure about his same size came in right behind him. At the sight of the second man, Aldi quickly, but carefully got up from the couch and joined Jane at the door.

"Johnny!" Aldi said excitedly. "We are so happy to see you."

Johnny reached toward Aldi with both arms and hugged him. Then he turned toward Jane. "Don't be frightened. We've come to help."

CHAPTER 44:

DOUBLE-CHECK

≥∫

The drive back down the mountain was harrowing. Under the best of conditions, the road was dangerous with its steep grades and blind curves, some of which were posted at just twenty miles per hour. But under the present blizzard conditions, these hazards were compounded. It took all of Rick's concentration to keep the Jeep off of the rock wall to the left and out of the yawning drop-off to the right; frustratingly, he couldn't see either. Being as how they were well beyond the checkpoints when the closure went into effect, theirs was the only vehicle on the road. On the one hand, this was to their advantage as they had the entire road to themselves. On the other hand, it made the going even slower because they had to blaze their own trail through the accumulating snow. To complicate matters even more, night was upon them. Rick had to keep his headlights on low because the blowing snow in the high beams created the effect of thousands of tiny snow-missiles attacking him in an endless stream.

The slow progress was maddening, making Rick even more anxious than when he started this treacherous journey. He gripped the steering wheel with white-knuckled determination and leaned forward as if to will the Jeep to penetrate the wall of blizzard fury. He had to get back to his family, to rescue them, but this blasted storm was bent on keeping him from them.

Kozum-Al seemed oblivious to the peril. Mostly, he just stared out the windshield. Occasionally, he glanced over at Rick and grinned. By the looks of him, they could have been on a leisurely jaunt down a country lane on a warm summer day. Rick wondered if the man had ever been in a snowstorm before. Perhaps he simply didn't understand the danger they were in. Rick decided to let him rest in his ignorance. No use in both of them sensing death at every turn.

When they finally reached the bottom of the mountain where the road straightened and became four lanes, Rick breathed a sigh of relief. Though the snow was still falling heavily, he felt confident to speed up to about forty miles per hour. It seemed fast after hours of creeping along at a snail's pace. He settled back into his seat and tried to work the stiffness out of his neck and shoulders.

Kozum-Al noticed the change in Rick and took it as his cue to resume dialogue. "When we get back to your place, I want you to do exactly what I tell you. Aldi does not suspect you know the truth about him, so he won't have reason to resist you. This will be our advantage."

Rick gave him a sideways glance. All that silence had given him time to think about what Kozum-Al had said about Aldi and compare it to what he had observed over the course of the last eight months. He was beginning to have doubts about Kozum-Al's story. "So, you do this sort of thing often?" Rick asked.

"Yes, I have dealt with the Raphim many times. Many of them collectors like Aldi."

"What are you, some kind of bounty hunter?"

Kozum-Al chuckled. "Yes, something like that."

"You know, Kozum-Al, your English is very good. I mean, in some ways you've got a better handle on it than Aldi and Elsa-Eska."

"Thank you," Kozum-Al said with a hint of humility in his voice. "Your language is one of the more difficult I have encountered. I have enjoyed learning it."

"I didn't mean that as a compliment. More like a question. How is it that your English is better than Aldi's and Elsa-Eska's, yet you haven't been here as long as they have?"

Kozum-Al answered the accusation without hesitation. "They have had contact with only a few humans. I have spent all my time in your cities. I have encountered thousands of humans."

"I see." Rick had to concede that was a plausible answer. He and Jane had been careful to not use many English colloquialisms around Aldi and Elsa-Eska. Kozum-Al probably had been exposed to a much greater diversity of the English language in his travels. Rick eyed his passenger again. "You aren't very tall for a Klyvian."

Kozum-Al didn't miss a beat. "You are taller than most humans."

"Huh?" Rick did not expect so quick a comeback.

"The average human male is five feet, nine inches. You are over six feet tall."

"Meaning?"

"Meaning, humans are different sizes as are Klyvians. Actually, I am quite average by Klyvian standards. Aldi is the exception."

"And Elsa-Eska?"

"Most Klyvian women are taller than the men. Actually, I have found this to be the case with all the dominant species on the planets I have visited. Humans seem to be unique in this respect."

This bit of galactic trivia intrigued Rick, but he dare not allow himself to become distracted by it. There had to be something that Kozum-Al couldn't explain, something that would indicate he had fabricated the entire story. If Rick could just get him to hesitate, that would be enough to raise a shadow of doubt. The burden, after all, was upon Kozum-Al. He was the one on trial, not Rick. Though his story was compelling, he would have to convince Rick beyond that shadow of doubt before Rick would bring such a damning accusation against the man whom he considered his brother.

"How long have you been tracking Aldi?" Rick asked.

"It is hard to say in Earth years. Judging from the time I've been here, I'd say it's been about four or five of your years. I have tracked him on three other planets besides this one. This is the closest I've come to catching him."

"How far is Klyv from Earth?"

"I do not know how to explain it in a way you can understand."

"Aldi said the distance is so great that he was born on the way here and grew up onboard their ship. He said he's never seen his home planet."

At this, Kozum-Al started to laugh. "Now that's a new one. I assure you he's seen it and lived on it. I doubt he plans to ever go back."

"Why is that?"

"Too dangerous. If he ever showed up on Klyv, he wouldn't live long. When he acquired Elsa-Eska, he also acquired a price on his head. Her mother is one of the most prominent women on Klyv. You could say Elsa-Eska is royalty, like a princess."

The reference to Elsa-Eska as royalty struck a chord. He and Jane had often commented on Elsa-Eska's regal deportment. And now to hear Kozum-Al confirm their suspicions, it was too much to be a coincidence. "You mean to say that Elsa-Eska could return home to her family? I mean, you could take her there along with her daughter?"

The mention of Elsa-Eska's daughter seemed to catch Kozum-Al's attention, but he hid his interest well. "That is the reason I've come here," he replied. "And also to end the career of a most despicable collector."

"Okay," Rick said, this time with more confidence than he had before, "tell me what you want me to do."

The rest of the drive back to the Blackwell Ranch was spent going over the plan to catch Aldi and rescue the Princess Elsa-Eska. Rick listened as Kozum-Al spelled out every detail. He was confident he could do his part, and he was beginning to find trust in this man whom he had once held in suspicion. By the time they reached the road leading to the ranch, Rick could hardly remember why he ever doubted Kozum-Al in the first place. He was convinced that Kozum-Al was committed to justice as well as the protection of his family and the safe return of Elsa-Eska and Sara.

Rick's heart sank as they pulled up in front of his house and he saw that it was completely dark inside. Without thinking, he jumped out of the Jeep and sprinted through the shin-deep snow to the front door that was awash in the high beams of the Jeep's headlights. He threw open the door and called out into the empty house. "Jane? Jane! Are you here?" He listened for a second and then felt for the light switch. The power was still off.

The light from the Jeep streaming in through the open door cast odd shadows in the room. He made his way through the living room to the hallway that led to the bedrooms. It was much darker there. Rick called out again. "Jane? Are you in here?"

Convinced that the house was empty, he ran back outside to where Kozum-Al was waiting in the Jeep.

"They're not here," Rick said, panting through the fear and exertion of his search.

"I was afraid of that," Kozum-Al said. "I should not have allowed him to see me. I am truly sorry."

"That's okay," Rick replied. "There's no way you could have known he'd see you. I'm going to check the other house. There's a flashlight in the glove compartment."

Kozum-Al looked at him blankly.

"The glove compartment," Rick said, pointing to the space below the dash in front of Kozum-Al. "Pull that handle right there."

Kozum-Al pulled on the latch, releasing the glove compartment door.

"The flashlight is that thing on the right." Rick's voice was fraught with urgency.

Kozum-Al moved slower than Rick's patience could endure. When he offered the flashlight, Rick snatched it out of his hand and sprinted toward the other house.

In less than a minute, Rick entered the house, deduced that it too was empty, and returned to the Jeep. He pulled the door shut and let his head drop into his hands. The snow that had accumulated on his shirt and hair turned to little spots of water in the warmth of the

Jeep. Then, with a heavy sigh, he leaned his head back against the headrest and stared out at the snow falling through the beams of the headlights. "They're gone, Kozum-Al. We're too late."

Two minutes passed with neither man speaking. Rick was too devastated to give any thought to the bounty hunter sitting next to him. He racked his brain for something, anything else to do, but he had nothing. There was no one to call, no place to go, nothing to do. If the collector —he couldn't even bring himself to think the name— if the collector had taken Jane and Elsa-Eska and their two daughters, there just wasn't anything Rick could do to bring them back. He had not even the slightest hint as to where he might begin to look for them. And if this entire day had been part of the collector's plan, and the ship had come while Rick was gone, there never would be any place on Earth where he could look. The enormity of his loss fell upon him with a suffocating weight.

Rick was nearing the point of emotional paralysis when Kozum-Al spoke. "Take me into their house."

Rick did not move or blink. He just stared straight ahead. Then he felt something clamp down on his shoulder.

"Rick!"

Rick came to himself and realized it was Kozum-Al who had spoken. He let his head roll to the right where he saw the bounty hunter with his hand extended to his shoulder. "What?"

"Take me into their house. Perhaps there is something there." Then Kozum-Al's voice became compassionate. "It's not too late, but we must act now."

Had Rick been in his usual rational state of mind, he would have protested the effort. He could think of nothing that would give them any clue as to where the collector might have gone with his family. But Rick had reached the point of desperation where a man will do anything, even if he believes it to be a waste of time and energy. He nodded and climbed out of the Jeep and into the cold, dark night that now seemed an apt representation of his life.

The two men trudged through the snow toward the house where Elsa-Eska and the collector had lived. Inside, Kozum-Al asked to hold the flashlight. Rick gladly handed it to him and then slumped down into a chair. What else could he do but let the bounty hunter do his job? He watched with only a sliver of interest as Kozum-Al methodically inspected the living room and then the kitchen. As he worked his way to the bedroom, Rick forced himself to get up and follow. Inside the bedroom, he found Kozum-Al pulling something out of the closet—a long metal case.

Rick recognized the container. It had been months since he helped

Elsa-Eska and the other one move into their new home. Rick had placed the two cases in the closet himself.

Kozum-Al shined the flashlight along the edge of the case, looking for the way to open it. Rick, who had seen it opened before, reached down and worked the invisible latch. There was a click and the lid slid open. Kozum-Al reached for the lid, but paused just before his hand came in contact with it. He tapped it gently and then quickly pulled his hand back. It reminded Rick of the way Jane sometimes checked to see if the iron was still hot. Only then did he place his hand fully onto the lid and push it all the way open. Next, he shined the light into the case, taking stock of its contents. On the second pass with the light, he halted it on a small object. Carefully, as if he were reaching for a priceless artifact, he put his hand into the case. Again, he paused before coming in contact with the object. He tapped his finger on its shiny black surface. Then, satisfied that it was safe to touch, he carefully lifted it out of the case and handed it to Rick. Rick looked down at the object in his hands while Kozum-Al trained the light onto it.

"Do you know this?" Kozum-Al enquired.

"Yes. It's the device Al…the collector used to communicate with his ship."

"Can you activate it?"

"I don't know, maybe." Rick turned the object around in his hands until he was holding it in the same way he had seen Aldi hold it. He moved his right hand over the top of the shiny surface and then lightly touched it with his index finger. The device blinked to life with a series of lighted Klyvian symbols around the edges. As the light from the device illuminated the face of the bounty hunter, Rick saw a look of triumph spread across his face.

"Our adversary was careless this time," Kozum-Al said. "He was unwise to have left us so great an advantage."

"I don't understand," Rick said. "It's just a communication device. Once he's onboard his ship he won't need it. I don't see how it's any use to us."

Kozum-Al chuckled. "Oh, it's much more than a communication device. We can use this to locate the others and track his ship. We can use it to find your wife and Elsa-Eska."

Rick seemed pleased by this. "Great! What do we do now?"

Kozum-Al looked up from the communication device and locked eyes with Rick. "Do you have a weapon?"

CHAPTER 45:

THE TRIBE

Δ. ⋮

"Where are we?" Jane asked when Ed Tyler pulled the big truck off the road in front of a large cinderblock building.

Jane and Aldi, each with a sleeping baby in their arms, were in the back seat of the truck's crew cab with a shivering Elsa-Eska between them. It wasn't easy, but they managed to squeeze into the small space and find reasonably comfortable positions. With seven bodies in the small cab and the truck's heater blasting out hot air, condensation quickly formed on the side and rear windows such that it was impossible to see out. As a result, Jane missed Ed's left turn onto the main highway, away from Riverton where she assumed they would go for help. After an hour of driving, she couldn't even guess where they were.

Ed killed the truck's big engine and jumped out without answering Jane's question. She watched him shuffle off toward the building and disappear through the door.

Johnny, who was sitting in the front passenger seat, turned to face her. "We are at Fort Washakie. That's the school." He nodded toward the building. "Come. Let's get Elsa-Eska inside where it's warm."

As soon as Aldi pulled her out of the truck, Elsa-Eska cried out as if in pain from the cold air and blowing snow. Her condition was worsening. Her shivering was now so intense that an observer would have suspected she was having some kind of seizure. Aldi cradled her in his arms and made a dash for the building. Johnny and Jane followed close behind, each cradling a baby close to their bodies in an attempt to shelter them from the cold. Thankfully, it was a short distance to the building, and they were quickly welcomed into its warm embrace.

The air inside was heavy with the pungent scent of kerosene

lanterns and gas heaters, but it was warm and dry. There was an unexpected cheeriness about it. A small gathering of people was seated on blankets and sleeping bags on the floor in a circle around a collection of mismatched candles. There were ten people in all, including Ed Tyler who was receiving a thorough licking from Bonko. From a distance, the scene looked like campers around a campfire. Jane half-expected to see someone roasting marshmallows.

The group, which had been chatting noisily upon Ed's arrival, grew silent and turned to look at the newcomers. Jane suddenly felt awkward, like she was intruding on a sacred ceremony. Jalamin started to cry and would not be pacified by Jane's frenzied attempts to quiet her. Mother and child hung back while Johnny and Aldi approached the group.

As if on cue, everyone stood to their feet and opened the circle to receive them. Aldi gently laid Elsa-Eska onto a sleeping bag and settled himself onto the floor next to her. Then he gathered her into his arms again and held her close. One of the group, an elderly woman with braided gray hair, draped a blanket over Aldi's shoulders. A young woman offered him a cup of something hot. Then the two women joined the others who gathered around Johnny. The elderly woman received Sara, who was now wide awake and whimpering, and began to rock her from side to side. Johnny spoke to the group in a voice too low for Jane to hear.

A collective *oh* sounded from the small group and every head turned toward Jane. She took a step back, wanting to melt into the shadows. There were nods and quiet murmurings as the group, including Johnny, reformed the circle around the candles. There was no obvious invitation offered for her to join the group, though there was a space left open between two of the men. Jane stayed where she stood.

Johnny spoke again, his voice casual and his hands animating whatever it was he was saying. All eyes were focused upon him until he gestured toward Aldi and Elsa-Eska. Once again, there was a collective *aw* and the entire group turned to look at the two Klyvians. Jane's curiosity edged her closer, but by the time she got within earshot, Johnny had ended his speech. Whatever he told them must not have been too earth-shaking. It appeared to Jane that the group was settling back into its pre-interruption state with conversations popping up around the circle.

With hardly any notice, Johnny got up from his place and walked the long way around the circle. When he came to the young woman who had given Aldi the cup, he touched her on the top of the head, but did not stop. The young woman immediately got up and followed behind him. Johnny's path led him directly to Jane and Jalamin.

The old man's weathered face had a look of solemnity, but his eyes were alive with youthful energy. Smiling tenderly at Jalamin, he placed one hand on her tiny head and leaned down to whisper into the child's ear. Jalamin immediately stopped crying and gazed at him with wide eyes. Next, Johnny turned his attention to Jane, placing his other hand on her cheek. He held her for a moment and then pulled her close to him. "You are among friends here," he said in a calming voice. "There is no reason to be afraid." Then Johnny stepped back to allow the young woman to step forward. She bowed slightly and held her hand toward Jane.

"I am Sharon," said the young woman.

"I'm Jane." She positioned Jalamin onto her hip and took Sharon's hand.

The young woman was beautiful. Her large dark eyes and silky black hair gave her a mystique characteristic of her Native American heritage. Jane guessed she was maybe seventeen or eighteen. "Come," she said. "Join the circle." When she turned, her long hair trailed around her and settled gracefully down her back; it shimmered from the various light sources in the room.

Jane followed, partly because Sharon still had her hand, but also because she wanted to. She glanced back to see if Johnny would join them, but he was nowhere in sight. When they reached the circle, Sharon deposited Jane and Jalamin in the spot between the two men and then took her place next to the young man she was obviously with. They joined hands, lacing their fingers together the way young lovers do. Jane smiled at them and then took notice of the others. Normally, she would have felt uncomfortable in such close quarters, especially between the two men, but here she felt at home. Jalamin stared wide-eyed at the man closest to her and let out a contented sigh.

One by one, the conversations fell silent.

"I'm Kenny Lewis," said the man to Jane's right. "It's nice to finally meet you."

The greeting intrigued Jane, as did the last name. What did he mean by *finally*? Why did the name *Lewis* sound so familiar? "It's nice to meet you, too. Thank you for taking us in."

"Friends of Johnny's are friends of ours. Let me introduce the tribe to you." One by one Kenny introduced each member of the circle in a clock-wise fashion, pausing after each one to let Jane become familiar with them. He gestured to the man on her left. "This is Pete, a friend of the family."

Pete looked up and nodded at her, then returned his attention back

370   *Michael E. Gunter*

to the gurgling Jalamin.

"Next to him is my brother, Louie."

Louie was huge. He sat in traditional Indian style with his bare muscular arms folded across his barrel chest. The man would have been intimidating had it not been for his equally huge smile that seemed to light up his entire being. "Good to meet you, Jane." There was a kindness to the man's voice that didn't quite fit his tough appearance.

"Of course, you already know Uncle Ed and Bonk."

Ed and Bonko were in their own little world. Bonko had curled up in Ed's lap, sleeping soundly under Ed's gentle petting. Ed was leaning over the little dog, whispering quietly.

"Next is my grandmother. Everybody calls her *Mother*"

The elderly woman who had given Aldi the blanket nodded. Her face was lined with more wrinkles than Jane had ever seen on one person, yet her eyes were keen and bright. It was apparent that she had lived a hard life, but her countenance suggested she had discovered the secret of peace.

"And my father. You can call him Big Jack."

The man nodded and smiled warmly at Jane. "Welcome Jane Blackwell."

Jane thought it interesting that Big Jack was only half the size of his sons. Then she wondered if there was a Mrs. Big Jack.

Kenny continued. "These two rascals are my little brothers, Joshua and Thomas."

The teenage brothers nodded in unison. They did have a certain mischievous look about them, and Jane imagined them being the life of the party in another setting. But here, whether it was because of her presence or something else, they appeared subdued, almost shy.

"You've met Sharon," Kenny said. "We still don't know why, but she's agreed to marry my brother." Kenny winked at the blushing couple, and Joshua elbowed his brother in the side.

Aldi and Elsa-Eska were sitting next to Sharon. Jane had almost forgotten about them, she was so enthralled by these people who had welcomed her into their group. In the five years that she and Rick had lived on the boarder of the Wind River Indian Reservation, she had not had a single encounter with any of the people who called it home. She had seen them from time to time, but had always felt inhibited by the barrier (whether real or imagined) between their two cultures. Now, here amongst them, her prejudices began to melt like snow under the radiance of the sun. Jane noticed that Aldi and Elsa-Eska seemed right at home amongst these people who were so new to her, almost as if they were already part of the tribe. She also noticed that Elsa-Eska was sleeping more peacefully, her shivering having diminished to an occasional twitch. Questions started to form in her mind: *Why did these people welcome us so readily? Why do Aldi and Elsa-Eska seem so at home here? Is it possible that these people know who Aldi and Elsa-Eska are?* Jane began to follow her thoughts to their startling conclusion when Kenny's voice brought her back to the moment.

"And last, but not least, this is my lovely Katie."

Katie leaned forward to look around Kenny. "Welcome, Jane," she said. "We are pleased to have you with us." She looked down at Jalamin and then back up at Jane. "May I hold your baby?"

"Of course," Jane replied without thinking. Normally, she would not have been open to letting a stranger hold her Jalamin, but here she found it impossible to refuse.

Jalamin cooed softly as Jane transferred her into Katie's waiting arms. The child seemed reluctant to let go of her gaze upon Pete, but settled into Katie's arms as naturally as if the woman were her own mother.

"Thank you all," Jane said, addressing the entire group. "You are all so kind to let us intrude upon your…" Jane hesitated, not knowing what it was she had intruded upon. "…your evening."

"It's no intrusion," Big Jack said.

"Not at all," Louie added, sounding very much like his father. "We're just riding the storm out. Glad to have you."

"You are safe here," Big Jack said. "The man of trouble will not come to this place."

"Man of trouble?" Jane repeated. "What do you mean?"

There was a momentary pause as if the entire group took a breath and held it. Louie cleared his throat. "The man who is with your husband is a…he's not a good man. He has come to bring trouble to Aldi and Elsa-Eska and the child. But you are all safe here."

"I don't understand," Jane said, her sense of peace giving way to worry for Rick. "Who is he?"

"Johnny did not tell you?" Louie asked.

"No, he didn't say anything. What's going on?"

Louie glanced at his father. The little man gave him a nod, which Jane took as a gesture of permission.

"According to Shoshone legend, the mountains are home to little people called the Nunumbi. If you are struck by one of their invisible arrows, you will become very sick."

Katie stole a glance at Elsa-Eska, but turned away when she saw that Jane had noticed.

"You think this man is a *Nunumbi*?" Jane asked, trying hard to hide her skepticism. "He's not exactly *little*."

"No," Kenny said with a slight chuckle. "The Nunumbi are just a legend; a story parents tell their kids to keep them from wandering off. Although, there are a few who still believe in such things."

"Kenneth," Mother said in a parental tone, "mind your respect for the old ways. Even a myth contains a seed of truth."

"Yes, grandmother," Kenny replied sheepishly. "I'm sorry."

"Excuse me," Jane said, "but what does this have to do with William?"

"William?" Big Jack queried.

"Yes, that's his name."

The little man folded his arms across his chest and nodded as if that meant something.

"I don't believe this William is a Nunumbi," Louie continued, "but the seed of the myth may be real in him."

"I don't understand," Jane said.

"What I mean to say is that whatever spawned the legend of the Nunumbi might be at work in this man of trouble. That is what Johnny says."

Jane was about to pose another question when she was interrupted by a weak voice to her right.

"That man is not Nunumbi." The voice belonged to Elsa-Eska. "He is Hori."

Every head in the circle turned toward Elsa-Eska, Jane's more urgently than the rest.

"What is a Hori?" someone in the group asked.

"That can't be." Jane said once she found her voice. "Aren't the Hori still on…" She cut herself short.

An uncomfortable silence fell upon the group as if each was waiting for the answer to his or her own question.

Jane could no longer contain herself. In an attempt at discretion, she turned her head to the right and kept her voice low. "Aldi, when you told us of the Hori, you said they were from *another* place. You meant another place on…" She noticed Kenny and Katie looking directly at her, but she couldn't stop a second time. "On…um…where you're from, right?"

Kenny and Katie looked at Aldi to hear his response.

Aldi tilted his head at the question. He did not try to keep his voice low. "The Hori are not from Klyv."

At that, Louie got up from his place, walked around the outside of the circle and knelt down next to Jane. "Jane," the big Indian said, "come with me." He stood up and walked away from the group. As Jane followed, she heard murmurings as various conversations began around the circle.

When they were out of earshot of the others, Louie turned and smiled down at her. "It is better that we speak in private. Some of them are not ready to hear these things."

"What things?" Jane asked tentatively.

"Some of us know about Aldi and Elsa-Eska."

Jane looked back at the group, wondering which of them were part of *some of us*.

Louie seemed to read her thoughts. "My father, Mother, Sharon, and Uncle Ed, of course. Johnny says the others will know soon."

"Where is Johnny?" Jane asked.

The big man did not answer.

"*Who* is Johnny?"

"You don't know?" Louie hesitated and then said, "He is…not like us."

"What do you mean?"

Louie leaned close to whisper in Jane's ear. "He is a protector sent by the Before One."

Jane gasped. "You know about the Before One?"

Louie nodded.

"Do the others know who he is?"

"They believe he is an elder from another tribe. I believed that as well until Aldi told me a few weeks ago. I suspect my uncle might know. He knows much, but says little."

Jane looked back at the group. "You all are really Ed's family? I didn't think he had anyone."

"There are a great many in his family." A hint of sadness crept into Louie's smile as he looked at the small gathering. "But only these are with us. Pete is a long-time friend. Katie comes with Kenny. Sharon is the newest among us." He turned again to Jane and there was something about the way he looked at her that suggested a new thought had occurred to him. "Sharon is young, but wiser than her years. Perhaps you should get to know her."

"I think I would like that."

Louie smiled as if letting Jane in on an inside joke. "New love is a strong river. It can be difficult to navigate."

Jane glanced at the young woman and felt the beginnings of sisterly affection.

"Jane," Louie said, bringing her attention back to him. "The time is soon when you must confront the man of trouble. Johnny has already gone. He has asked that I bring you and Aldi. Jalamin will be safe here, along with Elsa-Eska and Sara."

Jane instinctively looked back at Jalamin. The child had a fistful of

Katie's hair.

"Jane," Louie said. "Rick needs you."

She felt a tug in her heart back to Jalamin, but there was an equally strong tug in her heart to go to Rick. She held her gaze upon Jalamin for a moment longer then looked up at the big Indian. She felt her head start to nod. "Let's go."

CHAPTER 46:

KOZUM-AL FRACAS

||||

"Tell me again why you believe they're coming back here," Rick said impatiently. He was sitting in the dark of his living room cradling a rifle in the crook of his arm. "We've been sitting here for over two hours. They could be anywhere by now, and I do mean *anywhere*. If the collector's ship picked them up, they could be halfway to the moon. Why don't we call your ship, use that communication thing, and go after them?"

Kozum-Al remained silent and continued to stare into the fire.

"Hey, Koz, did you hear me? We're wasting valuable time. Let's do something."

Kozum-Al didn't alter his gaze. He spoke softly. "I am doing something."

"How's that?" Rick leaned forward in his chair.

Finally, the bounty hunter turned to Rick. "You humans are always in such a hurry." There was something in his voice that demanded Rick's attention. "You are so eager to shoot that you cannot possibly savor the anticipation."

Rick shook his head scornfully and twisted impatiently in his chair.

"Think about it, Rick. Aldi believes he has the advantage. He believes you are still under his spell. Such blind confidence. Imagine the look on his face when he realizes he's been caught. Go ahead, play it out in your mind."

Rick leaned back in his chair and relaxed his grip on the rifle. Kozum-Al's voice was soothing, convincing.

"Aldi will come back here with that stupid grin on his face. Elsa-Eska will be following him like the pet she has become. And Jane will be with him as well. He will think he has won. But there you will be, waiting; ready to take back what is yours. He will never suspect what you know." Kozum-Al chuckled. "This is my favorite part. How will you enlighten him to the fact that his little scheme has come to an end? You could just tell him and see what happens to that idiotic grin. Or you could play with him for a while, listen to his lies with the light of your knowledge, and enjoy his ignorance of your superiority. Then, when *you* decide it's over, *you* take him out on *your* terms. You'll have your family back."

"I can't...I can't..." Rick mumbled. It felt like someone had injected Novocain into his brain, numbing his judgment, making him susceptible to strange ideas. His eyelids drooped sleepily. "I can't... kill him."

"Why not?" Kozum-Al whispered. "It wouldn't be murder. He's not even human."

"I won't." Rick shook his head in an attempt to clear it, but the numbness was settling in thickly like a warm blanket.

"Don't kill him then," Kozum-Al said. "Just make him think you will. Get him to confess. Then turn him over to me. I'll take care of him."

"Okay." Rick felt his head move up and down in agreement. "I can do that."

"Now isn't it better to enjoy the thought before you do the deed?" Kozum-Al eyed Rick in order to gauge the human's response. The human nodded again. "You see what I mean? You can almost taste it."

"Almost taste it," Rick said automatically.

Kozum-Al himself savored the unfolding of his plan. He was confident that Rick had been properly guided into the part he would play, but he couldn't resist putting the final piece into place. "Elsa-Eska will be grateful." The way he said it sounded like an afterthought.

Rick tilted his head. "Elsa-Eska. What do you mean?"

"She's been a prisoner for a long time. You'll be giving her back her freedom. Gratitude is a universal concept." He paused to let the words sink in. Then he added, "Klyvians are very affectionate, especially the females."

"Huh?"

Kozum-Al chuckled. "You don't have to pretend with me, Rick. I know you are attracted to her. Why wouldn't you be? She is a very desirable woman. Any man from any world would agree."

"I'm, uh...I'm married." His reply lacked the enthusiasm he might have intended.

"Monogamy," Kozum-Al said. "An amusing little anomaly among you humans. So far, I have encountered it only on this planet. Though I understand there are some here who have gotten over it."

Rick's mind drifted to that evening when he and Elsa-Eska danced together—the feeling of her embrace, the scent of her hair, the warmth of her breath upon his neck and the sound of her voice when she spoke his name. It all came rushing back upon him, reviving the desire he thought had been buried. Buried, but not destroyed. With as much clarity as Kozum-Al allowed him, Rick could see her. He imagined her standing before him in her Klyvian robe. She was smiling at him.

Kozum-Al got up from his chair and walked behind Rick. He placed his hands on Rick's shoulders and leaned down until his mouth was nearly touching Rick's ear. "It's time."

Without warning, the entire living room was awash with a blinding white light. Rick's attention was immediately drawn to the window through which the light was streaming. He stood to his feet and held his hand up to shade his eyes.

Kozum-Al spoke quickly. "I will be close, but out of sight. Enjoy this, Rick. Remember, it's all you. Just call out if you need me."

Rick didn't see where Kozum-Al went. He was suddenly alone in his living room.

When the front door flew open, Rick could make out the shape of someone silhouetted in the high beams and spotlights from Ed Tyler's truck. Before he could decipher the figure's identity, he was caught in a firm embrace. There was something familiar about it's size and shape and scent.

"Oh, Rick!" Jane said, burying her face into his chest. "I was so worried. Thank God you're home."

The sound of Jane's voice surprised him. The vision of Elsa-Eska was still lingering in his mind. Then another figure entered the room. When Rick saw it duck through the doorway, he knew exactly who it was.

Jane sensed Rick's body tense. "What is it?" she asked, pulling back to look into his face. "Rick, what's wrong?"

How will you enlighten him to the fact that his little scheme has come to an end? When it had been just Rick and Kozum-Al, the thought of slowly drawing the collector into the light of truth seemed the way to go. Now, with his adversary standing before him, he just wanted it to be over. "Jane," Rick commanded. "Get down."

"What?" She saw something foreign in her husband's eyes—fear, panic. Hatred. She glanced over her shoulder in the direction of Rick's stare and saw Aldi standing just inside the living room. Then she looked back at Rick. "What's wrong? It's Aldi."

In one swift move, Rick shoved Jane to the floor behind the couch and snatched the rifle that was leaning against the chair.

"Hey!" Jane exclaimed as she fell to the floor. When she righted herself, she saw the rifle in Rick's hands pointed directly at Aldi's chest. "Rick! What are you doing?"

"Shut up and stay down!" Rick barked at her. "And you," he growled at Aldi, "get out of my house!" He rushed the big man. Using the rifle like a push bar, he forced Aldi back out the door.

Aldi stumbled backward and fell down the steps, landing hard on his back in the snow. Rick was on top of him in a flash, forcing the rifle down across his neck. From the doorway, Jane could see the look of shock on Aldi's face and the look of pure rage on Rick's. With the snow whipping around the two men and the harsh light from the truck, the entire scene looked like a dream or a scene from a movie. Jane wanted to wake up or leave the theater, but she could do neither. This was real.

"Rick!" she screamed. "Stop!" She started to take a step out the door, but froze when Rick turned to face her. His face was so distorted with rage that she could barely recognize him as her husband. She looked quickly in the direction of the truck, expecting to find Louie and Ed, but she could see nothing for the blinding lights. Where were they? Why didn't they help?

"Rick," Aldi said, his voice surprisingly calm in spite of the rifle pressing down on his throat. "It's me, your brother."

"You…are…not…my…brother," Rick snarled through gritted teeth. He pulled back on the barrel of the rifle and slammed the stock of the gun against the side of Aldi's head. Then he jumped up to his feet, took a few steps back, and trained the rifle back onto Aldi. "Get up, Collector!"

Jane leaped down the steps and knelt down in the snow beside Aldi. She helped him sit up so she could examine the side of his face. Blood was already running down the side of his face in thin rivulets.

"Get away from him, Jane!" Rick shouted.

Jane turned at the sound of his voice. "What are you doing? I don't understand. This is Aldi, our friend."

Rick's eyes narrowed. "He's not our friend!" Rick shouted over the sound of the idling truck and raging storm. "He's been lying to us the whole time!"

"What are you talking about?" Jane pleaded.

"I know who you are, Collector! I know why you're here! We won't let you take them!" The combination of bitter cold and bitter anger caused Rick's voice to tremble. The rifle in his hands was also getting cold, causing his hands to ache as they gripped it too tightly.

Aldi slowly stood to his feet, pulling Jane up with him. He put his hands up and took a step toward Rick, trying to put some distance between himself and Jane. "Why do you call me *Collector*?" Aldi asked innocently.

"Ha!" Rick laughed out loud. "You deny it? Where's Elsa-Eska?"

"She is not well," Aldi replied. "She is safe with friends."

"You mean she's locked up in a cage with the rest of them!" Rick shouted back. "Well, you're not going to get away with it. We won't let you. It's over, Collector. You hear me? *OVER!* We're not going to let you get away with it any longer."

"Rick," Jane said, "you're not making any sense. Get away with what? Rick, look at me!"

Rick forced himself to transfer his attention from Aldi to Jane. His eyes were wide open, but there was no sight in them. In spite of the intense light from the truck's spotlights, his pupils were dilated such that his eyes were only black—black like death.

"Who's *we*, Rick?" Jane asked. "You keep saying *we*."

Rick glanced back toward the house and then back at Jane.

"Is someone else here?" Jane asked. She closed the distance between herself and Aldi. "Rick! Who is *we*?"

Rick edged his way back toward the house, careful to keep the rifle trained on Aldi. He moved backward up the steps toward the open door. "Kozum-Al!" he shouted into the darkened house. "Come on out. You can have him now."

Jane looked up at Aldi. They exchanged the same bewildered look. When she looked back at the house, she was surprised to see Rick standing with… "William?" Jane said aloud.

Rick and Kozum-Al walked toward Jane and Aldi, stopping less than ten feet from them. Kozum-Al glanced at Jane and then fixed his eyes upon Aldi. His expression did not match Rick's fierceness. Instead, he beheld Aldi with curiosity as if he were some strange animal. Jane could see that Rick was shivering from the cold, and she and Aldi were shivering as well, but the stranger seemed completely unaffected. He stood perfectly still with the storm raging around him as if he were immune to the elements of this world.

Jane wanted to confront the man, but Aldi had placed his hand on her shoulder and was trying to move her behind him. "Don't worry, Jane," Aldi said calmly. "We are protected." He took a step forward, positioning himself between Jane and the gun in Rick's hands.

"You have the same look," Kozum-Al said, his voice too civil for the situation. "I haven't seen it since…"

Rick cut his eyes toward Kozum-Al, confused by the man's words. Kozum-Al placed his hand on Rick's shoulder and whispered something into his ear. Rick returned his gaze to Aldi and became like a statue.

"I have never seen your kind," Aldi said confidently, "but I know what you are."

"Ah," Kozum-Al grinned. "All the more interesting. You know, Klyvian, you present me with a rare opportunity. The first time I encountered your kind, I underestimated them. I tipped my hand, so to speak. Do you know what that means, Klyvian? *Tip my hand?*"

Aldi did not respond. Jane was too fascinated to do anything but listen. Rick just stood there, still entranced.

"Never mind," Kozum-Al said, waving his hand dismissively. "It is the speech of these creatures. Now where was I? Oh, yes, the first time I encountered your kind, I made the mistake of revealing myself too soon. I suppose you know all about that, don't you?"

Aldi nodded. "Kalan and Dorran still talk about it."

"Liar. I watched them die."

"They speak to us in the Song."

"Oh, that's right. That silly little song you hold so dear. Pure fantasy. A fabrication. Tell me, Klyvian, do they still sing about my return?"

"Yes."

Kozum-Al clapped his hands and laughed. "Now that was genius. They said I waited too long. They said I should have acted sooner, like the one who turned this planet." He looked upon Jane like she was a child. "Human, are you familiar with the story of your Adam and Eve?"

Jane could not find her voice. She simply nodded.

"It's legendary, you know, as the first one should be. But it was easy. Just two naïve little children. Hardly anything compared to others. Still, it was the first, and I would have liked to have seen it." Kozum-Al looked over at Rick. "Are you getting all this?"

Rick continued to stare blankly at Aldi.

"No, I guess you wouldn't." Kozum-Al waved his hand in front of Rick's face. There was no response. "Don't worry, human, your mate's still in there somewhere. See what I mean, Klyvian? These creatures are so easily manipulated. But you..." Kozum-Al took a step closer to Aldi, examining him with a great curiosity.

"Say it, Hori," Aldi snarled. The anger in his voice was impossible to miss.

Kozum-Al's eyes widened. "Ah, a Klyvian with a spine. You are not like those weaklings I so easily turned on your planet."

Aldi glared at Kozum-Al. "You did not turn us all."

"Yes, Aldi, you speak the true." Kozum-Al let out a long sigh of annoyance. "Your family has been a bit of a nuisance to me. But that will soon be rectified."

"Hori," Aldi interrupted. "Speak plainly or be silent. Why are you here?"

"Very well," Kozum-Al said like a parent to a child. "Klyv is the last of the unfinished worlds. I'm going to finish what I started. The Despised One (the way he said it made it sound like an obscenity) has kept you from us…until now. Uh-oh, somebody let the untouchables outside of their protective bubble." He waved his hands around Aldi's head, laughing as he did it. "I was surprised at how easily I was able to get to Arkel and Jalamin. I have something more amusing planned for you."

Aldi leveled his gaze upon the Hori, but said nothing.

"Shall we begin?" Kozum-Al walked back to Rick and laid its hand upon his shoulder. "Rick," he said loud enough for all to hear, "the Collector has confessed. He plans to kill you and take your wife and daughter to his ship. I am sorry, but I cannot stop him. It's up to you now."

Rick's eyes fluttered and he came out of his stupor. The rage returned to his face and he leveled the rifle at Aldi's chest.

"No!" Jane screamed.

Rick flinched at Jane's scream, causing his arm to jerk as he pulled the trigger. The explosion from the rifle echoed between the two houses. Aldi grabbed his arm where the bullet passed through.

"Klyvian," Kozum-Al said. "The human is unleashed. If you don't stop it, it will kill somebody."

Aldi recoiled as he realized what the Hori was attempting to do. He tried to push Jane away, but she clung to him.

Kozum-Al turned toward Rick. "The Collector has turned your wife. Look, she is with him."

Rick saw Jane clinging to Aldi's arm and believed it to be true.

"It's too late for Jane," Kozum-Al said. "But you can still have a good life with Elsa-Eska."

Rick brought the rifle up again, this time taking aim at Jane.

"Careful, Klyvian," Kozum-Al called out. "If you don't stop him, he will kill her."

Aldi saw the determination in Rick's eyes and knew the Hori was right. Rick was fully under his influence. "Rick," he called out to him, stepping in front of Jane. "The Hori lies."

Rick turned the gun back onto Aldi. "Shut up, Collector!"

"Rick!" Jane screamed, scrambling back in front of Aldi. "Don't!"

The gun fell back onto Jane. "Don't come any closer," Rick said, his voice calm now, devoid of emotion. "You've made your choice. I've made mine."

The standoff continued, Aldi and Jane taking turns drawing Rick's attention away from the other. Aldi was trying to protect Jane from injury or death if the gun fired. Jane was trying to protect Aldi from the Hori's scheme.

"ENOUGH!!" the Hori shrieked.

Aldi and Jane froze at the inhuman sound of it.

"Rick Blackwell," Kozum-Al commanded. "Shoot them both."

Rick raised the gun and took aim at the head of the closest target—Aldi. He was just about to squeeze the trigger when a movement behind Kozum-Al caught his attention.

There was a loud crack and Kozum-Al's head pitched forward, but he did not fall. The Hori turned slowly to see a wide-eyed Ed Tyler holding a Louisville Slugger in both hands over his head like he was about to take another swing at a piñata. The Hori turned his head first to right and then the left, as if checking to make sure it still worked, but kept its eyes fixed on the trembling little human before him. Sensing no real threat from the pitiful creature, Kozum-Al turned back to the more pressing issue at hand. "Shoot them now."

Rick re-aimed the rifle at Aldi's head. He saw a flash of white light and then everything went black. As Rick slumped to the ground, the rifle fell harmlessly from his hands.

Ed Tyler looked down at the unconscious man and said, "Sorry, Kevin." Then, shuffling over to Jane, he said, "Sorry, dear, it needed doing."

"That's okay, Ed," Jane replied. "You did the right thing." She put her arm around his shoulder and drew him close.

Ed looked nervously at her and wriggled free from her embrace.

Kozum-Al bared his teeth and growled at them. Jane braced herself for a fight, but the Hori did not advance. It just stood there as if trying to decide what to do next.

"Aldi," she said, "what's it doing?"

"I'm not sure."

Suddenly, the Hori's eyes widened and he took several steps backward. Jane, Aldi, and Ed turned to see what had caused such an unexpected response. Johnny Two Feathers stepped into the light from the headlights of the truck.

"Don't be afraid," he said as he passed by. When he got to Rick's unconscious body, he knelt down beside it and placed his hand on Rick's head. He turned back to Jane and gave her a reassuring nod. Then he stood to his feet and stepped toward the Hori.

Kozum-Al started to walk backward to keep the distance between them. He did not see the other figure until he backed into it. Kozum-Al spun around and then jumped back at the sight of the big frame of Louie.

With Louie and Johnny Two Feathers advancing and Kozum-

Al retreating, the three formed a triangle. Kozum-Al's eyes flicked between the two and then settled upon Louie. A smug grin formed on his lips as he took a step toward the big Indian. "A mere human," he sneered.

"STOP!" Johnny shouted with a commanding voice that caused the Hori to freeze. "Once again, legend has slipped beyond your reach. Leave this place and do not return."

The Hori turned as if to face Johnny, but then slowly stepped outside the beam of the truck's headlights until it was absorbed into the darkness of the night. An unearthly howl rose above the sound of the storm, and for a moment it eclipsed all other sounds. Then it was silenced. Even the storm itself seemed to pause its own fury.

Johnny and Louie returned to the three who were now huddled around Rick's unmoving form. Johnny knelt down with them and placed his hands upon Rick's chest. Rick's head rolled to the side and he let out a grown as he regained consciousness.

Jane leaned down and spoke softly into his ear. "Rick, honey. It's me, Jane. Can you open your eyes?"

Rick moaned again and wrenched his eyes open. They were filled with confusion. "What happened? Why is it so cold?" He brought his hand up to his face and noticed the snow dripping from it. "Why are we outside?"

CHAPTER 47:

THINGS REVEALED

⊤

At first, it seemed like they were talking about someone else. Rick sat in his chair and stared at the floor as Jane and Aldi took turns explaining the horrible details of what happened. The last thing Rick could remember with any certainty was arriving back at the ranch and finding it deserted, but even that seemed like a dream. Everything else was hazy and disjointed. When Jane got to the part about Rick shooting Aldi in the arm, he brought his hands up to cover his face in shame.

"I just don't remember," Rick kept saying. "How could I have done such a thing?"

Johnny provided the disturbing answer. "You were under the influence of a dark force."

Rick looked up at the old Indian. "Dark force? What's that supposed to mean?"

"The man you were with was not who he seemed to be."

"I know," Rick replied. "He told me he was…" Suddenly a piece of his splintered memory came back to him. "He said he was Klyvian, and he had come here to…" Another piece fell into place. "He came to stop Aldi." Rick gasped as the whole memory came roaring back in all of its hideous detail. "He said Aldi was a Raphim collector and that you were going to take Jane away."

"Those were lies," Johnny said. "The Hori are highly skilled in deception."

"Hori?" Rick repeated in disbelief. "You mean like in that story about the time of trouble on Klyv? Why is he here? How did he get here?" Rick was reeling from the pieces rapidly coming together to form the picture of what had really happened.

"The Hori has come to stop the mission," Aldi said. "I do not know how it got here."

"He said they had a ship," Rick remembered. "He said there were more of them, I think ten."

"That could have been a lie, too, right?" Jane suggested hopefully. "I mean it could have been the only one."

"I don't know," Aldi answered.

"Why do you guys keep referring to him as *it*?" Rick asked.

Johnny stood to his feet and held up his hands. The room fell silent as all eyes focused on the little old Indian who now looked much younger than before. "I sense there is more to this than the mission. If the Hori had intended to simply eliminate Aldi, it would have had Rick ambush him when they arrived."

"Maybe it wanted to use Aldi to find the others," Louie suggested.

"Probably," Jane said. "But it also said it wanted to finish what it started. Remember, it said something about Aldi's family. Sounds to me like a vendetta."

"Whoa, wait just a minute," Rick interrupted. "I'm not following any of this. Finish what? Vendetta? And why do you keep referring to Kozum-Al as an *it*?"

Johnny paused before answering. He seemed to be assessing Rick's readiness to hear what he was about to say. "Rick, I sense you will find this difficult to believe."

"Try me," Rick countered. "Just give it to me straight."

"Okay," Johnny said. "Straight. The Hori are neither human nor Klyvian, nor any other species that might inhabit the planets of this reality. Their dwelling is in another place, another realm, but they do have the ability to cross over as we all saw tonight."

"What?" Rick ventured. "Kozum-Al is like some kind of demon or something?

No one said anything. Jane, who had already come to this conclusion, shuddered when she heard the word. Aldi simply nodded.

"Oh," Rick said. "I think I'm gonna be sick." He swallowed. "Does that mean…" Rick started to say, but he was having difficulty getting the words out. "Does that mean I'm…possessed?" Rick's hands were shaking.

Johnny beheld him with all the tenderness of a loving father. "No, Rick. You are not possessed."

Rick exhaled the breath he was holding.

"But you were easily brought under the Hori's influence," Johnny added. "It would not be good for you to encounter another one in your condition."

Rick resumed his examination of the floor in front of him.

"Johnny," Jane said, trying to draw the attention away from her husband. "Why did the Hori not attack Aldi directly?"

"It is not allowed." The way he said it sounded like this should have been obvious to everyone. He explained further. "The Hori have certain limitations. They cannot touch a Klyvian directly. And for some reason, they cannot operate technology."

"Does that mean we were never in any real danger?" Jane asked.

"No, it does not." Johnny glanced down at Rick who was still staring at the floor. "The Hori could not fire the gun itself, but as we have seen tonight, it didn't need to. The Hori are skilled in the manipulation of the weak."

Rick flinched at the implication. He knew that everyone saw him as the weak one, the liability. Without looking up, he posed a question that he already knew the answer to, but wanted to hear Johnny say it anyway. "Who determines what the Hori can and cannot do?"

"The Before One," Johnny said matter-of-factly.

At that, Rick looked up. Where Jane had expected to see skepticism or even defiance, there was only wonder. "Tell me, how is it you know so much about all this?"

Johnny eyed him knowingly and chuckled. "You ask that which you already know. But I will tell you. I have come from the Before One to watch over Aldi and Elsa-Eska. I have known the Hori for a very long time."

"So, I take it you guys aren't really Indians." Rick started to chuckle because it was better than fainting. "What are you, angels?"

Louie laughed, too. "Not me, man. I'm as human as you."

Johnny was laughing along with everyone else. Then he offered, "Would you like to see my true form?"

A hush fell upon them, and Rick put up his hands. "No, that's okay. I think I've had enough for one day. Besides, my head is killing me." He rubbed the lump on the back of his head.

Jane glanced at Ed Tyler who was chewing feverishly at a hangnail. She decided Rick didn't need to know it was he who had given him the lump.

A silent pause fell over the group as Rick, Jane, and Aldi processed the events of the night. Johnny returned to his place on the couch next to Ed Tyler. The normally skittish little man looked at ease next to him.

After a long moment, Rick got up from his chair and stood before Aldi and Jane. "I need to say something. Jane, Aldi, I can't tell you how sorry I am for everything that happened tonight. I'm still not sure exactly how it happened, but that doesn't excuse what I did. I hurt you both. I put you both in danger. I could have…" He couldn't finish for the lump that was forming in his throat.

"It's okay," Jane said, standing up to embrace him. "We know it wasn't really you."

"But I shot my best friend. Aldi, can you ever forgive me?"

Aldi joined her and placed his hand on Rick's shoulder. "Yes, brother. Look." He moved his arm up and down. "I think Johnny would make a good doctor. It doesn't even hurt."

"Thank you, both." Rick stepped back so he could look at the entire group.

"What is it?" Jane asked.

Rick looked at each of them one at a time. Then, clearing his throat, he said, "I truly am sorry for my actions, but more than that I am sorry for...for being the way I am. I know why the Hori was able to control me. I don't want that to happen again."

Jane felt tears welling up in her eyes and her lip start to quiver.

Rick continued. "I guess what I'm trying to say is I want to believe like you."

Jane lunged at Rick and wrapped her arms around him, her tears flowing freely. Aldi stepped forward and hugged them both. Rick felt other hands upon him as Johnny and Louie joined the huddle. Ed Tyler had gotten up with the two Indians, but he wasn't accustomed to hugging. He awkwardly put his hand on Rick's hand, patting it like he was burping a baby.

"Oh, my gosh," Rick said suddenly, breaking up the huddle. "I completely forgot. Where are Elsa-Eska and the girls? Are they safe?"

"Yes, they are well," Aldi said.

"They're at Fort Washakie," Jane added.

Rick was confused. "Who are they with?"

Louie stepped forward with his enormous arm around Ed's shoulder. Ed looked like a child next to him. "They are with family."

Rick waited for a fuller explanation, but there was none. "What family?"

"We'll explain on the way."

Ed Tyler could barely see over the steering wheel of his huge truck. He gripped the wheel at ten and two with a white-knuckled zeal that would have made any driver's education teacher proud. Leaning forward, his beady eyes were like two lazars penetrating the snow-whipped night.

"Jane," Rick whispered. They were crammed in the back seat along with Louie. Aldi and Johnny Two Feathers sat in the front with Ed.

"Where did this truck come from?"

"I have no idea. Ed and Johnny just showed up in it."

"Weird. I didn't know Ed could drive." He put his arm around her and pulled her close.

Jane snuggled into Rick's side, laying her head against his shoulder. It felt good to have him back. Several minutes passed before Jane spoke again, her voice barely above a whisper. "Did you really mean what you said back there? Are you really ready to believe in God?"

"I think I'm ready to believe in the Before One."

"They're the same, you know."

"They might be. But I've got a lot of questions and I think I'd like to talk to Aldi and Elsa-Eska first. You know, get their take. That's okay, isn't it?"

"I think so," she replied. "It's just that it's sort of unprecedented. I mean, a human trying to embrace the beliefs of people from another planet—I'm just not sure how that would work."

"But if there's no difference, as you say, what does it matter?"

"I guess it doesn't. But there might be some things that don't translate exactly the same from Klyvian to human."

"How about we cross those bridges when we get to them?"

Jane wondered what the first bridge might be. But for now, she was happy to have her husband back; more completely, it seemed, than ever before.

CHAPTER 48:

THAT MUST BE WHAT IT'S LIKE

TO KISS AN ANGEL

Three-month old Sara lay quietly in her crib staring intently at the object suspended above her. The thing was about the size and shape of a half-dollar, liquid-smooth and black as night. Set just between the center-point and the bottom edge was something that looked like a clear marble about the size of a pea. As the object rotated on its nearly invisible line, both sides were revealed to be identical. From a distance it looked like a piece of jewelry made of cut and polished onyx with a crystal inlay. Upon closer inspection, it was much more interesting. The larger stone, if that's what it was, resembled a puddle of ink floating in space. It was shot through with tiny flecks of silver that moved slowly in a circular fashion. The crystal was also moving, rotating slowly upon a vertical axis and revolving around the center of the blackness as if caught in a current along with the silver specks. Sara's gaze upon the object was not one of mindless entrancement, but rather inquisitive wonder.

"Good morning, Jane," Sharon said softly, getting up from the rocking chair next to the crib. "I did not see you come in."

Jane stepped all the way into the room and hugged Sharon. "I've only been here a minute." She nodded toward the crib. "I was just watching Sara staring up at the Ka-stone."

"She is quite fascinated by it. Have you noticed how her eyes mimic the movement of the silver specks?"

"Yes," Jane whispered. "It's almost like there's a connection."

"It is from her home planet. Maybe she senses it somehow."

"Maybe."

The two women watched the child a moment longer before Jane

asked, "How is Elsa-Eska this morning?"

Sharon sighed. "Not good. I checked on her about an hour ago. The cold keeps her awake all the time. I do not think she has slept longer than a few minutes in over a week."

"But it must be over eighty degrees in here." Jane could already feel beads of sweat forming on her brow. "Ever since the storm, each day is worse than the day before."

"It has been very cold since then," Sharon observed. "I think the high today is going to be thirty-nine."

Jane frowned. "It could be like this for another three or four months. I don't see how she can last that long."

Sharon's expression became grave.

"I'm glad you're here," Jane said. "I know you were hoping to spend more time with her, but you've been a tremendous help with Sara. Your being here allows Aldi to be with her."

"She does seem to do better when they are together."

Sara let out a tiny squeal and held her hands up to Sharon. Sharon picked her up out of the crib. "She's getting so big. I can tell a difference since I moved in."

"She likes you," Jane observed as Sara wound her fingers playfully into Sharon's long silky hair.

Sharon smiled and blushed.

"Any word from Johnny?" Jane asked.

"He appeared at Fort Washakie three days ago. There is still no sign of the Hori. Johnny has gone to Ireland and then Australia to visit the others."

"I hope that thing is gone for good," Jane said. "I'm getting tired of being on alert."

"How is Rick doing with all this?"

"Surprisingly well. He likes having the guys around. He's taken quite a liking to Louie and Kenny and Pete. The twins don't come around much, so he hasn't gotten to know them."

Sharon grinned. "Joshua and Thomas are restless spirits. They always have someplace to go."

"How are things with you and Thomas?"

Sharon became quiet.

"That's okay, I know you'd rather talk to Elsa-Eska. Maybe she'll be up for a chat later."

Sharon laid Sara back in her crib and began to tidy up the nursery. Jane took that as a sign she didn't want to talk about personal business. Although Sharon had been living with Aldi and Elsa-Eska for about a month, there was still a distance between her and the Blackwells. She was friendly, but guarded.

"Sharon, I know this is probably a silly question, but do the Shoshone celebrate Christmas?"

"That is not a silly question," Sharon replied. "Most of us do celebrate it. There is a dance and we exchange gifts. Why do you ask?"

"I was just wondering if you all would like to come here for Christmas. We'd love to have you."

"That is kind of you, Jane. I will ask the others." Sharon finished putting Sara's clothes away and folded the quilt she had used during the night. Then she changed Sara's diaper and put her into some play clothes. All this she did in silence while Jane watched.

"If you'd like, I could take Sara over to our house and feed her with Jalamin," Jane offered. "In case you have something you need to do."

Sharon paused at the door to the nursery. "May I come, too?"

"Yes, of course."

"Maybe you can help me with something," Sharon said. "I want to get Thomas something special for Christmas. Would you help me think of something?"

"I'd love to."

Jane, Sharon, and Sara met Rick on their way over to the main house.

"Is Aldi up yet?" Rick asked.

"We haven't see them," Jane replied. "We're going to feed the girls at our house."

Rick wavered between the two houses, taking a few steps further and then retreating. He was eager to see Aldi, but he didn't want to interrupt Elsa-Eska's rest.

"What's up?" Jane asked. "You look like you're in a hurry."

"It's December 14th." He said it like Jane should know the significance of the date.

"And?"

"It's communication day. The *final* communication day before the Enterprise warps out of here."

Sharon tilted her head questioningly and pulled Sara in closer to her body.

Jane interpreted, "That's just Rick's way of saying Aldi's people are about to leave. Today is the day they are suppose to make their final contact."

Sharon nodded her understanding.

Jane turned back to Rick. "Maybe if you just go in and wait, Aldi will hear you. Read a book or something, but please try to be quiet."

"Good idea." Rick tip-toed up the steps and quietly slipped in through the front door.

"Come on," Jane said, "let's get these hungry girls some breakfast."

Rick crept into the house and sat down at the dining table. He was careful to make just enough noise to get Aldi's attention should he be awake. Since most meals were taken at the main house, this dining table had been converted into a study area. It was organized into five sections of books and magazines across the middle of the table and two writing areas on either side.

Rick perused the book titles to see what Elsa-Eska and Aldi had been studying lately. The first was a stack of coffee table books with lots of photographs: *Beautiful Ireland, The Land Down Under, Mysterious Places, A Day in the Life of America, The Complete Guide to the Valley of the Kings.* The second section consisted of textbooks Jane had borrowed from the college: *Human Anatomy, Biology, Geology, Philosophy,* and *Astronomy.* Next to that was a stack of magazines: *Popular Mechanics, National Geographic, Field & Stream, Today's Woman, Sports Illustrated,* and a local publication titled *Wyoming.* The fourth section was of particular interest to Rick: *The Holy Bible, The Koran, the Vedas, The Four Noble Truths of Buddhism, The Writings of Josephus,* and *The World's Last Night & Other Essays,* by C. S. Lewis. The Lewis book was open to an essay entitled "Religion and Rocketry." The final section was a mismatched assortment of books that looked as if they had not yet been read and categorized.

At one writing place, there was a legal pad with what looked liked notes, presumably in Klyvian script. At the other, there was a book entitled *Signatures: A Theory on the American Evolution.* Rick was just about to open it to the bookmarked place when Aldi entered the room.

"Hello, Rick," he said, "I thought I heard someone. How are you?"

"I'm fine, but you look exhausted."

Aldi forced a smile. "I have not slept. Elsa-Eska had another difficult night."

"I'm sorry to hear that. Is there anything I can do?"

Aldi shook his head. "I have tried everything I know. We continue to sing the Song, the chippick is gone, and still she is cold. Nothing will warm her. She shivers so much, she cannot rest." Rick had never seen him look so haggard, so discouraged.

"We may have to take her to the hospital," Rick said. The idea had been firmly rejected by Aldi and Elsa-Eska every time it was suggested, but Rick felt they were running out of options, and Elsa-Eska was not getting any better.

Aldi sat at the table across from Rick and shook his head. "We cannot."

"Why not?" Rick pressed.

"Johnny said we must not allow a human doctor to examine her."

"But what if a human doctor can help?"

Aldi made no attempt to reply.

"Aldi, she's not getting any better." Rick did not want to utter his next thought, but he could see no way around it. "She could die."

"We cannot."

"Well, we can't just sit here and do nothing." Rick felt his emotions begin to build. "I can't...we can't just keep letting her suffer like this. There has to be *something* we haven't tried...something we haven't thought of yet."

Aldi let Rick come to the end of his trying and thinking before he spoke. "There is one thing we have not yet tried."

"What is it?" A glimmer of hope rang in Rick's voice. "I'll do anything."

"Will you let us go?" A note of sadness tainted Aldi's voice.

Rick blinked several times. "Let you go? What do you mean?"

"The Enterprise, Elsa-Eska will be well there."

Rick couldn't find his voice. As the ramifications of Aldi's words sank in, he could not escape the simple logic of it. Elsa-Eska would be well onboard the ship. She would be well among her people. "But just for a little while," he said, trying to put a positive spin on the unthinkable. "I mean, you'll come back, right?"

"I am sorry, my brother, no. The Enterprise will be leaving soon to continue the mission. If we go now, we will not come back for many years."

Rick stared blankly at the books on the table.

"There is just no other way," Aldi continued. "She cannot take the cold in this place. Even if she survived until the warm air returned, she would get sick again next winter. You are correct; if Elsa-Eska stays here she will die. Johnny has said the same."

Rick choked back the lump in his throat. "How long have you known this?"

"After Sara was born. Our people know this, too. We spoke of it at the last communication just before the storm."

"Why didn't you say anything to us earlier?"

"We hoped she would get better. We did not want to cause you worry for something we hoped would not happen. Our people are waiting for me to contact them with a decision."

"I...I can't believe it. Aldi, you and Elsa-Eska have changed my life. You opened my mind to believe so much that I thought was impossible. There's so much more I want to discuss with you. I have so much more to learn about the Before One. And there's so much more I want to show you of this world. What will I do without you?

You're my brother."

Aldi bit his bottom lip to keep it from quivering. "And you are my brother," he replied. "Yes, there is much more we would like to do and see and say, but this is what must be. I wish it could be another way, but it cannot."

"How much more time do we have?"

"I will contact the Enterprise today. They will send for Imtulon and Tyba to come for us in three or four days."

Silence fell upon them again as Rick tried to process the devastating news. Finally, he asked, "May I see Elsa-Eska?"

"She is awake," Aldi said. "Come. You can talk to her while I get the communicator."

Aldi led Rick into the bedroom. It was dark and very warm. Once Rick's eyes adjusted, he could see Elsa-Eska propped up in the bed beneath a mountain of blankets. The only visible part of her was her head supported by several pillows. Her hair was disheveled, and her eyes were darkened. She was shivering severely. Yet, in spite of her condition, she was still the most beautiful creature Rick had ever seen. Her eyes flashed golden when she saw Rick, and she managed a weak smile.

Rick tentatively approached the bed and knelt down on the floor next to her. It seemed the appropriate posture. "Hey," he managed.

Elsa-Eska lifted a trembling hand and placed it on the side of his face. Her hand felt like ice. "Hey," she replied through chattering teeth. "Good to s-s-see you, Rick."

"It's good to see you, too." Rick reached up and took her hand in his. "Not feeling so hot, eh?"

"Th-that's my problem—n-n-not even w-warm."

Rick tried to hold her gaze, but the pain in his stomach was so intense he had to look down, away from those piercing eyes. "Aldi told me you have to leave." He felt her other hand beneath his chin, lifting his head so that he had to look at her.

"Aldi s-speaks the true. Do you unders-stand this is n-n-not what we w-want?"

Rick nodded.

"B-but it has to b-be."

"I know," Rick managed.

"Do you..." Elsa-Eska was interrupted by a violent shiver. "Do you know h-how much you m-mean to us?"

Rick could do nothing but stare into her deep brown eyes with their swimming golden flecks.

Elsa-Eska tugged on Rick's hand, pulling him up off the floor and onto the edge of the bed. Then she placed her hands on either side of his head and pulled him toward her until their foreheads touched. The trembling in her hands ceased and her entire body seemed to relax. "I want you to know that we love you." Her voice was much steadier now. "Wherever we go, we love you and Jane. You are tolis anuk with us."

Rick started to sit back, but found that Elsa-Eska still had a firm hold on his head. She held him just inches from her own face, studying every contour as if she were memorizing him. Then, she tilted her head slightly to the right and pulled him to her, closing the gap between them until their lips touched. It was not the passionate kiss of lovers, nor the casual kiss of a friend, but something totally other. The kiss was completely uninhibited, yet it was far from reckless.

"Rick."

The sound of Aldi's voice brought Rick back to planet Earth. Strangely, he felt no awkwardness kissing Elsa-Eska in front of him. When he pulled away from her, she smiled and closed her eyes.

"The communicator is not here," Aldi said.

Rick joined him at the foot of the bed. "Did you check both cases?"

"Yes."

The sight of the open cases brought a forgotten memory back to him. "Oh, no. I know what happened to it." He slumped back down onto the foot of the bed. "How could I have been so stupid?"

"What is it?" Aldi asked.

"The night of the storm, Kozum-Al got me to show it to him. He must have taken it. Aldi, I am so sorry."

"This is not good." There was no anger in Aldi's voice, but he was noticeably concerned. "The Hori will be able to use it to locate the Enterprise. He will be able to find the others. I hope Johnny returns soon. We must tell him."

"I'm sorry, Aldi. Really, I had no idea what…"

"There is no need to apologize. The Hori was controlling you. You had no choice but to do what it wanted."

"But how will you contact the Enterprise?"

"We cannot."

"They won't leave without you. We'll find a way to make contact."

"They will not wait long. The time is small for them to make their way."

"You mean they'll just leave without hearing from you?"

"Yes. It is the mission."

Rick processed all he was hearing. "But how will they know Elsa-Eska needs to get back to the ship?"

Aldi's face was serious. "They will not."

CHAPTER 49:

ON THE THRESHOLD OF FAME

Jane listened somberly as Rick explained the dilemma. She was deeply saddened by the thought of Aldi and Elsa-Eska needing to leave, but quickly saw the logic of it. And when she learned of the missing communicator, she was eager to find a solution. Sharon, however, quietly excused herself. Tears were spilling down her cheeks as she left.

"Maybe we could build a new one," Jane suggested. "By that I mean you, Aldi. Didn't you say you and Arkel dismantled your ship's computers and put them back together? Surely you could build one."

"It's not that easy," Aldi replied. "There is not enough time. The Enterprise will be in range only today and tomorrow. If they don't hear from us by then, they will leave."

"I've got an old CB radio," Rick said. "We wouldn't get the video part, but we could at least broadcast an audio signal. You did tell us that your ship was able to detect a radio broadcast. We should at least try...for Elsa-Eska."

Aldi looked at his shivering wife and then at Rick and Jane. "I will try."

About a mile away, a green 1965 Mustang slowed to a near stop and turned onto a dirt road.

"There it is," said Carl Drake, "Blackwell Ranch. Do you see any sign of the reporters?"

"No," Dave replied, craning his neck to survey the surroundings. "Either we beat them here or they actually followed your instructions and are keeping out of sight. Are you sure this is the best way to handle this? What if this isn't the place?"

"It's the right place," Carl replied. "Say, you're not having second thoughts, are you?"

"No. I just want to make sure we don't go knocking on the wrong door."

"I called the Wyoming Bureau of Land Management. When I gave them the coordinates, they told me it was a ranch owned by a Rick and Jane Blackwell. That sign back there said *Blackwell Ranch*. It's got to be the place."

Dave shifted in his seat. "What are we going to say when we get there? I mean we don't really know what we're looking for. What if it's nothing?"

"Hey," Carl snapped. "Now you're starting to sound like Jimmy. Don't forget it was *you* who kept calling me after I told you that signal didn't prove anything. *You* convinced me to listen to it again. And *you* figured out how to isolate the audio part. You heard them as well as I did. They're here."

Dave slumped in the seat. Everything made perfect sense when they were sitting in Carl's living room. Now that they were so close, he wasn't so sure.

Carl continued. "No, I'm not sure this is the best way to handle this. I'd rather go in and see them for myself first, but we may only get one shot at this. We've got to make sure the media is here to get it on tape."

"Do you have that reporter's number?"

"It's programmed in my phone."

"Back-up would have been nice," Dave postulated. "Maybe we should have informed somebody besides the media; you know, somebody more official."

"Don't worry, David. As soon as the media gets wind of what's going on out here, this place will be swarming with government people. And once they get involved, you and I may as well head back home because we won't get anywhere near the aliens."

Dave let out an audible sigh. "I guess this is it then. ET, here we come."

The table in Aldi's dining room had been transformed from a study area into an electronics lab. Rick's CB radio lay dissected across its surface, and Aldi was working feverishly trying to reassemble the parts into a working transmitter that could reach the Enterprise. They spent nearly an hour with the CB, before the dissection, trying to hail the Enterprise, but to no avail. There just wasn't enough power in the antiquated device. Now Aldi was trying to boost the signal using the amplifier from Rick's home stereo, and direct it with an old television satellite dish from Coop's house.

"Okay," Aldi said. "Let's try again."

Rick plugged the amplifier into the wall socket and held his breath while Aldi spoke into the CB's microphone. Aldi tried for several minutes, transmitting the Klyvian call over and over on different frequencies. After the third pass through the frequency dial, he sat back in his chair and rubbed his eyes.

"I don't think this is going to work," Aldi said. "They may no longer be scanning for radio signals from Earth. We may be transmitting, but if they aren't listening..." He shook his head and set the microphone back onto the table.

"What now?" Rick asked. "Do we just give up?" Rick found it odd that he was the one trying to coax Aldi into action. Usually, it was the other way around, but Aldi was fighting against the fatigue of being up all night and the frustration of working with human technology. Rick also found it strange that he was pushing so hard to succeed at the very thing that would take Aldi and Elsa-Eska away from him. Without realizing it, Rick was beginning to see things from a point of view that did not begin with himself. "We've got to keep trying," he said. "Elsa-Eska needs this to work."

Aldi shook his head in an attempt to clear the fatigue and picked up the microphone. Moments later there was a knock at the door. Rick got up from the table and answered it. Standing on the steps were two men; the eldest was leaning on a pair of metal crutches.

"Can I help you?" Rick asked.

"Yes," replied the man with the crutches. "The lady next door said I could find a Rick Blackwell here."

"You found him." Rick looked toward the main house and saw Jane standing in the doorway shrugging helplessly. "What can I do for you gentlemen?" He noticed the man was trying to peek into the room, so he maneuvered his big frame to block his view of Aldi.

"Ah, Mr. Blackwell, my name is Carl Drake, and this is David..." Carl looked at Dave, suddenly realizing he had never learned the young man's last name. "May we come in?"

"Uh, this isn't a good time. You guys can go out the same way you came in." Rick made a move to close the door, but he wasn't fast enough.

Carl planted his crutches across the threshold. "Please, sir."

"Who are you guys?"

"Look, Mr. Blackwell, we've come a long way to speak with you. We will only take a moment of your time."

Rick placed both hands on the door jams, filling the doorframe with his body. "Again, who are you guys?"

"Sir," Carl persisted. "Just a moment of your time."

Rick sighed heavily and stepped out onto the small porch, closing the door behind him. "Now what's this about?"

Now that they had gotten this far, the weight of the next few moments bore down upon Carl. He had waited over half of his life for this, facing countless skeptics along the way. Although he had learned to plead his case boldly before the unbelieving scientific community, he was actually nervous to say it once more to the one person he was certain was also a believer. "Thank you, Mr. Blackwell. I'll get right to the point."

"Please do."

"I used to represent a community of scientists called SETI."

"Hold on," Rick said. "What did you say your name is?"

"Carl. Carl Drake."

"Hey, I know you," Rick said as the lights of recognition blinked on. "I've seen you on TV. You're..." Rick stopped as he made the connection. "You guys can leave now. I don't have anything to say to you." He turned to go back into the house.

"Mr. Blackwell," Carl called out. "I know what's going on here. I know who's in there."

Rick slammed the door and locked it.

"Mr. Blackwell." Carl rapped on the door with his crutch. "We know they're here. We've been monitoring their signals for months."

"That went well," Dave scoffed from behind Carl. "I think he'll turn them over to us any minute now."

Carl turned on the younger man. Standing on the top step, he was nearly the same height as Dave. "Why don't you just go wait in the car and let me handle this? I'm not done yet."

Carl heard the door open behind him and he saw Dave's gaze turn upwards over his head. He turned around and looked directly into the chest of the tallest man he had ever seen in his life.

Aldi looked down at the little man. His immense height was intimidating, but his smile was disarming. "Tell me about this signal."

"I, um, I mean we," Carl stammered, backing down the steps. "We detected a transmission between this location and...um...uh...well, the moon...or actually the vicinity of the moon."

"What did you use to detect this signal?" Aldi asked.

Carl was mesmerized by the man in front of him. He gazed up at him, unable to connect his thoughts to the speech center of his brain.

Dave noticed Carl's predicament and stepped forward. "Actually, I'm the one who first detected it. I work at a CIA listening station..."

At the mention of CIA, Rick started to push Aldi back inside.

"No. Wait, please," Dave urged. "I'm not CIA. I'm just an analyst at a listening station. We monitor radio transmission from all over the world. But that's not why we're here."

Rick paused to hear the man out.

"We detected an unusual signal, and we tracked it here. We just want to know what it is, that's all."

Carl tapped Dave on the leg with his crutch. Dave ignored it.

"Can you still detect it?" Aldi pressed.

"Yes, if it's still broadcasting."

"Can you transmit?"

Carl tapped Dave's leg again with his crutch and cleared his throat. Dave continued to ignore him.

"Yes," Dave said hesitantly, "but actually, we're just trying to identify its source. You guys wouldn't happen to know anything about this, would you?"

"David," Carl said, stepping in front of the younger man. "My partner is a bit on the eager side. Would you excuse us for just one moment?" He hobbled a few steps backward, pulling Dave with him. "What are you doing?"

"I'm trying to find out what these guys know about the signal."

"What are you doing?" Rick asked Aldi when he was sure the two strangers couldn't hear him.

"If this man was able to detect our signal, we can use his equipment to contact the Enterprise."

Carl stared at Dave in disbelief. "Don't you realize who that is? Dave shook his head. "No."

Rick stared at Aldi in disbelief. "Do know who those guys are? Aldi shook his head. "No."

Carl spoke quietly, but with a sense of urgency, "That's him. The tall guy is the alien."

Rick spoke quietly, but with a sense of urgency, "Those guys are from the government."

Dave and Aldi turned toward each other simultaneously. They both wore the same bewildered expression. In spite of Rick's efforts to hold him back, Aldi moved toward the two strangers. Rick's heart sank. After nine months of protecting Aldi and Elsa-Eska from public exposure, the cat was leaping out of the bag. When Aldi reached the two men, Dave took several steps backward, but Carl stared up at him in wonder. Neither human could make their vocal chords work.

"Can you take me to your radio?" Aldi asked.

Carl blinked and Dave swallowed.

Aldi looked at one man and then the other. "Can you take me to your radio?" he asked again.

"You're real," Carl said weakly. Then thirty-five years of questions came flooding out in rapid succession. "Where did you come from? How did you get here? Are there others like you? How did you find us? Have you been to other worlds? What is your world like?"

Aldi looked back at Rick for some assistance.

"Mr. Drake," Rick said, joining them. "I know this is a lot to take in all at once. Believe me, I know. But please, just listen to me without saying anything. You're right—my friend Aldi is from a world called Klyv. And these signals you guys detected, they were transmissions between Aldi and his ship that's been parked behind the moon since last March."

Dave edged closer, wide-eyed and open-mouthed.

Rick continued, assuming command of the situation. "I know it's amazing, life-changing even, but right now you guys are going to help us. You see, Aldi's wife is very ill. If she doesn't get back to their ship, she may die. We need you to take us to your radio so we can contact their ship."

"He has a wife," Carl mused to himself.

"Why do you need us?" Dave asked, suddenly drawn into the dilemma. "Why don't you just contact them like before?"

"That's a long story," said Rick. "The short of it is we can't. But you guys can, right?"

Carl spoke up when Dave hesitated. "Yes. We can help you."

"That is very good," Aldi said. "Can we go now?"

Dave just blinked, still not quite believing what he was seeing.

"Well, actually, our radio isn't here," Carl said. "It's in Nevada."

"Nevada?" Rick exclaimed. "No, no, that's too far. We need it now."

"Now?" Carl asked. "Why now?"

"Their ship is about to leave without them."

"If we go now, we might make it," Carl said. "Dave, can you make the arrangements by phone? Dave? You don't look so good."

The enormity of the moment finally caught up with Dave, causing his eyes to roll upward and his knees to buckle. Had Aldi not caught him, he would have fallen face forward all the way to the ground.

As Rick and Aldi carried the unconscious Dave into the main house, and Carl hobbled along behind them, Rick noticed the grin on Aldi's face.

"This reminds me of the first day you and I met," Aldi said.

"Uh-huh."

When Dave came to a few minutes later, he found himself in an unfamiliar room surrounded by mostly unfamiliar people. Carl, he recognized, and there was Rick Blackwell and the man he called Aldi. But the others, all women, were strangers to him. There was an Indian girl and two other women, one of which had the most unusual eyes.

"What happened?" he said, surveying each face until he landed on Aldi and the woman with the unusual eyes. They seemed to be together. That's when it hit him—the freakishly tall man named Aldi and his wife. He suddenly felt light-headed again.

"It's okay, David," said Carl. "David." He snapped his fingers in front of Dave's face. "David, look at me. It's okay. We found it, the source of your signal, it's here." Carl was beaming like he had just hit the lottery; he looked ten years younger. "Okay, now look at them." Carl turned Dave's head for him. "That's your signal. They're real. Don't you see what this means? They're real and they're right here."

"Wow." It was the only thing Dave could say.

Rick determined he would have better luck directing his questions to the older man. "Carl, what about that radio? Can we get to it?"

"What about it, David?" Carl asked. "Do you think we can get them into your listening station?"

"No way," Dave replied. "Even if I had a week, I don't think we could get them in. In case you haven't read the papers lately, we're kind of at war. Security's too tight."

Carl frowned, but then he looked as if he had an idea. "We could go to Elvis."

"Elvis?" Jane and Rick said in unison.

"That's what we used to call the listening station I manned when I was with SETI. We could go there."

Everyone in the room paused as the light above the table began to vibrate and the china in the hutch began to clink together. Soon the entire house was vibrating.

"Earthquake," Dave shouted and made for the nearest doorframe.

The vibration continued, but now the sound of something like a jet engine could be heard. Aldi stood up and went to the window at the back of the house.

"We no longer need a radio," Aldi announced.

"Why not?" Rick got up and joined him at the window.

In the middle of Rick's massive back yard, a jet-like craft was descending. Great clouds of dust billowed from beneath the craft as it touched down on the ground. By now, the others had joined Rick and Aldi at the window.

"Would you look at that?" Carl said.

"I don't believe it," Dave mumbled under his breath.

"How did they know to come here?" Rick asked, directing his question to Aldi.

Aldi hugged Elsa-Eska close to his side. "Johnny."

About a quarter-mile away, a man and woman stood on a ridge overlooking the Blackwell Ranch.

"Are you getting this?" the woman asked.

"Oh, yeah," the man replied, looking through the eyepiece of the large video camera balanced on his right shoulder. "Better get that award winning Channel 2 smile on, we're live in four, three, two…"

CHAPTER 50:

THE WORLD LEARNS OF BLACKWELL

ж

This is *Andrea Fox, Channel 2 News. Are space aliens living among us? That's what radio astronomer, Carl Drake, believes. And that's why I'm standing on this ridge overlooking this ranch some thirty miles north of Riverton, Wyoming. We are here in response to a call we received yesterday from Dr. Drake informing us that he was prepared to announce a major discovery that would, as he put it, 'end the search for extraterrestrial intelligent life.' It must be noted that Dr. Drake recently disassociated himself from SETI, where he worked on the forefront of the search for ET since the 1970s. The reasons for Dr. Drake's departure are not yet known, but we are left to wonder if it has anything to do with today's announcement. What we do know is that Dr. Drake is at this very moment with the residents of the Blackwell Ranch, and we are awaiting a call from him to move onto the residential compound. While we wait, I would like to show you some dramatic footage of a large military jet landing at the ranch just minutes ago. As you can see, the jet came in from the west, slowed to a stop over those houses, and then descended vertically to the ground. Several people have come out of the house and have congregated in front of the aircraft, but we have yet to see anyone exit. We will keep an eye on this developing story and report back as it unfolds. I'm Andrea Fox, Channel 2 News.*

"And we're off," said the cameraman, lowering the camera from his shoulder. "Great job, Andrea. And, if I may say so, you look extremely hot."

Andrea rolled her eyes and shook her head. "Just keep that camera rolling on that jet." Then she spoke into her microphone, "Hey, are you guys still listening to me? See if you can get confirmation from the military about activity in this area. I can't see any markings on that jet, but somebody owns it. Also, you might want to get a comment from somebody at SETI. See if you can find out why Drake left. And another thing, next time you send me out to God knows where, send a professional cameraman." She shoved the microphone into the cameraman's chest and walked back to the van. "Amateurs," she muttered loud enough to be heard.

"Diva," the cameraman shot back. When he looked back into the eyepiece of the camera, he could see that a ladder had been extended from beneath the craft. "Miss Fox," he called. "You better get over here. Something's happening."

Rick, Aldi, Dave, and Carl were gathered in a semi-circle just in front of the craft. Jane, Elsa-Eska, and Sharon watched from inside the warm house. Dave kept steeling glances up at Aldi, whose perpetual smile only served to confuse Dave's science-fiction based ideas of what a being from another world should be. Carl, who was more prepared than Dave, had gotten over his initial shock and was now riveted to the craft before him. Aldi and Rick entertained more practical thoughts about the unexpected arrival of the Klyvian shuttle.

When the first boot stepped through the hatch onto the ladder, Rick was surprised that it was not the clunky black boot attached to the bulky black jumpsuit he remembered from his first encounter with the Klyvians. Instead, stylish brown leather boots introduced a pair of tan, shapely legs. What followed caused the hearts of the three human males to race. Rick tried to avert his eyes, but he just couldn't believe what he was seeing.

The woman who emerged from beneath the craft was wearing khaki hiking shorts and a cut-off T-shirt emblazoned with an image of a Koala Bear. She had short, spiky hair bleached white with pink tips. Dangling from her ears were long feather earrings, and she wore several hemp bracelets on both wrists. Rick recognized her face from before, but this was a decidedly sexier version of what he remembered.

Aldi stepped forward and the two Klyvians touched foreheads.

There was a brief exchange in Klyvian, and then Aldi introduced the newcomer. "This is my sister, Tyba."

When Tyba smiled, there was no mistaking the family resemblance. "G'Day, Rick," she said. "Great to see you again." Her voice was heavily accented. When she stepped toward him, Rick expected the traditional Klyvian forehead touch, but what he received was a kiss that left him breathless and somewhat concerned. Tyba's kiss was nothing at all like Elsa-Eska's. It was skilled from what Rick could only guess was a lot of practice. A troubling thought entered his mind about the humans with whom Tyba and Imtulon had been living.

From inside the house, Sharon gasped and Jane let out a chuckle. Elsa-Eska saw no reason for either reaction. Outside, Carl and Dave blinked in disbelief. Much to their disappointment, Tyba greeted them with handshakes.

Imtulon's appearance was no less surprising. His bleached hair was cropped short and spiky. A small gold ring pierced his left earlobe, and he wore a strand of white seashells high around his neck. His hiking shorts and t-shirt revealed bronzed arms and legs that looked like they had seen many hours in the gym, and there were tattoos on both arms and the calf of his right leg. When he approached Aldi, he grabbed him in a brotherly bear hug, picked him up, and spun him around. Comparatively, Aldi actually looked smaller. Rick suddenly hoped Imtulon had not seen Tyba kiss him, for the man could have easily dropped him with one punch. He was relieved when Imtulon greeted him with a huge smile and hardy handshake.

"G'Day, mate," Imtulon said. "I remember you."

"It's good to see you, Imtulon."

"Call me Imi." He exhaled a great cloud of breath. "Oy! Feels like a three dog night. Can we go inside?"

"Yes, please," Tyba pouted. Her teeth were chattering and she was rubbing her hands on her bare arms.

"Yeah, sure," Rick said. "Right this way." Rick led the group to the house and held the door for them. The two new Klyvians entered first; Tyba winked at him as she passed. Carl and Dave followed, their expressions hard to read. As Aldi ducked through the door, Rick tried to interpret his perception of his sister's and Imi's interesting appearance. If Aldi was as surprised as Rick, he was hiding it well.

"Oh, man," exclaimed the cameraman, still looking through the eyepiece of his rig. "I don't think that's a military jet unless it's stolen."

"What are you talking about?" asked Andrea.

"If those two pilots are Air Force, sign me up. That is one good looking woman."

"Let me look at that." Andrea commanded as she moved toward the camera. "Play it back."

Inside the house, introductions were made. Rick could tell by the look on Jane's face that she was just as shocked as he was. Aldi skipped the pleasantries and got right to the situation at hand. He brought Tyba and Imi up to speed on Elsa-Eska's condition and gave them an abbreviated account of the Hori's attack; leaving out the part about Rick falling for its deception. Tyba and Imi responded with genuine sympathy over Elsa-Eska's illness and deep concern at the mention of the Hori. When Aldi mentioned that he and Elsa-Eska intended to return to the ship, Tyba reported that they had learned of the plan from Johnny Two Feathers and that they had already contacted the ship regarding their intentions.

"Very good," Aldi said in conclusion. "We will leave tomorrow."

The finality of Aldi's statement hit Rick and Jane like a slap in the face. They agreed in their heads that this was indeed the necessary course of action, but their hearts were aching for another solution— one that would enable Aldi and Elsa-Eska and Sara to stay. They looked helplessly at Elsa-Eska shivering next to Aldi. There just wasn't anything else to be done.

Carl and Dave sat stunned by all they had heard. The intrigue of it all was much more than they anticipated, and the Klyvians didn't fit their expectations. By the time Aldi finished speaking, they were drawn more into the urgency of getting Elsa-Eska and Aldi back to the ship than to the fact that they were indeed extraterrestrial beings. They had forgotten about their own plan, which had advanced well beyond the point of no return.

In the production room at Channel 2 News, a research hound named Jenny continued to stare at the video feed from the Blackwell Ranch long after the others returned to their desks. "Why do I feel like I've seen this before?" she kept asking herself. She played the footage over and over and then stopped the tape on a close-up shot of the front of the craft.

Just then, one of the broadcast techs walked by. "Hey, that looks like the UFO that flew over San Francisco last spring."

"That's it!" Jenny exclaimed. "I knew I'd seen it somewhere. Thanks, Tom."

"No prob."

Jenny grabbed the telephone and punched in a four-digit number. "Chuck, this is Jenny in the production room. I've got something you're going to want to see. Remember that weird plane that buzzed the Golden Gate Bridge last spring? The one that everybody thought was a UFO? Well, I'm looking at a video of it that was shot not thirty minutes ago….Yeah, it's sitting in the backyard of some guy's house in Wyoming….Okay, I'll see you in a minute."

There was nothing else to be said on the matter, the decision had been made, and the vehicle that sealed it was sitting just outside the back door. Aldi and Elsa-Eska would be gone by this time tomorrow.

After the discussion intended for human ears, the four Klyvians lapsed back into their own language. Interestingly, the Australian team's accent disappeared completely when they spoke their native tongue. Jane was able to pick up on the gist of their conversation at first, but they spoke so rapidly and she was so out of practice that she couldn't keep up for long. After a few minutes, the Klyvians decided to carry their conversation back to Aldi's and Elsa-Eska's house.

With Elsa-Eska out of the room, Sharon quickly decided that Jalamin and Sara needed to be played with elsewhere. That left Rick and Jane alone with Carl and Dave.

"Rick," Jane said, "would you help me in the kitchen?" She didn't wait for his reply, as it really wasn't up for discussion.

"You guys can just make yourselves at home," Rick said to Carl and Dave. Then he too was gone.

"What now?" Dave asked.

"I'm not sure," replied Carl. "They aren't really what I expected."

"I know what you mean. Why do you suppose two of them have Australian accents?"

Carl shrugged. "I guess the same reason why the other two don't. They must have picked it up from the people they've been living with."

"If I didn't know any better, I probably wouldn't believe they were aliens. They seem so…human."

Carl sighed. "I know. A little too human."

In the kitchen, Jane was absentmindedly putting the dirty dishes from the dishwasher back into the cupboards. Rick noticed, but said nothing. He just went to her and put his arms around her. At his touch, Jane fell into his arms and wept.

Rick held her for several moments while he dealt with his own emotions. Finally, he was able to speak. "It's hard to believe, isn't it? Everything was going so well. It was really working."

"Oh, Rick," Jane managed between sobs. "They changed us both, didn't they? They made us better people—better humans. What'll we do without them?"

"It'll be okay." Rick did his best to maintain. "Maybe this was part of the plan all along."

"What do you mean?" Jane pulled back to look him in the face.

"Well, we've been saying that everything else may have happened for a reason—their being here, us finding them, our girls being born so close together. Maybe they've accomplished their mission here and its just time for them to move on. Maybe I was their mission. Maybe the Before One sent them here to show me I could believe."

Jane stared at him through big tears. "They did that, didn't they?"

"They sure did."

"That still doesn't make this easy. Oh, Rick, I'm going to miss them so much."

"Me, too."

They held each other for several minutes.

"What about those two guys?" Jane finally asked. "Who are they?"

"Ugh, I almost forgot about them. They might be part of the reason Aldi and Elsa-Eska have to leave. I'm not sure who the younger one is, but the old guy is from SETI. I've seen him on the *Discovery Channel* a few times. Somehow they detected Aldi's communications with the Enterprise and they followed it here. I believe they mean to expose them to the world."

"Shouldn't we get rid of them?" Jane proposed.

"I don't think it matters anymore. By this time tomorrow, they'll have nothing but another alien encounter story with no proof."

Jane nodded and leaned back against the counter. Rick recognized the expression on her face.

"What is it?" He probed. "Something's bothering you."

"It's probably nothing," she said, "but did Tyba and Imtulon seem a little strange to you?"

"Tell me what you're thinking."

"I don't know. There's just something odd about them. I sort of understand why they're dressed like that. And while the accent was unexpected, I get it. But there's something else—there's a way about them that seems less Klyvian than Aldi and Elsa-Eska. Does that make sense to you?"

Rick nodded. "I sense it, too."

"I can't quite put my finger on it, but something just doesn't seem right. Do you think Aldi and Elsa-Eska noticed?"

Rick shrugged. "No telling. With everything else that's going on, I think they're pretty distracted. Besides, it's probably none of our business, and there's nothing we can do anyway."

"Should we trust them?" Jane asked.

"It's Aldi's sister. And Imtulon is like his brother. I don't see that we have much choice."

From the other room, Rick heard his name being called. When he and Jane walked into the living room, they saw that Carl and Dave had turned on the television.

"Mr. Blackwell," Carl said, "I think we might have a problem. Look."

It took a few seconds for the image on the television screen to register in Rick's brain. "Hey, that's us. That's here!" Rick sprinted out onto the back deck and scanned the horizon. He could barely make out the outline of the top of a news van parked on the ridge a quarter mile away. Entering back into the house, he turned on the two men sitting on the couch. "What have you done?!"

Dave wasn't much good at confrontation. He tried to sink deeper into the couch. Carl, on the other hand, was hardened from a life of hardship and ridicule. He exaggerated his efforts to stand up; it was a tactic he had learned early in life to play on the emotions of his opponents. It worked about half the time.

"I'm sorry," Carl said, "I notified them. But they were supposed to wait for my call before they started filming."

"Why would you do that?"

"Why would I not do that? Mr. Blackwell, I've spent my entire life searching for extraterrestrial life. Do you know what it's like to dedicate yourself to something most people call science *fiction*? The ironic thing is most people believe it, but they're too scared to admit it. Yes, I called them because I thought today was the day I would finally be able to prove it. I'm tired, Mr. Blackwell—tired of being laughed at, tired of being dismissed as a nut case. I'm just tired."

Rick did not expect the old man to stand up to him like that. He didn't know how to respond.

"Sir," Jane said.

"My name is Carl."

"Carl, I appreciate your motives, and I am truly sorry for how you've been treated, but can you just try to see our friends as people instead of a science project? Their names are Aldi and Elsa-Eska. They have a little girl. They named her Sara. They are a family not so different from us. Yes, they came here from another world, but in the last nine months they have made this world their home. They have learned our language and our ways and even a little of our humor. They are kind and good. They understand love and they are not afraid to express it. Carl, can you just try to think of them as people?"

Carl cleared his throat and shifted his weight from one crutch to the other. "Mrs. Blackwell..."

"My name is Jane."

"Jane," Carl forced a smile. "When I began my work with SETI, I wasn't interested in detecting a signal from outer space in order to satisfy some intellectual curiosity. I wanted to make contact. You see, I never wondered *if* they were out there. I wanted to know who they were. I wanted to know if they were like us. I wondered if they laughed and cried. I wondered if they made love and war. I wondered if they had hopes and dreams and fears. I wondered if they wondered whether they were alone in the universe. I thought that maybe there might be someone like me on some distant world staring out into the same space, but from the other side, having the same thoughts I had. I thought if only we could bridge the gap between us maybe we could be friends. Jane, I *want* to think of them in the way you know them. I envy the way you know them. I would give anything to have known them as you have. But I'm too late." He looked back at the television.

Everyone in the room watched as Andrea Fox of Channel 2 News broke the news to the world that Carl Drake was right. The image shifted from Andrea Fox to a picture of the Klyvian ship hovering over the Golden Gate Bridge and then to the live feed of the same ship sitting in Rick's and Jane's backyard.

"I'm sorry about all this," Carl said. "I can't undo it, but I'll do whatever I can to help your friends get out of here before the world gets to them."

Dave, who had been quietly taking everything in, stood up. "You guys do realize what's coming, don't you? This isn't some human-interest story. I'd say we've got about thirty minutes before your peaceful little ranch here turns into the biggest media circus in history…unless it turns into a military operation first."

"Don't panic yet," Rick said, looking out the window. "I think help just arrived."

Jane, Carl, and Dave joined Rick at the window. They watched as Ed Tyler and six Indians from Fort Washakie climbed out of Ed's truck. As the seven approached the ship, their number became eight. Seemingly from nowhere, a little old Indian joined them.

CHAPTER 51:

SHOWDOWN

♑

"Jane, take Carl with you and tell Aldi what's happened. Tell them they must leave immediately."

"But Rick," she protested.

"I know, honey," Rick countered. "But there's just no other way. They won't be safe here anymore. Dave, come with me."

Rick grabbed Dave by the arm and pulled him out the door. Joining the men from Fort Washakie, he brought them up to speed on the arrival of Tyba and Imtulon and the news story they had just seen on the television. When he pointed to the ridge from where Channel 2 News was broadcasting, Pete and the twins took off in a full-out sprint toward the unsuspecting news team.

Inside the other house, Jane and Carl found Elsa-Eska laying on the couch with Aldi, Tyba, and Imtulon gathered around her. Their hands were upon her and they were singing the Klyvian Song together. The two extra Klyvian voices added a new dimension to the Song that Jane had not heard before. Aldi and Imtulon were singing the same line over and over, their deep voices solid and strong. Tyba's soprano voice soared ethereally in what could only be called free form. It was both beautiful and haunting. Jane was momentarily distracted by it and she wondered what an entire choir of Klyvians would sound like. Carl looked like the man who suddenly discovered that the paper-wrapped box he had been carrying his entire life contained a priceless treasure.

Sensing Jane's presence in the room, Aldi motioned for her to join them. She took a few steps closer, stopped, and motioned for Carl to follow. At first, he shook his head, but Jane's persistence won him over. Together, they approached the Klyvians. Jane placed a hand on Elsa-Eska's arm and began to sing a part of the Song that she had never before sung. Aldi grasped Carl by the hand and pulled him closer. He guided Carl's hand into Elsa-Eska's and then placed his own hand on Carl's back. In that moment, Carl Drake experienced an extraterrestrial contact that made SETI's entire array of radio telescopes seem ridiculous. He felt like a child in the court of Kings and Queens.

The Song continued for another ten minutes, though to Carl it transcended his awareness of time. When the Klyvians and Jane stopped singing, he couldn't tell how long he had been standing there holding Elsa-Eska's hand. And strangely, the Song seemed to linger in his consciousness like an echo that refused to fade. He was brought back to the present when he felt Elsa-Eska's hand tighten on his own. He glanced up at her face to find that she was looking at him. Her weak smile was still dazzling enough that Carl felt his heart skip a beat.

"Thank you, Carl," she said.

Carl blushed and pulled his hand free. He could not find his voice to reply.

Jane seized upon the moment and began to tell the Klyvians about the news report. At first, they didn't grasp the implications. But when Jane told them that the televised report was certain to bring a parade of authorities, reporters, and curious on-lookers to the ranch, Imtulon understood.

"Jane is right," he said, his Australian accent switching on as he reverted to English. "We should go straight away."

Aldi hesitated. He looked from Elsa-Eska to Jane to Carl and back to Imtulon and Tyba.

"Come on, brother," Imtulon urged. "We cannot afford to be caught."

"Aldi," Tyba said. "Imi speaks the true."

Jane detected something within Imtulon and Tyba that resembled fear. It was an emotion she had never sensed in Aldi or Elsa-Eska. It was as if Tyba and Imtulon had experiential knowledge of what was coming. Jane suspected the Australian team may have received a more sobering introduction to humanity than Aldi and Elsa-Eska did. She glanced at Imtulon's muscular tattooed arms and Tyba's bleached hair, make-up, and jewelry, and felt a new appreciation for what they must have gone through. Though there had not been any mention of it, the thought occurred to her that they had not yet had a child. Had their experience among humans been such that they felt it necessary to delay such an integral part of the mission?

Jane's thoughts were interrupted by the sudden haste with which Aldi began to ready Elsa-Eska for their departure. In her weakened condition, Elsa-Eska could barely stand without support. She leaned heavily against Aldi. "Where is Sara?" she asked.

"Dag," groaned Imtulon. He was looking out the window. "Blue heelers."

Jane looked out the window and saw a police car parked next to her Jeep.

"Sara?" Elsa-Eska called out, and Aldi looked to Jane for help.

Tyba joined Imtulon at the window, assessed the situation outside, and assumed control. "Imi, get the flyer ready. Aldi, get Elsa-Eska onboard now." She looked down at Carl's crutches and sighed. "Jane, go find Sara. We'll wait as long as we can." As she headed toward the door that exited the back of the house, she called out to Imtulon, "I won't be long." And then she was gone.

"Where is Sara?" Elsa-Eska asked again, panic filling her voice.

"Um," Jane stammered. "I think Sharon has her and Jalamin at our house. You two get to the ship. I'll get her." She slipped out the same back door through which Tyba had disappeared.

"More coming," Imtulon reported from the window.

Carl, who had been watching helplessly, hobbled over to the window. "Excuse me," he said to Imtulon, trying to sound strong. "I'd like to help. Is there anything I can do?"

Imtulon towered over the crippled radio astronomer. In spite of the escalating emergency, compassion for the weaker man emanated from his tough exterior. He glanced over at Aldi and saw that Elsa-Eska was well taken care of. "Why not?" he said. "You can help me with the flyer." Imtulon went to the door and opened it a crack. "Aldi, when it's time, I want you and Elsa-Eska right behind me. Carl, make sure they make it."

Carl stood a little straighter as he accepted his mission.

Outside, the driveway in front of the Blackwell residence was turning into a parking lot. There was still just the one police car, but there was now a line of vehicles backed up as far as the curve around the barn. Several of the drivers had gotten out and were inching their way toward the spacecraft. Rick made a feeble attempt to turn them away, but with the encouragement of their growing numbers the advantage quickly fell to the crowd. Rick gave up and rejoined Kenny, Dave, Ed, and Big Jack to form a barrier between the advancing crowd and the ship. To his alarm, Johnny and Louie were nowhere in sight.

"Mr. Blackwell," the police officer called out, stepping from the driver's side of the police car. "Looks like you've got some company."

"Boy am I glad to see you," Rick said. "If you could disperse this crowd, I'd really appreciate it."

The officer assessed the crowd. "Just folks being curious, that's all. Now why don't you bring your new friends out so we can have a chat?"

"I'd rather not," Rick said. He noticed there was someone else in the police car. Suspecting it was another policeman, he thought it odd that he would remain in the car at what was quickly becoming a situation.

"Then perhaps we'll talk inside," the officer countered, taking a step closer.

Rick eyed the policeman. Something wasn't quite right. "No," he said. "I think you and I can talk right here. But not until you clear these trespassers off my land."

The cop looked casually at the crowd again and shrugged. "I don't see any trespassers here, Mr. Blackwell—at least not on this side." Then he pointed at the Klyvian ship. "I do see something out of place on your side, though. Now, I'll say this once more. You can either bring them out or I'll go in."

Rick was stuck. It was just the five of them standing between the Klyvians and what could easily become a hostile mob. Ed looked like he was ready to run, Big Jack looked like he was ready for an afternoon nap, and Rick still didn't know enough about Dave to know where he stood. If only Johnny and Louie were there.

"Mr. Blackwell," the officer said. "Our patience is growing thin. What's it going to be?"

The crowd, which had grown to about fifteen, had become interested in the exchange between Rick and the policeman. They must have believed the officer was speaking on their behalf because they had formed a semi-circle behind him.

"Yeah," someone yelled from the back of the crowd. "Our patience is getting thin."

"Bring 'em out!" someone else shouted.

"Yeah, bring out the aliens!"

Rick knew they had just crossed a line. There was no doubt now that the situation had become very dangerous. If something didn't happen soon to tip the balance back in his favor, he wouldn't be able to keep them from storming the house.

Up on the ridge overlooking the Blackwell Ranch, Channel 2 News was getting an exclusive interview with Pete and the twins. Hassling pale-faced tourists who wandered unaware onto the reservation was one of Pete's favorite pastimes. The twins were emboldened by his bravado. It wasn't exactly a fair match, and within minutes Andrea Fox and her cameraman were off the air and in their van. As the news team drove away, the twins gave each other a high-five. "Easy, young braves," Pete said. "Those were just the scouts. Looks like the cavalry's coming."

They followed Pete's gaze toward the direction of the road. Two police cars had pulled off the main highway, followed closely by another news van. From the south, a helicopter was approaching low and fast. Pete and the twins watched it fly over their heads. They could see a cameraman poised in the open side door.

"Look!" Thomas shouted, pointing to the east.

Pete and Joshua squinted in that direction and saw two dots growing in size by the second. Soon the dots took on their distinctive shapes as two fighter jets zoomed over them. A second later, the roar of their engines shook the ground. Pete and the twins spun on their heels in time to see the jets bank sharply to the right and climb to a higher altitude where they began to circle in a holding pattern over the ranch.

Rick ran out of ideas and time. There was no way his small band of defenders could stop the advancing mob, and it was obvious now that the policeman was not there to serve and protect. As if to make a point, he placed his hand on the grip of his sidearm. At the sight of the weapon, Team Washakie took a step back. Ed continued to fade backwards until he was safely hidden behind his truck. That left Rick, Kenny, Dave, and Big Jack to face the advancing mob.

"We've waited long enough, Mr. Blackwell," the police officer called out loud enough for the entire mob to hear.

"Yeah, we've waited long enough," someone echoed.

The policeman stretched his arms across his chest and cracked his neck like he was getting ready for a fight. He locked eyes with Rick and closed the gap between then with five long strides.

Rick did not anticipate the fist that caught him squarely on the nose. The added momentum of the officer's advance increased the force of the impact, sending Rick staggering backward. Before he hit the ground, he knew his nose had been broken. Falling hard on his back, his head smacked the ground with such force that his vision started to darken around the edges. He watched helplessly as the officer stepped over him toward the house.

The crowd was momentarily stunned by the unprovoked attack. Unsure of their part in this confrontation, they fell silent. If Rick's hoped-for balance tipper was going to come, now would be the time—and it did. From the far corner of the house, Tyba sauntered into view. She walked slowly, but deliberately toward the crowd of men, accentuating her feminine attributes. Someone from the crowd whistled, and the rest allowed their male instincts to focus their attention upon her. Dave also found it impossible to keep from staring at her.

Kenny saw her too, but he also saw the reaction of the distracted crowd. Impulse took over and he launched himself toward advancing policeman. He hit the officer from behind, wrapped his arms around him, and drove him to the ground.

The policeman didn't see the attack coming. He fell easily, but his years of close-contact training kicked in at once. Kenny had about thirty pounds to his advantage and he had been in enough fights to know how to handle himself, but it quickly became apparent that the policeman was better trained and stronger than he looked. After several punishing blows, Kenny realized he would not be able to last long with the man. He altered his strategy from subduing him to keeping him distracted. He hoped his Klyvian friends were quick enough to take advantage of the little time he was giving them.

They were. As soon as Kenny and the policeman hit the ground, Imtulon came out of the house. Aldi was close behind, carrying Elsa-Eska in his arms. Carl brought up the rear.

They made it halfway to the ship when someone shouted, "There they are!" Half the crowd pulled their attention away from Tyba.

From his vantage point, Imtulon knew they could easily make it to the ship before the mob reached them. But getting them all up the ladder would be difficult, especially considering Elsa-Eska's weakened condition and Carl's disability. Then he saw Tyba trying to make her way toward the shuttle without re-attracting the attention of the crowd. From the corner of his eye, he saw Rick stagger to his feet and wave them on just before he leaped onto the back of the police officer.

As the mob advanced, slowly at first, two men broke away from the back of the pack and drifted toward Tyba. Then the mob began to pick up speed at the urging of those in the front who were now running toward the ship.

Imtulon saw the determination of the mob and tried to pick up the pace of his little group. Leaving Aldi to carry Elsa-Eska, he circled around and grabbed Carl around the waist like a sack of potatoes. One of Carl's crutches clattered to the ground behind them. They made it to the wing of the ship and ducked beneath it when a loud roar drowned every other sound.

A large pickup appeared from behind the ship, Ed Tyler's head barely visible behind the wheel. The spinning tires sent a blinding spray of dirt and gravel into the mob, stopping them in their tracks. Ed whipped the truck around with surprising skill and made another pass, peppering the mob with another shot. On this third pass, Ed aimed the monster truck directly at the mob, dispersing them just as the police cars and news van skidded to a stop. Making good on the gift Ed had just given them, Imtulon propelled Carl up through the hatch and climbed up after him. Then he reached back down and hoisted Elsa-Eska up into the ship. Aldi followed.

The two men who had broken away from the mob managed to put themselves between Tyba and the ship. "Hey, sweetheart," one of the men called out. "Where you going?"

Tyba backed away, but had to stop as the other man circled around behind her, cutting off her escape route. She could tell by the look on their faces that these were bad men. She had seen the same look before.

A little more than a minute had passed since the police officer had thrown his first punch. Dave's self-preservation had driven him back toward the house where he witnessed the deteriorating situation from a relatively safe distance. He wanted desperately to go inside the house and shut the door behind him, but what little self-respect he possessed prevented him from turning away. At one point, he wavered between helping Kenny in his struggle with the policeman and going toward the ship. Rick's recovery and Ed's skill behind the wheel rendered those two feats of bravery unnecessary. The sight of Tyba and the two monsters, however, was more than even his weak resolve could stand. Something like steal shot up into his spine, and his heart became a machine. The increase of adrenalin pushed him from flight to fight. He squinted his eyes, set his jaw, clenched his fists, and drove himself full speed toward Tyba's assailants. When he got within ten feet of them, the scream of a Banshee erupted from deep within.

The sight of the crazed radio signal analyst caught both men by surprise. One of them took off like a frightened deer. The other one tried to raise his hands, but he was not fast enough. Dave launched himself at the man and they both tumbled roughly to the ground.

Tyba watched in amazement as the two men struggled. She didn't notice the tall figure come up behind her until a strong hand touched her shoulder. She let out a scream and tried to run, but she was caught in a strong embrace.

"Tyba! Kanah!" a man's voice exclaimed.

Tyba flinched and then fell into the arms of Imtulon.

The embrace was short. Imtulon aimed her toward the ship and told her to go. With Tyba safely on her way, he reached down and pulled the man off of Dave, lifting him completely off the ground. The man struggled to see what had him and came face to face with the giant Klyvian. When Imtulon let the man go, he nearly tripped over his own feet as he tried to run forward and look backward at the same time. Next, Imtulon helped Dave to his feet. "Thank you, human," he said. Then he turned and sprinted back to the ship. Moments later, the ship's engines ignited with an eerie whine, and a great cloud of dirt billowed out from beneath the craft.

The ignition of the engines brought everything outside the ship to a halt. Kenny and Rick let go of the policeman and retreated from the suffocating cloud of dirt. The cop, who had been spitting and swearing and threatening to arrest everyone, scrambled to safety behind the line of police cars. The once organized mob dissolved into silent onlookers. The four police officers froze in their places. An irate police chief could be heard over the radio demanding that somebody give him an update. The cameraman from the news van lowered his camera, but left it running. The field reporter gaped at the Klyvian ship along with the millions of viewers who were watching it all happen on their televisions. The only movement came from the news helicopter still circling low overhead. And further up, the two fighter pilots were tightening their holding pattern at the order of their commander who was watching the whole thing on television.

In the moment of this pause, the passenger door of the police car opened. A man in a police uniform stepped out and walked slowly toward the ship, seemingly oblivious to the crowd, the other police officers, and the news camera. He stopped in front of the ship and glared at it as if challenging it to make a move.

At first, Rick didn't think anything of the man, but then curiosity and the sense of familiarity drew Rick closer. He stopped when the officer spoke in a voice that Rick immediately recognized.

"Ah, Rick Blackwell," the man said. "I see the collector didn't kill you yet."

CHAPTER 52:

FOR SARA

_♌

"Sara!"

Elsa-Eska was becoming more frantic by the minute as Imtulon and Tyba readied the ship for departure. Aldi scanned the monitors that offered views of various angles outside. Mostly, he was searching for Jane, who should have been there by now, but he was also keeping an eye on the developments just outside the ship.

The Klyvians reverted to speaking only in their native language. Carl could not understand what was being said, but he could tell they were agitated. Aldi spotted something in the forward monitor, and Carl heard him say the word *Hori*. At the mention of the word, Tyba and Imtulon immediately became alarmed, and Elsa-Eska's eyes flashed brightly. She called out again for Sara.

Jane searched the entire house, but found no sign of Sharon and the girls. She checked again, looking in closets and bathrooms. Still nothing. She slipped stealthily back to Aldi's and Elsa-Eska's house and checked there. Both houses were empty.

"Where could they be?" she said aloud in frustration.

Jane went back outside to see if Sharon may have gone out to see the commotion. When she came back around to the front of the house, she saw the crowd, the police officers, and her friends from Fort Washakie all standing still, staring at the ship. Its engines were whining at a pitch so high that it was painful. Then she saw them— Rick and the creature she knew was a Hori standing equidistant between the police line and the ship. Her heart sank at the sight of the creature. Jane could see that it was speaking to Rick. A dread thought flashed in her mind that Rick might be falling back under its deception. But then she saw Rick shake his head and back away.

The Hori had tried and failed to pull Rick back to its side. Rick expected more of an effort from the creature or even an attack. Instead, it simply turned away from him and walked over to the officer who had punched him. It seemed to Rick that it was methodically testing its options— discarding the one that no longer worked and moving on to the one that would. It was evident now that the policeman was under the Hori's control.

Rick couldn't hear what the Hori was saying, but he could see it speaking into the officer's ear. The cop stared blankly at the ship, nodding his head. When the Hori stepped back, its puppet approached the line of other officers and relayed the orders.

Aldi observed all of this from inside the ship. He also found Jane and saw that she was empty-handed. He whispered something to Imtulon and Tyba and then knelt down next to Elsa-Eska.

"I am going to find Sara," he said to Elsa-Eska in English. "I told Imtulon to wait as long as he can."

Elsa-Eska struggled to lift herself into a sitting position. "Let me come with you."

Aldi shook his head. "You are too weak."

Elsa-Eska tried to get up again, but slumped back onto the floor. "I'm sorry, my Aldi."

"Don't worry. I will find her."

She nodded in resignation. "We will wait."

Aldi leaned down and touched his forehead to hers. "I won't be long."

Elsa-Eska reached her arms around his neck in one last effort to pull herself up onto her knees. Aldi slipped his hands around her back to help her up. Now face-to-face, they gazed at each other for a long moment. She pulled him toward her and kissed him tenderly on the lips. When she let him go, Aldi eased her back onto the floor.

"Aldi," she said, her voice quivering. "Tolis anuk."

"Tolis anuk."

Aldi found Carl sitting quietly in the back of the ship. He placed his hand upon Carl's knee and made eye contact, but spoke no words. Carl sensed something from the Klyvian—a word which had no meaning to him—and then watched him disappear through the hatch. When Aldi touched the ground, two strong hands grasped him by the shoulders.

"Aldi," Louie shouted into his ear. "Go around the back of the house. Jane is waiting for you." He spun Aldi around and aimed him in the direction opposite the police. When Aldi was clear, Louie climbed up into the ship.

Jane was the only one to see Aldi duck behind the house. When he reached her position, she caught him in an embrace. "I'm sorry," she said. "I can't find her anywhere. Sharon must have taken the girls away from here."

Aldi didn't panic, but Jane could see the anguish in his face. He closed his eyes and tilted his head back. When he reached for Jane's hand, she took it as an invitation to join him, though toward what end she did not know. She held his hand and closed her eyes and waited. She half-expected a verse of the Song to come into her mind, but the only thing she could hear was the sound of the ship's engines. Ten seconds later, she felt a nudge in the back of her mind, like a thought trying to reveal itself. The nudge persisted until she could tell it was a thought.

"It's Sara," Jane exclaimed. "I know where she is. She's at Coop's old place. How do I know that?"

"Ka-noa," Aldi replied. "You have made a connection."

As much as she wanted to talk about this new experience, there wasn't time. Still holding hands, Jane and Aldi took a circuitous route around the back of the crowd and down the line of cars toward Coop's old house. Everyone was so enthralled with what was happening in front of the ship that no one paid them any attention.

The line of police officers was advancing on the ship. With guns raised, two of the officers took up positions on either side of the fuselage, just in front of each wing. The other two officers ventured beneath the ship and stationed themselves on either side of the ladder. They were all business. Then the lead officer, with his own gun drawn, made his way to the ladder and began to climb up. He managed to get halfway into the hatch when his body went limp and tumbled backward off the ladder. The two attending officers assumed he had simply lost his footing until they saw the crutch lying on the ground next to their unconscious leader. The bend in the aluminum tubing matched the shape of his head. Both officers looked up to see what caused the fall only to find a large Indian dropping head first out of the hatch. Louie hooked a man in each arm and used them to cushion his landing. Standing up, he hollered up into the hatch, "Come on, Mr. Drake, we've got to get out of here."

As Aldi and Jane made their way along the long dirt road, a movement drew their attention skyward. Two black helicopters flew over them. They were close enough for Jane to see they were government helicopters, heavily armed.

When they arrived at Coop's old house, they rushed inside and found Sharon sitting in a chair, holding both girls in her arms. She looked terrified, but relieved to see friendly faces.

"I'm so glad you're here," Sharon said as she handed Sara to Aldi and Jalamin to Jane. "What's happening? Who are all those people?"

"There's no time to explain," Jane said, already heading back to the door. "We've got to get Aldi and Sara back to the ship."

When the lead officer regained consciousness seconds later, he saw that his two comrades were out cold. The whine of the ship had increased to a deafening pitch, and the thrusters were whipping the dust with tornado-like fury. Leaving his officers where they lay, he made his way back to the Hori. The creature shook its head in annoyance and placed a hand on his shoulder. Leaning close, it delivered the next set of instructions. The entranced man nodded and started waving the others to fall back. Once everyone was safely behind the cover of the police cars, he grabbed the radio from one of the cars and delivered the instructions.

Inside the ship, Imtulon saw the line of police officers back away and one of the helicopters reposition itself for attack. "Hold on!" he shouted in Klyvian. "We must leave now!"

"But Aldi and Sara are not with us," Elsa-Eska replied, struggling to sit up.

"The humans are about to attack!"

"Imi speaks the true," Tyba interjected. "If we do not go now, we will not make it."

"My Aldi," Elsa-Eska moaned.

"We will find them later," Imtulon said as his fingers danced across the control panel. Then he spoke in English, "Carl, you must leave us. We cannot wait any longer."

"My Sara." Elsa-Eska dropped back down on the floor and wept.

From over the ridge that separated Coop's old house from the main residence of the Blackwell Ranch, Aldi and Jane and Sharon felt the ground beneath them shake and saw a huge yellow ball of flame rise up into the sky. An ugly column of thick black and gray smoke followed it.

"Oh, no!" exclaimed Jane.

Aldi broke into a run toward the fireball, clutching Sara to his chest. Jane, still holding Jalamin, tried to follow. Sharon stood transfixed by the explosion. They ran until they were almost to the top of the ridge, and then stopped as the Klyvian ship emerged from the smoke and fire like a phantom. They watched the ship climb higher until it was clear of the smoke. It looked as if it would continue its ascent, but then leveled out and moved directly toward them. When it passed over Aldi, the ship hovered for a moment and began to descend. Jane fell back to give the ship room enough to land. Aldi held Sara close to his body, trying to shield her from the fury of the ship's engines.

The ship was only thirty feet from the ground when out of the smoke the two helicopters appeared. A second missile shot out from beneath the lead helicopter and exploded at the back of the ship. Fire rained down upon Aldi, Jane, and Sharon. As they all dove for the ground, Aldi and Jane struggled to shield the girls with their own bodies. The ship pitched forward violently and dipped to within ten feet of the ground before pulling back up. A third missile launched, missed its target by no more than a few feet, and slammed into Coop's old house. The structure evaporated in the blink of an eye, sending burning debris down upon the people on the ground.

The ship made another attempt to land but had to abort in order to evade a fourth missile. The impact of the missile into the ground sent a geyser of dirt and rock into the air. More fire fell all around Jane, Sharon, Aldi and the girls.

"We cannot stay here!" Aldi shouted. "Jane! Sharon! This way!" He led them out into the desert, away from the ship and the helicopters' violent attack.

The Klyvian ship righted itself from its last evasive maneuver and made one more attempt to get close to Aldi, but it was cut off by one of the helicopters. The ship hovered in place for several moments while Aldi and Jane and Sharon continued to put distance between it and themselves. Machinegun fire from the helicopter pinged off the surface of the ship, reminding the prey that the predator was still on the hunt. The second helicopter dropped into place beside its twin and joined the assault.

The ship faded one way and then the other, pitched upward and then back toward the earth. Each time, one or both of the helicopters matched its maneuver. There was just no way around them. Finally, the helicopters backed away from the ship in preparation for missile launch. The ship, anticipating the attack, turned suddenly and launched up and away from the helicopters.

The escape route put the ship directly into the path of the F-16s. As one of the fighters obtained missile-lock, it seemed impossible that the ship would escape this newest threat. But before the pilot could launch its payload, the Klyvian ship executed an impossible maneuver and disappeared. One moment it was there, dead in the sights of the fighter, and the next it was gone. The two jets shot straight through the space where the Klyvian ship should have been, peeled away from each other, and circled back around. Although their onboard radar systems detected no enemy aircraft in the area, the jets climbed back up to surveillance altitude and began patrolling the area in case the ship returned.

The helicopters had been ordered only to bring down the alien spacecraft. The people on the ground were of no interest to them; neither was the monster truck that appeared from around the curve. The truck jumped the ditch beside the road and skidded to a stop next to Aldi and the girls. Within seconds, the sky was peaceful again.

Aldi yanked open the passenger door and helped Sharon crawl up into the cab. She reached down and received Sara and Jalamin. Aldi lifted Jane into the cab and then climbed up after her. Ed jammed his foot down onto the accelerator, causing the big tires to dig into the desert clay. Instead of turning back toward the road, the truck headed out into the open desert toward Fort Washakie.

By now, several more police cars and two more black helicopters had arrived at the Blackwell Ranch. Rick could tell by the way the grim-faced government men approached him that he was in for one long night—maybe more. His only consolation, and it was a big one, was that all of the people he cared for were safely away.

CHAPTER 53:

HOME FOR CHRISTMAS

$\overset{\wedge}{=}_{\triangle}$

Rick awoke to the sound of clinking dishes and muffled voices from the kitchen. "Saturday Morning Kitchen Talk"—that's what he called it; the kind of talk he remembered from his childhood when he was allowed to sleep in on Saturdays. In the slow groggy transition between fully asleep and fully awake, he began to identify the voices. Jane's was unmistakable; it was the lead voice in the soundtrack of his life. Though he couldn't hear what she was saying, he could tell by the timbre of her voice that she was in a good mood. The other voice belonged to Sharon, who had become a semi-permanent fixture at the Blackwell Ranch. She and Jane made a connection on the night of the storm, and the connection became a bond in the days following what everybody was referring to as *The Blackwell Incident*.

The sound of a male voice brought Rick fully into the world of the awake. It was a voice he recognized, but had not heard in almost two weeks since *The Blackwell Incident*—that awful day when Elsa-Eska left and Aldi disappeared. Now his friend—his brother—was back. Rick threw off the covers and pulled on the pair of blue jeans he had left on the floor the night before. He ran barefoot out of the room, down the hall, and into the kitchen.

Aldi stopped mid-sentence at the sight of Rick. "Good morning, brother," he said as he picked Rick up off the floor in a breath-stopping bear hug.

Rick tried to speak, but there was no air in his lungs to push across his vocal chords.

Aldi set him back down and stepped back, his broad smile communicating volumes. "We have missed you all very much. It is good to be home."

We? An image of Elsa-Eska flashed through Rick's mind, bringing with it the hope that she might be waiting for them in the living room or at the other house. Then he saw that Sharon was holding Sara, and that hope weakened. "I can't believe you're here," Rick said, fighting to keep his voice from cracking. "After you and Louie disappeared, we thought maybe the ship had found you. I didn't think I'd ever see you again. Is Elsa-Eska…" Rick bit his lip to keep from losing it.

"Come," Aldi said, moving to the door that led into the living room. "There are things we must discuss."

Everyone followed him into the living room and gathered around the coffee table. Once they were all seated, Jane finished Rick's question. "Is Elsa-Eska back, too?"

Aldi's easy smile became forced. "She is on the Enterprise. And she is well. Ka-noa has revealed this to me."

"They'll come back for you, won't they?" Jane asked.

Aldi shrugged. "I do not know. It is too dangerous now. In time, maybe."

As much as Rick wanted to keep Aldi there with them, he tried to sound encouraging. "I'm sure once things calm down, they'll come for you. You can just lay low here until they do."

"Thank you, brother."

"Where have you been all this time?" Jane asked.

"I have been with Louie up in the mountains. Sara stayed at Fort Washakie with Mother and Big Jack."

"Just as well," Rick said. "This place was crawling with reporters and FBI agents for days. It felt like the *X-Files* around here."

"I would have sent a message to you, but we had to make sure the Hori believed we were all gone."

"Yeah, now that you mention it," Rick said, "I don't remember seeing that thing after the ship left."

"That is good. Johnny believes the Hori came only to stop the mission. It has no reason to remain in this place if it believes there are only humans here."

"So, it's gone for good?" Jane said hopefully.

"From this place," Aldi replied.

"Where did it go?" Rick asked.

"It will try to find Mallia and Kai-Tai. If it believes they are the only Klyvians left on this planet that is where it will go. They are its last chance to stop the mission."

"What will happen if it finds them?" Jane asked.

"Johnny believes it will try to use them to get to the rest of us. Then it will use us to find a way to the safe place on Klyv. If that happens, it might be able to finish what was started in the Time of Trouble."

The room fell silent as everyone considered the weight of this new information. Finally, Rick spoke up. "Then we'll just have to stop it. We'll find it and we'll stop it. Where do start?"

"We cannot," Aldi said.

"What do you mean we can't? We've got to try. What about Mallia and Kai-Tai? We've got to warn them." After his own run in with the Hori, Rick understood Elsa-Eska's strong reaction toward the creature. He had never met Mallia and Kai-Tai, but now that he was part of their mission, he felt compelled to protect them.

"They are safe for now," Aldi said. "And they know of the Hori. Johnny is with them. He will remain there to watch over them."

"But it has your communicator," Rick pressed. "It can use it to find them."

Aldi let out a chuckle.

"What's so funny?" Rick asked, surprised by Aldi's levity.

"The Hori cannot make it work," Aldi said, still chuckling.

"Why not?" Jane asked.

"The Before One has humor, too."

"What do you mean?"

"On Klyv, the Before One made it so the Hori cannot cross over the water that surrounds the safe land. The Hori fear water and so do the Raphim. On Earth, the Before One has made it so the Hori cannot operate any technology—Klyvian nor human. I don't know why, it just can't. I did not learn this until the night of the storm."

Rick thought back to the moment he first met the Hori. "But it fixed our Jeep."

"It could not have done that," Aldi said.

"But I was there."

"Yes," Jane said, "but you said you didn't see him actually do anything. Maybe there wasn't really anything wrong with it. It could have been part of the deception."

"There is a story," Aldi said, "about a Hori that could throw its influence."

"See," Jane said. "Maybe William, or whatever its name is, was able to deceive you from a distance."

Rick shook his head. "It used me."

"That is how the Hori work," said Aldi.

Rick was struggling to make sense of it all. "If the Before One can place restrictions on the Hori, why doesn't He just put an end to them once and for all?"

"The ways of the Before One are not our ways," Aldi explained. "I do not know why He doesn't stop the Hori, but I am grateful that He gives us ways to resist them. Rick, we must always know that the Before One is greater than the Hori. That is our hope. That is the

Hori's fear."

Rick, Jane and Sharon became quiet as they considered Aldi's words and his confidence in the protection of the Before One. Rick would have liked to explore the subject further, but a knock at the door interrupted him.

Jane was closest to the door, so she got up to answer it.

"Who is it, honey?" Rick asked.

"Oops. I forgot to tell you," she said with a nervous chuckle.

Rick got up to see what she was talking about. When he got to the door, he saw a small band of Shoshone Indians standing in front of his house—their arms full of sacks and wrapped packages.

"I'm sorry," Jane whispered. "I invited them to spend Christmas with us weeks ago. I didn't think they would actually come." She felt Rick's hand slip into hers.

"That's okay," he said. "Family is always welcome."

"Who is here?" Aldi asked.

Rick hugged Jane and looked over at his brother. "Tolis anuk."

CHAPTER 54:

HOMEWORLD SECURITY

L⊙

"Merry Christmas," Dave said as Jim slid into the passenger seat.

"There's nothing *merry* about it," Jim grumbled in reply. "In case you've forgotten, I'm supposed to be skiing right now."

"Oh, yeah, Christmas with the future in-laws. What happened?"

"As if you didn't know. That little stunt you and Carl pulled has put us all on alert. I'm sure you got the same call I did." Jim's voice morphed into a near-perfect imitation of their facility director: "Until further notice, all personal leave has been suspended. We are at war, people!"

"Hey, don't blame me," Dave replied in defense. "It's not my fault the world went crazy over the biggest discovery in history. Come on, you have to admit it's pretty cool. Proof that aliens are real, and we found it. They should give us an award."

"You could've at least clued me in on what you guys were doing. I still can't believe you went up there without me."

"Excuse me? You told me you wanted nothing to do with it."

"You could've at least called and let me tell you again." Jim turned the radio on and sat back, folding his arms across his chest. "I don't want to talk about it anymore."

They drove for several miles and let the music ease the tension between them. Jim was just starting to feel better when the announcer cut into the middle of a song.

> *We interrupt this programming to bring you breaking news from Wyoming. Rachel O'Neal of KTWO TV 2 is about to make an announcement regarding the Blackwell Incident.*

There was a pause and then a female voice began reading a prepared statement:

> *Reporting the events that shape our world is not an exact science. Each story requires us to make judgments about its authenticity and relevance to you, the listening public. Most of the time we get it right, and you receive news that is accurate, timely and important. Sometimes we make mistakes. When this happens, we accept the responsibility to admit our error and correct the information we report.*
>
> *Eleven days ago, we responded to a call from the former SETI radio-astronomer, Dr. Carl Drake, about a discovery that would, as he put it, "end the search for extraterrestrial intelligent life." We sent a news team to a ranch near Riverton where we were told Dr. Drake would reveal this momentous discovery. At the time, we felt that this event held significance beyond our local broadcast area. Following protocol, we alerted our affiliate stations and other news agencies in the U.S. and abroad. All of these agencies agreed with our assessment and began broadcasting our video feed. As our camera captured amazing footage of what we then believed was an actual alien spacecraft, the world was stunned by a dramatic sequence of events involving local police and the Air National Guard.*
>
> *Sadly, this was one of those rare instances when we got it wrong. We have just learned that this entire event was a fabrication. I repeat; the video we broadcasted on December 14 from the Blackwell Ranch near Riverton, Wyoming was nothing more than an elaborate hoax. We at Channel 2 are embarrassed by our hasty decision and offer our most sincere apologies to our affiliates and the world. Regretfully, we cannot undo the distress and panic caused by our irresponsibility. We are prepared to do whatever is necessary to make amends.*
>
> *I can report that those persons at Channel 2 who were involved in the decision to air this story have been either terminated or put on suspension pending further investigation. Also, we are cooperating with government agencies to identify the perpetrators of this hoax.*
>
> *For the record, Rick and Jane Blackwell, the owners of the Blackwell Ranch, who were initially charged with conspiracy to mislead the public, have been cleared of all*

charges in what is now being called a criminal act. They do, however, remain persons of interest and are cooperating with this investigation.

The primary suspect, Dr. Carl Drake, remains at large. Eyewitness accounts of the event put Dr. Drake at the scene, but he has not been seen nor heard from since. If anyone has information about the whereabouts of Drake, they are asked to contact their local authorities.

Again, we at Channel 2 express our sincerest apologies for our actions. We pledge to use this grievous error as a call to a higher standard in reporting the news. Thank you.

"*That was Rachel O'Neal, acting station manager of KTWO TV 2 in Casper, Wyoming. For a reaction to this stunning announcement we turn to...*"

Dave switched off the radio. "Can you believe that? There is no way that was a fake. I was there. I saw them. I *met* them. Man!" He slammed his fist against the steering wheel. "It's a cover-up. Somebody's trying to shut this down."

Jim scratched his chin, considering the news announcement and the reaction of his friend. Part of him agreed with Dave's suspicion. Part of him wanted the retraction to be genuine. They drove the rest of the way in silence.

When they arrived at the listening outpost, they were surprised to see two black SUVs parked in front of the building. Normally, the only vehicles at the outpost belonged to the radio analysts who were presently on duty. Dave and Jim both noticed that these vehicles had government license plates.

"What's this?" Dave asked as he parked next to one of the SUVs. "Are we scheduled for a review?"

"Not on Christmas Day."

As they were getting out of the car, they were met by a man in a dark suit exiting the building.

"Hey, guys," said the man cheerily. He acted as if he knew them.

"Hey," Jim replied. "What's going on?"

The man laughed. "Haven't you heard? The world's coming to an end."

"Excuse me?" Dave asked.

The man laughed again. "It's an invasion. Ooooo." He wiggled his fingers in a mysterious fashion.

"What are you talking about?" Jim demanded.

The man ignored Jim's question. "Say, nice Mustang you've got there. What year is it?"

"Sixty-five," Dave replied.

"Awesome," the man said. "Well, I'll catch up with you guys inside."
With that, he stepped around to the other side of the furthest SUV.

Dave and Jim exchanged glances and walked toward the building.

"Do you know that guy?" Dave asked.

"No. I thought you did."

The levity of the man in the parking lot was in stark contrast to the
mood of the men inside the building. When Jim and Dave entered
the control room where they eavesdropped on all the bad guys of the
world, they found the team they were supposed to relieve sitting still
and silent on steal chairs while two unfamiliar men were busy at the
controls. Three other men in suits like the one they met in the parking
lot stood like sentries about the cramped room. Had they been quick
enough, Dave and Jim could have made an about-face. But one of the
sentries was quicker and positioned himself between them and the
door.

"Identification," one of the men commanded.

Dave and Jim offered the man the credentials they wore around
their necks.

"David Phelps," the man said. "And James Calvani. Follow me."

The man at the door stepped aside to allow the lead man through.
He joined the other sentry and moved in behind Dave and Jim, giving
them no option but to comply. They followed the leader to another
room where they found the man they met in the parking lot. Not
surprisingly, his demeanor changed to match that of the other men.

"What's this about?" Dave demanded.

Jim flinched at Dave's uncharacteristic boldness in the presence of
four men who could easily beat the stew out of them.

The man from the parking lot looked as if he might answer Dave's
question, but then took a different track. "Which of you is Phelps?"

"I am, sir," Dave replied.

"We have recently learned that for the last six months you have been
monitoring an unidentified radio transmission on a regular basis. Is
that correct?"

"Not exactly, sir. We detected a signal, but it was much more than a
simple radio transmission."

"What are the coordinates?"

Dave's mind suddenly went blank. "I, um…"

"The coordinates, son." The man's tone softened.

"I don't remember the exact coordinates." Technically, it wasn't a lie.
He really could not remember the numerical coordinates of the signal.

The man approached the two radio analysts. He paused at Jim and then turned to Dave. "Mr. Phelps, were you able to identify Wyoming as one point of the transmission?"

"Yes, sir."

"And were you able to identify the other point?"

Dave swallowed and felt his forehead prickle with beads of sweat. "We, um, we believe the other point was in the vicinity of…um…the moon, sir."

"Very good," the man replied. "Did you report this to your supervisor?"

"Yes, sir. But we were instructed to disregard it."

"I see. Were you able to translate the signal?" The man's posture took on a decidedly more friendly tone.

Dave was drawn in by the technique. "Not much of it, sir; just a portion of the audio. It's way too complex for our equipment. I think it was three-dimensional. But something tells me you already know that."

The man turned to address the other suits. "I'll take it from here. Send me the other analysts. I only want to go through this once."

The three men nodded and filed out of the room.

"Please, have a seat. Sorry about the interrogation act. I had to know if you were going to be honest with me."

The door opened, and the other two radio analysts entered.

"Come in, guys. I was just about to tell Phelps and Calvani here about some changes to your facility. I'm Agent Ford from the Department of Homeland Security. You have heard of the Department of Homeland Security, haven't you?"

The four analysts nodded.

"Excuse me," Jim said. "Where's Director Shaw? Shouldn't he be here for this?"

Ford pursed his lips. "Director Shaw has been given another assignment. I'm your new director."

"That means," Dave said, making the connection, "we're part of the Department of Homeland Security now?"

"Not exactly. It's a bit more complex than that. Given your unique history with the Blackwell transmission, we intend to direct the entire resources of this facility exclusively to home-*world* security. Until we get to the bottom of it, you guys are, for lack of a better term, alien hunters. Think of it as a promotion…a promotion that will be compensated accordingly."

"Excuse me, sir," Jim said. "We just heard on the radio that the whole thing was a hoax."

"That's the complex part," Ford said. "You can't tell anyone about this."

"So it wasn't a hoax?" Jim asked.

Ford laughed like he did in the parking lot. "No, son. This is as real as it gets. But you've seen the news. You know how this sort of thing affects people. We had to contain it."

"But if it's the truth," one of the other analysts offered, "don't people have the right to know?"

"The truth can be very dangerous," Ford replied. "And the truth is, we don't know what we're dealing with. For all we know, that ship in Wyoming could have been a scout for a full-scale invasion. Until we make contact with these creatures and understand their intent, we've got to contain it. It's for the good of the entire planet."

Inside, Dave was shaking his head in protest, but outside he was trying to play it cool.

"Mr. Phelps," Ford said. "You're the one who discovered the signal. I'd like you to take the lead. Are you onboard?"

Dave felt his head nod and heard his voice say, "Yes, sir."

"What about the rest of you guys? Are you in?"

Jim and the other two analysts agreed as if they had a choice. Everyone in the room understood this meeting was just a formality. The decision had already been made before they got there. The only choice these men had was whether to cooperate or find themselves relocated to some undisclosed location for an indeterminate period of time.

"Now, gentlemen," Ford continued. "I cannot overstate the sensitive nature of this project. It is a matter of global security. We will work with each of you to establish a cover-story that you will communicate to your families and anyone else who might miss you."

"Sir?" Dave said.

Ford chuckled. "Oh, I'm sorry. I forgot to tell you the fun part. You'll be staying here for the duration of this assignment. Don't worry, we've arranged for suitable accommodations to be brought out here. You'll have everything you need, and some of the things you want. Think of it as incentive. The sooner we get to the bottom of this, the sooner you get to go back to your normal lives."

The four analysts stared at Agent Ford in disbelief.

"I know this is a lot to throw at you men. I'll let you have some time to process it. If you need anything at all, just ask one of the agents outside. They'll be more than happy to accommodate you." Ford stood up and knocked on the door. The lock clicked and the door opened. Ford looked back at the analysts. "I am deeply honored to be serving our country with you gentlemen." At that, Agent Ford disappeared.

The door closed with a slam and the sound of the lock clicking into place.

AFTERWARD:

ZERO GRAVITY

O⊱

"There you are, Carl," Elsa-Eska said as she glided toward him, her long hair and robe fanning out around her as if she were under water. "I have just spoken with Ido. We cannot take you back."

Carl stared out a large viewing porthole at a basketball-sized Earth.

"Ido says the humans are searching for us. If we try to go back now, they will find us. If we stay here, they will come."

"You don't have to worry about that. Our ships can't make it out this far."

"We still cannot take you back." Elsa-Eska paused and then added, "We cannot go back for Aldi and Sara either. Now that the humans know of us, it's too dangerous."

"I understand."

"I am very sorry, Carl. You will have to go with us."

Several moments passed in silence. Then Carl said, "It's really quite beautiful...from out here anyway."

Elsa-Eska floated closer to him and gazed out the porthole. "It's one of the most beautiful planets we've seen."

"Have you seen many?"

"No. But of the ones we have seen, I like this one the best. Carl," Elsa-Eska said, turning to look at him, "it comes into my mind that you do not want to go back."

Carl glanced at her and quickly looked back out the porthole.

"You had a chance to get out of the shuttle. Yet you stayed with us. Why, Carl?"

"I...I wasn't ready."

"But you will not be able to return to your home for many years."

"I never really felt much at home there anyway."

Elsa-Eska's face revealed her puzzlement.

Carl turned to face her. "I never fit in with other humans. That's probably why I got in with SETI. That's why I've spent my life searching for...well, for you. I always believed you were out there. Even after all those years, I never doubted. And then when I finally found you, I didn't want to leave you."

Elsa-Eska nodded slowly as she considered his words. "I understand your feelings. I did not want to leave Rick and Jane."

Carl looked down. "And because of me you had to leave your husband and daughter, too. If I hadn't called those reporters...if I hadn't tried to prove I was right...I wish I could..." His voice began to falter. "I wish it could be different. I'm so sorry."

Elsa-Eska placed her hand upon his shoulder, and his body turned in the zero gravity. Keeping his head down to avoid her gaze, he tried to back away, but the absence of gravity rendered him incapable of movement.

"Carl," Elsa-Eska said, laying her hands on either side of his face. "Look at me." She lifted his head, and his breath caught when he saw the golden flecks in her eyes begin to glow and swirl like two tiny galaxies. "I have a pain in my heart that I have never felt before. It is a pain I will carry until I am returned to my Aldi and my Sara."

Carl started to apologize again, but Elsa-Eska touched his lips with her fingers.

"Please, do not speak. Listen. It is not the way I want, but it is the way that is. I accept it as part of the mission, just as I accept the loss of my sister and Arkel. If you are to live with us, you will learn our ways."

Carl felt himself being drawn effortlessly toward her until their foreheads touched. From the point of contact, a warm sensation filled his head and moved down his spine. He waited for her to speak, but no more words came from her lips. Instead, he became aware of an idea that became a hope that grew into a certainty. Somehow, he knew beyond all doubt that he was loved.

When Elsa-Eska pulled away, there was moisture forming around the edges of the swirling galaxies. A tear welled up and floated away from her eye and hung in the space between them. Just then a voice sounded from somewhere in the room.

"That is Ido," Elsa-Eska explained. "We are ready to go. Hold my hands. The gravity generators are about to be activated."

Carl grasped her hands and felt himself being pulled toward the floor. Though the gravity was only about half of that on the earth, Carl stumbled under his weight upon his crippled legs. Elsa-Eska caught him and helped him to a nearby couch.

"Thank you," Carl said.

Elsa-Eska knelt down and gently adjusted Carl's legs into a more comfortable position. Then she stood to her full height. "I am going to see Tyba and Imtulon. Would you like to come with me?"

"I think I'll stay here awhile longer, if that's okay."

Elsa-Eska bowed and left Carl alone.

There was no sound or vibration or increased G-force when the Klyvian ship engaged its engines. Carl realized they were moving only when he happened to glance out the porthole and saw that the earth was no longer visible. He stared out at the vastness of space for a long time thinking of the turn of events that led him to this place. Then he noticed something on bulkhead next to the porthole—a drawing of a woman he assumed was Elsa-Eska. He looked at the drawing for a long time and thought of her and the others. He thought of the strange certainty of love.

Outer space doesn't care who you are. The thought came to him as a forgotten whisper from the distant past. Then another thought replaced it: *But that doesn't matter when you're with people who do.*

The End
(Until 2016)

ABOUT THE AUTHOR

For me, writing stems from a curious mind. For as long as I can remember I've had a strong desire to discover and understand things. As a child, I was particularly attracted to dinosaurs and outer space. Now I enjoy history and Christian spirituality. But always, I am drawn to the idea of mystery.

Human history is filled with mystery. Our past is fraught with amazing tales and myths and legends, most of which we moderns dismiss as too fantastic to accept as real. The future holds the greatest of all mysteries, but again we are prevented from gazing too far ahead by the millions of attachments that bind us to the here and now. How odd that we are surrounded by so much mystery, yet we fear delving too deeply into it. Instead, we protect ourselves by relocating mystery to the realm of entertainment. But stories, whether written or told, preserve this sense of mystery. They call us to the edge of our ordered and scheduled lives, and beckon us to take a peek into the unknown.

In this respect I can relate to Rick Blackwell. I too am a product of this civilized age, and I am also strangely drawn to the untamed.

I hope you enjoyed reading BLACKWELL as much as I enjoyed writing it. If you are interested in more of the story, you will be pleased to know that I am currently writing the sequel. It is entitled Song of My People, and takes place in the year 2016. That's all I can say for now. In the meantime, you can visit us at www.klyvian.com. Please feel free to write. I'd love to hear from you.

Michael E. Gunter
Richmond, Virginia
August 2011

Learn more about BLACKWELL and progress on upcoming books at www.Klyvian.com

Follow Me!
Facebook: pages/Blackwell
Twitter: @Michael_Gunter
LinkedIn: in/MichaelGunter
Blog: www.Klyvian.com
email:Michael@GunterBooks.com
Web: GunterBooks.com

OTHER WORKS
BY MICHAEL E. GUNTER

Non-Fiction

A Life Not Wasted (Gazelle Press, 2005)
The greatest of all tragedies is not a life cut short by an early death, but a life that reaches its end without becoming what God intended it to be. The solution to this tragedy is revealed by wrestling with four of Life's Big Questions. These questions are essential to any life not wasted, as their answers bring clarity about God, His world, and His desire for us.

Short Stories

"One of a Million Things"
Third Runner-Up in Colonnade Writing Contest at CJM Books, 2011
You've probably been asked, just for the sake of conversation, "What would you do with a million dollars?" When bus driver, Anthony Robinson, wins a seventeen million dollar lottery, the question becomes very real. Join Anthony for the ride of his life and find out what he does with his millions. You may be surprised.

"By the Sword"
We know that life comes to us one moment at a time, but what if it didn't? When a young punk takes a brief trip forty-nine years into the future, he discovers that great opportunity comes with a great cost, and tampering with the order of things can have dire consequences.

"Tilley's"
While looking for the perfect Christmas present, a man wanders into a charming old antique store. Surrounded by trinkets and photographs of the past, he gives in to the tug of nostalgia and finds that some memories, the really strong ones, refuse to be forgotten.

More on these works can be found at GunterBooks.com.